THE CHELSEA GIRLS

The CHELSEA GIRLS

A Novel

FIONA DAVIS

DUTTON

DUTTON

An imprint of Penguin Random House LLC

penguinrandomhouse.com

Copyright © 2019 by Fiona Davis

Penguin supports copyright. Copyright fuels creativity, encourages diverse voices, promotes free speech, and creates a vibrant culture. Thank you for buying an authorized edition of this book and for complying with copyright laws by not reproducing, scanning, or distributing any part of it in any form without permission. You are supporting writers and allowing Penguin to continue to publish books for every reader.

DUTTON and the D colophon are registered trademarks of Penguin Random House LLC.

LIBRARY OF CONGRESS CATALOGING-IN-PUBLICATION DATA

Names: Davis, Fiona, 1966– author.
Title: The Chelsea girls : a novel / Fiona Davis.
Description: First edition. | New York : Dutton, [2019]
Identifiers: LCCN 2019002424 (print) | LCCN 2019009375 (ebook) |
ISBN 9781524744595 (ebook) | ISBN 9781524744588 (hardcover)
Subjects: LCSH: Blacklisting of entertainers—Fiction. |
Chelsea Hotel—Fiction. | United States—Politics and government—
1945–1989—Fiction. | BISAC: FICTION / Historical. | FICTION /
Mystery & Detective / General. | FICTION / Literary. |
GSAFD: Historical fiction
Classification: LCC PS3604.A95695 (ebook) | LCC PS3604.A95695
C48 2019 (print) | DDC 813/.6—dc23
LC record available at https://lccn.loc.gov/2019002424

Printed in the United States of America
1 3 5 7 9 10 8 6 4 2

For the artists
whose dreams were lost

THE CHEL/EA GIRLS

PROLOGUE

New York City, March 1967

In the dead of night, during the dreary month of March, the Chelsea Hotel is a quiet place. The only sound that cuts through the silence is the squeal of a police siren, and that fades fast. Thick walls keep out the everyday noises of one's neighbors: the muffled swears after walking into a bedpost with a bare foot, or the generous moans of lovemaking. The ghosts of the Chelsea hide in the cement-filled brick walls during the day, and glide out during the violet hours to keep watch. Over time, their number has accumulated, from the refined gentlewoman who left behind four diamond rings, to the puffy Welsh poet sinking from alcoholic stupor to coma. The musicians chant quietly with vaporous breath as the former owner hovers mutely by, wringing his hands with worry.

One more to come, very soon. If the woman had more courage, she might jump from the roof. That would be the faster method, instead of this slow slide into oblivion, where every so often a futile panic makes *her want to call out, cry for help. But no one would hear, not here. The ghosts jeer at her and point, but she knows they'll eventually welcome her into the fold. And once she's gone, she, too, will keep watch over the residents, including her one true friend, who will sigh into her pillow as the apparition leans in close for an invisible kiss.*

ACT ONE

CHAPTER ONE

Hazel

Naples, Italy, April 1945

S he hated Maxine Mead, and Italy, on first sight.

When Hazel had first auditioned for the USO tour, back in New York, she'd imagined arriving abroad and gingerly stepping off a plane to a cheering group of GIs. The stage would be a grand opera house or something similarly picturesque, like what she'd seen in the newsreels of Marlene Dietrich and Bob Hope entertaining the troops. Hazel would be sure to call them men, not boys, as the USO Actors' Handbook advised. After all, many of them had been fighting for four years now. They deserved respect as well as some wholesome entertainment, a respite from the fighting.

Upon boarding the Air Corps plane at LaGuardia Airport, Hazel was informed that she'd be replacing a member of an all-female acting troupe who'd come down with jaundice. Not until the noisy tin can of a cargo plane was aloft was she told her destination: Naples, Italy.

After a bumpy landing, Hazel lugged her two suitcases off the plane and stood on the tarmac, exhausted and confused, waiting for someone to tell her where to go, what to do next. The stifling heat was made worse by the fact that she'd been given the winter uniform, including wool stockings and thick winter panties. Every inch of her from the waist down itched as though she had ants crawling up her sweaty legs. Her uniform—a greenish-gray skirt, white blouse, long black tie, and garrison cap that she'd admired in the mirror back in New York—was now a stinking, wrinkled mess.

Finally, a soldier pulled up in a Jeep and called out her name. He tossed her suitcases in the back before helping her into the passenger seat.

They lurched off over a road battered by potholes, passing demolished apartment buildings and churches. Several women picked through a pile of garbage by the side of the road, stopping to stare at Hazel with dead eyes before turning back to their work. A group of ragged, emaciated children, one of whom sucked on his dirty fingers, watched the scavengers. Yet across the street, a tidy line of schoolboys walked past the desolation as if nothing were wrong. The air smelled of rotting vegetables; dust kicked into Hazel's nose and made her sneeze. Early in the war, the newspapers had published aerial photos of the city that showed almost all of it up in smoke, annihilated by relentless bombing. While many of the inhabitants sought safety deep underground in the ancient Roman aqueducts and tunnels, at least twenty thousand people had been killed.

She tried to envision what it would be like if New York had been similarly decimated, she and her mother out with their shopping bags, stepping over chunks of concrete, going about their day. She couldn't imagine it. "This is terrible. There's hardly anything left," she said.

The driver shrugged. "Naples was the most bombed site in Italy."

"The residents rose up and resisted the Germans, right?" She tried to remember what she'd read in the papers. "Looks like they paid dearly for it."

"Sure did." He made a sharp left, off the main road. "They told me to take you directly to the stage."

She would have thought they'd give her a moment or two to freshen up after her interminable trip. "Is the acting company rehearsing?"

"Nope. It's a show." He nodded at the men trudging along the side of the road in the same direction, smoking cigarettes. "This is your audience." At the sound of a low rumble above them, every helmeted head snapped up, scouring the skies. But it was only thunder, from a slate-colored cloud to the west, far out over the sea. The helmets snapped back down.

A show. Good. She'd have a chance to watch the other actors. In New York, she'd been given the script for *Blithe Spirit*, which had been a big hit on Broadway four years earlier, along with instructions to learn the maid's role, and she had managed to memorize some of the lines during the flight.

The lines were the easy part for Hazel, as she'd been a serial understudy for the past few years. Hazel's hope, when she first auditioned for the USO, was to be able to break out of her understudy rut and finally act onstage in a real performance. This was her chance to try something new, so that when she returned to New York, she'd be taken seriously as a major actress, not just a backup to be called upon when the leading lady got the flu. Which, with Hazel's bad luck, had never happened. She'd even established a reputation among producers: Hiring Hazel Ripley as an understudy guaranteed that your leading lady would never miss a show. Twenty plays now under her belt, without going on even once.

Every night, she'd feel a guilty flicker of relief as the star flounced through the stage door, healthy and raring to go, but Hazel attributed her own reticence to her lack of experience. Surely, once she'd gotten a taste of performing in front of an audience, she'd become just as competitive and eager to take center stage as her brother and father had been. She was a Ripley, after all.

Her mother, Ruth, thought that joining the USO tour was a terrible idea, listing off the names of entertainers who had been injured or killed while abroad, usually in plane crashes. "And let's not forget that pretty Jane Froman, who almost lost both legs when her plane crashed into a river in Portugal," Ruth had said. "Accidents happen all the time. You know that's true."

Hazel had changed the subject fast, recognizing the dangerous quiver in Ruth's voice. But she remained undeterred. The opportunity to get onstage while supporting her country was too good to pass up, and she viewed it as a way to honor her brother's memory while, at the same time, stepping out of his shadow. Not to mention the pay was ten dollars a day plus meals. She'd filled out a long questionnaire, had her fingerprints taken, and gotten inoculated for diseases she'd never even heard of. And now, finally, she'd arrived.

The Jeep pulled into an enormous field, where Mount Vesuvius could be seen smoking away in the distance. Soldiers had taken seats on long benches facing a truck. One side of the truck bed was folded down to expose a platform furnished with a small table and four chairs; a drab-olive canopy was strung overhead. A flag hung from one side, with the words USO CAMP SHOWS written in blue on a white background. This was the stage, although it couldn't be more than fifteen feet wide. A few hundred soldiers milled about, chatting and smoking cigarettes, with hundreds more still making their way across the field.

"Over there." The driver pointed behind the truck, where a large tent had been erected. "That's where the performers are." He helped her out and handed her the two suitcases. One held the remaining dastardly uniform and other sundries, while the other was full of her best dresses. The Actors' Handbook had listed a series of dos and don'ts: *For the stage, bring dresses that you'd wear on an important Saturday night date. Travel as a unit at all times. If you behave properly, you'll increase your chance of making the better tours and improve your living and feeding conditions.* Made them sound like livestock, that last one.

"I'd walk you in, but we're not allowed inside." The driver's neck turned red at the very idea. "Good luck."

"No! Don't say that."

The soldier's eyebrows knitted together with concern. "What?"

"You're supposed to say, 'Break a leg.'"

He broke out in a wide smile. "Right. Break a leg."

Hazel nodded goodbye and slid through the opening in the tent flap backward, awkwardly maneuvering her suitcases inside.

"Well, it's about time."

Hazel blinked, her eyes adjusting to the dark interior.

A woman around her age, with hair the color of fire, did a slow turn, the better to show off a curvy figure that oozed out of a green silk dress. Behind her, three women perched on low stools in front of a splintered mirror, applying the final touches of stage makeup.

The redhead's lip curled. "Hazel Ripley, where the hell have you been?"

At least she knew she was in the right place. "I came straight from the plane." She shrugged, lifting the suitcases a couple of inches to prove it.

"Get out of that and into something pretty. They just called ten."

"I'm sorry?"

"They just called ten minutes. That means it's ten minutes until showtime." The redhead took a dramatic pause. "Have you ever even acted before? I swear, Jaundiced Jenny is out, and in her place we get Hayseed Hazel."

The other women giggled.

Hazel stood tall. "I've acted before. I know what it means. But I can't go on."

"Why not?"

This must be some kind of joke they played on all the newbies. "Because I haven't rehearsed and don't know any of the blocking." She put down her suitcases and brushed the dust off her skirt, realizing as she did so that it made her seem like a prissy schoolmarm. She let her arms fall to her sides.

"You're the maid. How hard can it be? Do you know your lines?"

"I studied them on the plane."

"Then you'll be fine. Just enter and exit when you're supposed to."

A voice came from outside the tent. "Miss Mead!"

"Yes?" the redhead called back.

"Someone to see you."

She looked at her watch. "Hayseed, get some makeup on and get out of that uniform. See you ladies in the wings."

Hazel waited a beat. Surely these women would all burst into laughter, now that the joke had been played out, but they just turned back to the mirror.

The redhead seemed familiar. Maybe Hazel had seen her in a show or at an audition back in New York. "Who *is* that?" she asked.

"That's Maxine Mead. Our fearless leader." The speaker, a tall brunette fitted out in a lemon-yellow dress, stood and shook Hazel's hand, introducing herself in a deep alto as Verna.

"Do we have a leader?" Hazel was still waiting for an acknowledgment of the prank. "I thought we were all second lieutenants."

"Maxine runs the show." Verna shrugged and introduced the other two ladies. Phyllis was a rotund milkmaid type with rosy cheeks, and Betty-Lou was a tiny slip of a girl, perfect for playing kids' parts, most likely.

"She's joking, right? About me going on?"

Verna shook her head. "No. We've been holding the curtain, waiting for you. You can get ready over there."

But this was ridiculous. No rehearsal at all? Hazel didn't even know which actress was playing which character. A lump lodged in her throat at the thought of all those men out there, waiting for the entertainment to begin. This had been a terrible idea. She'd be put on the next plane home, back to doing crosswords in the understudies' dressing room.

Trembling, Hazel changed into one of her plainer dresses, as befitting a maid, and tied the apron Verna tossed over around her waist. She turned away so the other girls wouldn't see her hands shaking as she looped the ends into a bow.

After standing in the wings for countless shows, watching others perform, *this* would be the first time she'd actually step onto the stage? Before thousands of people, with no rehearsal? She yanked the script out of her bag and leafed through the first scene, trying to imprint the cues in her head. The words swam around on the page as her heart pounded in her rib cage.

Another loud clap of thunder. "Will they cancel it if it rains?"

"You kidding?" said Phyllis. "Some of these men walked miles to get here. They ain't going anywhere."

Hazel followed the other girls behind the big truck. The rain was holding off, but probably not for long, judging from the soggy feel in the air. Hazel longed for a bolt of lightning to hit the truck and cancel the show. Anything to not have to go onstage in front of this sea of men, in a strange country, when she hadn't eaten or slept in what felt like a week.

She waited in the wings, which was really a small set of stairs that led onstage, forcing back tears. Betty-Lou handed her a tarnished silver tray. "Here's your prop." Hazel couldn't even whisper anything back—by then, her throat had closed up. She'd wanted desperately to act in a play, but not like this.

Even worse, her character had the first entrance.

The lights went up.

She couldn't go out there. Into the spotlight.

"What are you waiting for?" A solid shove from Maxine, who'd silently reappeared, propelled her up the stairs. Hazel placed the tray on a table downstage as Verna entered from the other side. Hazel had no idea what Verna said, her mind had fuzzed over, but she answered with "Yes'm," her first line. She managed to utter the next few, hoping she got them in the right order, before scampering like a dog with its tail between its legs back to the safety of the wings.

The soldiers roared with laughter. Backstage, Betty-Lou gave her a pat on the shoulder. "Not bad."

The show continued. The other members of the cast were loud and confident, especially Maxine, who was a force of nature as the psychic Madame Arcati. The two male parts were played by men, presumably soldiers who'd volunteered. Each time Hazel ventured out, she relaxed a little more.

When she wasn't onstage, she watched the eager faces of the

soldiers in the first few rows. The men were desperate for entertainment, for something else to think about besides the war, and even when the rain began falling in sheets, no one stirred.

Unfortunately, in spite of the men's rapt attention, her performance was far from perfect. She stepped on the other girls' lines instead of waiting her turn to speak, and missed a couple of entrances.

But she'd done it. She'd acted on a stage, in front of people. Terribly, no doubt about that, but as the men whooped and whistled during the curtain call, Hazel managed a proud smile.

✦

"Up and at 'em, ladies."

Verna's voice boomed across the pup tent.

Hazel groaned and sat upright. After being driven back to the base the night before, Hazel had skipped dinner and retreated to her assigned cot, the exhaustion from her journey and the sheer terror of performing having caught up with her.

Sure, she'd stunk last night in the show. But what had they expected with no rehearsals?

Better to come clean, try to start fresh. "Listen, everyone. I'm sorry about how awful I was. I didn't expect to go onstage so soon."

"Don't worry about it." Betty-Lou's voice came out a sweet squeak. "We all had a period of adjustment. It's to be expected."

"Yeah," agreed Verna. "The thing about this gig is that you'll get a do-over. And another. And another."

"I'm so sick of *Blithe Spirit*." Phyllis yanked a stocking over a thick thigh. Everything about Phyllis was solid and grandmotherly, even though she couldn't have been more than thirty years old. "The men love it, but they love anything. What's the schedule today?"

Verna looked up at a ragged calendar posted on the bulletin board. "We're off this morning, then shows at four and eight."

"I'm serious." Betty-Lou put her hands over her face. "I can't do this play again. Please don't make me."

Maybe there was something Hazel could do to make up for last night. She pulled her suitcase out from under her cot and popped it open. Digging through the dresses, she found the book she was looking for and held it up.

"I brought this with me. *Twelve Best American Plays from 1936 to 1937.* Maybe one of these will work instead."

Betty-Lou let out a shriek. "Amen! I thought we'd be waiting another month for a new script. Now we have twelve. Maxine, look."

Maxine, who'd been uncharacteristically subdued, reading a book on her cot, swung her legs over the side. "Let's see."

Hazel tossed it over.

"Not bad." Maxine thumbed through it. "We can work with this. Good job, Hayseed."

Hazel refused to let that nickname stick. "Look, I really don't want to be called Hayseed during my tour. I've paid my dues."

"In what way?"

"Well, I've worked on Broadway since 1939."

Maxine studied her. "Why don't I remember you, then? When I lived in New York, I went to everything."

"I was an understudy."

"Huh. Did you ever go on?"

Hazel swallowed. "No."

"Wait a minute." Verna snapped her fingers. "I heard about you. Didn't you understudy for something like two dozen shows and never once perform?" She didn't wait for an answer. Not that Hazel wanted to give her one. "That's right! The producers loved you because the audiences were never disappointed. It was in the *Post*."

Hazel's mother had read the article aloud the day it came out, while Hazel's ears burned with embarrassment. "What a shame," Ruth had said. "You standing in the sidelines while real actresses like Fay Wray and Betty Furness get the spotlight. Seriously, Hazel. Your brother would've been very disappointed."

A man's voice called out from the other side of the tent's flap door. "The facilities are ready for you, ladies."

Hazel, relieved by the interruption, followed the girls outside, clutching her helmet and a towel. They were led to the washing area, where a board with circular cutouts lay across two wooden horses. The women stuck their helmets under the faucet and filled them with water before laying them in the holes, a kind of makeshift sink. Hazel washed her face and hands and brushed her teeth before dumping out the water and wiping the inside of her helmet with a towel.

She'd hoped that she'd have the morning to get her bearings around the camp but instead was told to report back to Naples to fill out more paperwork, with Maxine assigned to accompany her. She wished it had been one of the others.

Hazel held tight as the Jeep careened back toward Naples over roads that were no better than those in the Dark Ages must have been. Above the narrow streets, laundry hung limply from precarious-looking balconies. They took a right, coming to a small plaza, where a crowd blocked the way.

"What's going on?" asked Maxine.

The driver stood up to get a better look. "Stay here, in the Jeep." He climbed out and was soon swallowed by the crowd.

Hazel and Maxine pulled themselves to standing to get a better view. The focal point of attention seemed to be a beautiful, very pale boy with full cheeks, his blond hair swept off to one side. For a moment, Hazel almost called out her brother's name. The resemblance was uncanny: Even the way the boy tossed his head to get his hair out of his eyes was the same. When her brother used to do that, girls swooned.

But no, it wasn't Ben. This kid was too young, for one, and when he turned his head, the profile wasn't quite right, the nose slightly turned up at the tip. He had one arm flung around a slightly older boy sporting the beginnings of a mustache, who seemed to be near tears.

The swarm pushed in, jostling the boys closer together. The blond boy looked defiant, his light complexion a stark contrast to that of his olive-skinned companion.

A rock flew out of nowhere and struck the blond in the forehead. He winced but didn't speak or cry out. A shock of red blood oozed from just below his hairline.

Hazel gasped, shielding the sun with her hand for a better view of the scene. "Why are they attacking them?"

An old Italian woman standing next to the Jeep, her head covered by a green paisley scarf, answered in accented English. "They were caught trying to steal bicycles. One refuses to speak. Probably a German, the other a *collaboratore*."

"Jesus," said Maxine. "What will happen to them?"

"They die." The woman spit on the ground before allowing herself to be sucked forward with the surge of the mob like liquid mercury.

Hazel tried to spot their driver. He'd made it about halfway to the boys, but the pack had tightened and wasn't responding to his commands to step aside. Hazel pointed to a group of kids who were collecting rocks from the rubble of a bombed-out wall. "They're going to stone them to death!"

This primitive system of justice outraged Hazel, but the energy emanating from the crowd was like a living, breathing monster, unstoppable. The blond boy seemed resigned to his fate, but held on tightly to his friend as others tried to pull them apart. The dark-haired one shook his head, tears streaming down his face, as a man near the edge of the crowd lifted an enormous cement block above his head and, staggering under its weight, headed in the direction of the boys.

In one swift motion, Maxine climbed over to the front seat of the Jeep and slid behind the wheel. She laid hard on the horn, shifted the gears, and gunned the engine.

Hazel clutched the side of the Jeep and stifled a scream as Maxine drove forward. This was madness, driving straight into danger. Distracted by the horn, the crowd parted, some of them barely stepping out of the way in time.

Their driver, who'd finally made it to the boys, looked up and spotted the vehicle. The look of relief on his face was quickly replaced by an angry snarl directed at the Neapolitans around him. He grabbed both boys by the scruff of their jackets, like a couple of puppies, and yanked them in the direction of the Jeep. As Maxine tumbled back into the rear seat, revealing a flash of pale upper thigh, a man standing at Hazel's elbow said something in Italian and tried to reach inside. Hazel swatted him off and gave him a good thunk on the forehead with the meat of her palm for good measure. Finally, the driver got close enough to shove the dark-haired boy into the front passenger seat and the blond one next to them in the back, before taking the wheel.

He reversed up the street to a crossing, executed a quick turn, and sped away. Hazel breathed in great gulps of air, thankful to be free, as the dark-haired boy sobbed into his hands. The blond one, grimacing, allowed Maxine to dab at his forehead with a handkerchief.

Maxine said something quietly, under her breath, and the boy, eyes wide, responded in kind. In German. The suspicions of the crowd had been correct.

Hazel leaned over. "You speak German?"

Maxine addressed Hazel without taking her eyes off the boy. "My grandmother is German. I learned some from her."

No one with German or Italian parents was allowed to audition for the USO tour. Hazel supposed grandparents were all right, although she doubted Maxine would have been crazy enough to volunteer that information.

Hazel noticed the driver watching them closely in the rearview mirror. The rest of the ride, the boy spoke fast and furiously, Maxine interrupting every so often to ask a question.

"What is he saying?" Hazel couldn't wait any longer.

Maxine spoke loudly, so the driver could hear as well. "His name is Paul, his father was a senior colonel in the German army, who sent for him and his mother to join him in Calabria early in the war. I don't think the woman was married to him, more of a mistress. Paul befriended this Italian boy—Matteo, he's called—and says they both worked with the Italian resistance, against the Germans."

"Against his own father?" Hazel glanced ahead at the driver, who remained stone-faced.

"That's what Paul says. He and his mother were left behind, abandoned by his father when the German army retreated. His mother was killed soon after. Paul went into hiding, protected by his friend's family."

The German boy addressed Maxine again. She nodded. "He

says he can prove that he was part of the resistance, if they reach out to Matteo's father."

Matteo nodded. "*Mio padre*, in Calabria."

"What are they doing here in Naples?" Hazel asked.

"It was becoming too dangerous in the countryside, Matteo's family was threatened, so the two boys ran off to try to make it to the Americans in Naples. The idea was for Paul to turn himself in and explain his story. They stole bikes and traveled by night. Until they got caught."

They pulled up at a large square called the Piazza Municipio, ringed on three sides by official-looking buildings in a deep ocher. If their story were true, the boys had made it to safety, just barely. But Hazel had a suspicion that they weren't in the clear just yet, as did they, judging from their terrified faces.

Maxine addressed the driver. "What happens to them now?"

"I'll take care of them. You go up this way." The driver nodded toward an arched doorway. "Through there."

The German boy grabbed Maxine's arm and rattled off something fast.

"He says he's only fifteen, that he never hurt anyone."

The driver gave her a dark look. "He's a prisoner. Not a pet."

They had no choice but to watch as the boys were driven off, but Maxine and the German boy locked eyes until the Jeep rounded the corner and disappeared.

Inside, Hazel filled out her paperwork in triplicate while Maxine explained to the major in charge what had happened, trying to convince him to look further into the situation.

"The German one, Paul, says he was brought here when he was just eleven," said Maxine, "and that he can prove that he's been part of the resistance if you reach out to the father of the other boy."

The major barely contained the scorn in his voice. "What

makes you think you can trust some German kid, take his words at face value? He's just trying to save his hide. Probably a regular soldier who got stuck behind enemy lines. They'll say anything to stay alive."

"He's too young to have been a soldier. After all, the Germans retreated two years ago. Will you at least look into his story?"

Maxine's bravery in the square, as well as now, with the major, astonished Hazel. She wished she were that brash. But she wouldn't dare question an authority figure. Always the understudy, in life as well as in art. The thought smarted.

The major didn't answer Maxine's question. "You said you spoke German to him?"

Maxine responded with a barely perceptible nod. "My grandmother is German. But she's lived in America forever. She has nothing to do with the old country."

"Huh. Don't go anywhere. I have to check something." He disappeared into a back room.

Hazel looked over at Maxine, whose face had turned white. "Are you all right?"

"Let's hope they don't haul me off, too." She laughed but it didn't reach her eyes. "I couldn't help it. They were so young. Just boys."

The haunted look on Maxine's face stirred Hazel's memory. She'd seen a woman on her brother's arm wearing a similar expression, years ago. That must be why Maxine looked so familiar: Her brother had dated a striking redhead for a couple of months, whom Hazel had met only briefly. The realization almost knocked the wind out of her.

"Did you know my brother back in New York?" The more she studied Maxine, the more convinced she became. "You did, I'm sure of it. I saw you with him. A couple of times."

"What on earth are you talking about?" The color had crept

back into Maxine's face, and her usual look of annoyance had returned.

"My brother was named Ben Ripley. I'm sure I remember him introducing you around to his gang at a coffee shop downtown, his friends joking that you were way above his pay grade. And another time, when we were all at a demonstration in New York. Something against fascism, I'm pretty sure. Or maybe against the Spanish War. There were so many protests back then." Along with her brother and all of their friends, Hazel had marched practically every weekend, signed every petition. Anything to stop the wave of authoritarianism sweeping the world. Ben had shown up to one rally with the exotic-looking redhead. The crowd had been rowdy, and after a short while, the girl had yanked Ben away. Hazel hadn't seen her since.

Maxine cocked her head. "I dated a guy named Ben, an actor, for a New York minute. You're his sister?"

"I am. I knew it! That's where I know you from. It's been bugging me since I arrived."

For a moment the boys in the square were forgotten. Maxine let out a bark of a laugh. "Ben Ripley. Sure thing. I thought we were going out for a picnic in the park, but the guy dragged me to some demonstration. I couldn't get out of there fast enough. He was way too full of himself for me. Still is, I'm guessing?"

Hazel wasn't sure how to respond. She shook her head. Even though it had been three years, the words never came out right.

"No. Not anymore."

CHAPTER TWO

Hazel

April 1945

Maxine stayed silent for a moment, before putting her arm around Hazel. "Oh God, I'm so sorry. My big mouth."

Hazel finally got the words out. "Ben was killed soon after he enlisted, in a plane crash."

"If I remember, he was a talented guy, right?"

What an understatement. Ben had been the boy wonder, a natural mimic. He took after their dad, a former vaudeville star brought down by a stroke when Hazel was twelve. Ben, always up for a challenge, had entertained their father, enlisting Hazel as his stooge in skits that made him laugh, although it only showed on the good side of his face. Even before their father's stroke, it was assumed that Ben and Hazel would go into acting, that the Ripley name would carry on through the children. After all, this was the family legacy. While other families passed down a dry-cleaning business or a hardware store, their inheritance was their father's brilliance in the footlights, and his name.

From the fading glory of their vast Upper West Side apartment, where scripts and old newspapers littered the living room, Ben—older by three years—worked on auditions and scenes for his acting classes. Hazel dutifully signed up for the same ones as soon as she graduated from high school. Ruth, who had managed her husband's career from the very beginning and liked to take full credit for his success, was determined that the family become as famous as the Astaires or the Lunts. "The Ripleys of West End Avenue," she'd proclaim.

The first time Hazel performed a scene in acting class, she worked on the role with her mother until late the night before. Her head spinning from exhaustion, yet jittery with excitement, Hazel had waited with her scene partner as the teacher—an elderly Russian man with wild hairs sprouting from his ears and nose—reminisced for a good five minutes on Ben's uncanny take on O'Neill before allowing Hazel and her scene partner to proceed. From the corner of her eye, she'd noticed the instructor slumping farther and farther into his seat as they stumbled through the scene, which made her forget all the coaching her mother had given her. Once they'd finished, the instructor had focused all his commentary on her acting partner, before dismissing Hazel with a mere three sentences: "That was a perfectly fine interpretation of the scene. The problem with 'fine' is that it's boring. You bored us." While she knew she wasn't the best actress in the room and had a lot to learn, it wasn't fair to compare her first attempt with that of her brother after three years of intensive study. Hazel had scurried out as soon as class was over to avoid the sympathetic-yet-gleeful looks of her classmates. She'd been resigned to living in the shadows ever since.

But her brand of boring appealed to producers casting for understudies. They preferred a chameleon who'd blend seamlessly into the production, who wouldn't dare tamper with the blocking or line readings in an effort to outshine the star. Secretly, Hazel didn't mind waiting in the wings, watching the best scenes before retreating to the understudies' dressing room with a good book. But to say so out loud would tarnish her father's legacy, as well as her brother's lost dreams. She had to do more, be more.

She'd first heard about the USO tour from a couple of actors at the counter of Hanson's Drugstore on Broadway, where she was killing time before slinking home after yet another pointless understudy rehearsal. She'd signed up to audition for the tour on a whim, figuring that it would make her parents happy to see their daughter follow in Ben's footsteps, both on the stage and in service to the country. How wrong she'd been: Her mother had hated the very idea, terrified that she'd lose her daughter as well as her son, and said she prayed each night that Hazel would be rejected.

The day that Hazel was to depart on her tour, she'd stepped into the kitchen, wearing her uniform, only to see the ghost of Ben reflected in her mother's eyes. Her father's naturally lopsided countenance slid into a grimace as her mother ran from the room, one hand clutching her mouth as if she was about to be sick. No matter what Hazel did, it turned out terribly.

Maxine rubbed Hazel's back. "Sorry to have spoken ill of your brother. I barely knew him."

The major returned, accompanied by a wiry man with a pipe sticking out of his mouth.

Maxine and Hazel exchanged looks. No doubt Maxine had overstepped her place by advocating for the two boys.

"Which one of you speaks Kraut?" asked the wiry man.

Maxine raised her hand, as though they were in elementary school. To see Maxine cowed made Hazel even more nervous.

"Come with me. Both of you."

As they walked deeper into the building, the man introduced himself as Colonel Peterson, the head of radio programming. "We're in
charge of all the music the soldiers listen to, as well as propaganda
broadcasts. That's where you come in. What's your name again?"

Maxine introduced herself, then added, "And this is Hazel Ripley."

"Maxine, huh? This way." The colonel didn't even look at Hazel. But she was used to that by now, and she'd already noticed
that being in close proximity to Maxine was the equivalent to
disappearing into thin air.

They entered a small soundproofed room where a microphone
sat on a desk, next to some fancy equipment with lots of dials.

The colonel picked up a bundle of papers. "The soldier who's
been doing the propaganda broadcasts got transferred, and we've
been looking for a German speaker to fill in. Radio waves, unlike
newspapers or television broadcasts, aren't deterred by borders or
front lines, which gives us a direct line of communication with the
enemy population. You're a girl, but I figure it might be even better that way."

"What exactly do you want me to do?" asked Maxine.

"Make your voice nice and pretty, and read off this list of German POWs." He pointed to a single piece of paper beside the microphone. "Then say that the boys are safe and sound, in German.
Once that's done, pick some articles from these"—he tossed down
a few copies of *The Stars and Stripes*—"and condense it for a German audience."

"Condense it? I'm not sure I understand."

He pointed to a headline. "Choose three or four articles that
emphasize American values, American strength, and summarize
them. We want to plant doubt in their minds. Make them wonder

if the Fuehrer is not all that he's cracked up to be, if they're not being told the whole truth."

"Right." Maxine didn't sound convinced. "I'll take these back to camp with me and figure out what to say."

"You don't go anywhere. First broadcast is today, as soon as you're ready. If you do a good job, we'll have you on once a week."

"What on earth? I can't just speak off the cuff, I have to have something in front of me to read. I'm an actress. I need lines."

The colonel wasn't listening. "We'll call you Lina aus Amerika." His accent was terrible. "Lina from America. Don't make it too heavy-handed. No calls for surrender, no ridicule. We're just reinforcing what they know deep down, that they're on the losing side. Got it?" He didn't wait for an answer. "I'll be back in thirty minutes."

"But we've got to get back for a show—" The door slammed before Maxine could finish the sentence. She stared after him, aghast. "I can't do it. What do I talk about?"

Hazel grabbed the newspaper and picked up a pen. "I can help you. And if we get this right, we'll be back next week. That'll give us a chance to find out more about the boys. Maybe we can reach someone higher up who'll listen to us."

"Good point."

They sat down together at the table, studying the front page. "This one's all about the dive-bombing of rail bridges in Northern Italy, backed by ground forces," said Hazel. "I'll strip out the basic ideas for you and write them down, so it's a condensed version."

Maxine nodded. "Great. Then I'll just translate it off the page. What about this one? It says that the British forces are fifteen miles from Hamburg, which is Germany's largest port."

"Sure, that'll work."

"*Reader's Digest*'s got nothing on you."

Writing so fast, on the fly, made Hazel's heart race. Figuring out how to pare down a complicated sentence, or simply racking her brain to find the right word, was a mental challenge—like memorizing lines, but more interesting. They'd summarized three articles by the time the colonel came back into the room with a technician.

"Remember, keep it light and pretty," he said, as the technician handed Maxine a set of headphones. "Lean in close to the microphone."

Hazel held her breath as Maxine read through the list of POW names, her voice soothing and calm in spite of the guttural German consonants. She stumbled on the commentary for the second news item, and glanced over in panic. Hazel gave a nod of encouragement and Maxine kept on, the abrasive sounds of the language mellowed by her delivery.

After the last news item was announced, Maxine said a few lines in German, then signed off with a kiss. "*Danke fürs Zuhören.*"

They tiptoed outside the room as the technician put on a record.

The colonel beamed down at Maxine. "Well done. Come back next week. Same time." He looked her up and down. "Maybe we'll get some photos taken, fire them over the lines so they can get a long, sweet look at our girl Lina. This could really be something big."

"I'm thrilled you're pleased." Maxine drew close. "Maybe you could do something for me." She went on to describe the story of the boys they'd rescued on their way into town. "We were hoping you could follow up, make sure they're properly seen to, in case it turns out that they did work for the resistance. It would mean the world, if you could inquire."

"I suppose I can look into it. A German and an Italian, you say?"

"Yes. Paul and Matteo."

"Fine, fine." He took his leave, even shaking Hazel's hand. "See you gals in a week."

Out in the bright sunshine of the plaza, Maxine let out a deep laugh. Hazel couldn't help but join in from relief.

Maxine elbowed Hazel in the ribs. "I couldn't have pulled it off without you. Looks like Lina aus Amerika's new fans are getting two girls in one package: I'll be her voice and you'll be her brains."

To think that, twenty-four hours earlier, Hazel had written off Maxine as a bossy witch. Now they were linked as comrades in arms. She hoped her brother had made a similar friend in the short time before his death.

"You look a little wiped out." Maxine led her to a fountain where a trident-wielding Neptune stood watch over lions that, before the bombing, had spewed streams of water. Instead, their empty mouths gaped, as if they were uttering silent roars at the destruction of their city. "Let's sit over here a minute."

Hazel scanned the streets. Their ride was nowhere in sight. "I hope we make it back in time for the show."

"The soldiers will still be waiting, no matter how late we show up."

The giddy bubbles of relief slowly faded, replaced by the memory of the angry mob earlier that afternoon. Hazel spoke quietly. "Do you think the colonel will follow up like he said?"

"I don't know. Hopefully, we'll have more news next week." Maxine waved an arm out in front of her. "Every person here has a story, and most of them will probably end more pitifully than the ones we got a glimpse of today. Children dying of hunger while their mothers watch, unable to help. The world is a horrible place, and in the frenzy to be right, to force their will, these armies trample over each other. Trust me, I've been out here since last year and the one thing I've learned is that we're all at the mercy of the powers that be."

Maxine's view was so tragic, Hazel couldn't agree. She got the distinct impression that under the grand speechifying lurked the same fear for the boys' safety that gnawed at Hazel. "Once Hitler is stopped, and all the newspapers say that might be any day now, we'll be able to right all these wrongs," she insisted. "Fix what was broken. Take care of the children."

As the Jeep pulled up, Maxine stood and straightened Hazel's tie. "Enough with all this gosh-shucks optimism, Hayseed. For now, you just worry about not missing your entrance cue again."

❖

A week later, the news broke that Hitler had committed suicide, lifting the spirits of the soldiers, but Hazel detected a hesitancy behind the celebrations. The war in the Pacific was still raging, and no doubt the troops would soon be shipped east to join in the battle against Japan. Even after four long years of war in Europe, the fighting wasn't over.

The book of plays had warmed Hazel's welcome among the actresses, to her grateful delight. During the next week, they rehearsed in the mornings, filling in the men's roles with soldiers who had some acting experience, and often learned their lines faster than the professionals. Hazel's confidence grew with every show. Her knees stopped quaking before she stepped out onstage, and she could be present, in the moment, for most of her scenes. As the latest addition to their motley troupe, she didn't get the leading roles, but that was fine with her. Better to have Maxine or Betty-Lou garner the loudest applause at the curtain call.

Not that it was perfect. She noticed that sometimes Maxine

went off the deep end, overplaying her lines, but the men loved it when she swaggered about with a singsong cadence, even if it had very little to do with the character she was portraying. Betty-Lou often forgot what she was supposed to say next, but she shrugged it off with a good-natured squeal, while Verna had an annoying tendency to drift too far upstage.

At least half the soldiers had never seen a legitimate play and were intrigued by the whole concept. With an average age of twenty-six and a hunger for drama, they reminded Hazel of what she'd read about Shakespeare's audiences, the groundlings, who stood out in all weather and had no qualms about letting their enthusiasm rip. The USO tour's sets were basic, with scenery painted on fabrics that could be easily switched out between shows, and the minimum number of stage props. Yet for a few hours, there was no doubt the men were instead imagining the grand interior of an English manor house or a tiny village in Andalusia.

When Maxine and Hazel arrived back in Naples a week later, Colonel Peterson was in a good mood, Lina's propaganda broadcast having pleased his superiors immensely. Once they'd wrapped up the session, he shook both their hands. "Well done, ladies."

"Glad you enjoyed it," said Maxine. "Now. Can you tell us any news about the boys? You know, from last week?"

The colonel hesitated a beat before explaining that the Italian one was on his way back home, accompanied by two soldiers who would inquire into the validity of the German's story. The German, he said, was being held in a jail two blocks away so the Americans could interview him further. If he truly was the son of a high-ranking officer, as he claimed, he could be valuable.

"What if Maxine offered to help interview him, since she knows German?" said Hazel.

Maxine jumped in. "Right, I'd be happy to help."

"Sure, sure. We'll let you know."

A dismissal, if ever Hazel heard one. Normally, she'd back off, cowed by his authority, but she couldn't acquiesce this time. What if Paul had a sister back in Germany, one who wondered what had happened to him or if he was safe? A sister who would never get an answer, not if he was chewed up by the maddening bureaucracy of the war. It didn't help that every night, the image of a blond boy flicking his hair out of his eyes emerged like a ghost in Hazel's dreams. Sometimes it turned out to be her brother, sometimes Paul.

"We made a strong connection with the boy," said Hazel. "We would really like to assist."

"I can see that. You've made yourselves clear." The colonel reached out and shook their hands. "In the meantime, thank you. Lina was a big hit and we appreciate your service."

"I'm sorry, do you mean that you don't need Lina anymore?" Hazel exchanged looks with Maxine.

"Hitler's dead, there's no point, the German soldiers know it's over." The colonel popped a pipe into his mouth with one hand and lit a match with the other, waving the flame over the tobacco before inhaling deeply. The smoke ghosted up over his face, obscuring his features for a moment.

Without the broadcasts, there'd be no excuse to return to headquarters. Hazel racked her brain. "Well, what about the American soldiers? What if we do something for them?"

"Like what?" The colonel took another long drag on his pipe.

"What about we profile a soldier each week, talk about where he comes from, that kind of thing?" She sensed Maxine nodding beside her, encouraging her. "I'll write it, and Maxine can read it as herself, not Lina, to cheer our boys up and do our part to support the war effort."

The colonel looked over at Maxine. "I guess we could try it. What the hell. Go ahead, write something up and come back next week. If I like it, you can broadcast it."

Maxine squeezed her arm as they exited the building. "Quick thinking, Hazel."

"I hope I can pull it off," said Hazel, settling on a bench to wait for their ride back.

"What do you mean? You flew through those write-ups for Lina."

"That was just rewriting. Here I have to come up with something from scratch. I'm an actress, not a writer."

"You kidding? You're our secret weapon. Besides, I know tons of writers and they all feel the same way you do, that they're not up to snuff. Goes along with the territory."

"How do you know tons of writers?"

"From when I was in New York, living at the Chelsea Hotel."

"That's the one on Twenty-Third, right?"

"Yes, exactly. It's full of artists and people like us, a Shangri-La for new bohemians. You can't turn a corner without running into a poet or a playwright or a novelist, the place is simply bursting with wordsmiths." She counted on her fingers. "Thomas Wolfe, Edgar Lee Masters. Trust me, you're just as good as they are."

Maxine was being generous, but Hazel appreciated the support. The idea of a hotel filled with creative types was certainly appealing. "How long did you stay there?"

"A couple of years. There's an actress named Lavinia Smarts, who brought me into the fold. She's like the den mother of the place."

"I've heard of her, she's an amazing talent."

"Sure is."

Hazel sighed. "I just wish there was something more we could do to help Paul. The colonel didn't seem very interested in us getting involved."

"Well, since our ride back to camp is nowhere in sight, how about we take a quick walk?" Maxine gave her a long look. "He said the jail was only a couple of blocks away."

They asked the guard out front for directions, and hustled over as fast as they could.

An Italian soldier stood at the entrance of a massive three-story building dotted with small, barred windows. Maxine explained in a mixture of mime, English, and a few words of Italian that they wanted to see the *tedesco*—the German. The Italian soldier didn't speak much English but, by making the universal sign for a bottle of beer, made his point clear. Maxine promised to bring some alcohol back the next week, although Hazel wasn't sure how she'd pull that off.

As they walked away, Maxine glanced back, then gripped Hazel's arm hard. "Look."

Hazel turned around and followed Maxine's finger. A pale face stared down at them from the third floor, hands tight around the bars of the window.

Paul. They waved with both arms, and he responded with a lift of his chin and a wave of his own before retreating from view. They couldn't explain that they'd be back, or that they were trying to help, but at least he'd seen them. Paul's defiance, his proud bearing, reminded Hazel so much of Ben. But she didn't want to think about that.

That evening at dinner, the soldiers had a surprise waiting for the acting troupe. As the men clapped and whistled, the five actresses were escorted to a table in the middle of the mess tent that had been laid with a white tablecloth, a bouquet of flowers, and cloth napkins. Hazel turned beet red but the other girls whistled right back.

"What's all this for?" asked Maxine.

"For reminding us of our girls back home," said one of the men. "For giving us hope."

Hazel looked about. So many of these men had never ventured out of their small towns before they were shipped off, and she could imagine the depths of their homesickness. How horrible it must've been when their idealized versions of the war, of heroic feats and brotherly love, were twisted by reality into fatigue, hunger, and grisly sights that would never fade from their memories.

After dinner, the women sat around the table, now joined by ten or so soldiers and a young kid with a sketch pad who offered to do caricatures of the men.

"Who is that?" Hazel asked Betty-Lou.

"Floyd. He was sent over, like we were, to entertain the troops."

"With art?"

"You should see him, he can whip up a portrait in no time. I kept mine. I'm going to frame it when I'm home. He gave me a waist to die for."

Hazel laughed. The boy had red pimples on his forehead, while his feet and hands were way too big for his thin frame. "He looks like he's about twelve."

"Kid's got a gift."

The boy ripped a page from his pad and handed it to Maxine. She held it up so the rest of them could see. In the drawing, her curves were slightly exaggerated, but not enough to be crass, and her red hair cascaded down her shoulders like a waterfall of lava. She came off as voluptuous and tough, her lips pursed together and her eyes peering off to the side, as if a lover had just walked into the room.

Hazel's attention was soon taken up by the man to her right, who hailed from Kansas. He talked so fast sometimes she wasn't sure what he was saying, but that didn't seem to matter to him at all. Something about sending home letters to his girl and did she think she'd still be waiting for him.

"Of course. What's your girl's name?" Hazel asked.

"Eileen. I write to her every week, without fail. But I haven't heard from her in three months. Do you think I've done something wrong? Or maybe she hasn't gotten my letters and thinks I'm dead? I don't know if I could stand that."

Hazel thought of her brother, who hadn't had a girl back home. Who hadn't had time to send even one letter to his family before they got word of his death. Her mother had opened the door to the two men in uniform and brought them into the living room, where Hazel sat reading to her father in his wheelchair. She remembered thinking that she hoped the soldiers weren't shocked by what they saw, the scripts and books lying about, the missing button on her father's cardigan, the dust motes dancing in the sunlight. That's what she remembered most about that moment. The dust motes, as she willed the men not to speak.

"Benny's all right, yes?" Her mother's chin wobbled.

They'd launched into a prepared speech. Said he'd been killed in a plane crash behind enemy lines. Said that he had not survived. Said that he was a hero.

"Where did it happen?" Ruth asked.

"We're not at liberty to say, ma'am," answered one of them.

"Was it quick?"

"Yes, ma'am."

But Hazel could tell the answer was a lie. They didn't know the circumstances, any more than she and her parents did. It was all a haze, like the stifling air inside the room.

The family came apart without Ben. He was the glue, the silly clown, the sweet prince that Ruth doted on. Hazel's father didn't show much emotion, and his disability made it difficult in any event. But Ruth emoted enough for the three of them put together, except for once at the wake, when Hazel looked up from pouring out cups of coffee to see her mother studying her intently, her eyes clear and dry. "I guess you'll do, God help us," Ruth had said, before retreating into the living room to weep in the arms of strangers.

As if he'd picked up on her thoughts, the boy from Kansas began to tear up. Hazel shifted her chair closer, asking him questions to distract him from the girl Eileen. About his favorite K rations, and what made him laugh. What were his favorite films? Who did he look up to and admire?

As they talked, she realized that this was how she could create the soldier hero for the broadcast. By interviewing the men and summing up their stories of bravery and humility. She couldn't wait to get back to the tent, pull out her notebook, and jot down some notes from the conversation.

"Hey, look, Hazel!" Verna pointed from across the table. "Floyd's done you, too."

Hazel hadn't even noticed the kid had pulled up a chair nearby. He carefully ripped the paper from the pad and handed it over.

He'd gotten the basics right. Her shoulder-length blond hair, with its curled tips. Her blue eyes and arched eyebrows, which she had to pencil in. Unlike Maxine's portrait, hers was not even a caricature, because nothing about her stood out.

What surprised her was that she didn't mind, really. The work she and Maxine were doing for the army, as well as their personal mission to get justice for Paul, was suddenly bigger and more vibrant than everything else in Hazel's life. She had never been the type of girl to fixate on her appearance, but now it was an afterthought at best; she was far more interested in what she was doing than what she looked like.

She smiled and thanked the boy for his drawing, rolling it up just as Maxine wandered over, carrying a box that clinked as she carefully set it down.

Their bribe had been procured.

CHAPTER THREE

Maxine

May 7, 1945

We managed to get into the jail to see the boy, Paul. They locked us inside his tiny cell with him while we talked, probably to keep us safe from the other prisoners, whose shouts and whistles echoed off the stone walls.

Right after we got back to camp, I dictated the basics of the conversation to Hazel and we sent it off to the colonel, convincing one of the drivers to hand deliver it today.

Now we wait, but I can't get him out of my head. Our report didn't say everything, like how the Italian guard eyed me up and down as I handed over the bottles of beer, and how glad I was to have Hazel next to me at that moment. That the cell Paul was kept in smelled like rancid meat.

So I'm writing it down myself. I have to, or I'll go mad with the waiting. We're not supposed to keep diaries, but I have to get these images out of my head and onto the page, so they don't haunt me anymore.

Inside his dingy cell, Paul talked with great detail, straining to make the story as vivid as possible, knowing that Hazel and I were most likely the only people who cared what happened to him.

The report didn't say that the first thing he did was pull out a ragged photo of his mother from his pocket, the words "Greta, Age 28" scribbled on the back. She had pale hair and eyes and looked like a ghost, and he told of his father's cruelty, how the beatings were more frequent as the German forces lost their hold. Greta disappeared two days after they'd been abandoned by his father, having gone out to find them some food. Rumor was she'd been drowned in the river by some villagers, held down until she stopped squirming. Paul had sought shelter in the home of his friend, Matteo, and they'd hidden him away, kept him safe.

The report didn't talk about the stretches of boredom as he cowered in the basement, staying quiet when a neighbor dropped by unexpectedly, of playing card games with Matteo to pass the time. Of their deepening friendship, and how worried he was that Matteo wouldn't be delivered home safely from Naples.

Before, when the Germans were in control, Paul would creep into his father's study late at night and copy the maps laid out on the oak desk as best he could. He'd bring them to Matteo, who'd pass them on to the Italians fighting against the Germans. I asked him why he did this, and he said it was revenge for his father's cruelty toward his mother, for the suffering of Matteo and his family. A way to sabotage the Nazi war machine from the inside.

I wondered if he'd been drafted into the role of spy—if Matteo's family had homed in on him as someone to be manipulated into doing the bidding of the resistance. He talked about Matteo as if he were his own brother, how their bond was unbreakable. As his tears fell in dirty tracks down his cheeks, Hazel asked what he was saying and I told her. She said to tell him that one day maybe he and Matteo would see each other again. I didn't bother translating that back to him. I didn't want to give him false hope.

A blind rage seized me in that moment, out of nowhere, at the fact that this kid had been dismissed by his own father. I knew that feeling well, but at least my grandmother had stepped into the void and made my childhood bearable. Paul was so young and vulnerable, yet had been so brave.

I recognized the pride in his voice as he spoke of channeling his confusion and distress, becoming a fighter for a cause he believed in. I understood his pain.

Paul told of traveling by night on stolen bicycles, how the freedom of being out in the world, of the scents and sounds of the earth, gave him courage. Until Naples, when they'd been flushed from their daytime hiding place and quickly surrounded.

The report was full of details of the maps he'd copied, the plans he'd handed over, and the names of the people who might vouch for him. It didn't say that since being put in the jail, he'd been kept in solitary confinement. The report didn't include the way he reached out as we got up to go, wanting to touch us but knowing that he was filthy and unwashed and that we'd be repulsed. Or how Hazel marched right over and held him close anyway, and then I did, too, stroking his hair as he wept.

"Have you heard the news?"

Betty-Lou burst into the tent, brimming with excitement. Hazel and I exchanged looks. Neither of us had felt like venturing out that day, not after seeing Paul so wretched. At least Hazel's script for her "American Hero" idea impressed Colonel Peterson to no end, which meant we could keep going back. The subject was a sweet kid from Kansas who has a girl back home, can't wait to see her, aw shucks, happy to be righting Hitler's wrongs in the meantime. Bringing order to chaos. It started out corny but by the end I was stifling a sob on air.

I tucked the diary under my mattress and stood as the cheers of the soldiers radiated across the camp. "What's going on?"

"Germany has surrendered!" Betty-Lou shrieked, her arms

clenched to her chest and her fists curled up tight like a baby's, before bouncing back outside. We followed. There were cheers, hugs, the men lining up to give me a squeeze. I was happy to provide what comfort I could. Some of these boys haven't felt a woman's arms around them in years.

With Hazel, of course, they were more circumspect, preferring to get into a deep conversation, spill their guts. She's got this girl-next-door quality—it's as if she were wearing pigtails and overalls, not a uniform. They may like to look at me, but they want to get to know her. I have to admit, when we first met, I thought she was a prude, and an insecure one at that. If I hadn't pushed her onstage that first day she showed up, I suspect she would have run for the coast and swum her way back home.

But now I see that she's stronger than I gave her credit for, and bolder, too.

With the celebrations in full swing, that night the five of us girls hit a Neapolitan nightclub, an after-hours joint on the second floor of a restaurant. The place was just how I like it: dark, music blaring, a mob of movement. The liquor poured freely and they asked me to sing, so I got up on the makeshift stage and belted out "That Old Black Magic." The band had my back, we shook the town. That's where the power is, when you're onstage, untouchable, and on fire. That kind of attention is like rocket fuel to me.

After, I stepped down and joined the girls at the table.

"You're so courageous," Hazel said. "Do you ever get nervous or doubt yourself? I can't imagine pulling off a song like that."

I admit, the compliments warmed me up. I told her the truth: "I never get nervous. I figure if I mess up, I'll just shimmy my way out of it." I performed a quick shoulder shake, and the soldier walking by us tripped on his feet. "Works every time."

When a young waiter brought over another round of drinks, Hazel examined him closely. The nightclub was staffed by POWs, and I knew who she was thinking about.

"Are you sure Colonel Peterson got our report?" I said. "What if he's mad that we met with Paul?"

"I don't care if he was mad, I'm glad we did it." She added that she'd even dreamed of Paul last night.

I didn't tell her I had, too, Paul's face as pale as a specter. And how my grandmother had appeared in the dream, trapped in the cell with him, screaming for help.

When my grandmother moved in with me and my parents when I was just a little girl, none of our neighbors wanted a Kraut nearby. Before coming to Seattle, she'd lived alone on tiny Vashon Island, a crazy hermit that the other islanders just barely tolerated. But my mother was sickly, and needed help raising me. Grandmother didn't make things easy on herself, speaking English only when necessary, defiant as ever.

My father, a failed salesman and successful inebriate, raged every evening against the world or his boss or both. I stayed hidden as much as possible, my grandmother bearing the brunt of his anger. At my mother's wake, when I was just five, one of his coworkers pulled me onto his lap. I could smell the liquor on his breath and it reminded me of my father. Shocked by the unexpected warmth of a man, the arms wrapping around me, I softened into his embrace.

I remember looking up at the man's face, the one who'd pulled me close. He kissed my forehead and pulled my hips in tighter. Into something that felt very wrong.

My grandmother appeared out of nowhere, yelling at him in German and yanking me by the arm. He'd crossed his legs and arms and called her a bitch, a Hun.

At my mother's wake.

"So tell me, do you have a boy back home, Maxine?"

Hazel's question, clearly an attempt to lighten the mood, snapped me back into the room. The nightclub was emptying out. Without the crush of bodies, the room's charmless decay was exposed, and depressing. My performance, like all performances, had vanished without a trace once the spotlight was turned off.

"No. No boy."

A man. But I'd never tell her that. He and I had made a pact not to tell anyone our secrets.

Sometimes I miss him so much I don't feel like I can keep it in, but I must. Although he's been part of my life for so long, I can't even write him letters home, knowing that the arrival of a letter from abroad will arouse suspicion. Yet I know he'll be waiting for me when I return. He promised.

"No one special?" Hazel was slightly drunk. She blinked a couple of times, trying to focus her gaze.

"No one special," I repeated. "How about you? Any beaus back in New York?"

"No. But that's fine. I was always too busy working."

The heat in the room was stifling and the mood of the remaining men had shifted, ever so slightly, from celebratory to predatory. The other girls had left to return to camp, leaving Hazel and me on our own.

That's when Colonel Peterson appeared, looking like he'd had as many drinks as we had, his cheeks as red as apples.

"Ladies, I received your report."

We both froze, unable to speak.

"It was surprisingly helpful. We were able to compare it to the report from our contacts in Calabria, and it appears that the boy's story checks out."

We whooped and hugged each other. I asked him what happens next.

"He can't go back to Germany, nor stay here. We'll have him released to the British forces, and taken to England."

Paul will be safe. That's what counts. While I'd love to see him again and say goodbye, wish him well, at least we know he'll be safe.

I know why Hazel got so tied up with Paul, even if they don't share the same language: She sees her dead brother in him. We don't speak about that, of course. For me, it's also personal.

I was out with my grandmother, when I was fifteen. We were shopping downtown, and I was proudly wearing grown-up shoes with a heel for the first time. I tripped over my own feet, splattered down on the sidewalk. My grandmother shrieked, then rattled off a scolding about picking up my feet when I walked, that I should stop scuffling along like a mule.

But in her frustration, she'd spoken German.

Before long, we were surrounded by angry men. I began crying, and they thought it was because I was afraid of a German stranger who'd pushed me. My grandmother stepped away from me, fear-stricken at having revealed herself, her nationality. A few men spat at her, called her a Kraut.

The injustice enraged me, and my teenaged embarrassment of drawing attention to myself faded fast. "*Nein. Sie ist meine Groß-mutter.*"

The crowd grew silent. I repeated the words, in English. "She's my grandmother."

Of course, that was the wrong thing to say, as it only incensed them further. Then a woman stepped into the crowd, a woman with a deep voice like thunder and the stature of Cleopatra, and mouths dropped. That was how I met Lavinia Smarts. I'd fallen on my face right in front of the theater where the actress was playing Lady Macbeth, and she took our hands and led us inside, to safety. Just as I'd saved Paul. I'm still not sure how I had the nerve to get into the driver's seat of the Jeep and slice through the crowd, but it was like an invisible line connected me to those boys. I remembered Lavinia's determined expression as she plucked me and my grandmother from danger, bringing justice to the world, and I couldn't let her down.

The Seattle Repertory Playhouse, run by a kindly couple named Florence and Burton, became my refuge. The plays they put on were fancy, with lots of poetic lines—Shakespeare and Chekhov. But I watched every rehearsal and helped out at the box office before landing a couple of small parts as a reward for my industriousness, eventually winning bigger roles. The professional actors passing through, including Lavinia, regaled us with stories of New York City, and I decided then and there to head east after high school.

My father told me the choice was teaching or nursing. No way would he have a daughter in the theater, exposing herself to ridicule. One evening, my grandmother stole into my bedroom and sat beside me on the bed in the dark.

"You want to go to New York? Leave me behind?" She spoke in German, knowing my father wouldn't understand us.

"I want to make something of myself. I love the theater."

"What do you love about it?"

I considered the question before answering, nestling into her the way I'd done as a child. "I love the way the actors treat each other, the way a play comes to life. That there are all these moving parts to a show that are entirely separate at first: the actors, the scenery, the lights. Slowly, they all come together and become something bigger. And then, after the applause dies down, it disappears. It's magical."

She smelled like peppermint as she reached down and kissed me on the forehead. "Your mother loved watching plays when she was young. We'd go to the puppet shows and she'd insist on climbing behind the stage after the performance, to see how it was put together. She wanted to touch the strings."

"That's what I want, as well. I want to touch the strings."

"Then you go."

She gave me enough money to get across the country and I checked into the hotel that Lavinia had told me about, a safe haven for artists, for activists, for freedom: the Chelsea. Fifty years earlier, it had been at the center of the theater district, but the Broadway houses had since moved uptown to Times Square, leaving the Chelsea behind. The room I stayed in was tiny, with a balcony decorated with cast-iron sunflowers and a wonderful view overlooking Twenty-Third Street.

Lavinia took me under her wing and got me a job as an usher at one of the smaller theaters, as well as an agent. Eventually, I began getting roles in touring productions. Somehow, though, I could never break through to the big time and land a part on the Broadway stage. Even though I tease Hazel about her serial understudying, part of me is jealous she's worked on the Great White Way. She got to watch Gene Kelly and Uta Hagen from the wings, had the chance to show up at opening-night parties and hobnob with the big-time critics, producers, and players. Better than singing your heart out in Cleveland for peanuts, then packing up and doing it all over again in another town, another state. To a bunch of nobodies.

It's funny, but sometimes I feel more for Hazel than I have for anyone else in my life, and other times I want to strangle her. I suppose this is what it must be like to have a sister.

How tenuous the line is between friends and enemies in a world at war.

❖

Hazel's crying on her cot, inconsolable.

We went to Naples to do the broadcast, secretly hoping for a chance to say goodbye to Paul, to wish him well. Colonel Peterson looked up from his desk but didn't rise, just pointed to the chairs and suggested we sit.

"There was a miscommunication," he said. "We gave instructions to release the German boy to the British. Either they didn't understand or they chose not to, but instead he was released into the general population of the jail."

My stomach lurched at the thought. A German teenager among Italian convicts.

"What happened? Is he all right?" I asked.

No. He wasn't.

As soon as the prisoners had been herded out into the courtyard for fresh air, two of them had dragged Paul over to a far corner, the colonel told us. One by one, the others drifted over to punch, kick, or stab Paul with whatever weapons they'd hidden from the guards. Never enough movement to draw attention in the crowded enclosure, but enough to brutalize. When they were called back into their cells, Paul lay crumpled in the dirt, breathing, but barely. He died on the way to the hospital.

We saved him from one mob, but he was torn apart by another.

Hazel hasn't stopped crying since. She paused once in her tears to wonder out loud what was it all for, why we even bothered. I didn't respond. Because I know that it wasn't fruitless, it just wasn't enough.

I thought of the war still raging, and of my grandmother back home, and vowed to not stop fighting.

CHAPTER FOUR

ℋazel

August 1945

B y August, the heat was unbearable, and news of atomic bombs being dropped on Japan only increased everyone's anxiety. The crush of the unknown seemed to get worse every day, as the entire camp waited to find out where the next posting would be. Hazel was still haunted by the terrible fate of Paul, but she and Maxine didn't discuss it, as if it were an infected wound, too raw to be exposed to the air. Silence was the only way to bear whatever came next in the war and not go mad.

Every so often, though, she'd look up and catch Maxine blinking rapidly, overcome by emotion, and Hazel would step in front of her, shielding her from the view of the other girls. Once, during a show, the line "All we have is our hands and a hole in God's earth" stopped Hazel cold. She couldn't remember what to say next, or why she was even standing onstage, but Maxine had picked up her cue and carried on with the play. As they crossed paths center stage, Maxine had laid a hand gently on Hazel's arm. No words were necessary between them.

"Where do you think they'll send us next?" Betty-Lou propped herself up on her cot, fanning her face with the script for tonight's performance, a compilation of Hazel's soldier tales. Colonel Peterson, entranced by her stories and looking for any way to keep the men entertained during the wait, had insisted that the acting troupe read them out loud, onstage. The girls were pleased, as it meant they didn't have to memorize anything new, just stand center stage and speak.

"I wouldn't mind being posted to a tropical locale," said Verna as she added next week's shows to the calendar with a black pen. "When you're surrounded by palm trees, the heat doesn't seem so bad. Maybe one of the Pacific Islands."

"I've had enough." Phyllis wore only her brassiere and panties, broken up by pink rolls of flesh. She'd stripped down as soon as they'd returned from breakfast, overcome by the flies and the sun. "I want to go home. I can't do this anymore. I don't want to offer comfort and distraction. What about *our* comfort and distraction?"

Hazel stopped scribbling in her notebook. "We haven't had to go out and kill people. No one's tried to shoot at us and kill us. Think of what these soldiers have been through."

Betty-Lou moaned. "Hazel with her halo, always doing good. Give it another few months, you'll be complaining like the rest of us."

Hazel took the teasing with a good-natured smile. "Yes, I'll be moaning with the rest of you wherever they send us next, I promise."

"I just want to be somewhere that there's orange juice. That's what I miss most." Phyllis sat up. "A fresh glass of cold orange juice."

"With bits of pulp so you get the burst of flavor," added Betty-Lou.

Verna cried out. "Stop, you're making my mouth water. This is so cruel. When I go home, I'm going right back to Los Angeles, where you can have an orange tree in your own backyard."

"What are you writing, Hazel?" Maxine asked. "I thought the latest script was final."

Hazel placed a hand over the page, not that Maxine could read it from where she was hanging laundry on the makeshift clothesline, filling the tent with the smell of wet stockings and Shalimar.

This morning, an idea for a play had come to Hazel in a rush of images. She didn't want to have to explain it, though. "Just a letter home."

"Ladies, mail for you!"

The artist boy, Floyd, popped in after Phyllis slid on a robe and gave him the all clear. He'd made himself the acting troupe's little helper ever since the fancy dinner in the mess tent, surprising them with boxes of Good & Plenty candy and, once, a bottle of White Horse Scotch. His devotion had only increased when Maxine and Hazel had come across some soldiers roughhousing with Floyd one day, making fun of his "artistic ways," and threatened to ban them from future performances if they continued the teasing.

Floyd walked over to Maxine and handed her an envelope with a grand flourish. "For you, Miss Mead."

Maxine took a deep breath, like she'd been splashed with a bucket of cold water, before tearing it open. Maxine never got mail, and as she read the letter, Verna snuck up behind her, taking a quick peek over her shoulder.

"Ooo, it says 'Meet me in the City of Angels,'" Verna crowed. "Maxine's got a rendezvous."

Maxine whirled around and for a moment, Hazel worried she'd lash out. But she caught herself, offering up a cheery smile. "Guess I'll have an orange tree in my backyard as well."

Before they could question her further, Floyd called for everyone's attention, standing tall in the middle of the space, gangly and blushing. Clearly proud to be noticed, yet utterly terrified of making a fool of himself. "I have news for you ladies."

"What's that?" Hazel asked, eager to encourage his bravery. She found him endlessly endearing, like a younger brother she had to protect from the big, bad world.

"We're not performing on the truck tonight."

"We're not performing?" echoed Phyllis, her eyes shining at the thought of an evening off.

"I didn't say that." He grinned so wide it was as though his face might burst. "We're performing at the Teatro di San Carlo."

Soon after Hazel had arrived, a driver with a love of opera had pointed out the grand theater, telling her it had been built in the 1730s, even before La Scala in Milan. Damaged by bombs a few years ago, it was one of the few buildings quickly restored after the liberation.

Even Betty-Lou perked up at the news. "A real theater. Where I won't get bitten up by those awful bugs that come out at night."

"Where people sit in actual seats, not on benches," added Verna.

"Be ready by five," said Floyd. "This is gonna be your biggest show yet."

Hazel stood and gave him a kiss on the cheek. "You're the hero of the day, bringing us such good news."

The theater was even grander inside than Hazel expected. Box seats rose five stories in a horseshoe shape, capped by a painted ceiling where robed figures floated on clouds. After playing under the actual sky for so long, no matter what the weather, it was a relief to have a fake one instead.

Hazel spent time with the crew before the house was opened to the audience, trying to explain what kind of lighting she wanted for the evening's performance. A soldier who spoke Italian translated, but the stagehands were pushing back, saying it couldn't be accomplished. Hazel didn't back down. She kept at it, talking to the interpreter, gesturing like mad, until they all were nodding.

Maxine approached her after the group broke up. "What's going on?"

"I could tell they were just going to point a spot at whoever's speaking, and that won't work at all. It has to feel inclusive, warm."

"I've never heard you so passionate about lighting before," Maxine teased.

"This is different."

"Because you wrote it."

"No. Because *they* wrote it." She pointed out to the empty audience. "It's their play. That's why it has to be perfect." After what had happened to Paul, her eyes had been opened to the harsh realities of war, and she knew every soldier out there had gone through a similar awakening, one that must be respected and honored.

At exactly eight o'clock, the colonel gave a brief speech about what the evening entailed. Verna read first, and the soldiers seemed more subdued than usual, perhaps intimidated by the lush setting or because this wasn't a normal performance, just a series of speeches. But by the time Verna had finished her story, the soldiers were dabbing at their eyes. The men ate it up, giving her a standing ovation.

Next up was Betty-Lou. Hazel hovered backstage in the wings with Maxine, watching Betty-Lou reduce the audience to helpless laughter as she told a soldier's story about trying to tame a local piglet, when Colonel Peterson appeared.

"We have to stop the show." He held a piece of paper in his hand, and Hazel could have sworn he was shaking. "Stop it at once."

"We can't stop the play." Maxine gestured to the stage. "They're having a ball."

"Stop the play and read this to the men." He shoved the paper into Hazel's hand. "Orders of the CO."

"The commanding officer?" Hazel's eyes grew wide. Something terrible must have occurred. Or maybe it was news of their next posting. Either way, it was unfair to make the performers the bearers of bad news.

Before Hazel could inquire further, Colonel Peterson shoved her onstage, just as Maxine had done her very first day. Betty-Lou looked over, confused. Murmured complaints from the audience at the interruption washed over Hazel as she took center stage.

"I'm sorry." Hazel spoke quickly, hoping to get this over with fast, whatever it was. "I've been told we have important news from the CO."

A hushed silence fell over the expanse.

Hazel unfolded the note and gasped. She glanced over at the colonel, who nodded. Her voice shaking, she read out loud.

"The war with Japan is over."

Tears filled her eyes as she looked out over the men.

"The war is over. We're all going home."

ACT TWO

E ach room at the Chelsea remembers the people who've passed within its walls, as if the names and dates have been etched on the grubby doorframes. This one had held the bloated poet who trod over discarded candy wrappers and dirty shirts, rolling himself onto the bed with a groan as the springs of the mattress answered with high-pitched creaks. He took a swig of whatever sat on the bedside table, coughing and retching, then another to swill away the taste of his own bile.

His girl, assistant, lover, slept quietly beside him, and he didn't blame her; he was the cause of her exhaustion. But he was wide-awake: The hallucinations returned, frightening him, the swirls of phantoms circling closer and closer. A gentlewoman stretched out her hand, her rings glistening like tears, while the long-dead painters studied the scene as they would a pietà. The hum of musicians grew louder, the vibrations flowing through plaster and stone. The poet had sighed and let go and drifted up, joining the others.

Years later, the room would prepare to swallow one more soul. Already, the breaths of the woman on the bed were becoming increasingly jagged.

The poet joined hands with his fellow wraiths, and together they waited.

CHAPTER FIVE

Hazel

New York City, May 1950

"All right, everyone. We're live in thirty seconds. Hazel, this will be your big moment."

Jack Singleton, the director of the hit radio program *Cavalcade of America*, looked her way. Hazel returned a solemn nod.

They recorded in the NBC Studios at Rockefeller Center every Friday, an 8:00 P.M. show followed by another one for the West Coast at 11:00. In the weeks Hazel was called in to work, she was able to watch great actors and writers in action, big names like Robert Sherwood and Mickey Rooney. Even Cary Grant, once.

She huddled with four of her fellow actors around one microphone, script in hand. Each episode brought to life a historical event, with the emphasis on inspiration and uplift. This evening's reenacted how the death of a tubercular cow led to the pasteurization of milk and saved millions of lives. Not a topic Hazel had ever imagined being dramatized, but why not?

The ON AIR sign lit up and the announcer launched into the

DuPont slogan, "Better Things for Better Living through Chemistry," before offering up an introduction to this week's episode.

The actors straightened, at the ready.

The director nodded and the first section of dialogue between the cow's owner and a veterinarian began, the actor Melvyn Douglas speaking with a clipped authority as the owner.

The director raised his eyebrows at Hazel, lifted his finger, and right on cue Hazel moved closer into the mic and took a deep breath.

"Moo."

She mooed like a cow a few times more, before joining the others with general barnyard noises.

The director nodded his approval.

The highlight of her week. Acting like a cow.

When she'd first come home from the war, her mother had welcomed her back, eager to hear about her travels abroad. But once Hazel had run through all the stories she could muster, they fell into old habits. Her mother had made lists of theater producers Hazel ought to see, shows she should audition for, just as she'd done with Hazel's father and brother, when the last thing Hazel wanted to do was put on makeup and high heels and beg for an audition. The work seemed trivial, after what she'd done in Naples. After what she'd seen. She'd eventually been offered the job at the radio show, although the work was intermittent at best, and far from challenging.

The past few years, she'd continued to work on the play she'd started in Italy after learning of Paul's brutal murder. The main characters—a young Italian man hiding a German who'd turned against his homeland, and the German himself—had haunted her nightmares since the events in the plaza in Naples, and she'd put it down on the page in the hopes she could tame the violent memories that spooled in her head. Still, something was wrong with it, but she was too nervous to show it to anyone else and get advice. The setting—an Italian village in the countryside—limited her enormously. What did she really know about small-town Calabria? Not much beyond the scenery. She kept at it, though, trying to make it come to life.

After the radio program wrapped, everyone clapping one another on the back and offering congratulations as if they'd won the World Series, Hazel grabbed her coat and handbag and headed for the door. In spite of the odd subject matter, she'd been inspired by some of the dialogue, and couldn't wait to get home to tweak her own work accordingly.

She never played anything grander than a voice in the crowd, but with each broadcast, she learned something new about structure or timing. Hazel absorbed these lessons as if she were an apprentice instead of an extra, lingering behind the director as he gave notes to the leads or brainstormed with the writer to come up with a better ending.

She stepped outside into the warm spring evening. The streetlamps threw down shimmering ribbons of gold on the wet pavement and sidewalks. The walk uptown, even at this late hour, was safe and quiet.

At home, Ruth sat alone, hunched over, nursing a cold tea and a grudge at their linoleum table. Without Ben to divert their mother's attention, Hazel received the full onslaught of pressure to perform. She'd considered finding her own place, even walked by the Chelsea Hotel a number of times and gazed up at the balconies, wondering which room Maxine had stayed in.

They'd exchanged letters for a while after the war, Maxine's full of Hollywood gossip, Hazel with updates on the theater scene and her attempts at both acting and playwriting, but after a while, Hazel found it easier to stop replying than admit how dull her life had become. Meanwhile, she'd read all about Maxine's exploits in Hollywood in the magazines, how she'd landed several decent parts in movies, been photographed in front of palm trees and on breezy beaches.

The Chelsea Hotel felt like a link to the Maxine she'd known in Naples, the girl who'd suffered with her at Paul's death, who'd shared the horror and, at times, the strange joy of war. On top of that, the place tantalized her with creative promise, with the knowledge that so many actors and writers had stayed there and found inspiration. But Hazel couldn't leave her mother, not after Ben had left and never come back.

Hazel hung her coat on the hook and took off her gloves. "Did you listen tonight, Ma? What did you think?" Hazel added an extra dose of enthusiasm to her voice, hoping that might change the course of the conversation.

"It was fine." Ruth took a loud sip of tea. "I have no idea which one you were."

No way was Hazel going to volunteer that she'd voiced a bovine.

"I made a list of casting calls for you for next week." Ruth pointed to a notebook on the table. "First one is Monday at ten, for a revival of some Thornton Wilder one-act. Make sure you wear something pretty, put on some makeup. We've got to land you a theater job soon, or you'll be out of the running completely."

"That's the wrong way to look at it. Radio and television are all the rage these days. There's a ton of new opportunities."

"I don't know about that. The stage was good enough for your brother. By now he would have been starring on Broadway. Don't forget, I know how this is done. After all, I built your father's career. Without me, he'd never have hit the big time."

No one could forget that fact, as Ruth brought it up every chance she got: that she had been his assistant at first before gradually taking over every aspect of decision-making—from choosing the color of his shirt to the part in his hair—and turning him into a major name. His helplessness later in life sealed her role as compassionate caretaker. Every neighbor who stopped by for coffee knew to praise Ruth for her self-sacrifice if they wanted an extra slice of cake.

Whenever Ruth got prickly, Hazel reminded herself that her mother lashed out only because she was terrified of losing another child the way she had lost Ben. Hazel had already disrupted her mother's life once by impulsively auditioning for the USO tour, and Ruth would brook no more foolishness.

One evening, though, Hazel had seen a different side of Ruth, when she'd awoken to a strange sound and watched silently from the darkness of the hallway as her mother sobbed into her father's lap. She was half kneeling on the cold tile floor, clutching his knees and weeping into his skinny thighs as he patted her head with his good hand, as one would an old dog. Her father lifted his eyes and met Hazel's gaze. Even though he hadn't said a word since the stroke, she knew exactly what that look meant. Do not enter, do not catch her in her grief. Go back to bed and leave her to me.

Hazel tried again. "The good thing about being on the radio is that no one knows how old you are, which opens up a lot of great parts."

"Voices age just like faces. Don't fool yourself."

"Well, sure, eventually they do. But I'm only thirty."

"You think thirty's young?"

"Not young, no. But I don't mind aging into leading lady territory. Much better than being a ditzy ingenue." Hazel winked, trying to force Ruth into more lighthearted territory. If she could steer her mother into a laugh just as her rant gathered steam, the tension between them might fizzle. Hazel had used this method of circumventing Ruth's tirades for years, but lately it hadn't been working very well.

"What do you know about it?" Ruth scowled. "You've never played an ingenue."

Hazel sighed. There would be no avoiding any tension tonight. "Mom, enough. I may not want to work onstage anymore. I may not even want to act."

Ruth flinched, her lips in a long, hard line. "You don't want to act? It was good enough for your brother."

"But I'm not Ben. I'm not going to be Ben. I have to find my own way."

"Exactly what do you think you'll do instead? You're in your room all day, typing away, like Hemingway. Do you think you can be a Hemingway? That's not what's in your blood. What's in your blood is the theater." She stood and dumped out the rest of her tea in the sink. "At this rate, you'll be playing old harridans before you know it."

Enough was enough. "Then I might as well stick around and learn from the best."

The slap came as a complete surprise. Ruth had never raised her hand to Hazel before, and for a moment, Hazel wasn't sure exactly what had happened. She put her hand to her cheek and then looked at her fingers, as if the answer could be found there.

"I'm sorry, Hazel. I didn't mean it."

Her mother tried to hug her, to pull her close, but Hazel stepped back, hands in the air, to block her. She needed space, time to think, without her mother fussing about and telling her what to do every minute of the day. Enough was enough. And there was one place where she might be able to find this reprieve.

As her mother's apology slid into tears, Hazel packed a bag and jumped in a cab. She gave the driver the name of the Chelsea Hotel and stared out the window as the taxi pulled up to the redbrick building, a handsome melding of Victorian Gothic and Queen Anne styles that loomed over Twenty-Third Street.

Her plan was to stay there for a few days and collect herself, cool off. She wasn't called in to work this week anyway, and she needed a break from her mother's self-pity and recriminations.

In the lobby, she examined the eclectic mix of art on the walls. One was signed *de Kooning*, and she remembered seeing his first one-man show a couple of years earlier. Victorian flourishes filled the foyer, including a massive mahogany fireplace that wouldn't be out of place in a Scottish castle. Tables with gleaming marble tops reflected the circular chandelier. The furniture was too big for the size of the room, but the high ceilings helped manage the scale.

A young couple stood at the front desk, chatting with the clerk. The woman tottered on heels so high Hazel was amazed she'd been able to navigate the foyer, and had a purple fascinator perched on her head that matched the suit clinging to her slender frame. She turned around and gave Hazel a tentative smile.

The woman was a man. With five-o'clock shadow and thick eyebrows. In women's clothing. The couple disappeared into the elevator.

"All right, miss." The man behind the counter tugged at the brown bow tie around his neck and motioned to Hazel, entirely unperturbed by the strange sight. "What can I help you with?"

She tried to remain unruffled, as if being here were perfectly normal. Maxine had warned her the place was eccentric. "I'd like a room, please. Nothing fancy. I'll be here for a few days."

He looked at his register and frowned. "We're almost fully booked. Who are you, exactly?"

The question threw her. "I'm sorry?"

"Who are you? What do you do?"

"I'm a writer." She'd never said that out loud before. Never dared to. The words hung in the air.

The man perked up considerably. "We've had a number of famous writers here. O. Henry in room 412, Edgar Lee Masters in 214. Thomas Wolfe wrote *Look Homeward, Angel* in 829. Mark Twain lived here as well. You a novelist?" He spoke with a vaguely European accent that Hazel couldn't place.

"No. A playwright."

"Huh. In that case." The man scribbled something down in his register. "What's your name?"

"Hazel Ripley."

"Sign here."

She did so, and snapped open her pocketbook.

"No need for that yet," he said. "Let's get you settled first. You seem like a nice enough girl."

"Thank you, sir."

"Full name's David Bard. At your service. You got any problems, you just come to me. My office is around the corner." He plucked a key off a hook and led her to the elevator. His upbeat manner and ill-fitting suit endeared him to her immediately.

A weathered bellhop appeared, wearing a frayed navy uniform that looked about as old as he was. He picked up her suitcase and followed them inside the elevator.

"This here is Percy," said Mr. Bard. "And in case you need anything fixed, ask for Krauss."

She reminded him that she was only there for a few days. "I doubt I'll need a handyman."

He just smiled.

They got out on the fifth floor and walked past a wide marble staircase that spiraled through the middle of the building, its railing studded with bronzed-iron passionflowers.

Mr. Bard opened the door to one of the rooms at the very end of the hallway, and Hazel gasped. Rows of handsome bookcases lined one wall, with a fireplace opposite. A solid rosewood beam separated two open spaces, the walls of one painted a robin's-egg blue and the other a sunny yellow, with golden wood floors that ran on the diagonal. Matching red brocade chairs flanked the fireplace, but the rest of the furniture trumpeted mismatched patterns and colors that unexpectedly blended in with one another. Stained glass in the transom windows topped off the room's riot of colors and textures.

To the left was a small kitchen. A bedroom sat just off the main room, its decor only slightly more subdued than that of the salon.

She thought of her meager savings. "This is beautiful, but I can't possibly afford it."

"I'm afraid it's all we have. But you're only here for a few days, you say, right? Let's agree on fifteen dollars a night and call it a day." He laughed at his joke.

"Are you sure? Once I'm here, I may never want to leave."

He smiled. "Won't be the first time. Price is cheaper by the month, by the way. If you're a true artist, and I can tell just by looking at you, you are, this is the place for you. Back when it was built, the plan was to make it a utopia for creative minds, whether poor or rich. The Chelsea was the tallest building in New York City until 1902. We still have a roof garden where you can enjoy the view."

Hazel let him ramble on at length. This was obviously a man who enjoyed his work.

After he left, she unpacked the few items she'd brought with her and placed her typewriter and manuscript on the small desk. In the kitchen, she checked the icebox, which was empty, and poured a glass of water from the sink, realizing after the first sip that the cold tap ran hot water, and vice versa.

One window looked out west, across the roof of the synagogue next door, while the French door in the main room faced north. She turned the knob and stepped out onto the narrow, lacy balcony.

Five stories below, traffic zoomed along Twenty-Third Street.

With a start, she realized what was wrong with her play: the setting. It was far too specific and unwieldy. What if she set the story in a grand hotel, like the Chelsea, but one that's crumbling away in a war zone, under siege, with only a handful of guests left? Forget nationalities, make it a war story that's not tied to any particular war, so the characters are stripped down to their essence. They suspect there's an enemy in their midst, an enemy who insists he works for the resistance. It would raise questions of patriotism and nationalism, faithfulness and betrayal, everything that had churned inside Hazel from her time in Italy.

Hazel reconsidered the strange person she'd observed in the lobby. What if one of the leading men was actually a leading lady, but her gender wasn't revealed right away? Hazel thought of Shakespeare, who often had girls wearing drag in order to remain safe in a dangerous world—Rosalind, Viola. If she layered in a love story between the two leads, the whole thing would truly sing.

She practically skipped back to the desk and rolled a fresh sheet of paper into the typewriter. Fingers poised on the keys, she considered how many other writers had stayed here, in this hotel. She could almost feel the ghosts of former guests pressing around her, encouraging her. This place was a living, breathing muse, one that coddled its guests and kept them warm while they scribbled away. Or, from the sound of the piano she'd heard in the hallway and the artwork in the lobby, composed or sang or painted.

She'd come this far, and her only goal over the next few days was to rework the play, following this new inspiration. That accomplishment might spur her on to pursue a different path, a way out of the grind of playing barn animals on the radio. Once the play was ready, she even might work up the courage to gather together some actor friends to read through it, and get a sense of what worked and what didn't. For now, though, in the quiet of her room, she would take it page by page.

❖

On Hazel's second day at the Chelsea Hotel, a desk clerk called her over as she entered the lobby on her way back from a quick lunch at the corner Automat. She'd been up all night, fueled by coffee and the words that tumbled out of her fingers onto the pages, and was eager to get back to work.

"Miss Ripley? You have a message." He plucked a piece of paper from one of the cubbyholes.

It was an invitation to a cocktail party later that evening, up on the seventh floor, signed *Miss Lavinia Smarts.*

The actress who knew Maxine. "I've never met her. How does she know who I am?" she asked the clerk.

The clerk laughed. "Mr. Bard, of course. He's been talking you up all around the place. As our new writer in residence."

Considering Mr. Bard had never read a page she'd written, his enthusiasm was certainly misplaced. Still, she couldn't help but puff up a little.

She'd planned on writing all evening. Going to a party might disrupt the flow of creativity that had invigorated her the past two days, the clacking of the typewriter the only sound other than the honks from the cars far below. Her revisions were almost complete.

The clerk shook his head, as if reading her mind. "Best not to decline. There are rules of etiquette at the Chelsea, you know."

"What rules?"

"One never knocks on the door of a room during the day, when the writers are writing or the artists are at work. Instead, messages should be left down here. Once evening falls, all rules are off and you'll find folks tripping from room to room as if it's Mardi Gras. Oh, and never turn down an invitation from Miss Smarts."

"I won't know anyone. I'm not sure I'll fit in."

"You do already, my dear."

She wasn't sure from his raised eyebrow whether that was a good or a bad thing, but she decided she must attend. It would give her a good story to tell, and who knows who she'd meet? A few hours later, after another furious bout of writing, Hazel reluctantly pulled herself away. She put on her favorite lilac dress and powdered her nose before taking the elevator up to the seventh floor.

The party was already in full swing. Miss Smarts's apartment was similar in layout to her own, but in the center of the salon stood a grand piano, piled with sheets of music spilling onto the floor around it. A drink was placed in her hand without her asking—a martini—and she made her way to a velvet couch, hoping to observe the goings-on without having to interact.

No luck.

Two older women, identical twins wearing matching dresses and bright pink shoes, plunked down on either side of Hazel and introduced themselves as Winnifred on the left and Wanda to her right. "You're the new writer Mr. Bard is talking about, right?"

"News spreads fast."

"Sure does," said Winnifred. "We've lived here for ages. Anything you want to know, just ask us."

Hazel looked about. "Where's Lavinia Smarts?"

"She likes to make a grand entrance once the party's in high gear," answered Wanda. "In the meantime, let me tell you who *is* here. That man over there is Virgil Thomson, the composer."

She pointed to a pear-shaped man standing by the piano, with a wide forehead and a grim look on his face. He was listening to an older man, handsome, who Hazel recognized as a well-regarded artist. "Is that the painter John Sloan?"

Winnifred gestured around the room, beaming like a proud mother. "She's full of famous people."

"The hotel, you mean?"

"Exactly."

The Chelsea Hotel. A "she," like a lumbering redbrick ship filled with foolish dreamers.

Hazel would have to use the phrase somewhere in her work.

"Oh no, watch out for fireworks." Wanda and Winnifred spoke in tandem and giggled at each other.

"You dare to show your face, Ben Stolberg!" The words came from a woman of around seventy who appeared from the bedroom, with thick, swept-up hair and a profile that belonged on a Greek coin. Even though her skin was wrinkled and stippled with age spots, her mouth was still generous and her eyes a vivid green, matching the wrap that she tossed dramatically over one shoulder. Lavinia Smarts was even taller in person than she appeared onstage, a fact that surprised Hazel.

Miss Smarts glared at a man who'd just arrived through the

front door and looked to be in his late fifties. The man opened his mouth to offer a retort, but someone turned up the music, so Hazel couldn't hear his reply.

Wanda shouted into Hazel's ear. "That's your hostess, Lavinia Smarts. She and Ben are always at each other's throats."

"Why?"

"Politics. When things get crazy, everyone goes up to the roof to avoid getting decked by a flying ashtray."

The music grew even louder, the sounds of violins drowning out any attempt at conversation. Across the room the argument carried on, like a silent movie. Hazel secretly rooted for Lavinia Smarts to win.

"Lavinia Smarts was a communist but is now a socialist," shouted Wanda. "That's what the fight's all about. Ben Stolberg finds her political views abhorrent, whether communist or socialist."

"He hates all 'ists,' really," added her sister.

"Are you a communist?" Wanda asked politely when the orchestral music quieted down.

Hazel didn't answer outright. "Why?"

"We have a number of them organizing on the first floor, if you're interested."

The thought made her smile. "Back in the day, my brother was active in the CPUSA. I went along for the ride, really." Ben had joined the Communist Party of the USA in the thirties, after droning on and on at home about the imbalance of wealth during the Depression and the rise of fascism in Europe. He'd call her into his room to read from some Communist text or other, and she'd sit at the end of his bed, cross-legged, nodding as if she understood but really just enjoying his attention. He'd had the lashes of a girl, long and lovely, but the rest of him was all boyish exuberance, quoting

Karl Marx the same way he'd once carried on about the Hardy Boys mysteries.

"I suppose everyone has a right to an opinion," offered Hazel to the twins.

"Maybe not for long."

Wanda had a point. In the years since the war had ended, political sentiment in the United States had turned hard to the right. Mr. Stolberg turned off the record player with a sharp scrape that made Hazel put her hands to her ears.

"Listen, Miss Smarts," he said. "You want to know why the Screen Actors Guild insists that all members take an oath of loyalty? Because the entertainment industry is filled with pinkos."

Miss Smarts wasn't cowed. "Says who? Joseph McCarthy? He's just making it up as he goes along. How can you not see that?"

Mr. Stolberg wagged a plump finger in her face. "The commie spies have already made inroads throughout America. It's only a matter of time before they take over and destroy democracy forever. We must fight back."

"How? By invading Korea? It's on the other side of the world, for God's sake. It has nothing to do with us." She looked around the room, currying support, and Hazel nodded vigorously.

"Korea is only the beginning." Stolberg was turning red. "We have to defend ourselves from the incursion."

"You mean send more boys out to die? Enough, I've heard enough. You must leave at once." She extended one arm out, finger pointing to the door, and Mr. Stolberg did a dramatic bow before exiting. Obviously, this was a repeat performance, and neither seemed to take it personally, Mr. Stolberg rolling his eyes on his way out, and Miss Smarts taking a long swig out of a glass and twirling around.

"Where's this new writer we have on board?" She came to a stop in front of the sofa, jutting out one hip.

Hazel got to her feet, noting that Miss Smarts was taller by at least five inches. She introduced herself and thanked her for the invitation.

"Please, call me Lavinia," she insisted. "I remember your father fondly, as well as your brother. You Ripleys are a talented bunch."

"Thank you." The theater community was so small, Hazel immediately felt comfortable with Lavinia, as if she'd known her for years. "We also have a friend in common," she added.

"Who is that?"

"Maxine Mead."

Lavinia clapped her hands together, her eyes twinkling. "A delightful child. I remember her well, from my days on tour. I hear she's off in California making movies. How is she doing?"

"Sounds like she's doing quite well," Hazel answered vaguely. "From what I can tell, Hollywood agrees with her."

"Word at the Chelsea is that you're a playwright. What have you written?"

"Nothing yet. I'm trying to write a play. About my experiences in a USO touring company, during the war."

"A girl writing a war play, I like what I'm hearing. Send it to me, please."

"Send it to you?" Hazel must have heard wrong.

"Yes. Call downstairs and have them deliver it up to me tonight. I'll have it back to you tomorrow morning by nine."

A terrible idea, for many reasons. It was Hazel's only copy. She hadn't finished revising the last scene. It wasn't ready. Yet Lavinia's offer, her eyebrows raised in bemusement, was quite generous.

But what if she hated it? Would Hazel be able to withstand the blow of harsh criticism? Then again, no matter what Lavinia thought, by refusing her, Hazel might never get another opportunity.

God, she was making herself crazy. Meanwhile, Lavinia was staring at her, waiting for an answer.

"I'll do that. Thank you, Lavinia."

Hazel dashed back to her room to continue working, finalizing the draft before wrapping some twine around the finished pages, tying it off, and ringing down to the porter to pick it up.

The next day, she reluctantly began packing up her few items of clothing, watching as the clock ticked closer and closer to nine. Maybe Lavinia had tossed the script aside after the first page and completely forgotten about it. Of course, Hazel could call up to her room and inquire, but she didn't want to come off as pushy.

What a mistake, to let the pages out of her sight.

She sat at the bare desk, the typewriter packed up in its case on the floor beside her, and stared out the window. No matter what the outcome, she'd make good on her promise to finish it. For Paul's sake. For her own sake.

Promptly at 9:00 A.M., there was a knock on her door. A porter handed the script back, with a note tucked inside the twine.

This must be mounted. Am talking to a producer forthwith. Remain in place.

Hazel sat down on the sofa and looked about, the bright colors of the pillows and rug swirling dizzily around her.

Looked like she'd be staying on at the Chelsea Hotel.

CHAPTER SIX

Hazel

May 1950

W ho are you? Did you really write this?"
Lester Canby tossed Hazel's play on his desk and eyed her from above his spectacles, perched midway on a bulbous nose. His face was long and thin, with hollow cheekbones, topped by an enormous bald head. His enlarged cranium and bulging eyes reminded her of an octopus she'd seen in an aquarium as a child.

Hazel had turned up at the producer's office in Times Square not knowing what to expect. Four days went by after Miss Smarts's directive to remain in place, and Mr. Bard had inquired, ever so politely, about the rent. He'd called her into his office at the front of the building, formerly the ladies' reception room, where angelic plaster cherubs looked down with unabashed delight at the chunky adding machine and endless reams of paper that covered his desk. Hazel promised she'd pay up on Monday, once she'd had a chance to cash her check from the radio show, and he'd beamed like she'd told him he'd won the lottery. She'd hate to disappoint him.

Luckily, the invitation to meet with Mr. Canby arrived soon after. Hazel had been in his office before, as a struggling young actress making the rounds in her finest outfit and brightest lipstick, inquiring whether there were any roles she might audition for. Mr. Canby had seen her a few times but never cast her in a part, dismissing her with a loud bark. She hoped he didn't remember.

She wasn't sure how to respond to his question about the play's authorship. Her name, after all, was on the title page. "I did write it. The play was inspired by my experiences as a USO tour performer."

"I love the part where the guy turns out to be a girl. I didn't expect that twist."

She couldn't help but beam.

"It's a fresh take on war, and I also love that we don't know what country the hotel is in, or even what side some of the characters are on, at least at first. Terrific." He leaned back, teetering on the back legs of his chair. A habit, from the looks of the indentations on the wall behind him, that lined up perfectly with the two round finials rising over either shoulder. "This isn't my usual cup of tea. My audiences love spectacles. Revues, that sort of thing. I had a troop of whirling dervishes from Turkey booked at the Biltmore this summer, but I just found out they're not coming. So I need a replacement. Fast."

She'd figured she'd been called in as a courtesy to Lavinia Smarts. But no. He needed a replacement. Mr. Canby was actually considering her play for a slot in a Broadway theater.

"You mean, me?"

"Maybe." He slammed his chair back down. There were probably a couple of divots in the wooden floor as well.

She had to set him straight on one point. "This is a drama, not a spectacle."

"Fine with me. Look at *Death of a Salesman*. Nothing spectacular about it, yet it won the Tony. I read that play and said to Miller, 'What kind of title is that? You're giving away the ending, what the hell are you thinking?' So I passed." His irritation at having done so was obvious. "What a mistake. After that, I decided that I should go against my instincts. If I think something's a bore, I should book it. What's your play called again?" He squinted at the title page.

"*Wartime Sonata.*"

"Exactly. Who would want to see a play with that title?"

"So you think that my play is a bore?"

"Don't take it personally." He leaned forward. "I cried. Don't tell anyone else that. If you can make me cry, think of all those weepy housewives out there. That's what I'm banking on. We'll do a table read in two weeks, onstage at the Biltmore. It's one of the smaller theaters, which means I'm not taking that much of a risk. I gotta hear it out loud, then we'll do casting and get it up by July. I got an empty theater and I gotta fill it, or I lose money. You in? Don't go shopping this around on me. Any questions?"

He wanted her play. Barring any surprises at the table read, her play was going to Broadway. For a moment she was struck dumb; then she asked the first thing that came into her head. "Um, how do I get paid?"

He laughed. "I like the way you think. Like a man, not a girl. Here's the deal: We give you an advance of one grand. I'll have my secretary cut you a check today. Once the show makes money, you'll get four and a half percent of the take, minus the advance. Got it?"

He held out his hand and Hazel shook it. One thousand dollars. An unimaginable amount, considering she'd thought the ten dollars a day she'd made on tour was a decent wage. Even better, she'd be able to stay on at the Chelsea.

All those words she'd typed and retyped over the past five years since her return from the war had finally paid off, in spades. She thought of the thousands of pages of dialogue that she'd reworked and then tossed aside in her effort to find just the right phrase, the right joke, the right mood. This play was a culmination of serious study and hard work, but still, after all that, she'd simply been in the right place at the right time. At the Chelsea Hotel.

Right off, she sent Lavinia an enormous bouquet of flowers to thank her for the referral, and told the folks at NBC that she had booked another job. The hardest part was telling Ruth, who considered her decision to stay at the Chelsea Hotel and not return home a personal betrayal. Ruth had said she was crazy to break away from acting, called the play a dangerous distraction, and warned that Hazel would regret not taking her advice. Hazel had stood firm, though, the memory of her mother's hand on her cheek still fresh.

The day of the reading, Hazel knocked on the stage door of the Biltmore and was ushered inside to the house, where plasterwork in creams and light blues rose to an enormous dome. A long table had been set up in the center of the stage; a bare bulb atop a pole stood sentry near the wings. A group of actors had been assembled for the workshop, and Hazel knew from experience that they all hoped to get the roles they'd been temporarily assigned. They clapped politely as she was introduced, and she took the empty seat next to Mr. Canby.

The director, a short man with a nasal voice, named William Williams, stood to offer a welcome speech. "This is a remarkable play by a woman about war. I want the audience to feel the bullets, the fear, to smell the sweat. Make it big, don't be afraid, my soldiers. Let us begin."

Not the words Hazel would have used to describe her play, but she stayed mum. Let the professionals do their jobs. She'd given herself a pep talk before walking into the theater, telling herself that she had as much right to be here as anyone, and to take a seat at the table with confidence. But no one had really noticed her, even now.

"Act one, scene one," read the stage manager.

Hazel cringed as the actress playing the female lead burst into high-pitched crocodile tears only a few lines into her first scene, when she was supposed to be pretending to be a man. The actor playing opposite her shouted to the rafters and gesticulated wildly as they hid from the search mob storming the hotel. Not the most effective choice. Thank goodness this was just a workshop.

Hazel raised her eyebrows at Mr. Canby, but he just nodded and leaned back in his chair, staring at the lighting grid in the rafters.

The revisions she'd done to the play held up, at least. Once she convinced the director to take it down a notch, she was certain it would work. She looked out at the empty seats. So many people to attract, to convince to buy a ticket. To entertain. This was her big chance, and she'd have to make sure she held the reins tightly so Mr. Williams didn't run off in the wrong direction. But that's what rehearsal was for.

They took a break after the second act. Hazel tried to explain her take on the play to Mr. Canby, but he just laughed and told her that the playwright always thought he knew best. But in this case, they would have to trust in the director, who, as Hazel would do well to remember, was the most experienced and successful artist in the room. Hazel knew then that her only hope was to appeal to Mr. Williams.

She discovered their illustrious director off in the wings whispering with the lead actress. They both jumped when she approached.

Mr. Williams shook her hand, squeezing hard. "Miss Ripley, we were just remarking on what a terrific work you've come up with, on the first try. Bravo."

"Thank you, I am quite honored to be here, of course. But I was wondering, as we delve into the final act, what if you asked the actors to lower the tone a bit? I think the play will work even better. After all, the subject matter is serious."

"Now, don't you worry, little lady. I have it well in hand. You know, I've directed twenty-five shows on the Great White Way."

"Twenty-six," added the actress with a sly smile. Brandy Sainsbury was her name. Hazel had run into her on previous auditions, where she had a tendency to tap-dance in the waiting room, ostensibly to calm her own nerves, but more likely because she knew it would irritate and fluster her competition.

"Right. Well, just a thought."

Hazel returned to the table. She'd never been in this position before, one of authority, and was unsure. Should she assert herself now, making her preferences and demands known right off? Or was it better to wait until they had an actual cast and were in rehearsal? It was less immediate pressure if she chose to wait, but was that just a cop-out?

By the time she'd convinced herself to speak up, they'd launched back into the play. Too late.

Emboldened by Mr. Williams, the actors went all out, offering up over-the-top line readings and, a couple of times, silly voices. She'd have to add in slamming doors and tripping on rugs, now that her play had turned into an English farce.

Finally, the stage manager intoned, "Curtain."

Hazel tried to catch Mr. Canby before he left, but he said he had a lunch to get to at Sardi's and he'd see her tomorrow at the auditions. She asked if he had any notes about the play, any suggested changes, and to her surprise he made a good one, switching around two scenes in the second act. Easy to execute, and an improvement. Maybe today's reading hadn't been for naught.

She walked back to the hotel, where a half dozen men with cameras slung around their necks had gathered just outside, smoking and talking among themselves. A strange sight, more suited to the fancy hotels uptown like the Plaza or the Waldorf. She made her way through and headed for the elevator.

Mr. Bard stopped her.

"You have a guest, Miss Ripley."

Hazel wasn't expecting anyone. She looked about the lobby, but all the chairs were empty.

"I didn't think she should wait down here, so I sent her straight to your room with an extra key." He looked positively giddy, like a schoolboy who'd aced a test.

She imagined her mother showing up, demanding that she return home. "Who is it?"

"She said I was to not tell you, to let it be a surprise. Don't you love surprises?" He clapped his hands together. "Up you go. She arrived a few hours ago. Do let me know if she requires anything. We can send up anything you need."

What on earth was he talking about?

Hazel braced herself and headed up. Her door was unlocked, and at least seven suitcases were strewn across the Oriental rug, several opened and the contents bursting forth, as if they'd been dropped from a great height. She recognized one of the dresses from the tent in Naples.

"There you are!" Maxine popped her head out from the bedroom, her shoulders bare. "Just changing, I'll be with you in a bit."

Maxine Mead had arrived.

⁂

Hazel didn't have to wait long before Maxine rushed into her arms, wearing only a silk slip and smelling like lemons. Memories flooded back, of sand and mud, of uncertainty, and deep belly laughs at the silliest things. And of the boy in the cell, petrified and alone.

"Are you surprised?" asked Maxine.

Hazel stared at her friend, amazed. "I am. I didn't even know you were in town."

"A last-minute decision. Gosh, it's boiling in here. Can we open a window or something?"

An early hot spell had settled on the city the past two days. In the dark quiet of her rooms, Hazel barely noticed. Somehow the hotel seemed to keep the humidity low by the sheer thickness of the walls, but just having Maxine in the room caused the temperature to rise considerably.

"Ugh, I can't breathe." Maxine clawed at her throat. "We have to get out of here."

"There's a pack of reporters out front. Are they part of your entourage?" It was almost as though Maxine had been flown in from another planet. What she was doing here at the Chelsea Hotel instead of at the fancier hotels uptown was anyone's guess.

"Can't seem to shake them. I came to New York for some peace and quiet. Didn't realize the frenzy would follow me here."

"We could go up on the roof."

"Splendid idea. Let me put on some clothes."

While Maxine dressed, Hazel looked in the icebox for a bottle of wine and grabbed two glasses. They took the stairs instead of the elevator, winding their way up to the top floor. Hazel shoved open the heavy metal door at the top and squinted in the bright sunlight.

The various chimneys and gables, including a pyramid-shaped turret that sprouted in the middle of the building, were festooned with vines and softened by potted trees and grasses. Hazel and Maxine settled in a corner that faced west, where the ships glided down the Hudson River. Over in New Jersey, a line of gray clouds paralleled the horizon.

Maxine plopped down in one of three Adirondack chairs. Hazel took another and pulled the cork from the bottle. "I assume you need a drink."

"Do I ever."

They toasted to each other's health, and then Maxine rested her head against the back of the chair and closed her eyes. Her cheeks were slightly fuller than Hazel remembered, but the added padding suited her. Maxine seemed to gain weight in even proportions around her bust and hips, whereas Hazel's thickened waist made her feel older than her years.

"What brings you to New York, my friend?" she asked. "From what I can tell, you've been working nonstop out in Hollywood."

Maxine turned her head to face Hazel and sighed. "Yes. I've had a good run. But I had to get away. Professionally and personally."

"Man trouble?"

Maxine didn't answer, but Hazel could tell she'd guessed right.

"The same man who wrote you the one letter back in Naples?"

Maxine raised an eyebrow. "Of course you'd remember that. Always watching what everyone is up to."

"You just so rarely got letters."

"The story of Arthur. It's a boring one, really. We've heard it all before."

"Who's Arthur?"

"A man I met ages ago. Before the war. He's married."

So that was the big secret. That explained Maxine's reluctance to discuss him, even though the girls had shared so much. "Have you been having an affair all this time?"

"It was one of the reasons I went overseas. To get away."

"But then you went back?"

"He wrote and asked me to come to California. Said he knew he wanted to be with me, and put me up in the sweetest cottage in the Hollywood Hills, hidden away from prying eyes." She shielded her eyes with one hand and looked over at Hazel.

Underneath Maxine's usual swagger lurked an unsettling vulnerability. This was a different girl from the one who'd driven a Jeep into a hostile crowd.

"Tell me more."

"When we first met, it was like a bomb going off." Maxine's words tumbled out. "I saw him and he saw me and we knew we had to be together. He's a businessman, food packaging. Sounds boring, right? But he's not boring at all. He's funny, kind. We clicked. His wife—I've nicknamed her Zelda—has some kind of serious mental problem." She caught the look Hazel threw her. "No, it's true. She should be in a home, but he continues to care for her. He can't get a divorce because she's not mentally competent to sign off on it. So he's stuck."

Hazel couldn't help but play devil's advocate. "How do you know that's true?"

"I followed him home one time, back to his house. She'd locked him out, and was leaning out of the window, screaming at him, throwing his clothes into the garden."

"That sounds like a wronged wife, not a lunatic."

"She almost climbed out the window herself. He finally broke in and pulled her inside."

"Okay. That might be honest-to-goodness crazy."

How complicated Maxine's life was. Hazel wasn't surprised. She was a touch envious, to be honest. Hazel had gone out on dates with some lovely boys since the war, but they were just that. Boys. Actors who loved the sound of their own voices and carried on as if they were Marlon Brando. She'd told herself she had no time for boyfriends, that her work came first. And for the most part, that was true. Yet here was Maxine, juggling a successful career and a passionate love affair. Even if it was with a married man.

"Sounds like a reasonable setup, in a way," said Hazel. "You can have your career and not have to deal with taking care of a man."

"Oh, there are plenty of men who want to be taken care of, believe me."

"What do you mean?"

Maxine frowned. "Out there, it's not like New York. It's as if the casting couch is the only way to get a good role, to jump to the top of the line." She didn't elaborate further. "I miss what we had in Naples. We didn't have to listen, and got away with breaking the rules."

Indeed, that had been one of the few refreshing things about being abroad. There were no meddling middlemen and limited self-indulgence on the part of the actors, as there was no time. Learn your lines and get onstage. It had been a valuable lesson, one Hazel hoped she could apply to her own play. But maybe now it wouldn't be possible, with Mr. Williams in charge.

Hazel poured herself some more wine. Maxine was trying to communicate something important, though she was having trouble being direct about it. No wonder, as it had been at least a year or two since they'd corresponded, a decision that Hazel now greatly regretted. Maxine was here because she needed Hazel, in some way, and had sought her out.

"I have to apologize, Max."

"Whatever for?"

"I didn't write back, I pulled away from our friendship, and I'm so sorry." She waved away Maxine's response, knowing she had to finish. "I felt dull next to your glamorous lifestyle, like I was treading water while you performed tricks from the high dive. I was jealous, I suppose."

"Well, that's all water under the bridge, to continue your aquatic metaphor."

They both laughed, before Maxine grew serious. "After you go through what we did, with Paul, you're bonded for life. Besides, you're the only one who can see me as regular Maxine, and not the facade of a Hollywood star. I'm glad we're reunited."

"Me, too," said Hazel. "But it's terrible that you have to deal with all that other baloney. You don't deserve to be treated like that, either by this Arthur fellow or by those producers."

"I was trying so hard to please Arthur whenever we met, knowing that our time was precious. I bent over backward. He'd show up and I'd have his Scotch ready, dinner on the table, ready to take care of his every need. He was paying my rent at the beginning, after all. I was utterly dependent on him. Then I'd go to auditions and do the exact same thing, smile and flirt and play the game. I wasn't myself in either situation, always acting." She took a slug of wine. "On my last audition, for a doozy of a role, I refused the producer's advances and lost the part."

"I'm so sorry."

"Marilyn Monroe sure isn't. They announced the casting a few days ago."

Maxine was up against the likes of Marilyn Monroe? Hazel couldn't help but be impressed. "I'm sure you'll get the next one. On your talent, not your availability."

"Anyway, Arthur and I had a terrible fight. I said awful things to him"—Maxine's voice hitched with emotion—"and he was awful back. I jumped on a plane heading east and here I am."

"I'm sorry." They sat quietly for a moment. Hazel knew something was missing from Maxine's story, but whatever it was, Maxine had shut down and wasn't about to volunteer more. "What would you like to do while you're in New York?"

"Not sure. See some plays. Lay low."

The door to the roof slammed and Lavinia came into view, carrying a straw hat with an enormous brim, a script tucked under one arm. Hazel waved her over and both girls stood as she neared.

Lavinia's face brightened as she recognized Maxine and enveloped her in a warm hug. "What a surprise, my dear! It's a true delight to have you back."

Hazel could have sworn that Maxine had tears in her eyes when she pulled back from Lavinia after a few long moments in her arms. She hadn't realized how close they were.

To give her friend time to gather herself, Hazel thanked Lavinia again. "Lavinia was the one who got my play on Broadway," she explained to Maxine.

Maxine nodded. "I read all about your show in *Variety*. I'm sorry I didn't congratulate you sooner. I got so wrapped up in all of my silly problems, I forgot to tell you how happy I am for you, Hazel."

Lavinia settled in one of the chairs. "A terrific play, even if there wasn't a part for me in it." She pointed a finger at Hazel. "Next one, promise?"

Hazel nodded.

"How is your grandmother, Maxine, still going strong?" Lavinia asked.

"She is, thank you. Sends you her love. And how's the Chelsea holding up these days? The twins still roughing it? Or has their father allowed them back into the fold?"

Lavinia laughed. "They're not going anywhere, those two."

"Roughing it?" echoed Hazel.

"The hotel's guests can be divided up into several categories," explained Lavinia. "The twins belong to the herd of black sheep, dilettantes who've been tossed out of wealthy families for not following the rules. Winnifred and Wanda were brought up in a mansion on Long Island's gold coast, but they had some kind of a spat with their dad and moved in here. They're up on eight. Down on the first floor are all the left-wing organizers, like the Peace Information Center."

"I'm sorry, what's that?" asked Hazel.

"It's headed by W. E. B. Du Bois; they're fighting against nukes. They share the same floor as the Eastern European refugee families who were temporarily housed here by the Catholic Charities but never left. The rest are creative types: artists, writers, musicians, designers, actors, several photographers. All overseen by David Bard and his Hungarian syndicate, who are constantly wheeling and dealing. I'm told that even the building's plumber, Krauss, has some kind of ownership stake in the Chelsea. Quite a stew, when it comes down to it."

Maxine threw back her head and laughed. "I'm so happy to be here, I can't tell you."

"How long do you think you'll stay?" Hazel asked.

Maxine swatted her arm. "You worried about all those suitcases taking up space in your tidy room? Who knows? But don't worry, I'll talk to Mr. Bard about getting my own room. He said one down the hall is free. I'll be close, but not too close."

Hazel was thrilled. She could use a friend right now, and Maxine might bring a little lightness into her life. Without the distance between them, she could see her jealousy of Maxine's Hollywood dream life was unfounded and that their friendship mattered more than that, anyway. She had no doubt they'd pick up right where they left off.

Together, they'd dive headfirst into the delicious stew of the Chelsea Hotel.

CHAPTER SEVEN

‎ℳaxine

May 23, 1950

The shock of being back at the Chelsea, of seeing Lavinia and Hazel, has driven me to pick up a pen again, to keep a record, like I used to during the war. But just in case the hotel maids are snooping, I'm keeping some secrets to myself. After all, a girl needs her privacy.

I felt bad, dumping my sob story on Hazel like that, watered down as it was. I'd hoped that in coming to New York I could flee the sickly perfection of Los Angeles and get some gritty New York dirt under my nails. Just like when I flew off to Europe with the USO and found an anchor in the plays and the women around me.

That article in *Variety* about Hazel's production was like a lighthouse beacon at my lowest moment, where I could escape the humiliation of botching that audition and get a breather from being in Arthur's grasp. Hazel getting a show on Broadway. No mean feat. She'd obviously changed from that sweet, scared girl who'd shown up in Naples. There was a sturdy capability about her, a no-nonsense demeanor. When her eyes focused on you and only you, it felt as if she was the only person who understood you. Arthur was like that, too. In the beginning. I get now that he used that particular ploy to reel me in, but Hazel has different intentions. Her desire to connect comes from a kindhearted, unselfish place.

Seeing her again brought up all kinds of emotions: pride at her accomplishments, jealousy at her uncomplicated life—at least compared to mine—and, above all, a love for her. I loved the way she looked at me, like she didn't quite believe whatever was coming out of my mouth, and called me on it, when necessary. My grandmother is the same way, someone who truly understands me.

I suggested we go out and celebrate her good news. We put on our posh frocks—I wore my fiery-pink Balenciaga. Whenever I put on that dress, I feel divine, but then Hazel stepped out of her bedroom in a strapless white number, stunning in its simplicity, that made it seem like there was a halo around her. How does she do that?

"I hope there aren't any photographers still waiting outside," said Hazel as we stepped off the elevator.

No such luck. I counted four, that I could see, and had steadied myself, like I was about to dive into a pool filled with alligators, when Mr. Bard popped into the lobby from a side hallway.

"You don't have to go out that way, if you don't want."

"Is there a back door to this place?" Hazel asked.

"Not exactly," he said. "Follow me."

We took a staircase tucked beside the lobby phone booths down one flight to the basement, past the laundry. The maids stubbed out cigarettes and began loading sheets into enormous dryers as soon as we came into view.

Their lackadaisical work ethic didn't seem to bother Mr. Bard, who kept up a running commentary as we zigzagged through the narrow hallways. "Back when the hotel was built, in the 1880s, we had a billiard parlor, wine cellar, and butcher shop down here." Hazel rolled her eyes, she'd clearly heard all this before. But Mr. Bard had a giddy hop in his step, leading us deeper into the basement, to a narrow door, which he opened with a flourish. "The servants used to be housed in a brownstone on Twenty-Second Street, but now it's empty. This tunnel connects the two buildings."

We entered a dank, dark hallway, lit by bare bulbs spaced widely apart. Strange to think we were directly underneath the ragged courtyard that separated the Chelsea from the row houses to the south. I wouldn't want to come down there on my own. I was sure rats and other critters used it as a highway when the humans weren't about.

We eventually emerged inside a small cellar. Up five steps and we were out on the street, not a camera in sight.

"Well done, Mr. Bard," said Hazel. He grinned with delight. I blew him a kiss as we jumped in a cab, and in no time we arrived at the Russian Tea Room. Nothing classier than that, I've always thought. The place was jumping, the red leather banquettes full up and golden samovars gleaming in the low light. I blended in just right. Showy but with a purpose. That's me.

"Hazel, over here."

A man whose shiny bald pate rivaled the gleam of the samovars stood and waved his arms. "You must join us."

Hazel looked uncertain, worried. "We could get a more private table upstairs," she said out of the side of her mouth.

"Nah. Let's meet your friends." Something was holding her back, and I was curious to find out what it was.

The older man turned out to be Mr. Canby, the producer of her play, who sat next to the director, Mr. Williams. A hussy with glossy lips was squashed up against Mr. Williams like a barnacle.

"This is Miss Brandy Sainsbury," remarked Hazel. "She was kind enough to do a reading of the show earlier today."

We ordered Moscow mules and got acquainted. At first, Miss Sainsbury pretended to not know who I was, before doing a wide-eyed double take. "Wait a minute, weren't you in that movie with Linda Darnell? I can't remember the name. Well, gosh almighty."

What a liar. Any aspiring actress with Hollywood dreams knows every last thing about the film business—who's in, who's out, the names of all the speaking cast members on the silver screen, from the stars on down. Miss Sainsbury knew exactly who I was, but she preferred to try to diminish me in front of these men rather than admit it. It was the oldest power play in the world, and she probably sensed it was a waste of effort from the get-go. At this table, there was no denying who was queen. Or maybe little Brandy's objective was less to establish the upper hand than to telegraph how much she already hated me. The feeling was entirely mutual.

The director and the producer, on the other hand, cozied up to me big-time. Theater folk love to think they might end up in Hollywood, however much they pooh-pooh the film business. Usually, I'd luxuriate in the attention, but instead, I turned the subject right around to the play. This was Hazel's town, not mine. For now.

"We're planning on opening in July," said Mr. Canby. "It's fast, but I've been telling investors that our playwright is the next Lillian Hellman, another lady writer great with a turn of phrase." He lit a cigarette, pleased with himself. "I tell you, it makes people swoon."

"Lillian Hellman, that's a lot to live up to," said Hazel. "We've still got to cast the thing. That'll be the key, to get the right people in the leads."

I noticed she avoided looking at Miss Sainsbury as she spoke.

"Now, how do you two know each other?" Mr. Canby asked.

"We acted together in the USO tour." I put my arm around Hazel. "In fact, that's where our soon-to-be-famous playwright first put pen to paper. She wrote up news items that I translated over the radio to the Germans as part of the propaganda effort, known as *Lina from America*. I was the voice of Lina, but Hazel was the brains."

Mr. Canby swiveled his head around to Hazel, his eyes popping. "Then there we have it."

"Have what?" Hazel fixed him with a strange expression.

"Your character in the play is named Lina. This is Lina." He gestured to me. "Obviously, Maxine Mead is our girl."

I blinked in surprise, but already my excitement was building. I could list a dozen reasons why this appealed to me. It could be a chance to prove myself as a real actress, on a Broadway stage. A way to leave the sordid life of L.A. behind for a few months. And an opportunity to reconnect with Hazel. Not to mention—

I was jolted back to the present when Hazel offered a weird half smile. "I see how you might think that, but the Lina I wrote isn't Maxine." She put her hand on mine. "Please don't be offended, you know I adore you. But this character is more of a tomboy. The actress who's cast in the part has to be able to play a man believably. You're too recognizable, too womanly. You understand, right?"

I knew I was more bombshell than boyish, but still, her speedy dismissal hurt. We did God knows how many shows together, catching each other when the lines failed to come because we had so many plays stuffed inside our heads. We played in thunderous rain and sticky heat, and I never failed to bring down the house. "Sure, I understand."

It was as if Canby never even heard us. "We can use this in all the publicity. The reunion of two wartime heroines, from the USO to the Great White Way. It's perfect. Done. You've got the job."

Both Hazel and Mr. Williams shifted in their seats, tense. From the way little Brandy was staring at Mr. Williams, it was quite evident she'd counted on getting the job.

The director spoke first. "We have auditions set for tomorrow. We can't just cancel them."

Mr. Canby would have none of it. "Of course we can. For a rising star like Maxine Mead, that's exactly what we'll do. She's the next Kim Hunter or Tallulah Bankhead."

News to me, but I'd take it.

Hazel began to speak, but the young actress slammed her beaded handbag on the table. A couple of the tiny beads came loose and rolled along the tablecloth. "That's not fair. Not at all." She turned to the director. "You promised."

"Promised what?" asked Hazel, her eyes narrowed. "An audition or the part?"

The director paled. "An audition, of course."

"No, Willy." The girl's voice shook with rage. "That's not what you said. You said the part was mine."

I sat back; things were getting interesting.

Hazel grew cold. "You had no right to do that, Mr. Williams. This is my play, not yours."

"As your director, I know what works." The poor guy was caught between two very angry women, and I almost pitied him. "You're too close to see it. That's what we tell all the writers. To leave the decision-making up to us. Canby, tell her."

Miss Sainsbury let out a whimper.

Mr. Canby smiled, still coasting on the genius of his great idea.

"It's true, the writer can gum up the production if not held in check. But I want Maxine."

Mr. Williams looked at Miss Sainsbury and back at Mr. Canby, his face red. "That won't do. I won't stand for it." I noticed Miss Sainsbury's hand sliding across his thigh as a reward for his courage. "Either I get control of this production or I quit."

"Yeah, he quits," echoed Miss Sainsbury.

Mr. Canby held firm. "Great. Quit."

Hazel looked panicked, and I could understand why. Her show was falling apart fast. She opened her mouth to speak, but Mr. Williams cut her off.

"I cannot believe I'm being treated like this. Trust me, I will complain to the union about having to suffer such an indignity. Being fired before I've even begun, it's unheard of!" He carried on with his diatribe as he and his chippy exited with as much dignity as they could muster, not easy when it involved sliding out of a banquette.

After they'd left, I turned to Hazel, who'd gone white. "Good riddance, I say."

"What now?" she said, to no one in particular.

"Don't worry, there's a line of directors down the block eager to take on this project." Mr. Canby, unconcerned, ordered another round of drinks.

"But the auditions start tomorrow at ten," she said. "They'd still have to read the play before then."

The answer came to me like a shot. "You should direct it."

I knew I was right the minute I spoke the words.

"What?" Hazel pushed her drink away. She was probably regretting she'd ever agreed to bring me into her circle.

"You directed us on tour." I cut her off when she started to speak. "Maybe not at first, but definitely by the end. You stepped up and took over. Remember the show at the Teatro di San Carlo?" I turned to Mr. Canby. "She wrote it and directed it, the whole shebang. Just like what we're proposing today."

"That was just a matter of making sure we all didn't collide onstage," Hazel protested. "Hardly directing. More like being a traffic cop."

"You could do it. I know it. You're bossier than you think."

Got a smile out of her with that one. I could see she was warming to the idea.

Canby spoke up. "I don't know, maybe we should interview some other possibilities first, just to be safe."

"Since she's green, you won't have to pay her as much," I volunteered.

Mr. Canby's eyebrows lifted. I'd found his weak spot. No doubt he was thinking of the savings in salary compared with a pricey veteran like Mr. Williams. Less overhead, more profit for him. "That's true, I can't pay Hazel as much. On top of her being a girl."

Hazel's eyes flashed. Now she really wanted the job. "I'm certainly not the first woman director on Broadway, by a long shot."

"That's true." He snapped his fingers. "Let's do it. As long as Maxine Mead plays Lina."

I could have sworn Hazel winced, but it was too late. After some back-and-forth, Hazel and Mr. Canby shook hands. The deal was done. She was a director, and I had my first Broadway leading role.

Hazel was quiet during the cab ride. We passed the front of the hotel, where a few photographers lingered. "Take us to Twenty-Second Street," she told the driver. I waited for her to thank me for acting as her de facto agent over what turned out to be a lucrative business dinner, but she wasn't in the mood to talk.

We took the reverse route back into the Chelsea. I used the key that Mr. Bard had pressed into my hand earlier that evening to get into the basement door of the brownstone. Once in the tunnel, the only sounds were our footsteps and occasional drips of water, like we were in a cave deep in the earth.

Hazel walked ahead of me, her shoulders back and tight.

I couldn't stand her freezing me out. "Look, I'm sorry if I got ahead of myself at the Tea Room," I offered. "I know I don't match what you picture in your head for Lina. But I can do it, I promise."

"You're wrong for the part. Entirely. She has to be able to blend into the background, at least at first."

"I can blend into the background."

"How? By putting yourself up for the part less than two minutes after meeting the creative team?"

"I didn't do that. Canby did. I got you the job of directing, by the way. No thanks for that?" I tried to make her see the big picture the way I did. "Being a writer and director is a giant career leap, and it'll serve you well going forward. And in the meantime, you get to work with an old friend. Is that so bad?"

"Look at you." She gestured from my feet to my head. "You couldn't look like a boy if you tried."

Her rejection stung. If she only knew.

There was one way I could prove it to her, but it would take all the courage I had. I reminded myself this was Hazel, a friend. And I wanted this part, more than anything. I lifted my hand to the top of my head and gently tugged, letting the wig slide off. I held it by my side while she gaped at me.

My hair had been chopped off, each irregular piece no longer than a few inches. The color wasn't the red I got from a rinse, but my natural color, more of a dirty blond. Her face reflected exactly what I feared: Without my mane, I was a wretched, ugly girl.

"What happened to you?"

"Arthur got angry. He held me down and cut it all off. That's why I fled to New York. And that's why I can do the role." I paused. "I can play a boy, like this. I can play a girl playing a boy. You have to give me a chance, that's all I ask. One chance."

◆◆◆

We talked well into the night.

I told Hazel that Arthur had become increasingly cruel over the past year, taunting me and pushing me to fight, then apologizing and swearing he'd never do it again. He'd been under a lot of stress, and while we'd always had arguments in the past, they'd begun spiraling out of control. This last time, after we'd both had too many drinks, I'd confided to Arthur that the movie producer had pawed at me, offering up several guesses as to the size of my brassiere at the film audition, the one that had just been announced as going to Marilyn Monroe. Arthur said something snide about how I shouldn't be so precious about sleeping my way to the top, since my talent obviously wasn't enough to get me there on its own, and I'd tried to smack him. Bad mistake. That only made him angrier, and before I knew it, he'd grabbed a fistful of my hair and was dragging me to the bathroom. He picked up a set of shearing scissors and, with a knee to my chest, snipped off two thick locks of hair before coming to his senses, collapsing on the floor beside me. We both wept. I told him to get out, and once he was gone, I finished the job, doing my best to even it up as tears streamed down my face.

"He's horrible. I'm glad you're free of him," Hazel finally said.

"There's more to me than a vamp. I can do the part of Lina, I swear I can." I stayed still while Hazel studied me.

"Why don't we read through Lina's part together, up in my room?" she suggested.

"Tonight?"

"Why not? Time is of the essence."

Hazel and I worked until dawn. She spoke of the character's desires, and her weaknesses. Scene by scene, we picked apart the motivations, focusing on Lina's desire to be with the man she loved, while hiding her true identity from the others. Around five in the morning, I read the character's final monologue, and when I looked up, Hazel's eyes were shining.

"Yes. You should play Lina. I never should have doubted you. This role is yours, and I'd be honored to have you involved."

"The honor is all mine."

Hazel invited me to sit in on the auditions a few hours later. The morning was spent finding the right actor for the character of the male lead, Matthew, and we had more than enough to choose from—the talent pool in New York was tremendous—but everyone agreed on a man named Jake Simmons, who hit all the right notes of desperation and desire.

During a coffee break, Mr. Canby said he'd invited a potential costume designer to stop by to meet Hazel, so I stepped off to the side to grab a donut, which I almost dropped when Hazel let out a screech like she was being attacked by bees.

She was hugging someone, and as they disentangled, I screeched as well.

Floyd, our artist from Naples. The boy who had done our caricatures had grown into a lovely young man in the past half decade, with an easy smile yet still sporting a slight hunch to his shoulders, like he was afraid of taking up too much space.

Turned out, he'd come to New York after the war, taken costume design classes, and landed a few decent gigs. Hazel's eyes widened as he listed some of the shows he worked on. "Those costumes were excellent! You're a real rising star."

"Well, I owe it all to you two ladies." He shoved his hands deep into his pockets, while his face turned scarlet. "After the USO shows, I decided I wanted to get into theater, too, and here I am."

Hazel pulled Mr. Canby aside and they shared a quick whisper. She looked over at us, beaming. "Floyd, you've got the job. See you next week at the first rehearsal."

After we'd all hugged again and he'd taken his leave, we got another surprise guest, Brandy Sainsbury, the girlfriend of the ex-director. Or ex-girlfriend of the ex-director, apparently. She showed up at her appointed time, all meek and mealy, and asked to read for one of the smaller roles. Hazel, that saint, allowed it and Brandy wasn't half-bad, so I wasn't surprised when Hazel offered her the part. Floyd's arrival had put all of us into a good mood.

I spent the rest of the week getting my New York life in order, setting up the room Mr. Bard had offered me down the hall from Hazel's. Much to Hazel's relief, I'm sure. She was such a neat little girl, her desk perfectly arranged with her typewriter, a stack of paper, a thesaurus, and nothing else.

At the first rehearsal, I stepped through the backstage door and was handed a key for my dressing room, but before heading up, I snuck into the back of the house to catch my breath. The Biltmore Theatre is gorgeous, with plasterwork like ornamental lace on the walls, and a ceiling that soars high above the balcony seats. Hazel and Mr. Canby were standing at the foot of the stage, waving their arms about and doing whatever it is directors and producers do. How strange, to not be on the same level anymore. Now I was working for her. Still, it was way better than being in Arthur's clutches, any day.

"All right, everyone, let's begin." Mr. Canby clapped his hands.

I grabbed my script and let a stagehand guide me up onto the stage from a temporary set of steps at the end of the aisle.

"We'll start with the scene where Lina and Matthew are confronted by the other hotel guests," said Hazel.

Not my first choice, as it gave me no chance of easing into the role. My heart began to pound like I was a newbie. If I didn't relax, my throat would tighten up and make my voice sound strange, but the very thought made me even more tense. A merry-go-round of disaster.

We did the scene once through. Then again. Jake Simmons, even this early in the rehearsal process, was committed, passionate, while I came off like a stick figure. Both times, Hazel gave us guidance, but I could tell Jake's advice was only for show, to make me feel better.

"This time, let's heighten the stakes, okay?" said Hazel. "We can always bring it down."

That was the problem, though. I only had two speeds as an actress, a shortcoming that I hadn't really understood until now. On a film set, I could bring it down to almost zero, let my eyes do the work. I barely speak above a whisper, but the microphone picks up my words as the camera captures my every emotion. Does the trick every time, just as it did with Hazel when we read through the scenes at the Chelsea. My other speed is full throttle. Put me out in front of a thousand soldiers and I can make them laugh and sway in their seats as I belt out "That Old Black Magic." But this play required me to run in second or third gear, and I wasn't sure how to do that.

In fact, I was completely at a loss. Every line landed with a thud. Hazel's initial reluctance to cast me had been spot on, she knew me better than I knew myself. I simply wasn't up to the task.

Out of the corner of my eye, I saw Mr. Canby run a hand over his head and sigh loudly, while Brandy smirked just behind him. Jake looked panicked for me, which only made matters worse.

"Let's all take a break," said Hazel. "Ten minutes, please. Maxine, come with me."

Oh God. A dressing-down my first day on the job. Part of me hoped she'd fire me and put me out of my misery.

As she led me up the stairs stage right, I filled the silence fast. "I'm sorry, Hazel, it's just a bad day. You know I'll figure this out."

She didn't look at me as she climbed up another flight. "We have to find you another way. Your old bag of tricks won't work in my play."

Of course, she knew exactly what was going on. That's what happens when you share a tent and sleep under each other's laundry.

"Do you trust me?" she asked.

I nodded.

We stepped into the hair and wig room. She dismissed the crew and closed the door. "Take off your shoes and dress."

I did so.

"And the wig."

"I'm not sure about that. Not just yet. Give me a week and I'll do it." I tried to hide the pleading from my voice. She was asking me to give up all my defenses. On the first day of rehearsal. I'd figured around week three I'd shock the cast and crew with my wigless head, once we'd all gotten to know each other and I felt safe. Not day one.

I deserved this, though. Everyone else in the cast was better than me. I was terrible, a fraud, a vampy whore who would be shown up. That awful Brandy Sainsbury popped into my head. I imagined her reading the reviews, crowing at my bad notices, proclaiming that I'd ruined the production with my wooden line readings.

I took off the wig.

Hazel grabbed a roll of cloth and told me to lift my arms while she bound my curves down, circling around me and around me, her eyes focused on my torso. Then she handed me a man's suit, one that had been recently brought up from storage, by the sour smell of it, and I put it on.

"Shoes."

I stepped into a pair of men's Oxfords. The comfort of being able to wiggle my toes perked me up. Much better than heels.

"Let's go back down and try again. You can't coast in this role, Max." She leaned in and put her hands on either side of my face. "From now on, when we're rehearsing, you must wear these clothes and take off the wig. Lina has to act like a man to make herself heard. She can't use her feminine wiles, which means neither can you."

We walked back down to stage level, Hazel leading the way, holding my hand and talking in a low, soothing voice, as if I were a horse about to bolt.

I couldn't do it. I couldn't show everyone how awful I looked, what a mess I was. What Arthur had done to me. I wanted to pretend that he never existed, and now it was as if he was standing right behind me, jeering and laughing.

Hazel kept talking. "Remember when we first saw the boys in the plaza? Their faces, one defiant and one near tears. What was Paul thinking? What made him sling one arm around his friend, like they were two kids heading off for a summer's day of fishing? Not about to be torn apart by a mob. When have you felt that way, Maxine? Defiant when you should be terrified?"

The answer came to me right away, although I didn't speak it out loud.

The day that Lavinia had rescued me and my grandmother, ushering us inside the foyer of the Seattle theater, where it was silent and dark, the air sweet with pipe tobacco. As Lavinia and the others huddled over my grandmother, who'd been on the verge of fainting, I'd turned back to the glass doors and stood, legs spread wide, hands on hips, glaring right back at the unruly mob outside like a sheriff in a Western. Rage surged through my body, like I was on fire.

Hazel and I walked back onstage. I hardly noticed as the stagehands and cast gasped at my physical transformation. I touched Jake's arm, briefly, to connect and let him know that I was in this one hundred percent.

We began from the top, and this time I didn't think about my posture, or what to do with my hands. The emotion inside me, the image of my grandmother's cheek glistening with spit, was the engine of the scene now. Everything else followed suit, and before I knew it, we'd reached the last line.

Applause filled my ears. I'd found her. I'd found Lina.

CHAPTER EIGHT

Hazel

June 1950

After that first tweak with Maxine in rehearsal, which came to Hazel in a rush of inspiration and panic, the cast and crew settled into a rhythm. She and Maxine fell into an easy alliance onstage, just as they had in Italy. Artistically, Hazel knew what she wanted and what she was doing. Whenever she had a logistical question, she counted on the grizzled stage manager to answer it and guide her forward. From her stints understudying, she knew that a good stage manager—who acted as the glue that held the cast, crew, and production team together—was the key to a smooth ride when it came to wrangling the strong personalities of the theater world.

Mr. Canby sometimes stopped by rehearsals but generally kept out of Hazel's way, other than making sure she had everything she needed, and after a couple of days, she no longer thought twice about piping up to offer her opinion, whether with the set designer or the wardrobe mistress. A dramatic shift between Hazel and Maxine, almost a role reversal, had clicked into place after Maxine's tearful, terrible confession. In Naples, at least in the beginning of their friendship, Hazel had hung back, observing, while Maxine ruled as queen bee, and now Hazel was the trailblazer and Maxine the vulnerable one. Hayseed Hazel had taken the wheel, with Maxine along for the ride, and so far the dynamic was working nicely.

Back at the Chelsea, Hazel was usually exhausted after a day of rehearsing, but Maxine never lagged. She could often be found wandering the halls in the evenings in a silk caftan and turban, popping from room to room, checking in on the twins or Virgil Thomson. Or she'd force-march Hazel up to the roof, where Lavinia held what she called her "sunset happy hours." The three would talk shop as the lights of the city twinkled around them.

Meanwhile, the entire city pulsated with a strange new energy. The threat of another war, this time with Korea, loomed in the papers and the news. America had slain the fascists, and the communists were next, according to the politicians. Hazel had made some minor changes to the play, subtle parallels with what was going on now, in the hopes that her words might make her audience reconsider this headlong rush into another fight.

One Thursday night after rehearsal, she wished desperately to go back to her room and lie down, but Maxine insisted she join them at Sardi's. "You have to show the cast that you're one of us, not just the girl who tells everyone what to do and bosses them about."

"I'm the *woman* who bosses everyone about, and that suits me fine," Hazel couldn't help teasing, but she agreed to go.

Usually, walking into a room with Maxine set off a quiet roar. She knew how to make an entrance. But not this time. In fact, the entire restaurant was unusually subdued. A smattering of actors and Biltmore crew members had gathered around one end of the bar, and a few glanced over at Hazel and Maxine with tight smiles. Odd.

The group opened up to include them. Maxine nudged Floyd and pointed out the hundreds of caricatures of theater luminaries that hung on the restaurant's walls. "Maybe I can get you to do mine again when our show is a smash hit, right, Floyd?"

Floyd nodded and smiled, but didn't answer.

"What's going on?" asked Hazel. "Is something wrong, did someone die?"

"Just some political inanity," said Floyd.

"What on earth are you talking about?" Maxine put a hand on her hip. "You all are looking like we got panned before we even opened."

Brandy Sainsbury handed over a thin booklet. "This just came out."

Hazel studied the cover over Maxine's shoulder, an illustration of a red hand about to clasp a microphone. *Red Channels: The Report of Communist Influence in Radio and Television.* Hazel read the lines at the bottom of the page out loud: "Published by *Counterattack*, the newsletter of facts to combat communism."

"Came out today." Floyd spoke quietly. "It lists people in the entertainment industry who are linked to communism."

"Like who?" asked Maxine.

Brandy rattled off names. "Aaron Copland, Pete Seeger, Orson Welles, Lillian Hellman, Arthur Miller, Dorothy Parker. A hundred and fifty-one people in all."

"And you." Maxine, who had been leafing through it while Brandy spoke, held up a page to Hazel.

"Me?"

Hazel took it from her. Like the other names, hers was followed by a list of "offenses," all of which had occurred in the 1930s: signing a petition for the Scientific and Cultural Conference for World Peace, attending an anti-fascist rally, being a member of the Actors' Equity Association, having signed a congratulatory telegram to the Moscow Art Theatre, and donating to a clothing drive for Spanish refugees. A couple of the entries were incorrect, listing organizations she'd never even heard of.

"What was wrong with attending an anti-fascist rally?" Hazel looked to Maxine, confused. "That's who we went to war against."

"They say these are all communist fronts." Brandy again.

"Look at this last one." Hazel pointed to a line on the page. "It was a clothing drive. I gave away an old coat. This is utterly ridiculous."

"So it is." Maxine took the booklet from her hands and tossed it onto the bar. The others stared at it as if it were radioactive. Maxine shook her head. "This will all blow over."

The more Hazel thought about it, the more outraged she became. "But it's not right. Who published this?"

"A company called American Business Consultants." Brandy shrugged. "Their heart is in the right place. They don't want communists to infiltrate our country and destroy democracy."

Hazel disagreed. "But you can't go after people who are innocent in order to scare everyone else out of their wits. It's just fearmongering."

Floyd spoke quietly. "They're not kidding about this stuff. Look at what happened to the Hollywood Ten." Three years earlier, in a challenge to free speech, a group of Hollywood screenwriters had refused to reveal whether or not they were communists. The case had made its way through the courts, but lost a chance to appeal when two Supreme Court justices died within a couple of months of each other, tilting the Court to the right. Several of the

Hollywood Ten had recently begun serving prison sentences for contempt.

"They're trying to scare us," Hazel said. She didn't have to add that it was working. "They're basically saying that if you wanted to help out with war relief, or if you were for a good relationship with Russia—back when we were allies of Russia fighting on the same side, I might remind you—you're now an enemy of America. That, my friends, is what's un-American. Not this stupid pamphlet of rumors and falsehoods."

The people around them burst into applause. She hadn't meant to make a speech, but she was their director. If she didn't speak up, who would?

"That's right," said Floyd. "If Hazel's a communist, then I'm one, too. We must all stand together."

More cheers.

"Um, Hazel, can I talk to you for a moment?"

Brandy had sidled up to Hazel, and linked arms with her. Hazel allowed her to pull her off to the side, away from the group.

"What's going on, Brandy?"

"Everything's great. I love the play, it's amazing, I mean, you're *so* talented."

"Thank you."

"I consider myself so lucky to be part of this team, really lucky."

Hazel waited.

"I hate to complain about anything, but—" Brandy took a breath. "Well, it's about my costume. Floyd showed me the sketch and I just don't look good in that color, and trust me, I have a really good eye. I know what works on me and what doesn't. I tried to explain that, but he said my first choice didn't fit with the show's palette."

"What's your first choice?"

"Tangerine."

Hazel smiled. With all the drama going on in the world, it was a strange relief to have to consider the color of a dress. "Well, you know it's really up to the costume designer. They get the final say, as they have to make outfits that work together onstage. If they allowed every actor to have a preference, the play won't look as good, it would be visual chaos."

"I would think you have the final say. As director, and all."

Floyd was staring at them from across the room, on the alert. Obviously, they'd already had some kind of tiff. Hazel nodded for him to come over. She didn't want Brandy to think she could bulldoze her way into getting what she wanted. Or Floyd to think she talked behind people's backs.

"Ladies?"

"Floyd, Brandy was explaining that she has an issue with the color of her costume."

"You mean the aubergine dress that will fit her like a glove?"

Brandy shook her head. "In the sketch, the dress is purple. I hate purple, it makes me look sallow and fat."

"It's a lush, deep hue, I promise," insisted Floyd. "The color of a sweet plum, just like you."

The flattery was lost on Brandy. She crossed her arms. "I look much better in bright colors. Like tangerine."

Floyd shook his head. "Orange? No, I cannot have you parading around in orange. The rest of the cast is in cool tones. You'll stand out like a garish citrus fruit."

"Better than an ugly eggplant."

Hazel had to shut down this verbal food fight. "Let's wait and see the dress once Floyd is finished with it, all right? If you really don't like it, we'll reconsider."

Brandy reluctantly agreed before flouncing off.

"That girl is used to getting her way," said Floyd. "Should I just dye the dress in a big vat of orange and get it over with?"

"Not at all. I'll handle her, don't you worry. Let's just hope this is our biggest dilemma."

❖

Three days later, North Korea declared war on South Korea.

Hazel tore through the newspaper articles, alarmed at the thought of another war. The North Koreans were backed by Russia, the South Koreans by America. The country would become a proxy for a larger conflict, communism versus democracy, of that Hazel had no doubt.

For her brother and his friends, who came of age in the 1930s, communism as a philosophy was all the rage, and Ben had jumped on the bandwagon right off, following the lead of brilliant writers like Clifford Odets and Albert Maltz. Practically everyone who was in a creative field looked to communism as a way to even out the gross misbalances of society, especially after the Depression exposed the wide rift between the rich and the poor.

At least once a week, Ben knocked on her bedroom door, some petition or other in hand, and asked her to add her name to it. Most of the time she never even bothered to read it. Everyone was taking up causes and trying to impose change, and she was happy to follow Ben's lead and take part.

At his urging, she'd joined in marches, like the one to support the Spanish Republicans against Franco. News of the violence and horror in Spain, of executions of anyone thought to be communist, including priests, had spread to the United States, and Ben and his buddies had embraced the cause. That afternoon, they'd marched and shouted, and then crowded into someone's basement apartment to go over next steps. She'd never seen her brother so engaged, his face shining with purpose, until he'd been drafted into the army and was heading off to his own war. And his own death.

Now there would be more boys sent abroad to a foreign country, who'd never traveled anywhere outside of the United States and would be in a strange land, told to fight and kill people. Like the soldiers she'd met in Naples.

Shaking off the dark thoughts, she headed down to the hotel lobby to meet Maxine for brunch. Mr. Bard stood in the middle of the space, overseeing two workers who were hanging an enormous oil painting above the fireplace. She stopped and studied it. "Very nice."

"By one of our sixth-floor tenants. Couldn't pay rent but I figure this will cover a couple of months."

His graciousness touched her. "That's very kind of you."

"Did you see the Feds outside?"

"What?"

"Been there the past week or so, on and off. Could be any one of our guests who they're after, other than Mr. Stolberg, of course. Wonder if he's the one who sent for them." He scratched his chin and surveyed the painting. "Pull the right side up two inches." He nodded. "Great."

"Has anyone asked them what they're doing there?"

The workers climbed down their ladders and folded them up. "Watch that, don't scratch the floors." Mr. Bard turned back to Hazel. "Nah. Why bother? They go through the garbage, they tap our phones. We know it and they know we know it. Just like Hungary, where I came from. I'm used to it. You Americans think it's all so free. But no one's free."

Out on the street, Hazel peered around. A black sedan was

parked next to the fire hydrant, unoccupied and unticketed. Maxine stumbled out of the hotel, a scrape of mascara down one cheek, which Hazel wiped off with a handkerchief. "Long night?"

"The usual." Even Maxine managed to look alarmed when Hazel told her about the Feds staking out the hotel, listening in on their phone calls. She glanced at the car before taking Hazel by the arm. "I don't know about you, but I could use a sangria."

"Unbelievable. You never stop, do you?"

They did an about-face and headed into the street entrance of El Quijote, the Spanish restaurant located in one of the hotel's former dining rooms. The interior decor was best described as Iberian bordello, featuring red leather seating, a long, dark bar peppered with fake Tiffany pendants, and rough adobe-style walls that would leave a scratch if you got too close. The place was huge, with rooms off of rooms. They grabbed a couple of seats at the bar. A few tables were filled with folks who looked like they'd accidentally stumbled in, but the place was otherwise empty. This was way too early in the morning for the restaurant's usual clientele.

Lavinia Smarts sat at a table way in the rear, talking to an older man. She waved at them before turning back to her conversation.

"She's so regal," said Maxine, sliding onto a barstool. "That's what I want to be like when I'm her age. A doyenne."

"No one messes with Lavinia," said Hazel.

As she said the words, she spied a man in a black suit in a shadowy corner of the restaurant. He was scribbling in a notebook, and when he wasn't writing, he was staring right at Lavinia.

She elbowed Maxine. "Don't be obvious about it, but that man seems like he's surveilling our friend."

Maxine pretended to drop a napkin and eyed the man as she picked it up from the floor.

"That was so obvious, Max!" Hazel almost laughed. "Seriously, no one would ever guess you were an actress."

The man turned away, so they couldn't get a good look at his face.

"You're worried for nothing. He's probably an accountant who wishes he was a writer, and comes here to soak up the poetic atmosphere," said Maxine.

Lavinia rose and hugged her friend goodbye, before disappearing through the side door that connected the restaurant to the hotel lobby. As she did so, the man snapped the notebook shut and pulled out his wallet, tossing a few bills down on the table before trailing her.

Hazel stood, pulling Maxine along with her. "No. He's up to no good."

In the lobby, there was no sign of either Lavinia or her tail, and the elevator was slowly ascending. Instead of waiting, they hoofed it up the stairway. At the third floor, Hazel peered up over the railing. She loved this view, straight up, the ornate railing wrapping around and around and disappearing into the blinding whiteness of the skylight. Fancy and overdone, as if she were in Paris or London.

But this time, a few floors above, the man in black was looking right back down at her.

She withdrew fast and whispered to Maxine. "He saw me, he's up there."

They picked up the pace, trying to walk as quietly as possible, but as their steps quickened, the man's did, also. Around and around they went, until they heard a bang.

"The door to the roof." Hazel stopped. "We have him trapped."

"I'm not sure we should follow him. What if he's got a gun?"

Hazel thought of Lavinia. The very least they could do was

show these men that they weren't afraid, that the hotel residents would stand up for one another and resist such intrusion. "We're just a couple of girls getting some sun. Come on."

They pushed through the heavy door.

The man stood near one of the gables, looking down over the avenue as if he was searching for his ride. When he saw them, he took off his hat and fanned his face, an attempt at nonchalance. Hazel looked about. No one else was up there with them.

She made a beeline for him. "Who are you?" Up close, he was younger than she'd expected, and rather skinny. His nose was slightly too big for his face, above rose-colored lips that belonged on a girl. His unruly thatch of brown hair could use a barber. This guy sure didn't seem like a Fed.

He looked from Maxine to Hazel, as frightened as a chicken.

Hazel stuck her hands on her hips. "Are you a Fed? If so, you're a disgrace to the agency, going after a sweet old lady. We saw you, and the residents of the hotel don't tolerate being spied on."

"I'm not a Fed." His voice was deeper than Hazel expected.

"Oh, please, everyone in the hotel knows we're being watched." Hazel studied him. Even though the morning was cool, sweat beaded down the man's temple. The walk up the stairs had winded Hazel, but not that much. "We saw you taking notes about Lavinia Smarts."

He tugged at his collar, as if trying to catch his breath. "I'm not a Fed." The words were barely audible. "I work in the private sector."

"What does that mean?" Maxine asked.

He grimaced, as if he had some kind of tic, but didn't respond. Something was off.

"We seem to have stumped him," said Maxine.

To Hazel's surprise, the man slowly listed to one side before sliding to the ground, a clump of boxwood breaking his fall.

Not what Hazel had expected. "What on earth? Did he just faint?" They bent low over him, unsure of what to do next.

"He passed out," said Hazel.

"No. He's having a fit."

Maxine was right. The man had gone rigid, his mouth parted, eyes open and looking off to the side. His body shook as if he were in a washing machine, and his lips began to turn blue.

Hazel turned to Maxine. "Go down and call for someone. Have them send for help."

"I'll be right back." Maxine rushed off.

Hazel had no idea what to do. She tried to hold his head, to keep him from hitting it on the base of the planter. He was unreachable, his eyes rolled back and a horrible grimace on his mouth. She knelt down, the gravel of the roof digging into her knees, her mouth dry, and pulled his head and shoulders onto her lap. As the man's vibrations coursed through her, she murmured calm words, as soothing as possible, to try to draw him out of his trance.

CHAPTER NINE

Hazel

June 1950

The man lying in Hazel's lap seemed only to get worse. A trail of drool dripped down the side of his chin, and the sound of his teeth grinding set her own on edge. She looked around, desperate for help, even though she knew she was all alone on the sprawling rooftop. For a while he fought against her, as if trying to get to his feet, so in a low voice she told him to quiet down, that everything was fine.

With a great gasp, he sat upright, almost knocking Hazel in the head as he did so. He wasn't fully conscious, but his breathing began to return to normal, and the color slowly came back to his face.

"Where am I?" When he finally spoke, his voice was low, weary. Like that of a much older man.

"On the roof of the Chelsea Hotel. You had some kind of a fit."

He blinked a couple of times and looked about. "God, no."

She kept her hand on his back, unsure of what to do next. "You fell pretty hard. Are you hurt?"

"I don't think so." He rolled his shoulders a few times.

"Someone's gone for help. What happened to you just now?"

He looked defeated, worn. "Epilepsy."

"Is it because we chased you up the stairs?" Hazel couldn't believe she was actually feeling bad for the guy.

"It just happens."

"Does it happen often?"

He put one hand on the back of his neck and rubbed it. "Not in years, since I was in high school. It's what kept me from the draft."

She guided him onto a nearby bench and sat beside him, like a couple of strangers waiting for a bus. Uncertain, she said the first thing that came to mind. "You were following Lavinia Smarts, right?"

He nodded, barely.

"Why are you spying on people? There's no one evil or dangerous here. Just a bunch of artists and writers and actors."

"I'm not spying. I was just inquiring. We're trying to keep America safe." His face fell. "Apparently, I haven't done a very good job of it."

"That was pretty terrifying."

"I'm sorry you had to see me like that."

She knew she should let him recover, but in her nervousness, and her relief that he was okay, she couldn't seem to stop talking. "How old are you?"

"Twenty-five."

"You seem younger."

He took out a handkerchief and wiped his mouth. "I guess it doesn't help when I'm drooling like a baby."

"You only drooled a little." She patted his knee, then immediately regretted it. "I hardly noticed."

The corners of his mouth rose slightly. "I appreciate that."

The door to the stairway banged open and Maxine and Mr. Bard appeared.

"What's your name?" asked Hazel.

"Charlie. Look, I really don't want to cause a scene, I'll lose my job. Again, I'm sorry about this. I'll just go."

By the time Maxine and Mr. Bard reached them, Charlie was back on his feet. He tucked the handkerchief into his pocket and addressed Hazel. "Thank you for helping me. I appreciate it, but I must go now."

His strides lengthened as he crossed the rooftop, then disappeared into the black hole of the stairway.

"What should we do?" asked Maxine.

Mr. Bard shrugged. "What can we do? We're the little people, they're the ones in power. We do what they say."

Hazel spoke up. "He's not a threat, believe me. He's mortified by what happened. My guess is we won't see him around here again."

"If you say so," answered Maxine.

"In the meantime, should we go and tell Lavinia what's going on? She'll want to know."

Downstairs, Lavinia was nestled in an apricot-colored armchair in her living room, a script spread open on her lap and a pair of reading glasses perched on her nose. Winnifred and Wanda sat at a table near the window, playing a game of checkers.

Lavinia listened to Hazel's recounting of the morning's events without interrupting, glancing over at Maxine every so often.

"I don't think we'll see him again," said Hazel. "He was awfully embarrassed, but I bet there's more where that came from."

Lavinia closed the script and set it on the floor. "What bothers me most is not that I'm a target, but that by infiltrating the hotel, they're destroying everything the Chelsea stands for. Where people with opposing opinions can mingle and mix without forcing one side or the other to leave. It's the beauty of the place, has been so for decades. The same goes for Broadway."

Maxine leaned back in the sofa. "Broadway—and New Yorkers—won't put up with this insanity for long. It'll blow over fast, I'm guessing."

"I'm not so sure," said Hazel. "The House Un-American Activities Committee successfully crushed the Hollywood Ten, which has only encouraged that awful Senator McCarthy in his fanatical hunt for communists in the government. Who knows who's next after that? Artists, musicians? We're right in the HUAC's crosshairs. I can't help but think that if we band together, we can show them that we won't be bullied," said Hazel.

"You mean, like the Hollywood Ten banded together?" Wanda's voice was barely a whisper. Winnifred finished her thought. "They ended up going to prison."

The sisters had a good point.

"What about going to our unions?" said Hazel. "Aren't they there to protect us?"

"Good luck with that," answered Lavinia. "The Screen Actors Guild caved three years ago, and I have no doubt AFTRA will do the same." She looked dolefully down at the script on the floor. "No doubt I'm next, with my history. If I get named, there goes my starring role on the small screen."

"What starring role?" asked Hazel.

"I'm to play a family matriarch in a new television series on NBC. A juicy part, to say the least."

Congratulations rang out around the room. "What will become of us if the classically trained Madame Lavinia stoops to television work?" teased Maxine.

"I'm getting old. Older. It would be nice to cut down on travel, do less regional theater. Although I'd miss your grandmother's apple cake." Lavinia turned to Hazel. "Maxine's grandmother made all the treats that were sold during the intermission at Seattle Rep. I still dream of that cake."

"Being German, and something of a battle-ax, my grandmother didn't have many friends," added Maxine. "But she was always welcome at the theater, and has a special place in her heart for Lavinia. She'll be very sorry if you stop performing there."

The apartment door opened and Virgil Thomson walked in. "What on earth is going on in here?"

Hazel gestured around the room. "We're trying to figure out a way to fight back against the blacklist."

"A ghastly premise for a get-together." He patted her on the head. "On principle, I don't tolerate discussions of politics or religion. I don't tolerate complainers. It all bores me to tears."

"We're not complaining, we're standing up for something."

But he'd already wandered over to the bar cart, and didn't hear a word she'd said.

❖

The soothing repetition of rehearsals helped Hazel move forward.

The play was gradually taking shape under her hand. The process was no different from that of a sculptor, but instead of wet clay, she maneuvered actors around a stage. First, the table read: A scene was discussed and characters considered from all angles, usually a demonstration of pseudo-intellectual posturing, although every so often a small nugget of truth hit home. Then the actors took to their feet and stumbled around onstage, bumping into one another, struggling with words, a mangled mess of a thing that left everyone panicked. This week, though, the actors had been told to be "off book." No more scripts.

The fear of not knowing the lines overcame nearly everyone, with actors calling out for help from the stage manager when they lost their way, apologizing profusely as the scene ground to a halt. But by the third or fourth run-through of a scene, the emotion under the words began to bubble to the surface. For a minute or two, speech and movement coalesced into a sublime tension. Whenever that happened, the cast would turn to Hazel afterward with the expectant smiles of good schoolchildren waiting to be patted on the head.

The only cloud in the creative process was Hazel's worry that her listing in *Red Channels*, and the threat of others being listed, was dividing the cast. When a couple of the actors whispered in one corner during a break, every so often looking up and scanning the rest of the group, she couldn't help wondering if they were merely gossiping, or guessing at who was a communist sympathizer. Another time, when Brandy and Hazel started walking toward the stage door at the same time during a break, Brandy said she'd forgotten something and suddenly turned back. Did she not want to be seen to the outside world as being too chummy with Hazel?

Hazel tried to shrug it off as her own silly insecurities.

Until Mr. Canby showed up early to a meeting of the show's designers at the theater with a grim look on his face. He tossed the latest issue of *Variety* on the worktable, where Floyd's sketches were scattered around a model of the set.

"They're closing in."

Hazel picked it up. "Who is?"

"Read the headline."

She did so out loud. *"Un-American Activities Group Probing Radio, TV, Stage."*

"Stage. That's us." Mr. Canby took out a handkerchief and wiped his brow.

She scanned the first paragraph.

The House Un-American Activities Committee is heading east, and soon will be initiating a probe of communism within the Broadway theaters of New York City. Committee investigators are already on the ground in the Big Apple investigating suspected actors and writers, as well as gleaning information from others claiming to have facts about commie influences in Manhattan's showbiz.

The pattern for the Broadway probe will be no different from that of the Hollywood hearings. The HUAC expects several former members of the Communist Party to come forward and purge themselves by answering questions and naming those they knew in the Party.

"Purge." Mr. Canby let the word hang in the air. "That's some word. They've already started interviewing people in secret."

Floyd and the set designer were downstairs in the basement, checking to see if any old props could be retooled for the show, and Hazel was grateful they weren't in earshot. She didn't want them to see Mr. Canby so anxious. "I don't know anyone who's been interviewed."

"Because they're secret, doll."

The article would certainly strike even more fear into the hearts of the theater community, everyone wondering if a rival was turning on them, if they were a target. If they'd go off to jail and lose everything. An insidious, poisonous fog was drifting down Broadway, across stages and into producers' offices and rehearsal rooms, making everyone suspect and scared.

"What can I do to help you? To help our production?" she asked.

He shook his head. "Nothing. I mean, that's what you should do. Nothing. Don't speak out, don't talk about it with other people. Lay low."

"What about the radio interview Maxine and I are supposed to do this afternoon?"

Canby had arranged for an on-air interview at NBC, and Hazel hated to admit how eager she was to return to the studio as a budding playwright, as opposed to a cow.

"You'll still do that, of course. We need all the good press we can get." Canby's expression softened. "Don't get me wrong. I believe in this show. This is the best thing I've produced in decades. Screw Butterfield Supermarkets."

"I'm sorry. What?"

"Butterfield Supermarkets, some upstate grocery chain owned by an amateur blacklister. He enjoys organizing boycotts of anything slightly pinko. Laurence Butterfield has decided the theater is his next pet project."

Floyd and the set designer emerged from the wings just then, preventing Hazel from asking any more questions. She dove headlong into the agenda, knowing that they had only an hour before the rest of the cast reassembled, and Mr. Canby headed off after giving the nod of approval to both sets and costumes.

As Floyd and the set designer were packing up to go, the rest of the cast drifted back in for the afternoon's rehearsal.

The air in the room seemed to chill even before Hazel realized that two men in dark suits were charging down the aisle.

This could not be good. She desperately wished Mr. Canby were still here.

"Yes? Can I help you?" Hazel tried to stay calm, put a neutral expression on her face.

"We're investigators with the FBI." The one who addressed her had an angry landscape of razor burn across his neck. In tandem, the men flashed their badges before tucking them back into the inside pockets of their jackets.

"What do you want?"

"We were informed that Floyd Jenkins is here."

Floyd stepped forward, clutching a folder with his sketches in front of his chest like armor. "Yes? You want me?" His voice rose almost to a falsetto.

The other man, a bear of a guy in a too-small suit that pulled at the seams, nodded. "We'd like to ask you some questions, downtown. Come with us, please."

"What is this all about?" said Hazel. "You can't just come and take him away, we're working here."

"Actually, ma'am, we can. If you'll come with us, please, Mr. Jenkins."

The room froze. "Floyd, let me call Mr. Canby, don't go anywhere," said Hazel, starting down the steps from the stage.

"No, no." Floyd waved his hand. "It's fine. It'll be fine." He handed the folder to Hazel. "See that these get back to the costume shop, to my assistant. Tell her we have the green light and to get to work."

"No, Floyd."

"It's fine. I'll answer their questions and be back in no time."

With the agents flanking Floyd on either side, they disappeared up the aisle.

"Maxine Mead, you are an absolute delight." The host of the radio program leaned in close to his microphone. "I know all our listeners out there are entranced, and if only they could see you like I do, they'd be panting like dogs."

Not exactly the way Hazel would have liked him to put it, but at least so far the radio interview had gone smoothly, with all the focus on Maxine. Hazel hadn't been able to reach Mr. Canby to tell him of the FBI spiriting Floyd off to be interviewed, but their own interview had only five minutes to go, after which she could head right over to his office.

"Now, Miss Ripley." The host swiveled around to Hazel. "You've come out of nowhere, it seems, and now will be not only directing your first Broadway show, you also wrote it. How can you explain your good luck?"

"Well, you have to remember I understudied on Broadway for several years, so I know the theater world pretty well. And as Maxine explained, it came out of our experiences during World War II, in Naples."

"Right. Now, tell us what your little skit is all about."

Unbelievable. She doubted they'd call a male playwright's work a "little skit," even if it were a debut. She soldiered on. "It takes place in a formerly grand hotel in an unnamed country that's under siege, and the guests are trapped inside by the fighting. They start turning on each other, in fear and desperation, and make assumptions about each other that aren't necessarily true. I'd say the general theme touches on the dangers of making assumptions about someone's identity and political beliefs."

"Intriguing. That's a big subject to tackle, especially now. I hate to bring this up, but your name turns up in *Red Channels*, which if our listeners don't know, is a list of people suspected of being communist sympathizers. What do you have to say to that?"

She looked over at Maxine, who'd turned gray. "I advise everyone to ignore it, it's all hearsay."

The host was only getting started, it seemed. He pulled a sheet of paper from his notes. "I also have here a letter from a producer in the Theatre Guild, saying that you shouldn't be directing a Broadway show since you've been listed in *Red Channels*. It says that a half dozen Theatre Guild subscribers were unhappy to see the employment of a controversial artist."

This was news to Hazel. The incriminations seemed to be coming faster and faster. She couldn't help but wonder if William Williams wasn't behind this, trying to stir up trouble ever since he'd quit as director.

"I won't bother to defend myself against the spurious allegations you just mentioned," she said. "In fact, I'm surprised, as a member of the press, you'd give them any credence without checking your facts first."

"I'm just repeating what I've heard."

After watching Floyd be taken away, Hazel couldn't take Mr. Canby's advice and stay under the radar. Not when she'd just been ambushed. This time, she'd channel Maxine's innate courage and speak the truth, loud and clear. "May I remind you and your listeners that we have something called the First Amendment, the right to free speech? Directing a play should have nothing to do with my political views. America is a free country, after all. Am I right?"

Before he could respond, Maxine launched into a long monologue about the difference between acting in a movie and acting onstage, not letting the host get a word in edgewise. The clock ticked down until there were only ten seconds to go. "So be sure to come see *Wartime Sonata*," Maxine said. "Previews start July twelfth, opening night is July twenty-first. See you at the theater!"

Hazel threw her headphones down on the table, with Maxine following suit, and together they walked out without another word.

CHAPTER TEN

↵Maxine

June 26, 1950

Hotel living definitely has its perks, especially when I camp out in the lobby and watch Mr. Bard's reactions to every tenant passing by. You can tell immediately those he loves and those he abhors. If he loves them, he calls out a nickname, sometimes "dearie" and other times some kind of Hungarian endearment that sounds like it consists of all consonants. If he hates them, he'll scurry into his office rather than suffer their presence. Worse off are the folks who owe him rent money. Those he'll follow to the elevator, standing too close as it makes its slow descent, and speak about their "monetary delinquency" in a stage whisper that I'm sure he hopes will shame the poor resident into ponying up.

I was waiting in the lobby because I was tired of staring at my phone upstairs, wondering if it would ring. Not surprisingly, Arthur had resurfaced. More than once. The first time, he was standing across the street from the Biltmore, wearing a black fedora and matching raincoat. My eye went to him immediately, it always has. He nodded but didn't beckon to me, and I jumped into a cab and escaped as fast as I could, heart pounding.

He was outside the Chelsea the next time, holding a bunch of flowers. Peonies. My favorite. We spoke, briefly. He was back in town for business, but said he couldn't let me go, that he'd do anything to make it up to me. We made a date to talk further, and it was then he pulled out all the stops, bringing me to a glitzy nightclub, ordering champagne.

My grandmother had adored Arthur from the start, even though I was only sixteen. "I met your grandfather when I was a teenager," she told me. "It's better that way." I asked her why, and she just smiled. She kept a photo of them on their wedding day on her bureau, and I used to creep into her room and study it. In it, they were looking at each other, laughing, my grandmother's profile as delicate as a movie star's and my grandfather's eyes filled with longing. The same way Arthur looked at me that evening at the nightclub.

Arthur talked of our shared history, pleaded with me to not let our story end like this. Promised that he'd changed and we were meant for each other. Even though I knew it was only a matter of time before he wore me down and we were back to performing our sordid duet, I'd said I wasn't ready, and walked out.

❖

"What are you doing, lurking in the lobby?"

Hazel appeared out of nowhere, wearing a prim shirtdress with a matching cardigan. Like she was off to church or something.

I avoided her question with one of my own. "Where are you headed this fine evening?"

"Family dinner. Would rather jump in the Hudson, but duty calls. My mom's still sore that I moved out, although I stop by once a week, to try to make it up to her." She let out a funny sound, a cross between a hiccup and a gasp. "Hey. You should come along.

Do you want to meet my parents? My mother will love you." She didn't wait for me to reply. "This is perfect. Come on."

I agreed, curious. Not that I had anything better to do.

"Any news on Floyd?" I asked as the cab roared uptown. Yesterday, we'd hightailed it over to Canby's office right after the radio show, and found him already on the phone with NBC, chewing them out for their attack on Hazel. He'd taken the news about Floyd badly, throwing a coffee mug across the room, and promised to track him down, do whatever it took.

"Nothing yet. I'm sure we'll hear soon, though."

I didn't answer. None of us knew how these new rules worked, where someone could be taken away for questioning and then disappear. As if we were living under siege in some authoritarian state, not America.

The taxi dropped us off outside one of those grand Upper West Side apartment buildings that take up the whole block. Hazel nodded to the doorman keeping guard just inside the gates and we took a sharp left, up a flight of wide stairs. She shoved open a door and we were standing inside what felt like a rambling country house, not a New York apartment. An expansive foyer with a mosaic floor opened up to a dark wood library on one side and some kind of salon on the other, both with big fireplaces. Hallways led off other hallways, a maze of sharp turns and hidden nooks.

Hazel hung her hat and coat on the rack and I followed suit. "This is your home?"

"Yes. Back in the 1920s, when they moved in, it wasn't a big deal. Everyone lived like this. Lucky for them, it's rent-controlled, otherwise they might have to move in with me." She rolled her eyes.

"Oh, Mr. Bard would adore them, I'm sure."

Inside the kitchen the aroma of a roast chicken greeted us. Her mother was stooped over, lifting it out of the oven, and when she caught sight of me, she squealed and dropped the roasting pan with a large crash.

She left it there, the chicken half in the pan and half on the floor, and dashed over, wiping her hands on her apron. "You're Maxine Mead. A true star, here in our home." Hazel's mother had the same blue eyes as her daughter, but they darted back and forth, studying me closely. Her jowls hung heavy on her face, as did the skin under her eyes, forming translucent half-moons.

Hazel was on her knees, cleaning up the mess and wiping the chicken's backside with a towel. "This will be fine. It wasn't on the floor for long."

I moved to help, but her mother held me firmly by my elbows. "Maxine Mead, in the flesh!"

"Nice to meet you, Mrs. Ripley."

"That's right, Hazel said she acted with you in Italy." Mrs. Ripley turned to her husband, who sat in a wheelchair by the table. "Remember? Hazel acted with Maxine Mead in the USO tour."

Her father, a skinny man with bony knees under his too-big slacks, nodded but stayed silent.

Hazel made the introductions and then Mrs. Ripley was off to the races, offering me a glass of wine and asking all about Hollywood. I swear she used the word *starlet* at least four times. We sat down and ate dinner, me answering her questions and Hazel looking quite pleased with herself and not saying a word. Unlike me, that girl shied away from attention, and now I knew why. Attention in this household was fierce.

"Hazel wanted to be an actress, but she wouldn't listen to me." Mrs. Ripley passed me the bowl of peas. "If she had taken my advice, she'd be in your position, doing movies and the like. I made Mr. Ripley's career, you see, so I know of what I speak."

I looked over at Hazel, who stayed silent. "Hazel is a wonderful actress," I offered.

Mrs. Ripley shook her head. "I wouldn't know. I've never seen her act. Not once. She's a bit of a joke in the theater world. 'Always the bridesmaid,' you know that saying?"

I was well aware of Hazel's run as an understudy, and resented her mother for throwing it in her face. She seemed to take it personally, as if Hazel had refused to go onstage to spite her. There was no inquiry into her daughter's play, or acknowledgment of the fact that Hazel's work was soon to be performed on Broadway. The blinders on that woman annoyed the hell out of me.

After dinner, Mrs. Ripley attended to her husband, and I wandered around, eventually finding Hazel sitting in one of the bedrooms, looking out the window onto the rooftops of the city, the sky lit up with the last blast of sunset.

The room still smelled slightly boyish, a lingering hint of sweat and hormones. Or maybe that was just my imagination. "Was this Ben's room?"

Hazel nodded, her hands folded in her lap. "How did you meet him?"

We hadn't spoken much of him. I didn't want to, as I barely knew her brother at all. I'm sure she wanted some dramatic love story, but that's not what it was. Far from it. We were just kids, moving along in the world.

"In a coffee shop, downtown. We dated here and there, but it wasn't anything serious. I don't really remember much about him, to be honest. I'm sorry."

"What about the other man? He's back, isn't he?"

Of course Hazel would know. She'd been watching me onstage, day after day. Surely the resurgence of Arthur registered in my body language, my voice. Hazel of all people would know that.

"He is. Arthur's in the city on business. I tried to fend him off, but he's persistent. I finally agreed to meet him and we talked. He feels awful about what happened."

"Why do you like him so much? He doesn't respect you."

"Why don't you tell your mom to respect you? She's awfully rude."

I hadn't meant to be so abrupt, but Hazel considered her answer before speaking. "She believes she knows the best way to go about things, and gets frustrated when I don't listen. She was upset when I moved into the Chelsea, and feels abandoned. First Ben, then me."

"You're only a cab ride away, and you're an adult, for God's sake. Does she really feel abandoned, or is it just that you made an independent decision without consulting her?"

"What do you mean?"

"Your mother is one of those people who comes across as selfless and caring, but only so others will recognize and laud her martyrdom. She craves control."

"That's a horrible thing to say." Hazel's tentative delivery didn't match the admonishment. She had to know it was true, deep down. "At least she doesn't hurt me."

The dig at Arthur hit home. "You so sure of that? It doesn't just have to be physical, you know."

We sat quietly, a détente of sorts. "My mother has been through so much," she finally explained. "I guess I see it as my daughterly duty, and try not to let it bother me. How did you and Arthur meet?"

I appreciated Hazel maneuvering the conversation to a less fraught subject. "He knew the couple who ran Seattle Rep, and would often stop by and help out. All the girls had a crush on him." I couldn't help but smile at the memory. The smell of the theater— a mix of wood shavings and pipe smoke—came back to me in a rush. "I was sixteen, and he was twenty-one, with this curly dark hair and blue eyes, what a combination. A tough guy, all muscles and cragginess, except for those eyes. Anyway, I'd finally gotten a decent role in a play, where I had to sing and dance. No one expected me to land that part, but I'd been practicing day after day, really putting in the work. The other girls hated me for getting it and tortured me to no end. Whispered backstage as I was rehearsing, hid my costumes and makeup."

"That's terrible." Hazel sat back against the headboard and wrapped her arms around her knees. "What did you do?"

"What could I do, really? The night of the first performance, they smeared lipstick on my shirt. I tried to get it off best I could but then I had to go onstage, wearing this white blouse with a huge water stain over my chest. My grandmother and father were in the audience. This was my chance to prove to them I could act, that I was worthy of going off to New York City after school. Instead, I froze. I warbled out the tune, feeling the tension in the room rise with every note, feeling horribly exposed. After, I ran into an empty dressing room and crawled under the counter, crying my eyes out."

"Oh, Maxine. I'm so sorry."

"Eventually, the door opened and I hoped it might be my grandmother, but no, it was Arthur. He didn't say a word. Just sat on the floor with me and placed a hand on my ankle. My ankle, of all places." The pressure of his hand had been wonderfully warm and calming, like he was staunching the flow of my shame. "Once I was okay, we headed out the back door and found a diner and drank milkshakes. And that was that."

I could tell Hazel wanted to ask more questions about why I tolerated Arthur's bad behavior, about his marriage, but I didn't want to discuss it and ruin all those lovely memories.

Back in the kitchen, Mrs. Ripley was wiping Mr. Ripley's chin. Even though she was a loud, brash woman, the way she gently cleaned her husband, dabbing at the corners of his mouth, moved me. I wondered if Arthur would take care of me like that, if it came down to it, and regretted my earlier harsh words.

"Where did you girls get off to?" asked Mrs. Ripley.

"I was just showing Maxine around the apartment," said Hazel. "We really should go, though, it's been a busy day."

"Can't be that busy. It's not as if you have to memorize any lines, since you're not acting anymore." Mrs. Ripley finally acknowledged the play we were both working so hard on.

"A director has just as much work, if not more."

Mrs. Ripley stepped forward and planted a kiss on Hazel's forehead, her hands on either side of her cheeks. "I just wish you were onstage with Maxine, not hiding in the back of the theater."

Hazel shook free. "I'm not hiding in the back of a theater. That's not what directors do."

I couldn't help myself. "Your daughter runs the show. She gets paid more money than the actors, gets to say what she wants and how she wants it. You really ought to be impressed."

"A lady director? I don't know."

Hazel placed her hands on her mother's shoulders and stared hard into her eyes. "I am the boss, Mother. You get it? Just like George Abbott, Moss Hart."

Her mother began to say something smart, but Hazel shook her head. "No more dismissing this. It's a big deal. You can come to opening night, but only if you are there to be pleasant and say nice things to me. Period. Otherwise you can stay home."

Her mother frowned but remained quiet. Hazel swept away, grabbing our coats and hats from the rack in a fluid motion and letting the front door bang hard behind us.

As we walked outside, she hugged me. "Thank you."

"You were great. Your best role yet."

"Believe me, I wasn't acting." She took a deep breath, pleased with herself. "Now it's your turn. Next time you see Arthur, you tell him what's what. I've got your back."

If it were only that easy. But I didn't say that. I just nodded and whistled for a taxi.

Mr. Canby pulled me aside at rehearsal the next day. Not just aside, he yanked me into the house manager's office near the front of the theater, kicked out the house manager, and closed the door.

"Am I fired?" I was only half joking, but Mr. Canby laughed hard and loud. Nervous laughter, forced.

"No, of course not."

I'd hoped he might have some news about Floyd, but I was wrong.

"I have a favor to ask of you, Miss Mead. I've arranged a meeting with you and an important person, someone whose approval is crucial to our little play here."

"An investor?"

"Not quite. After that disastrous radio interview, he reached out, saying he wants assurance that all is on the up-and-up. I'm hoping you can tell him that it is."

Strange choice of words. I was intrigued. "Isn't Hazel the right person for this?"

"No, I want star power. You need to dazzle him with your Hollywood glitter."

"Darn, I forgot to pack it in my handbag this morning."

More fake laughter. Whoever this guy was, he had Mr. Canby shaking in his shoes.

"No need to mention it to Hazel, she has enough on her plate as it is. He's at the Pierre hotel."

"Swanky. How will I know who he is?"

"Just ask for Laurence Butterfield."

Now it was all coming into focus. "This is the Butterfield with the supermarket empire? The same lunatic who crusades against commie sympathizers?"

Mr. Canby blanched. "Please don't put it like that. Look, he heard the radio broadcast and is threatening the show with pick-eters, and I was hoping you could convince him to back off."

"Why don't you have Hazel meet him, and let them talk like two grown-ups? I bet she'd love a chance to put him straight."

"First of all, that's the last thing we need. You know Hazel will go on the attack, like she did during the interview."

"Can you blame her?"

"No, no, of course not. But we need a level head. Butterfield's got a direct line to a lot of people at the top, including the FBI."

I knew he was thinking of Floyd. And I knew I'd do whatever I could to help. While I hated going behind Hazel's back, I could see Mr. Canby's point.

⁘

The somber clerk behind the desk at the Pierre directed me to a suite on the thirtieth floor, where a woman sporting a bouffant hairdo that resembled cotton candy dipped in ink opened the door.

"Please, come in," she said, without a trace of welcome. I followed her into the living area, where a slight man with a crew cut sat reading the newspaper. He folded it up carefully as he saw me coming, and we sussed each other out. His suit was too large for his frame, as if he was trying to emphasize shoulders he did not have. His profile disappointed further, with a chin that receded into his neck.

But when he stuck out his hand, an entirely different energy emanated from that skinny scaffolding. His grip was firm, and he spoke with a baritone that almost rattled the teacup next to him.

"I'm Larry Butterfield. Pleasure to meet you, Miss Mead."

"Likewise."

He ordered his wife to pour us tea and she did so, before leaving the room and closing the door quietly behind her.

"Miss Mead, I'll get right to the point. I was listening to my favorite radio show and was very disappointed."

"How so, Mr. Butterfield?"

"Don't get me wrong, you were marvelous—I've seen a few of your movies and enjoyed them very much—but I didn't like what I heard from that director girl."

"I'm sorry to hear that, but you see—"

He cut me off. "Canby says you know Hazel Ripley quite well, professionally and personally."

"Yes. We met in the war, in Naples. She's a talented actress, and a skilled writer."

"I see. Her show—your show—opens soon. I'm surprised you'd be involved, a movie actress of your stature."

"Have you read it?"

"I don't need to read it, I already know everything I need to know about it." Mr. Butterfield took a sip of tea and pursed his lips. Or maybe that was his usual tea-tasting face. "Canby's making a huge mistake. Don't think I don't know what he's up to, sending along a pretty gal to try to convince me otherwise. Let me tell you, your playwright-slash-director is not to be trusted."

"Hazel? She's one of the best people I know."

"I'll tell you a secret." He leaned in close. I had to stop myself from recoiling. "She reminds me of my wife back when we first met."

That made no sense at all. The mousy woman who let me in?

"She was a journalist, wrote about garden clubs and the like, before getting caught up in the women's right to vote, with all that pseudo-political grandstanding. When I asked for her hand in marriage, I explained I wouldn't tolerate any of that rubbish, and now she's a proper wife, a proper mother."

I tried to keep my expression neutral, not let on how horrified I was. The way the story spilled off his tongue, it was obvious he told it frequently.

"I know a thing or two about the world that you ladies simply cannot, by virtue of your sex. I fought in the First World War—I was considered a war hero, if you must know—and after the war I told Coolidge to keep an eye on those Germans. I told that to anyone who would listen, but no one believed me. Proved right, I was, and before we knew it, we were immersed in another world war." He stared out the window, where clouds scudded across the sky. "For years now, my gut has been telling me that the Russians are next, and every day I'm proven right a little more. This time, I won't just talk. This time, I'm taking action to stop our country from attack."

This clearly wasn't a man to be underestimated. I tried a different tack. "I appreciate your service, sir. I can only imagine the things you've seen. But we're just trying to put on a play, a little entertainment. I promise it's not an attack against America, not in the least."

He shook his head. "I've been working closely with the American Legion and we believe there is a terrible threat out there. A threat to our very way of life. We've seen the impact of the Hollywood Ten, we know that these tainted artists have infiltrated television and radio. Broadway is next."

"If I may, Mr. Butterfield, what was the last show you attended on Broadway?"

He rolled his eyes. "Oh, I couldn't possibly recall the title—it was years ago. My wife and I don't enjoy the theater, as a general rule. Matter of fact, several years ago, a local theater group in Syracuse tried performing some lefty propaganda, and the minute I got wind of what they were up to, I had the entire production shut down, the group banned. I vowed to my wife that we would never step foot in a theater again."

I took a deep breath and remembered why Mr. Canby had sent me. Not to fight, but to flatter. "Tell me what you're trying to do here in New York, if you don't mind. I'm not sure I understand exactly."

He brightened at the invitation. "I've made it my mission to ensure that *Red Channels* is in every advertising executive's desk drawer up and down Madison Avenue. If they hire or represent someone who's on that list, then I threaten to boycott all the products hawked by that particular ad agency."

"You mean you won't stock their cigarettes or toilet paper or whatever?"

"Exactly. Or sometimes, I keep a few of the products in stock, but I put them out on the shelves with a note for all the customers to see, so that they know they're supporting the Communist Party if they purchase that particular product."

"That seems extreme."

"It's my store, and my right to express my opinion."

"Just as it's the right of the artists to express theirs."

"Not if they're spies. We're organizing a fight on all fronts, and I won't rest until every last dirty Red has been exposed and brought down. I don't care if we're talking about a girl director, a producer like Canby, a musician, or an actor."

He scared me, to be honest. I took a deep breath, softened my shoulders, and leaned forward conspiratorially. I would placate this madman, for Hazel's sake.

"Look, Mr. Butterfield, would I be working with someone who was a tainted artist? Of course not, I'm American through and through. When Hazel and I were entertaining the troops in Italy, we saw the fight in our soldiers' eyes, felt their love of our great country. That's what inspired Hazel to write the play, which is far from un-American, by the way. You really ought to read it."

"I don't need to read it." But my patriotic words had soothed him. He ogled me, breathing heavily. This was way too easy. The more uptight the man, the faster they fall under my spell, I've discovered.

"You've got to see our quandary, then," I continued. "If you won't read the play, or even come to the theater to see it once it's running, what can we do to convince you that everything's on the up-and-up? You must see how you've put us in a bind. Hazel's a good person, she's been unfairly targeted."

"Unfairly targeted? Huh. Anyone who thinks so is free to visit the offices of American Business Consultants and request to clear their name."

I sat back. Could it be that easy? "Well, then, I'm sure Hazel will want to do so."

"You seem like a smart lady, Miss Mead. You must understand that we're surrounded by a spiderweb of subversives that grows and grows. There are some nights I can barely sleep. I have children, I hope to have grandchildren. I want them to be safe." His voice cracked. "Don't you want that, too?"

"Of course I do." I stood to go. I'd heard enough and if I stuck around any longer, I'd tell Mr. Butterfield to go to hell and toss his tea in his face. And if I did that, without a doubt, the show would be surrounded by picketers and close before it had a chance to open.

But with Butterfield placated, we'd have a chance.

"If Hazel goes to American Business Consultants to clear her name, will you give us a little breathing space, Mr. Butterfield?" I forced myself to let my hand linger on his arm as he showed me to the door.

"I just might, Miss Mead." He offered up a slow, vicious smile, revealing a mouth of crowded teeth. "I very well just might."

CHAPTER ELEVEN

Hazel

June 1950

First thing tomorrow, I'm going to go right uptown and confront Mr. Canby. How dare he put you in that position with Butterfield?"

"No, you can't." Maxine grabbed Hazel's arm, pleading. "He made me promise not to tell you any of this."

It had taken only a couple of drinks for Hazel to get Maxine to spill the beans as to what was going on. Hazel had known something was up when she came down from the mezzanine level earlier that day, having just checked the sight lines for the play's final scene, and spotted Mr. Canby and Maxine slipping out of the house manager's office, neither saying a word to the other and practically tiptoeing away. They were up to some kind of intrigue, and Hazel was determined to find out what.

So she'd invited Maxine to El Quijote that evening, where they'd gossiped for a bit before Hazel asked her directly what was happening. Eventually, Maxine had filled her in on her meeting with Mr. Canby, followed by the one with Mr. Butterfield. Hazel shook with anger. What the hell had Canby been thinking, sending Maxine into the lion's den like that? Maxine had assured Hazel that she'd slowed him down and sweet-talked him into backing off, and he'd even opened up the possibility of Hazel getting "cleared" from all charges.

"So you see, it was a good idea after all," said Maxine. "First thing tomorrow, you can go down and get your name taken off the list."

Hazel called for another drink. "Still, the two of you had no right to go behind my back."

"I know, and I'm sorry. Look, once the show's open and ticket sales are through the roof, Butterfield will have lost what little power he wields."

They simultaneously knocked on the wooden bar with their knuckles, and laughed. The knot of worry in Hazel's gut released and she assured Maxine that she'd not turn on Canby for using her leading lady in his attempt to make nice.

First thing the next morning, after a sleepless night, Hazel headed to the offices of American Business Consultants, located in a skyscraper across from Bryant Park.

She took the elevator up but paused a moment outside the door, unsure. Anger would only inflame the problem, not help it. She took a couple of deep breaths and reminded herself of the goal: to clear her name, not create more drama. Face-to-face, they wouldn't be able to deny the inconsistencies and inaccuracies. She hated to stoop to their level, but she wanted to save the show from even the threat of picketers, from being shut down.

As the director and playwright, she was accountable for over a hundred jobs, another reason she hadn't been able to sleep the night before. She didn't want to disappoint anyone.

Secrets were dangerous. Better to have it all out in the open.

A secretary took her name and disappeared. The place wasn't particularly grand or bustling, the floors scuffed and the walls empty. Hazel counted only four office doors off the small waiting area, where copies of *Red Channels* were fanned out on a glass table. Hazel stifled the impulse to snatch them up and bury them in her purse.

"Miss Ripley. In here."

The secretary held open a door with the name Vincent Hartnett on it. Mr. Hartnett had thinning hair that had been unartfully draped across his scalp, a coiffure that probably took longer to arrange than her own.

"What can I do for you?" He closed a folder and placed both elbows on it, hands under his chin.

No handshake, no niceties. Fine. Hazel sat in the chair opposite. "My name is Hazel Ripley. My name is listed in *Red Channels*, and Mr. Butterfield suggested I come by. The entry about me is erroneous and I wish to clear things up."

"I see." He opened a desk drawer and took out the booklet. "Ripley, did you say?" He rifled through the pages until he found the right one, and then took a moment to study it while she stayed silent.

Someone knocked on the frame of the open door. "Mr. Hartnett, just wanted to let you know I'm heading out."

Hazel turned her head and let out a small "oh."

Charlie—the man from the roof of the Chelsea, looking much healthier than when she'd seen him last—stared back at her.

Hazel had assumed he was a Fed, but obviously not. He hadn't been lying when he said he worked in the private sector; he was one of Hartnett's lackeys. Judging from the shocked look on his face, he was as stunned as she was.

Charlie gave her a barely perceptible nod before turning to Mr. Hartnett. "I didn't know you were with someone. Sorry to interrupt."

"Do you two know each other?" Mr. Hartnett eyed Hazel.

"No, we don't know each other." Charlie's answer was firm.

He was probably more than eager to keep the rooftop episode from his employer. This was the only hand she had, and she had to play it. "Are you sure? You seem quite familiar."

Charlie looked as if he was about to have another fit. He blinked a couple of times at her and she knew exactly what he was trying to convey, a desperate plea not to tell his boss about his illness. "No, I don't think so."

For now, she relented. "I guess not. Although, as a writer, it's my job to notice things, observe people. I rarely forget a face."

Mr. Hartnett shrugged and made the introductions. "Miss Ripley, this is Charlie Butterfield. Why don't you join us, Charlie? Miss Ripley is interested in getting cleared."

Butterfield. He shared the same name as the supermarket monster. Hazel took a deep breath, absorbing the news.

Charlie Butterfield took the seat next to her, carefully, as though the room were a minefield, as Mr. Hartnett read off the list of Hazel's so-called offenses. When he was finished, he closed the booklet and stared hard at her. "What do you have to say about this?"

"Almost all of those occurred before the war, when it was a very different time." She paused. "My older brother was quite active in political causes and I followed his lead."

"Your brother, you say?" Mr. Hartnett picked up a pen. "What is his name?"

"Ben Ripley." She let Mr. Hartnett scribble it down before adding, "He died in the war."

"I see. A soldier?"

"Yes."

"Well, I'm very sorry to hear it."

"Mr. Hartnett, if you don't mind my asking, how did you compile the information in *Red Channels*? Some of it is incorrect, you see."

Given Hazel's assumed status, the man was surprisingly willing to share his methods. "We study old photos of May Day parades and peace marches, see who we recognize and who comes up over and over. Or we look at people who have signed petitions fighting the good work of the HUAC, and unveil their hidden agendas."

"But what if what you gather is incorrect? For example, I never even heard of the World Federation of Democratic Youth, and it says I 'sponsored' activities for them, whatever that means."

"No, no. Nothing is incorrect. I served in the naval intelligence, I know how to tell facts from fiction. Besides, we have staff"—he looked over at Charlie Butterfield—"who do reconnaissance out in the field."

Right. What a pigheaded dolt Mr. Hartnett was. "You have to give those you're accusing the chance to defend themselves before you publish, I would think."

"We do, we do. The more-well-known ones, we'll send a letter and ask if they have changed their views. If they have, I give them an opportunity to clear their name." He cleared his throat. "Have you changed your views, Miss Ripley?"

"That fascism is bad and that refugees should have coats to keep them warm? No. I haven't. And also, that American democracy is the best form of government there is? Again, no."

He gave an irritated sigh. "You clearly don't get it. I'll spell it out for you, how to exonerate yourself. Do you want to know? Or do you want to quibble with me?"

She made herself sit back in her chair, as if this was just any other business negotiation. "I want to know how."

A pomaded strand of hair had fallen across his forehead. He licked one finger and smoothed the lock back into place. "I'll review your file again, and we will have a conversation. Once you convince me that you are not a member of the Communist Party and have never been, I will pass your file on to the FBI. They'll interview you, and you'll tell them anyone else you think might be a communist sympathizer. Once we're all on the same page, I'll take your name off and give the green light that you're hirable." He paused. "It costs two hundred dollars."

She sat quiet, stunned. The fury built back up, unstoppable. "You're telling me that you created this list of names of people who can't get work because of rumors and innuendo you disseminate, who then have to come to you and pay you"—she raised her voice—"*pay you*, to get cleared off the list? This is a racket. A moneymaking scam, plain and simple."

"How dare you, Miss Ripley. We aren't playing games here. There are subversives out there in the entertainment industry tainting the minds of innocent, God-fearing Americans. People like Uta Hagen, Judy Holliday, Dorothy Parker."

His list consisted only of women, a warning if ever she'd heard one. She should never have come. This was a labyrinthine trap and she'd fallen right into it. But this scheme was outrageous. Someone had to say something.

Hazel addressed Charlie, hardly concealing the threat in her voice. "You've been awfully silent. I'm surprised you don't have anything to say about this."

Charlie avoided her gaze, but turned to his boss. "Mr. Hartnett, I'm sure there's another way to approach this. Miss Ripley seems to be on the up-and-up. After all, she came here of her own volition."

Mr. Hartnett looked from Hazel to Charlie, curious. "I'm surprised at how easily you're swayed, Charlie."

"I have nothing to hide, nothing to defend," said Hazel.

"I have an idea." Charlie broke through the icy silence and stared hard at Hazel, as if he were trying to send a signal, some kind of warning. "If you truly have nothing to hide, if your production isn't a cover for subversive behaviors, then perhaps you wouldn't mind allowing it to be monitored."

"Monitored?"

He nodded. "Observed, if you like. I'll drop into rehearsals and production meetings, and report back any untoward behavior, any suspicious contacts. Or the lack of same."

"What? No. Absolutely not." Hazel wanted to slap him. After practically saving his life, this was how he repaid her?

"Yes. Brilliant." Mr. Hartnett jumped on the idea. "Why would you say no if you have nothing to hide?"

"Because it's ridiculous."

"You may think so, but I'm sure Mr. Canby would be happy to reach a compromise."

Mr. Hartnett was right on that count. Mr. Canby would agree in a heartbeat. Anything to take care of this threat and get into the good graces of Daddy Butterfield and his minions. She had to get something out of it, though. "If Mr. Canby and I consent to being observed, then you tell Laurence Butterfield to back off, and take me out of *Red Channels*."

Mr. Hartnett considered the idea, taking his time before answering. "If you agree to our plan, I'll request that Laurence Butterfield ease up and consider taking you out of *Red Channels*, depending on what sort of feedback we get."

With that, he stood and dismissed them both. The meeting was over.

⁘

Hazel had hoped to lose herself in the mob of office workers churning along the sidewalk, but Charlie Butterfield caught up with her before she crossed Sixth Avenue.

"Look at you, still unable to trail someone without tipping your hand." Her words came out with a caustic edge.

"I'm not following you. I'm attempting to walk with you. Please, slow down."

She did so, only because she didn't want him to have another fit in front of her. Hazel made a sharp right and he followed suit, as if a magnet joined them together. "Why did you make that ridiculous suggestion?"

"I don't know if you're just completely out of it or deliberately chose to ignore the facts, but Hartnett was ready to throw you to the wolves. What on earth were you thinking, talking back to him like that? That's not the way it's done."

"I thought I'd be clearing up a misunderstanding. I didn't expect to be shaken down for two hundred dollars."

"It's not like that."

"No? How is it not?" She didn't wait for him to answer. "I could have told him everything, by the way. About your epilepsy, that we'd met before. I should have."

"I just did you a huge favor, Miss Ripley."

"You really think so? You've got to be kidding, Mr. Butterfield."

She ground to a halt as a crowd gathered outside a theater at intermission stymied her progress.

"You can call me Charlie. And I just bought you a huge amount of leeway."

"First off, I'm not calling you anything. Second, rehearsals are closed, for a reason. We don't need the actors worrying about what they're saying or doing. It's a free space, a creative space. Having a minder will get in the way of that." She peered into his face. "How are you related to the supermarket guy?"

Charlie swallowed. "I'm his son."

"Great. Just great."

A dinging sound echoed from inside the theater, the signal that the intermission was over. Hazel changed direction, joining the theatergoers inching their way inside.

"Where are you going?"

"Away from you."

"No, you're not."

The crowd crammed though the front doors, like a squirrel squeezing through a tight opening in a fence and miraculously emerging out the other side intact.

"But we don't have tickets," whispered Charlie from behind her.

Hazel didn't answer. She needed time to think and figure out her next steps, and the cool interior of the theater beckoned. Luckily, her brother had showed her how to "second act" a play when they were young. They'd wait until the lights went down, and then grab any empty seat. It didn't matter that they'd missed the first act. As struggling actors in New York City, they took what they could get. She dashed up to the mezzanine level and scanned the rows of seats as an usher walked by.

Hazel turned to face Charlie, as if they were a couple of ticket-holding audience members just stretching their legs. "Your father is making serious trouble," she whispered. "I don't see how you can be part of that."

"Make no mistake, there are people out there trying to forward the Communist Party's agenda. They may not be official members, but they're most certainly fellow travelers."

"*Fellow travelers.* That's a ridiculous term. Same with *friends.* You have all this code-speak for treason. No more euphemisms. Why not just call all us artistic types 'traitors' and be done with it? Here's why: Because then we could fight back. Instead, you throw out insinuations, get the rest of America good and paranoid, and watch as the country turns on itself."

"You've got your head in the sand. There's a giant network, a conspiracy forming out there. Heck, it's already formed. Open your eyes before it's too late."

"If you're so sure about that, why aren't you with the FBI instead of slumming it with the likes of Hartnett?"

"Actually, I've already applied and am waiting to hear back."

The news just kept getting better and better.

The lights dimmed, saving Hazel from further conversation. She spied an empty box seat and darted over, taking the one in front as Charlie shuffled into the one behind her. This had been a stupid idea. Now she had him staring at the back of her head for the next hour. For a fleeting moment she wondered if her hair looked all right, before dismissing the thought as frivolous. Still, she reflexively lifted a hand to smooth it into place as the curtain rose.

What to do? She couldn't see any way out of it. Mr. Canby would get the call from Mr. Hartnett about having Charlie lurk about, and not be bothered one whit. Not if it meant no picketers, no controversy. Of course, she had nothing to hide. But it was the principle of the matter, the slippery slope into censorship, that irked her to no end.

By the end of the matinee, which turned out to be a riveting opera about fleeing European refugees, Hazel's racing thoughts had finally settled down. Her play, like this opera, was timely and powerful, and audiences were obviously eager to be challenged. Hazel's sole purpose was to get *Wartime Sonata* staged, and if that required Laurence Butterfield's son to lurk about during the rehearsals, so be it.

She turned to face him as the rest of the audience filed out. "So, what did you think of the play? Russian propaganda?"

"I'd already seen it before, to be honest. I loved it then and I loved it today. You should catch the first act next time."

"You go to the theater?"

"I do. I see practically everything that comes out."

"What does your father think of that?"

"He doesn't know."

So Butterfield's son was a theater buff. Maybe this would work, after all. Hopefully, he was dopey enough that she'd be able to manipulate him into giving the production a green light, while also putting her in the clear in terms of the blacklist. "Not that I have much choice, but I'll allow you to sit in on the rehearsals. See you tomorrow morning, ten o'clock, sharp."

"See you then, Miss Ripley."

The next day, at rehearsal, Mr. Canby briefly introduced Charlie Butterfield as a consultant, one who was helping him assess various protocols. Perfectly vague and innocuous. Hazel had to hand it to him, Mr. Canby's success in the cutthroat world of Broadway was in no doubt due to his ability to obfuscate when needed, either sweet-talking investors or puffing up the egos of the talent.

Most of the cast didn't give Charlie a second glance, but Maxine bristled with anger. She shot Hazel a dark look and followed her to the table where a coffee urn stood. "I don't like this idea one bit. Wolf guarding the sheep and all that."

Hazel poured herself a cup and added some milk, keeping her voice low. "We have no choice. Trust me, this is the last thing I want. But we have to live with it, at least until opening night. Try to keep your Bolshevik declarations to a minimum."

Maxine cracked a smile, in spite of herself. "Very funny."

"Better to have him in sight, to be able to control what he hears and sees. Don't you think?"

"You're acting like you're the guilty party."

"Right. I'm a spy."

Maxine's eyebrows raised. "Stop it. You're going to get yourself into even bigger trouble." She sighed and poured herself a cup as well. "But I guess you're right."

"I am. Besides, he's a big theater buff, apparently, sees everything."

"Interesting. His father bragged to me about shutting down a theater company upstate. There must be a lot of friction there."

"Let's see if we can't use it to our advantage."

The run-through was rough, to say the least. The actors kept on having to call out "line" and have the stage manager feed them their words, and two of the men playing soldiers fumbled their prop guns. To be expected, Hazel knew. At this point in rehearsal, the actors were overloaded with sensory information: where to stand, what the overall arc of the scene was, and the fear of forgetting the next line. Which of course made them forget the next line. Over the next week, Hazel hoped, the stage directions would become second nature, the lines would become embedded in their pretty heads, and the acting would feel less forced.

As a playwright, to hear her words mangled was painful

enough, but she tried to keep her director hat on and let the mistakes go. Right now the cast needed confidence.

Charlie sat in the very back row of the theater for the entire morning. But that afternoon, as they returned from lunch, he plopped himself in the seat next to her.

"Yes?" She was scribbling some notes in her script and didn't look up.

"Is it all right if I sit here?"

"You are the consultant, you can sit wherever you like, I suppose." She wasn't about to give him an inch.

The cast launched into the final act. Whether they'd been energized by lunch, or the break, the scene took off with a bang. Maxine was on fire, and her energy invigorated the other actors. Finally, the play in Hazel's head was beginning to match the one being performed on the stage.

"Fantastic, everyone. Take fifteen."

"Wow. Just wow." Charlie remained motionless, still staring at the stage.

"No subversive dialogue for you to report?"

"It's amazing. That's a great finale to the whole thing. Poor Lina . . ." He didn't finish the thought. "Terrible, but it makes perfect sense."

"Well, thank you." She hated to admit it, but his praise pleased her to no end. If she could impress this guy, then the audience of ticket payers would be a breeze.

"Although I have to say the second lieutenant was facing upstage too much. There were times I didn't hear what he said."

Hazel tried, and failed, to bite her tongue. "Everyone's a critic, I guess."

"No, no. I'm not saying anything bad. I mean, you probably knew that already."

She didn't let up. "I get it now. You're a budding artist yourself, aren't you? Let me guess, you acted in a couple of your high school plays."

Even if she didn't know it already, his bright red cheeks gave him away.

"I was in the drama club. I couldn't do sports with my condition, so ended up building sets, hanging lights, that kind of thing. I even got cast in *Waiting for Lefty* at a community theater upstate."

Now she understood his father's fury. The Odets play was all about striking cabdrivers and communists. Talk about making Laurence Butterfield's blood boil. Her respect for Charlie went up a notch. "That was very brave of you."

"Not really. My father had the company shut down and banned from ever performing again. Everyone hated me."

"Your father, as I have said before, is a beast." She stood and walked up to the stage, leaving him to stew. She wasn't here to babysit, there was a job to be done, a play to put on.

Poor kid, though. The humiliation obviously still stung.

She gave some notes to the cast and then they ran the final scene one more time. The juice wasn't there, not like the last time, but that was fine. Ups and downs were to be expected.

As the second lieutenant walked onstage and delivered his lines, she braced herself. She'd told him to not upstage himself, and moved him farther away from Maxine so that he'd naturally have to speak up.

Charlie turned his head to look at her. Even though she kept her eyes glued on the stage, there was no avoiding his triumphant grin.

CHAPTER TWELVE

Hazel

July 1950

Floyd finally resurfaced—sort of—the next week. Hazel's phone rang in her room at the Chelsea, where she was going through the script again, trying to figure out some clunky transitions in the second act. Her relief at hearing Floyd's voice on the other end of the line was enormous.

"How are you? Where are you?"

Floyd's voice was weaker than usual. "I'm fine. Listen, I have to take a step back from the production. They are asking lots of questions and I have to keep a low profile."

"Who's they? The FBI? What kind of questions?" She suddenly remembered that the phones were tapped. "No. Wait a minute, be careful what you say. Do you understand, Floyd?"

"I do." She heard him swallow. "Let's just say that I'm perfectly fine, but I'll be unreachable for a few weeks. My assistant knows what needs to be done, you're in good hands."

"No, that's unacceptable, Floyd. Why do you have to go into hiding?"

A pause. "Not hiding. Just unavailable. I'll explain later, but for now, be careful yourself, okay? And be careful what you drink."

"What?" What was he talking about?

"That drink, just be careful. Don't pair it with tangerine. Very dangerous."

Brandy.

He was saying that Brandy had turned him in.

Would Brandy have done something like that, just because she didn't like the color of her costume? It seemed crazy. Yet just yesterday, Maxine and Brandy had gotten into an argument about the blocking. Previews for the show, which were open to audiences but not reviewers, would begin next week, and everyone was on edge. When Hazel intervened, Brandy spat out, "Of course you take Maxine's side, she's your friend."

The way she said the word *friend*, emphasizing the double meaning, wasn't lost on Hazel or on the rest of the cast. Even worse, Hazel had spied Charlie hovering in the wings, observing the exchange. Hazel, tired and irritable herself, had lit into Brandy. The girl had approached Hazel later for stepping out of line and apologized. Her words may have been warm, but her eyes didn't convey a jot of remorse.

"Floyd, take care of yourself and let me know if there's anything I can do. Maybe we can meet somewhere and catch up?" She hated to leave it like this, so open-ended.

"No. Don't worry about me. Take care of yourself. And be careful."

What a mess. This day off, which would be followed by another tomorrow for the Fourth of July, was endless. Hazel wanted nothing more than to get the show back in motion. The late-afternoon sun streamed through the windows of her room at the Chelsea. She had to get out.

She strode over to Maxine's room to see what she was up to, but a strange sound made her pause before knocking.

"Maxine?" She rapped quietly. "Are you all right?"

Maxine opened the door a sliver. "I'm fine. Do you need me?"

"I'm not here as your director, silly. I heard from Floyd. He said he's lying low, for now, and that we should be careful of Brandy. I think she's the one who turned his name over to the FBI."

Maxine drew her inside and cleared off some room on the settee. While Hazel's rooms were neat and tidy, Maxine's looked a lot like when she'd first arrived, with clothes strewn around and silk scarves hanging over lamps. Whether for mood lighting or because that's simply where they landed, it was hard to tell.

"Brandy, huh?"

"Yes."

"I wouldn't put it past her. Can you fire her?"

Hazel shook her head. "Not without cause, without proof that she's done something wrong. Otherwise we're just like the other side. However much I'd like to."

"The union would have something to say about it, no doubt," added Maxine. "She wouldn't go gently."

For the first time, Hazel noticed that Maxine's face was red and puffy. "Max, what's going on with you?"

She was fairly certain she knew the answer. That man.

"Arthur. I know, I know. Messing around with a married man will break a girl's heart."

"What's the latest?"

"I really am fine. I don't want to bother you with this, especially now. I've been trying to keep it all out of the play so that it doesn't affect anything that's going on with us, with the show."

"We're friends first, remember? I'm sorry he's making your life difficult." She slung an arm around the back of the settee. "He hasn't hurt you again, has he?"

"No. None of that. He promised it wouldn't happen again. And it hasn't." Maxine delivered the words with a calm certainty.

"Then, what?" Hazel asked.

Maxine began laughing. "Don't make fun of me, it's so silly. Really."

"What?"

"It's my birthday." The laughing turned to crying and back to laughing, which made Hazel join in, until the two of them were doubled over in a fit of giggles. Finally, Maxine grabbed a scarf off the nearby lamp and wiped her eyes. "I sound like a baby, like I'm some five-year-old who didn't get a birthday cake."

"Everyone deserves to be recognized on their birthday." Hazel pulled her close. "Happy birthday."

They hugged. "Thank you. I was hoping he'd call, but I haven't heard anything yet."

"Wait a minute, you were born on July third? That was Ben's birthday."

"It was?"

"Yes, he always said he wished it had been a day later, as then he could say all the fireworks were in his honor." The memory made Hazel smile. The fact that he and Maxine shared birthdays brought her a strange bit of solace, as though he was right there with them.

"Well, happy birthday to him." Maxine took Hazel's hands in her own and kissed them. "In the meantime, how's your shadow?"

"Charlie? He's fine. Innocuous."

"You really believe that?"

"Yes. I think he really likes being in a theater, he's even started giving me notes."

Maxine made a face. "You've got to be kidding."

"I'm not. I mean, we have nothing to hide, so having someone looking over my shoulder doesn't bother me a whit anymore. Not if it means we keep his father at bay."

"Please don't tell me you let down your guard with him."

"Of course not. But, really, what is there to guard? I'm not doing anything illegal or wrong."

Maxine's mouth stayed in a tight line. "We both know that doesn't matter much these days. He's a good-looking guy, don't let that get in the way of your scruples."

"He's not that good-looking." Charlie's nose was too large for his face, although his eyes were rather sweet, the irises brown like coffee. He was a bit scrawny for her taste, to boot. "Like you're one to talk about scruples, seeing a married man." Hazel punched her lightly in the shoulder.

"Listen to us." Maxine threw up her hands. "The whole point of me being here at the hotel and working together is to keep all the nonsense away, and I'm wallowing in it."

"You mean boy nonsense?"

"Yes. Boy nonsense."

"Then let's get out of here. No more wallowing. I'll stop fixating on every detail of the play and driving myself mad, and you stop waiting around for a boy to call."

"Where will we go?"

"Trust me on this. Put on a fancy dress and meet me in the lobby."

Maxine looked like a new woman when she stepped out of the

elevator, wearing a tightly cinched silk with a low-cut V-neck, where a pretty brooch drew all eyes to her cleavage. Hazel wore a dress from before the war, a navy blue chiffon that draped around her torso, offering the illusion of curves. Unfortunately, this wasn't something you could fake. Next to Maxine, she looked like a frump.

Maxine looked her up and down. "That's pretty, but we're going to have to find you something smashing for the opening of your play."

"If you could advise, I'd appreciate it. My wardrobe is in desperate need of an update, but I've been too busy writing to shop."

In the cab, Hazel explained that Mr. Canby had given her two tickets to the opening of a new Broadway play that evening, some kind of silly musical revue on a patriotic theme. She hadn't planned on attending, but figured it might be a fun lark for a birthday celebration. The crowd in front of the theater dazzled. Men in tuxedos escorted women in clingy dresses under the marquee as photographers' flashbulbs popped furiously around them. Just before they stepped inside, Maxine was waylaid by a fan who insisted on getting her autograph.

Maxine scribbled her name on his program and handed it back, but even then he refused to let her go, gripping her arm to keep her in place as he whispered into her ear.

What a creep. Hazel broke between them, making excuses. "I can't let you out of my sight," she murmured to Maxine as they walked down the aisle.

"I'm popular, what can I say?" Maxine looked back, distracted.

They were shown to their seats, only a few rows from the stage, a reflection of Canby's standing in the theater community.

Maxine looked at her watch. "They're running late."

"They always do for openings. Gets everybody worked into a tizzy by the time the curtain goes up."

The show was just as Hazel expected, light entertainment, a crowd pleaser. At the intermission, Maxine took off like a shot—"Gotta beat the crowd to the ladies' room"—while Hazel stayed put, chatting up the managers, press agents, and columnists who approached, inquiring how her play was going. Only one mentioned her listing in *Red Channels*, whispering in her ear to "stay strong." The fact that he didn't dare say it out loud was worrying.

She turned around, hoping to see Maxine's red wig bobbing back down the aisle. She was probably being mobbed out there in the lobby. Hazel shouldn't have let her go alone.

The chimes for the second act sounded, but still Maxine didn't appear. Hazel was about to bolt out of her seat to check on her, when the lights dimmed. She was trapped, unless she wanted to make some kind of scene.

Finally, after another hour and a half of Yankee Doodle Dandy, the cast came out to take their bows. Hazel took the opportunity to slip out.

She found Maxine in the alleyway tucked into one side of the theater, smoking.

"What on earth? I was worried about you."

"Sorry, I couldn't get back in. I didn't want to cause a fuss."

"Let's hope the newspapers don't mention that you walked out. It makes us look bad, like we're above everyone else."

"I didn't walk out, I just missed the bell."

"Why?"

Maxine stayed silent, and finally Hazel realized the missing piece of the puzzle.

"Arthur, right? Did he follow us here?"

Maxine threw the cigarette down and stomped on it, hard. "He did."

"Between Charlie Butterfield and your beau, we can't get a break. What did he say to you?"

"The usual. Listen, I've got to go."

Hazel could feel her friend slipping away, drawn back to this awful man. She didn't bother hiding her disappointment. "After everything we talked about, you're meeting up with Arthur tonight?"

"Please, Hazel, it's my birthday. Let me have this."

Maxine's gaze darted over Hazel's shoulder, across the street. Hazel whirled around. A tall man in a dark suit quickly looked away.

"Is that him?" She turned back to Maxine and gestured with her thumb over one shoulder. "That your darling Arthur?"

Maxine nodded.

"I want to meet him."

"No. That's not a good idea. I don't want to get you involved."

"I'm your director. And your friend. I'm already involved in everything you do. Let's go."

Hazel marched up to Arthur and stuck out her hand.

"I'm Hazel Ripley, a friend of Maxine's," she said.

He shook her hand carefully, as if he were afraid she was going to punch him. Which she really wanted to do, to be perfectly honest. How dare he torture her friend this way? Arthur glanced briefly over Hazel's shoulder at Maxine, but Hazel couldn't get a sense of the message behind it, warning or worry.

"I'm Arthur Tunney." He didn't smile, his face a neutral mask. "It's a pleasure. I've heard so many wonderful things about you. What do you say we go out to dinner, and celebrate Maxine's birthday?"

He looked to be in his mid-thirties, the lines whispering out from his eyes barely noticeable. And those eyes. Baby blue, with thick black eyelashes, a contrast that softened the sharp angles of his face. A face made for the movies. She could see why Maxine was having a hard time getting over him.

Hazel checked in with Maxine, who nodded. "That sounds like a good idea."

He took Maxine's arm and they walked to a nearby bistro, taking a table near the back. Hazel took off her gloves and perused the menu, and when the waiter came over, they all ordered the coq au vin special, with Arthur requesting a bottle of Chianti for the table.

"Maxine tells me the play's ready for opening day." Arthur straightened his cutlery.

"We hope so. It'll be here soon enough." Hazel couldn't stand the tension, or the small talk. "Why are you going after Maxine after she asked you to back off?"

He looked up at her, shocked. "To back off?" he repeated.

"Hazel, really, let's not get into this now." Maxine laid a hand on the table.

Hazel ignored her. "I am worried about your effect on my leading lady, Mr. Tunney."

"Please, call me Arthur." He cleared his throat. "It's been a mess. I admit that, and I've asked for her forgiveness and although you and I don't know each other and we've only just met, I will ask for yours as well. I behaved badly. Very badly."

The waiter poured the wine for Maxine and Hazel, but Arthur put his hand over his glass. "None for me, thank you."

After the waiter stepped away, Arthur continued. His voice shook with emotion. "I was drinking then. My wife, you see, wasn't doing very well. The doctors finally agreed that she should be put into a home."

Maxine sat back, a stunned look on her face. He clearly hadn't told her the news yet.

Hazel kept on. "What is wrong with her?"

"Her brain's not right. She can no longer take care of herself, and I can't ask her for a divorce. She isn't competent to make that decision, and while it breaks my heart to not be able to be with Maxine as husband and wife, I must keep caring for Caroline. Even if she no longer recognizes me. Back in California, with Maxine, I was under terrible pressure. That's no excuse, but it got out of control. I've promised her that will never happen again. I'm ashamed."

The hurt and fear in his eyes seemed unforced, real. It was hard to imagine this man violently cutting Maxine's hair off. Drink could do that to a person, Hazel knew. She'd seen plenty of baby-faced soldiers turn into snarling maniacs after a few drinks in Naples. But she wasn't ready to let down her guard with him. Obviously, Maxine already had.

"What do you do, Arthur?"

"I'm in food packaging. Not very exciting, I know, compared to your professions. My hope is that I can be a stable force so that Maxine can lead the life of a movie star, knowing that I'm behind her all the way. Not that she needs anyone, I understand that now."

He began asking questions about the show, and Maxine shared some silly gossip about finding the wardrobe mistress and a stagehand making out in the basement, which made them laugh. By the time the food came, the mood at the table had lightened ever so slightly.

"How long will you be in town, Arthur?" Hazel asked. "Are you planning on attending the opening?"

He looked at Maxine, and she nodded her approval. Hazel appreciated that he'd checked with her first. A promising sign. "I'd love to come. I'm flying back and forth from California a lot, but will make sure I'm here then."

"Maxine says you met at a theater in Seattle?"

They looked at each other and laughed. Arthur spoke up. "I was taken by her the minute I laid eyes on her. But I didn't get up any nerve to talk to her until I saw her in the box office, counting receipts."

Maxine cut in. "I was counting the take from the performance under my breath, and he wandered over and started messing with me, saying random numbers out loud to mix me up. I couldn't believe the gall."

"I had to do something to catch her eye."

"Oh, please, you had your pick of the girls. Everyone was in love with you." Maxine leaned into him. "And a few weeks later he came and found me when I was at my lowest, and took care of me."

"I bought you a milkshake, that's all I did."

"It meant the world."

"And now I've asked her, begged her, to take me back. I'm off the sauce, and with Caroline settled, I'm a new man."

In spite of her initial reluctance, Hazel found herself wondering if it wasn't all right for Maxine to give this guy a second chance. It wasn't as if Hazel was one to give advice on love, anyway. She'd cloistered herself from the very thought of romance for a long time now. First, her excuse was her focus on her career, or more specifically, what her mother wanted out of her career. No getting sidetracked. Then again, her girl-next-door looks tended to fade into the background in the theater circles she traveled in, where nearly everyone did their best to look fabulous and flashy. Like Maxine.

Later, as she focused on writing the play, she didn't go out as much as she had before the war. Her day was filled with imaginary characters and scenes, as if a movie were playing out in her head side by side with the real world. She could be walking down the street to the drugstore, but in her mind two characters were hold-ing a conversation in the scene she'd been working on earlier that morning. A couple of times, another resident from the hotel told her they'd said hello in passing but Hazel had seemed to be in a dream, a daze. She was. All of her energy went into her writing.

Only recently, as a director, had she interacted more with eligi-ble men. But she could never let down her guard, not even a little. She had to claim her spot at the top of the hierarchy, to prove that she deserved the title of director and writer, and so refused to flirt or joke with any of the talent or creative team. One of Mr. Canby's investors, early on, had placed his hand on the small of Hazel's back and suggested they meet later, in his hotel room. She'd told him that under no circumstances would she ever do such a thing, and warned him against trying anything like that with her ac-tresses. He'd straightened right up and never touched her again.

She had to work twice as hard to preserve her hard-won status and never let herself show vulnerability. The last time she'd been close—physically and emotionally—to a man was when Charlie had that fit up on the roof of the Chelsea Hotel. They'd looked at each other without filters; he'd been at risk and defenseless, and that had brought out a softer side of Hazel. But only for that mo-ment. Ever since then, she'd stayed guarded whenever he was around, which was often.

He was the enemy, not to be trusted. She laughed at herself, picking the most inappropriate person to consider.

"What's so funny?" Maxine looked like a fiery angel in the can-dlelight, the copper hues glowing around her white skin.

Hazel didn't reply, just smiled and turned back to her meal.

CHAPTER THIRTEEN

Maxine

July 4, 1950

I waited for Arthur outside of the hotel, looking my summery best. I'd been asked to judge the strongman contest at Coney Island—another of Canby's ploys to get some press for the play—and had picked out a pretty pink-and-green floral dress and a straw hat with a wide brim for the day's outfit.

Arthur finally pulled up in a green Chevy and honked. I leaned through the open window and gave him a wide smile. "Looking for a date?"

He told me to jump in. For a moment, I considered telling him to get out and open my door like a gentleman, but I wanted our outing to get off on the right foot.

As I settled in, he snarled that I looked like his mother-in-law's couch.

So that's the way he was going to play it. Why was I surprised? Life with Arthur was a series of dips and rises, and right now we seemed to be headed into a dip. He'd be nasty or cut me down, and then the guilt would kick in and he'd fall over himself to right the wrong and make me feel safe and good again. We'd been through this before.

The first time Arthur lost his temper, I was completely unprepared.

We were returning to my very first room at the Chelsea—he was visiting from California for a few days—and his arms were full of wine and groceries that we'd picked up. The plan was to spend all weekend in bed together. As I fumbled with the lock, his patience ran thin, and after two exasperated sighs, he shoved his elbow into my back and bellowed, "Open the goddamn door!"

Shaking, I tried again and much to my relief the dead bolt slid away. I held the door open for him.

Once we were inside, his temper disappeared, and he actually hummed to himself as he put away the groceries.

I figured he was just stressed about work. After all, Arthur had never spoken to me like that before. He'd delighted in me, he'd said, over and over. Told me that I made him believe that anything was possible. And it wasn't a big deal, really. I got better at sensing when he neared his breaking point, and did what I could to distract him: make him laugh, seduce him. Only recently had I started to call him out on his bad behavior.

***

In the car, I threw Arthur a hard look. "I thought we were done with the cutting remarks, now that you no longer drink."

"It was a joke." He leaned over to give me a kiss, but I turned my head. "Sorry, love. I was out of order. Thought I was being funny. Please forgive me." He ran his fingers up my bare arm and I shivered.

I kissed him back, taking his prompt apology as a sign of progress.

"Hey, isn't that Hazel?" He called out to her, practically blowing out my eardrum.

Hazel walked over. "Hey, guys. Where are you off to?"

"Coney Island," he said. "You should come. Our movie star here is judging the strongman contest."

Arthur's invitation threw me. I thought we were supposed to be spending the day together. I glanced over at him, and Hazel probably picked up my hesitancy.

"No, I'm just heading back upstairs." She took off her sunglasses and smiled. "Now, don't get a sunburn today, Max. We don't want you all pink onstage."

Previews began next week. I was nervous, and I knew Hazel was, also. She could probably use some diversion. "You have to come along. It'll be fun."

Hazel looked me in the eye. "Really?"

"Please."

She jumped in the back seat and we were off. Arthur kept Hazel laughing the entire time, talking about the food packaging business, of all things. By the time we hit the Ocean Parkway, I had relaxed, partly from hearing Hazel's laughter from the back seat and also because that bitter edge had disappeared from Arthur's voice. He'd reached over and rubbed my hand a couple of times, as a way of asking additional forgiveness.

The boardwalk was packed with families loaded down with blankets, chairs, and beach toys, the heat shimmering off the planks. I considered heading down to the beach and putting my feet in the surf to cool off, but one look out to the ocean put me right off that idea. Every inch of sand was taken up by sunbathers—it was as if a herd of flesh-colored seals had flopped out of the ocean to loll in the bright sunshine, braying every so often when stepped upon.

The contest was silly. I basically clapped and gave the winner of the contest a smooch on the cheek, but the announcer mentioned the play twice and had us take photos for the newspapers. After, Hazel, Arthur, and I walked by the entrance to the freak show, where a sign touted a peek at Anita, the elephant-faced girl, and Olga, the headless one.

"Wanna go in?" asked Arthur. I noticed him checking out décolletage on the drawing of the elephant-faced girl. Men.

"I doubt it's cooler inside than out here." Hazel fanned her face with her hat. "Maybe we should get something to drink?"

"Let's head to Nathan's." Arthur took each of our arms in his. "You'll love Nathan's, it's a New York institution. If we're lucky, we can catch the hot dog eating contest." He pointed to a huge booth set up across the boardwalk for the occasion.

Halfway across the boardwalk I stopped, bringing the other two to a halt. "Well, look who it is."

Charlie Butterfield stood beside a small stand where a sign proclaimed CONTEST CONDIMENTS SPONSORED BY BUTTERFIELD SUPERMARKETS. He caught sight of us around the same time I did him. For a minute, I thought he was going to slink away, but instead he nodded and straightened up.

"Who's that?" asked Arthur, the edge coming back into his voice.

"That's my shadow," said Hazel.

"Shadow?"

I filled Arthur in as we approached. Arthur stuck out his hand and shook Charlie's as Hazel made introductions.

"You here shilling for your dad?" I asked.

Charlie, to his credit, looked miserable. "We do this every year on the Fourth of July, it's a family tradition."

"I bet it is." I glanced down at the pamphlets scattered on the stand's countertop: *Americans, Don't Patronize Reds*, screamed the headline. No doubt Mr. Butterfield considered the Fourth of July the perfect day to promote his nasty cause.

I plucked one from the pile and read it out loud. "*The Reds of Hollywood and Broadway have always been the chief financial support of Communist propaganda in America. Right now, films are being made to glorify Marxism and being piped into your living room via your TV set, and poisoning the minds of your children under your very eyes.* Really, Charlie?"

Before he could reply, the elder Mr. Butterfield and his mousy wife came into view, Mr. Butterfield's face as red as a tomato. I whispered a warning to Hazel. "That's Charlie's father."

When Mr. Butterfield spotted me, he let go of his wife's arm and straightened his tie.

"How do you all know each other?" Mr. Butterfield waggled a thick finger at us. He shuddered—actually shuddered—when told who Hazel was.

Charlie stammered out an answer. "Um, I've been assigned by Mr. Hartnett to keep an eye out on the production of *Wartime Sonata.*"

"*Wartime* what?" bellowed Mr. Butterfield.

"The play that Miss Ripley is directing and Miss Mead is acting in."

"That travesty. I'm sorry, what exactly does 'keeping an eye out' entail?" Mr. Butterfield stuck his chin forward.

Charlie hadn't told his dad what he was up to, and I almost felt sorry for him. "I make sure there's nothing subversive going on and report back to Mr. Hartnett what I observe." He dug his hands deep into his pockets, like a teenager who'd come in late for curfew.

"You're saying that Hartnett is paying you to watch a play all day?" He let out a spiteful laugh. "I get you that job and you end up flitting around with theater folk? Again?"

Next to me, I could sense Arthur surveilling the scene, figuring out how to play it. "I respect what you're doing, Mr. Butterfield," he said. "You never know what's around the corner, what's going to happen in the international scene, never mind the domestic one. I respect the fact that we have to put up barricades against the communists. No one is safe."

I thought right there and then Hazel was going to lose her mind. I put a hand on her arm, warning her to step down, let Arthur do his thing. There was no point getting this guy's nose all out of joint, it would only harm the play.

"I think we're all on the side of America," Hazel said.

"Don't assume anything, little missy," said Mr. Butterfield. He turned to Charlie. "So this is why Hartnett told me to ease up on that play? Wish I'd known. You can find your own ride back to the city. I don't want you in my car."

Charlie's mother, who so far hadn't said a word, looked from her husband to her son, concerned. "Larry, no."

Charlie kissed her on the cheek. "Don't worry about me, I'll take the subway. Go with him, Mom."

Hazel glared after the pair as they walked away. "I'm sorry, Charlie, but your father's a bully."

"You showed admirable restraint," I said to Hazel. "You could have taken the Coke bottle and smashed it over his head. But you didn't."

Arthur put an arm around my waist. "By the way, I know I laid it on pretty thick with the rah-rah America stuff. I hope you know I was only trying to help you girls."

"Why did you encourage him, Arthur?" Hazel said. "Do you actually think he's right?"

"These days, you've got to be flexible, not make waves. I got him to back down, didn't I? Isn't that what we all wanted?"

"I disagree completely." Hazel was stone-faced. "And I don't think he was placated. Far from it."

I pointed up. "Hey, let's all hit the Cyclone. Think of the sea breezes up at the top. I think we all could use some cooling off." Anything to stop this conversation.

Charlie and Hazel exchanged a look.

"We'll wait here," she finally said. "I don't think my stomach can manage it."

Hazel had bragged on the flight home from Naples that she had a stomach of steel, as the rest of us turned green after a turbulent takeoff. No doubt she was covering for Charlie, who probably wasn't able to go on it because of his fits. She'd realized it right off and made up an excuse so he wouldn't lose face in front of Arthur. Why she cared so much about the guy baffled, and worried, me.

"Your loss," I said.

The roller coaster was the perfect antidote to Mr. Butterfield's venom; I was sorry Hazel didn't join us. The steady climb, the clicking of the wheels, up to the very top, where I grabbed Arthur's arm hard and then we were flying down and around curves and back up and back down. I loved every minute of it, Arthur laughing and me screaming, and when we stepped off, we were giggling like kids, all cares forgotten.

A long roll of thunder cleared the boardwalk like a bulldozer. In the excitement, I hadn't noticed the skies had gone black. A storm approached fast from the west, building to a crescendo of rain that poured down. We joined Hazel and Charlie under the awning of Hyman's Bar & Grill. The two of them stopped whatever deep conversation they were having as we approached. Hazel explained that she'd offered Charlie a ride home with us.

"Of course," said Arthur.

"I like the beach better now than before." Hazel pointed out to the sea. The only person left was a young boy dragging a sack behind him, picking through the detritus of the beachgoers. I hoped he wouldn't get struck by lightning, but he didn't seem concerned and the storm did seem to be settling down. A steady rain drummed on the boardwalk, and the hollow sound of raindrops on the awning provided a watery symphony in stereo. The heat had dissipated and a cool, briny breeze lifted off the water. Arthur pulled me under his arm and I snuggled into his embrace.

"So are you nervous about your play, Hazel?" Arthur asked. His effort to make nice was pretty obvious, but I was glad he was trying.

"I'm as fine as I can be," Hazel said. "I don't think there's anything that can calm my nerves at this point. We're all in."

"Hey, I'm jittery, and I'm not even a part of it." Charlie laughed, watching Hazel for a response. When she smiled, he looked away, pleased. Something was going on between these two.

"I hear this guy's been your secret weapon," said Arthur, nodding to Charlie. "Maxine mentioned that he'd offered up some good advice."

"Maxine!" Hazel poked me in the ribs with her elbow. "I can't believe you."

"What? I was just repeating what you'd told me."

"Really, you think I helped?" Now Charlie was practically incandescent. On one hand, I was relieved that Hazel had him wrapped around her finger so tightly. That was where we wanted him. On the other, was it a good idea to be that close to your minder?

The rain was beginning to ease. I stuck my hand out and captured a couple of drops on my open palm.

"I've enjoyed watching the show come to life." Charlie turned to Arthur. "And Miss Mead is terrific. You'll love what she does onstage. There's this moment in the second act—"

"No!" Hazel covered his mouth with her hand, then quickly withdrew it. "Have I taught you nothing?"

"Sorry." He put his fingers on his lips, where her hand had just been.

"What? What's going on?" asked Arthur, perplexed.

"If he says something," explained Hazel, "it means that next time Maxine does the scene, she'll be thinking about re-creating that exact moment, not discovering it fresh. That's why it's never a good idea to read reviews, good or bad. The words get stuck in your head and then you're doomed."

I pretended to pout. "But I want to hear it. You know how I feel about compliments."

"Not a word," warned Hazel.

"Not a word, *maestra*." Charlie nodded. "I promise."

CHAPTER FOURTEEN

Hazel

July 1950

While Arthur and Maxine roared around on the Cyclone, Charlie again apologized for his father's behavior.

"You should be angry at him, too," answered Hazel. "I can't believe he left you behind."

"He doesn't like to be crossed. Once, when I was eight years old, I complained about something and he made me walk four miles home from my grandmother's house."

Always the city kid, Hazel did the calculation: Four miles was eighty New York City blocks. Almost unimaginable. "That's horrible."

"He's not exactly the warm-and-fuzzy type."

"My mother isn't either. Although she'd never send me on a forced march like that."

He stared out at the sea, avoiding her gaze. "You made up an excuse about the roller coaster for me, didn't you? Because you knew I couldn't ride it?"

"I just figured it'd be easier that way. You shouldn't be embarrassed."

"Thanks. It's just, around a tough guy like Arthur . . ." He didn't finish the sentence. "How long have he and Maxine been together?"

"A long time. Years, apparently. The more I get to know him, the more I can understand why Maxine is drawn to him, even though there are aspects of him that I don't like. He's complicated, but then so is Maxine, who no doubt can be difficult at times."

He lifted a brow. "You don't say."

She couldn't help but laugh. "I know, she's a diva. But she's more insecure than she lets on."

"She's not like you, then."

"Me? I'm very insecure."

"You don't show it."

"I can't afford to. Not when people like your father call me 'little missy.' I have to stay on my guard."

"You are as far from a little missy as they come. Trust me."

"I'm not sure how to take that."

"It's a compliment."

His gaze was sweet, warm. She was used to seeing him in a suit, and his casual outfit—khakis and a short-sleeved linen shirt—made him seem far more approachable. "Have you read the play *All My Sons*?"

"I saw it on Broadway."

"You should read it. There's nothing like reading a play to understand how the theme gets woven through. I have a copy, I'll bring it to rehearsal."

"It's about a son realizing the truth about his father. I already know the truth about my father, trust me."

"Then why don't you step out from under his shadow? Make your own way in the world?"

For a moment they stared at each other, as if trying to figure the other one out. He was about to answer, when Maxine skipped over, trailed by Arthur, beaming with exhilaration from the ride.

Rain poured down hard the whole drive back from Coney Island, and Hazel was happy to not have to make conversation above the din. Back in New York, Arthur dropped Hazel and Charlie off in front of the Chelsea and zoomed away with Maxine, off to a work party for his company up in the northern suburbs. While Hazel still had her doubts about Arthur, he did seem to be on his best behavior, and it wasn't worth falling out with her friend and lead actress by making a fuss and insisting Maxine come back to the hotel with her, especially when she knew she wouldn't listen.

Besides, she wanted to continue her conversation with Charlie.

"You didn't answer my question," said Hazel as the sedan pulled away from the curb. "About your father."

"I know exactly who my dad is, I don't have any delusions about that. The work I'm doing now is only to help me get into the FBI."

"So you can arrest actors, instead of just intimidating them?"

"It's more complicated than that."

"I doubt that."

He looked up at the building. "Let me come upstairs, you can give me that play, and I'll explain."

"I'd be thrilled to be enlightened."

Up in her apartment, she poured them both some Scotch and opened the windows to let in the post-storm breeze.

Charlie sat back on the sofa, drink in hand. "I'll be perfectly honest with you, I highly doubt the entertainment industry is rife with communists who are trying to overthrow democracy. That's all a ridiculous sideshow."

"Why on earth do you work for American Business Consultants if that's what you think? You're a part of the machine that's tearing us all apart." She thought of Floyd and Brandy, of the way baseless claims could be used to target innocent people.

"Because it's a professional stepping-stone. You need to have three years of job experience after college before you can apply to be a Fed, and when I was offered a position as an investigator with Hartnett, it seemed like a smart place to bide my time. I'm proving I have the skills the FBI looks for." He let out a sigh. "Look, I do think my father is partly correct about the threat we're under. He has connections in the Bureau, and they've told us without a doubt that secrets are being relayed to the Soviets, that a network of spies is in place and has been in place for years. I want to be part of that fight. I couldn't go to war, because of my epilepsy, but if the FBI will let me in, that's how I'll serve my country."

He continued on, gathering steam. "If I can prove to the FBI that we can catch the actual spies without a witch hunt, it'll all be worth it. Right now, yes, my father is persecuting innocents and has gone too far. I'm working to stop him from the inside, which, as his son, I know is the best way to change his mind. And if I can't change his mind, at least I can try to protect the artists he goes after, since I admire them immensely." He stared at her.

Hazel felt a blush spread over her cheeks. "Is that why you volunteered to watch over the show?"

"I felt I owed you, after your help on the roof. To be honest, I like being in the theater every day, watching as you whip them into shape."

"Well, your instincts are good. I know you don't say a lot of things because I've told you to keep it to yourself, but the ones I've let you offer up are pretty smart."

"Like my idea to play Charlie Parker during scene changes?"

"Yes. That one was a good one." She shifted so she was facing him, one leg bent across the couch and the other on the floor. Although she hated to admit it, Charlie was exactly the type of person who should be involved in politics or a government agency. Better him than the rigid, right-wing McCarthy any day. At least he talked sense. "You can see that we're harmless, right? Admit that. At the very least, admit that."

His jaw tightened. "You and your production, yes. I can admit that. But there's so much else going on out there. Things that you don't know about. That you shouldn't know about."

"Like what?"

"I can't say."

"Will we hear about it in the news one of these days? Or is this the kind of thing that's going to stay underground, all conspiracy theory and conjecture?"

"Soon. You'll hear something soon."

She leaned in. "Ooo. So scary."

He touched her chin with his index finger, lightly, like he was casting a spell. "Don't make fun."

The feather-like stroke rippled through her. He pulled back, placing both hands in his lap. Unnerved, she rearranged her features into a polite smile as the sound of firecrackers reverberated over the city.

"When I first came to the hotel, I was so worried about what my mother thought," she finally said. "We'd had a big fight, and I moved out for what I thought was a few days but turned out to be permanent. I don't regret it one bit. It was only the second time I went against her wishes—the first being the USO tour—and I'm glad I did. Maybe by working on the show you're declaring your own independence."

"I'm going to step out from under my father's shadow, one way or another." Charlie's voice was soft but firm. "What the hell, maybe if I get rejected by the FBI, I'll invest in your next production."

"Now you want to become a producer?" She was going to tease him, but the look on his face was so sweet, so hopeful, that she pulled herself up short. "I think that would be grand."

"You do?" He glanced out the window, at his drink, anywhere but at her.

She finally took his chin in her hand and made him focus. "Yes."

They stared again, but this time neither broke away. He leaned in and kissed her, pulled back and whispered, "Is this okay?"

She moved into him. "Yes."

For once, she wanted to be the bad girl, like Maxine. To let herself go and stop overthinking everything. Like the fact that Charlie was the worst possible choice as a lover, for many reasons. To just stop thinking.

They stayed on the couch for what seemed like hours, Charlie taking his time exploring her body and very slowly peeling off her dress, then her undergarments, until she was bare. The small part of her that was aghast at the exposure was quickly overwhelmed by her other senses. She became consumed by his inhale of breath, the touch of his fingers on her breast, the sting of Scotch on their tongues.

All thoughts of the play evaporated from her mind, just like the rainwater steaming off the black pavement of Twenty-Third Street.

CHAPTER FIFTEEN

ℳaxine

July 6, 1950

We're in tech now, which means long, painful days for us actors. We stand onstage, say a few lines, then Hazel stops us while the lighting designer fiddles about and the set designer does the same. A few more lines, more fiddling. Of course, it's not fiddling. Canby had hired master lighting and set designers who would transform the naked stage into a believably decrepit hotel in a war-torn country. But for the actors, it's something to endure. We're dying to run through the show with lights, sets, and costumes, but tech week ground all that to a necessary halt.

Floyd was missed, especially when we showed up for the costume parade at a cavernous warehouse in the West Thirties, where members of the cast dress in full wardrobe, for inspection by the creative team. Floyd's assistant had taken charge, but her boss's absence was palpable.

I worried about Floyd, about where he was hiding out, what was going on behind the scenes that none of us were privy to. He'd been such a sweetheart in Naples and I hated the thought that he was being bullied again, like he'd been bullied there. During the war, Hazel and I had been able to offer him a modicum of protection, but this time he'd pulled away, out of our orbit of safety.

I wanted to weep at the thought of Floyd lost and alone, fearing a knock on the door, with absolutely no one to turn to. I wanted to break things and inflict pain, but our enemies were unseen, amorphous. Evil.

As I walked into the space, the actors, still wearing street clothes, were huddled in one corner, looking at something that Brandy held in her hand, and every eye turned to me as I entered. Brandy, always the bearer of bad news, thrust an issue of *Counterattack* right in my face.

"You really should take a look." Brandy spoke louder than she needed to.

"Already seen it, this ain't new, dearie," I said. "Same folks who published the *Red Channels* rag, I hear."

"But you've been named."

I glanced down. It was another list of people deemed as threats to America. While many of the others had at least five lines of "offenses," mine only had one: that lousy rally that I went to with Hazel's brother eons ago.

Inside, I admit I was quaking, just a little. This was bad. I handed it back to her. "I've been called a lot of names in my time, and commie won't be the last, I'm sure."

Hazel clapped her hands and called for attention. From the rough edge in her voice, she'd already heard the news. "We're late. Everyone get dressed and let's get this show on the road."

Normally, a dress parade is an exciting event. The costumes make the show feel real. While we'd had a number of fittings over the course of the rehearsal period, this is when you see the big picture, the color palette, what visual delights the audience is in for. It also makes you look at your fellow actors in a new way, more as the character than as the person you got to know outside of rehearsal. Costumes are a blast. Usually.

This time, it was as if all the air had been sucked out of the room. We lined up in front of Canby, Hazel, and the assistant costume designer. Hazel and Canby walked up and back, examining buttons and silhouettes, whispering with each other, while we all held still. No joking, no banter. All business.

Brandy stood tall, a smug smile on her face, in her tangerine dress. She'd gotten what she'd wanted, after all.

We were finally dismissed, and I lingered around after changing back into my street clothes, hoping to talk to Hazel privately. Charlie Butterfield had arrived, unfortunately. When I came out from the dressing room, Hazel, Canby, and he were talking in the middle of the room.

I barged right up. "How bad is it?"

Canby rubbed his face. "It's not good. Not good at all."

Hazel crossed her arms. "Now we have two of us listed. There's nothing I can do about that, and trust me, I tried to get myself cleared. These charges are baseless."

Charlie shook his head. "I'll talk to Hartnett, try to find out what happened."

We already knew what happened. The scene on the boardwalk with Charlie's father was the reason for the escalation.

"What about me?" I couldn't help myself. "I was dragged to some silly rally years ago and that gets shoved in there? We were there for all of five minutes. When I found out what it was, I insisted we leave."

I wished I could take back the words as soon as I said them.

Hazel glanced over at me. "Can we talk alone for a second?" She held up a finger to Canby and Charlie.

I knew what was coming.

"Was that the rally I saw you at, with my brother?" Hazel kept her voice down as we walked into one of the dressing rooms.

I didn't want to answer. I didn't. But she could tell from the look on my face that I had been with Ben.

"This is terrible," she said. "I hate that he was the one who got you listed."

"There's nothing we can do about it now, except stay the course and see if this all dies down."

My words rang a little hollower every time I said them. I felt terrible for Hazel. This should be her shining hour.

Instead, the show's reputation was being sullied a little more each day.

We took a cab home together, both of us eager to put this day behind us. But as we waited for the elevator, a man who'd been sitting on the lobby's couch rose and called Hazel's name.

"Yes?"

"Are you Miss Hazel Ripley?"

"That's me."

He handed her an envelope with her name typed on it in capital letters. "I'm here to serve a subpoena from the House Un-American Activities Committee."

CHAPTER SIXTEEN

Hazel

July 1950

After Hazel checked into the Washington, DC, hotel recommended by her lawyer, she put on a silk bathrobe and hung up her dress for the following day. One didn't want to show up wrinkled in front of the House Un-American Activities Committee. She'd chosen a navy tailored suit with a relaxed silhouette that hit right below the knee, about as generic and unfeminine as one could get. Her aim was to meet the Committee, comprised all of men, of course, on their own level. Be straightforward. Not get pushed around.

Inside, though, she was terrified. If she angered the members of the Committee, her chances of getting the show mounted on Broadway would drop to zero. But if she placated them, she could never live with herself.

Everything had moved at lightning speed since the subpoena had been placed in her hand. She'd gotten the referral for her lawyer,

Andrew Z. Stone, Esq., from Mr. Canby the next morning. "You'll be in good hands with him. He's an honest man and is agreeable to representing blacklisted artists," Mr. Canby told her.

When she'd met Mr. Stone in his midtown office a few hours later, he'd made some calls in an attempt to get her a private meeting with the Committee, but had been refused. "In that case, the sooner you appear, the better," he'd advised. "They're thirsty for blood, and the longer you put them off, the angrier they'll become." The Committee members were feeding on the outrage generated by every appearance, getting nastier and less careful about legal propriety. So she'd agreed to appear the next Monday—the company's last day off before previews began—in front of a dozen or so politicians, with the press documenting her every word.

Which was the following morning at 11:00 a.m.

A knock at the door broke the silence of the room.

"Who is it?"

"Me."

She swept open the door and Charlie slipped inside.

"What on earth are you doing here? We said I'd do this on my own."

He didn't answer, but held her close. They'd decided after their first night together that the relationship had to be kept under wraps, at least for now, even from close friends like Maxine. No good could come from news of their alliance getting out, not with all the negative attention on Hazel, but they both hated the thought of being apart.

The feel of Charlie's arms around Hazel made her wilt inside, just when she needed her strength. To let go, and let someone else hold her up, was too much, and she began to sob.

He led her to the sofa and pulled her down beside him, offering up a handkerchief, which she gratefully took.

"How did you get up here? Did anyone see you?"

He shook his head. "I came in through the kitchen, no one said a word. I had to see you."

"You're crazy."

"That's true."

After they kissed, she settled her head on his shoulder. "All I want to do is write plays and put them up. That's it. I have no other agenda. But I'm trapped in this nightmare and if I don't do well tomorrow, if I don't put on the performance of my life, I may never work again. I'll lose everything."

"What does your attorney say?"

She sat up straight, all business. "I have three options. I take the Fifth—refuse to answer their questions—and get held in contempt, possibly sent to jail. Or I can be a 'cooperative witness' and give up the names of people who've been members of the Communist Party at one time or another. If I do that, there's a good chance I can continue on with my career, but I'll have placed others in the same precarious position I am in today." She rubbed her face with her hands.

"And the third option?"

"I tell them that I'll answer any questions about myself but none about other people. But here's the rub: If I do that, I'll have waived my rights under the Fifth Amendment and could be legally forced to name names. That's all they're after, more names. I'm supposed to prostrate myself before them, show that their paranoia is valid by offering up more sacrificial lambs, friends who've done nothing wrong. It's political purgatory."

"There, now." Charlie placed both hands on her legs as if trying to stop her from floating into air. Which is exactly what she felt like: a balloon that could be popped at any moment, before falling to the ground in jagged pieces.

"Stone considers the third option morally correct, but the Committee might still hold me in contempt."

"What's his advice, then?" His words were edged with exasperation. "Isn't that why you hired him?"

"Look, it's not his fault, he's trying to help."

"Of course. You're right. I just want to kill someone, specifically my father, for his part in this sideshow."

"Trust me, I know that feeling. But Stone's been helpful. He told me never to answer any question with a flat-out 'No.' I'm supposed to soften it with 'Not that I can recall' or 'It was so long ago, I'm afraid I don't remember.' If I try to defend the people they're asking me about, the Committee might very well produce testimony by others that contradicts what I say, catching me in a lie. Then I'll be charged with perjury. It's a twisted, sick game. I don't know what others who've appeared before me have said to the Committee, which makes me as paranoid as they are, and more likely to do whatever it takes to get out of the hot seat."

"You won't do that. You're stronger than that."

Charlie's support was a much-needed comfort. "I wrote up a statement, with Mr. Stone's help, saying that I would not object to answering any questions about myself but wouldn't impugn others. It was sent to them by messenger a few days ago."

"That seems reasonable."

She reached over to the coffee table and picked up an envelope. "It was delivered back to me today, unopened."

"So you'll have to do your talking yourself, not rely on the page. You can do that."

"I'm a writer, not a politician or a lawyer. They hold all the cards. Besides, they don't care what I say. They just want to get me in a bind and squeeze me hard so that they can prove to the American public that democracy is a minute away from collapse."

"By standing up for yourself, you'll prove that it's not."

"And go to jail. Lose everything."

"You won't, I promise. I love you, Hazel."

Ever since they'd made love up in her room at the Chelsea, Hazel had found herself desperate to be touching Charlie whenever he was near, either laying a hand on his arm as they passed in the aisle of the Biltmore, or shoulder to shoulder as they whispered back and forth in the house seats. Only with that touch did she feel that all was right in the world, that the problems were surmountable. It was as if her body had known she was in love with him before her mind had. But the connection wasn't only about physical passion, she knew now. She valued his ideas and opinions, shared his passion for the theater, and wanted more than anything to spend every moment they could together, laughing and talking before curling up in bed when the day was through.

The realization made her forget, for a moment, the nightmare she was trapped inside.

She pulled him close and stared into his eyes, already feeling the heat of their connection. "I love you, too."

❖

Hazel propped herself up with several pillows and watched as Charlie dressed in the morning light. His legs were solid but not thick—perfect, really—and she couldn't get enough of the way the small of his back curved up, the indentation of the spine that ran like a channel between his shoulders.

He kissed her goodbye and wished her good luck, promising that he'd see her back in New York, and after he'd gone, she ordered some coffee from room service and glanced again through the twenty-something questions her lawyer had given her to study.

As the letters floated around on the page, she remembered she'd had the typical understudy's nightmare last night—that she had to go on but hadn't had time to memorize the part—exactly what had happened that first day in Naples.

Here she was, back to learning lines instead of writing them, and her brain refused to cooperate. It might as well have been in Mandarin. In a cold sweat, she pulled off the hotel robe and threw it on the floor. She'd have called Maxine for comfort if the Chelsea Hotel's phone lines weren't tapped. Instead, Hazel was completely alone, treading water in a whirlpool of nerves.

She met Mr. Stone for breakfast at a corner table of the hotel restaurant, where he whispered further instructions. "You can take exactly one break, only if things get too difficult. And no jokes."

"Jokes? Why would I joke?"

"You'd be surprised what people do under that kind of pressure. A colleague of mine had a client who said he wasn't going to break, and ended up throwing all his friends' names out to the committee, including his college roommate and best friend."

"That won't be me, I assure you. Do I get to meet the loud-mouth Joseph McCarthy?"

Mr. Stone blanched. "I said, no jokes. You've got to be serious about this. No, you won't. He's focused on investigating the State Department for communist infiltration. For now. But I warn you, the HUAC is just as serious."

"Believe me, I know." Hazel looked out at the people on the street, going about their day, worried about a dentist appointment or what to buy for dinner that evening. How wonderful it would be to go back to that state of mundane, everyday bliss. Once this was over, if it was ever over, she'd appreciate the more modest joys of life. But wasn't that what everyone said, when their lives took a terrible turn?

The committee room in the Old House Office Building seemed like something right out of an Oscar Wilde play, with its dark wood, refined striped wallpaper, and globed sconces. Clerks passed official-looking papers back and forth, stenographers sat at the ready in front of their machines, members of the public took their seats and murmured among themselves, while photographers squeezed in wherever they could get the best angle.

Hazel and Mr. Stone took their seats and again she scanned the list of questions. Again, they floated around in her vision like fireflies.

"Here they come." Mr. Stone leaned close. "Take your time, speak slowly and clearly. Don't let them rattle you."

The members of the Committee, all scowling, middle-aged men, filed in and took their places on a raised platform. The chairman, Congressman John S. Wood, banged his gavel. "The House Un-American Activities Committee will come to order. This morning the Committee resumes its series of hearings on the vital issue of communist propaganda and influence in the entertainment industry."

The first questions were easy. Hazel supplied her name, where she was born, her current place of residence, her education, her occupation, the title of her play.

"Miss Ripley, are you a member of the Communist Party?"

"No."

"Were you ever asked to be a member of the Communist Party?"

"No."

The chairman shook his head after her reply, as if he knew something she didn't.

He looked at his notes. "Did you sign a petition for the Scientific and Cultural Conference for World Peace?"

She took a deep breath, remembering to answer with care. "At a rehearsal for a play, I don't remember which one, a group of young people approached me outside the theater and asked if I'd sign a petition so they could be representatives at a peace conference. I thought having a conference for peace was a great idea, so I did so."

"Did you question as to whether this so-called conference was a communist front?"

"Why would I?" Hazel sensed Mr. Stone twitch beside her, worried that she was getting riled.

"Answer the question."

"No. I did not."

"What about the anti-fascist rally you attended in 1938?"

"What about it?" She knew she shouldn't talk back, but couldn't help herself.

"Did you know that it was organized by the Communist Party?"

"I knew that I was against fascism, as we all were in those days. And are currently, unless I'm mistaken about the purpose and outcome of World War II."

The chairman looked down at the stenographers. "Please note that the witness refuses to answer the question." He glared at Hazel. "You also sent birthday greetings to the Moscow Art Theatre on its fiftieth anniversary, did you not?"

"The Moscow Art Theatre is a distinguished institution in the theater world, like the Old Vic in London. I got a phone call asking if I'd like to be added to the list of people offering congratulations, and I said, 'Sure.' The telegram had nothing to do with politics or the Soviet Union or communists."

"Who was the person who called you?"

"I have no memory of the caller's name."

"You are currently a member of the Actors Equity Association, is that correct?"

"Yes. If one wants to work on Broadway, one must be a member of the union."

"I see." His raised eyebrow suggested otherwise. "You appear to be associated with a number of organizations and causes that we know to be communist organizations or fronts." He fingered the gavel.

Another committee member, Congressman Richard M. Nixon, took over the line of questioning. "I'm going to ask you a question, and I'd like you to take a moment before answering."

She knew what was coming. The ultimate test of a witness's cooperation, naming names. The failure to do so would signify that she was protecting potential infiltrators, and was not a true American. A serious offense.

"Considering your extensive contact with people and organizations that spread communist propaganda," said Congressman Nixon, "do you know anyone who has been a member of the Communist Party? Fellow travelers, if you will."

"I'm sure you already have a long list of names of people who you consider to be fellow travelers. I am not interested in confirming, denying, or adding to it."

The members of the public gasped, giving the chairman reason to slam down his gavel a few times for good measure.

"What about your brother?" continued Congressman Nixon. "A Mr. Benjamin Ripley. He was a member of the Communist Party, am I correct or not?"

Once again, her beloved brother's name was being dragged through the mud. What these men were doing was no different than if they'd exhumed his bones and danced on them. Enough was enough. Hazel let rip. "My brother was killed in the war. He's not here to defend his name, and I am shocked you'd try to use him to get me to testify against others. You're not interested in discovering subversives, or uncovering some dastardly plot against America, you only want to push people like me around to prove how powerful you are. To publicly stigmatize and degrade."

The chairman lectured Hazel at great length after her outburst, while Mr. Stone asked for a break, which was denied.

But as the furor died down, a lone voice, a baritone Hazel didn't recognize, rang out from the back of the room. "Thank God someone is talking straight. Finally."

Once again, the room went wild. Hazel turned around but couldn't tell who'd said it. More yelling, more banging of gavels, and in that time, Hazel was able to regroup, pull herself together. That one voice, breaking out through the bitterness and allegations, made all the difference. She knew she wasn't alone in this madhouse, and that she was strong enough to manage what was next. She gave a silent prayer of thanks to her anonymous supporter.

Once again, after order was restored, the chairman resumed his questioning. "Do you know a Mr. Floyd Jenkins?"

"I do. We met in Naples and he designed the costumes for my play."

"Is he or has he ever been a member of the Communist Party?"

She remembered his rallying declaration at Sardi's, in front of practically the entire cast and crew: *If Hazel's a communist, then I'm one, too. We must all stand together.* Unfortunately, there seemed to be no tolerance for sarcasm in these dark days. No doubt the Committee already had Brandy's witness testimony, and if Hazel answered the truth, that Floyd wasn't, they could accuse her of perjury. "I am willing to respond to any questions that pertain to me or my activities. I understand from counsel that, under the Fifth Amendment, I can refuse questions about myself on the ground of self-incrimination. I don't need to take the Fifth, because, as I've shown, I'm willing to discuss my actions and intent. But I will not name other people, or answer questions about their actions or intent."

"You are not in a position to set the terms here, Miss Ripley. I will ask you again, Floyd Jenkins. A communist or not?"

"I refuse to answer on the ground that it might incriminate me. I will take the Fifth, because you refuse to agree to a reasonable request." She turned to Mr. Stone, forgetting that the microphone would pick up her every word. "As a theatrical production, this is first-rate. Right up there with Nick Bottom and the Mechanicals."

"Nick Bottom?" The chairman pounced. "This Nick Bottom you speak of, is he a communist?"

Hazel burst out laughing, as did several of the spectators. After a sharp look from Mr. Stone, she spoke clearly and succinctly into the microphone, for all to hear. "He's a character from Shakespeare's *A Midsummer Night's Dream*. A fictional character."

The room broke out in pandemonium. Again.

"Strike that from the record, this is a waste of time. Strike it off!" The chairman's neck, and then cheeks, turned crimson. He grappled with the papers in front of him and rose to his feet. "That's enough. We have no further questions."

The hearing was over. Mr. Stone grabbed her by the arm. "We have to get out of here fast. Follow me and don't answer any questions. Not one. Understand?"

They made it out through the scrum and leaped into a car that had been waiting by the curb.

"I may be wrong, but I think you did it." Mr. Stone looked like he was about to break into song.

"Did what?"

"You laid bare their political agenda, and embarrassed them to boot. The way Chairman Wood got flustered at the end there bodes well. He won't want this getting out." He switched back to sober, wary attorney. "I have to say, you were lucky. You pushed back, and I think that caught them by surprise, you being a woman and all."

"Let's hope you're right. Who was that man, the one that spoke out?"

"He's a reporter from the *Chicago Tribune*. I don't know whether that's good or bad for us. We'll find out soon enough."

Hazel leaned back, letting the relief wash over her and praying that Mr. Stone's initial assessment was correct.

That, at the very least, she had a chance of keeping *Wartime Sonata* on track.

CHAPTER SEVENTEEN

Hazel

July 1950

Hazel's nerves kicked into high gear as she arrived at the theater for the first preview. She'd had some oatmeal for breakfast, which threatened to come up, and retreated to the mezzanine level to take some deep breaths. At least the critics weren't coming until next week.

Charlie joined her, sneaking in a quick kiss. "How are you holding up?"

They hadn't had any time alone since she'd returned, although she'd given him, Mr. Canby, and Maxine a quick run-down after rehearsal yesterday. She wished she and Charlie could escape somewhere private and curl around each other, instead of having to stand at a distance and appear to be acquaintances in case any of the ushers came by.

"I'm doing fine, I suppose."

"Tell me what really went on in Washington. Everyone's talking about the article in the *Tribune*."

She took a deep breath. "My lawyer says I successfully embarrassed the Committee in public, and so far they've seemed eager to sweep me under the rug, not charge me with contempt. So that's good news."

"I would have thought it would be easier to sweep it under the rug if it *hadn't* been reported on."

"No, that journalist is a hero, in my opinion. He stood up and called them out on their monstrous behavior, then had the courage to write about it, depicting me as a linchpin in the battle for America's soul. Which I suppose made me untouchable, in a way. They can't arrest me without looking like they're trying to hide something."

"Then again, if you'd been arrested, it might have highlighted how unreasonable everything is and might have threatened the power of the blacklisters."

"You looking to put me in jail?" She was only half teasing.

He shook his head. "God no, not at all. Just following the logic."

"That's the trouble, there seems to be no logic, not with that crew. In any event, I'm still on the blacklist when it comes to television, film, and radio, so they've won in that sense."

"That won't matter, once the play's up and running. You'll be the queen of Broadway."

"Your confidence is premature. Don't jinx us, kiddo."

In fact, while Hazel's appearance before the Committee had made a splash for a day, the vitriol ran deep against anyone who refused to heed the call for blood, for informing on friends. Hazel didn't tell Charlie that she'd already started receiving hate mail, her cubby behind the counter in the lobby stuffed with bland-looking white envelopes filled with vile accusations, as well as anonymous threatening telephone calls, always from men. Mr. Bard had told the switchboard operator to take messages and stop putting them through.

"What if no one comes to the show because of my testimony?"

Charlie guided her back downstairs. "Why don't you run through the final changes, and then you can worry about all the stuff that's out of your control. Sound good?"

"As usual, you're right."

Down in the house, Hazel called for the actors to assemble onstage. While she waited for the last of them to appear from the wings, she and Charlie stood for a moment, smiling at each other and not saying a word, until Mr. Canby sidled between them.

"Hey, Charlie, can you check with the box office? Curious how many seats we've sold so far."

"I'll be back in five." Charlie headed up the aisle.

Mr. Canby waited until he was out of earshot. "Whatever you're doing with the kid, keep it up."

She tried to wipe the smile off her face, fast. Was it that obvious? "What do you mean?"

"Ah, come on. If it takes leading the kid on in order to get what we want, I'm all for it. I haven't seen a puppy face like that since, well, since never. He's an open book and he obviously adores you."

"He's a good person." She wanted to say that it was real, not an act, and that she wasn't leading him on in any way, but she knew better. Charlie's love was like a coat of armor she carried around with her everywhere, one that buffered her from the world's razor-sharp spears. She'd noticed, since falling in love, that she attracted more attention from men, from not-so-covert glances to unexpected flirtations. Her confidence had increased—knowing he was in her life, that she was loved—which in turn seemed to make her more appealing to the opposite sex. No doubt this was how Maxine, as a starlet, was treated every day, like a prize to be won. The power was heady.

When the stage manager called places at exactly eight o'clock that evening, Hazel hid down in the basement. She'd already stopped by all the dressing rooms and breezily wished everyone well, told them all to break a leg, but her nerves were shot. It was easier to be an actor any day, than a writer. You had a job to do, you got onstage, and you did it. As the playwright, she had to suffer through hearing the audience's reaction, or non-reaction, knowing she could no longer stop the show mid-performance and make adjustments.

The sound of the curtain lifting drove her out of her hiding place and up to the balcony, far above the stage, where Charlie was waiting. Only half of the seats in that section were filled. All this worrying, and most likely the show would sink without any fanfare at all.

Right after the second act began, she motioned to Charlie and they crept downstairs, standing at the very back of the orchestra level. At least most of the seats here were filled. Mr. Canby had probably handed out free tickets in Times Square.

The actors were all doing their jobs beautifully. Maxine had matured into the role and commanded the stage just as she'd done on the USO tour, but had layered in a hint of fragility that worked perfectly for Lina. Her leading man drew laughs with his silly entrances and exits, allowing the audience to let off some steam as the tension in the play rose, page after page. When he was killed, and Maxine mourned the loss of him before being sent to her own execution, Charlie nudged Hazel and pointed out to the audience.

Even though she could see only backs, several people were shaking with sobs. Handkerchiefs were out, noses blown, as the emotional vibrations echoed around the theater. In the last scene, the audience stayed rapt. The falling of the curtain at the very end of the play was met with silence.

Hazel waited, holding her breath. Maybe she'd read it all wrong, maybe they hated it for making them feel so awful. For reminding them of the trauma of World War II, which was over and done with. Maybe she'd failed, horribly.

But then one man near the front clapped twice. Others joined in, and within ten seconds, the entire theater echoed with shouts and clapping as the crowd rose to its feet en masse. Charlie grabbed Hazel and kissed her. "You did it. You absolutely did it."

Backstage, Mr. Canby surprised them with bottles of champagne. "You all worked hard," he said, as the stage manager popped a cork. "I'm happy to be able to announce that a new American playwright has arrived. One who isn't afraid to speak out, to speak up. Our very own champion of the arts, Hazel Ripley."

Hazel left the Sunday matinee in good spirits, looking forward to an easy stroll down Eighth Avenue. She liked walking home from the theater instead of hopping in a cab, as it gave her time to think about the play, what small directorial tweaks needed to be made, the best way to convey them to the actors or the crew. The show was coming together nicely, each performance building on the one that came before. There had been a couple of technical glitches, but that was to be expected, and they'd been addressed right off. She had to give it to Mr. Canby, he had a great team in place.

The guard at the stage door handed her a note as she left. It was from Charlie, asking her to meet him at the entrance to the Staten Island Ferry. She caught a subway downtown, wondering what this was all about.

Charlie paid two nickels for the fare and they boarded, surrounded by a mass of commuters. The playfulness that they'd fallen into was nowhere to be found, he was all business.

"What's going on, Charlie? Why bring me all the way out here?"

"I wanted to find somewhere we could talk but not call too much attention to ourselves."

They moved to the back of the boat, where the skyline of Manhattan slowly receded as the ferry chugged into the harbor. Hazel leaned over the railing and let the wind whip her hair around her face as the ferry picked up speed, charging through the choppy waters. Part of her wished she could escape the city entirely, leave it all behind her. Find a job selling clothes in a department store in New Jersey, say, and ignore the threats leveled her way. Writing the play had been a solitary endeavor, and she'd enjoyed every moment. But by mounting a play on Broadway, she'd exposed herself. In normal times, her biggest worry right about now would be the critics coming next week. Instead, she was caught up in a political storm.

She rearranged her scarf over her hair and tied it under her neck, partly to keep it from flying into her mouth and partly to obscure her face. The passengers around them weren't paying them any mind, but still. Was the businessman holding on to his hat listening in on their conversation? Were the couple with their arms around each other federal agents? She was becoming paranoid. She had to keep a clear head. "What is it, then?"

He turned away from her and rested both forearms on the railing. She did the same, their elbows touching. He took a deep breath. "They're about to make a big arrest. My guess is once that happens, the focus will turn to where it should be, on the actual spies."

"They are? Who's they?"

"The FBI." He lowered his voice so she could barely hear him above the churning of the ship's engine.

"How do you know this?"

"A high-up official at the FBI who was in the war with my father. He keeps him informed of what's going on."

The fact that Charlie had taken her into his confidence, entrusted her with what could be explosive information, was thrilling. At the same time, Hazel worried about being told secrets that could possibly land her in more trouble, just for knowing them. The risk was worth it, she decided. "Tell me what you heard."

"A few months ago, a scientist and an army sergeant were arrested on espionage charges. Both men were passing along atomic secrets, bound for the Soviets, but now the Feds have cornered the person who brought them together in the first place. It's a New Yorker, a member of the Communist Party USA. He's an electrical engineer named Julius Rosenberg, married, with a couple of kids. They're closing in on him, and the arrest will be announced any day now."

Hazel wasn't convinced. "How do we know the FBI isn't railroading an innocent man into confessing? Like Floyd, for instance. How do we know this electrical engineer hasn't been set up to take a fall, to show to the American public that they have reason for concern? I wouldn't put it past the HUAC or the FBI to manufacture an enemy to justify their overreach of civil liberties."

"They're passing along atomic secrets, Hazel. You've got to see how serious this is." He turned his head and gave her a hard look. "This is no longer theatrical, it's not a game."

"Trust me, it's just as dead serious when it's 'theatrical.' What's going on on Broadway is not a game, in any way."

"Of course it isn't, I didn't mean it that way. Sorry, my love."

She considered what he'd told her. If a real spy was exposed, maybe that would ease up the pressure on the artists, put focus where it should be, just as Charlie had said all along. Maybe this would be a good turn of events, and put a stop to the false incriminations. And if that happened, she and Charlie could take their relationship public, since they'd no longer be on opposite sides. All this speculation left her dizzy, confused.

Charlie laughed, almost to himself. "All because of Jell-O."

"What?" She was sure she misheard him.

"Apparently, that's how the two spies identified each other before the handoff. Each was given a ripped half of a Jell-O box top. The two halves fitted together."

"What flavor?"

He laughed again, louder this time. "Leave it to you to ask the least pertinent question. I'll check and get back to you."

"It's all too strange to be true." She quickly added, "I guess I believe it. I believe you, of course. But if the spy ring's techniques were that primitive, how effective could they have been at stealing atomic secrets?"

"During World War II, Russia was barely able to keep up demand for basic weaponry. These days, they're practically going toe-to-toe with us. There's a reason for this steep increase in technology, and it's not because they finally figured out the math. They've been fed it. And they'll use it against us, given the first opportunity."

"I hope you're wrong."

"I'm not."

They stood for a while, not saying a word, watching the seagulls dive and dip around them.

CHAPTER EIGHTEEN

Maxine

July 18, 1950

I was only called in for a quick morning rehearsal today, and looked forward to an afternoon of leisure. But as I was leaving the theater, Arthur pulled up in his car and motioned for me to get in. I did as directed, and he drove away fast, waiting until we were heading up Eighth Avenue before speaking.

"They got Julius."

I stayed quiet, digesting the information. I'd heard Arthur mention the name a few times before, but had never met him. "How did you hear?"

Arthur picked up a newspaper on the seat between us and hurled it at me. "Don't you read the newspapers?"

The front-page headline proclaimed, FOURTH AMERICAN HELD AS ATOM SPY. I glanced down the column, jumping to page eight for the rest. Near the top was a photo of a disheveled-looking man flanked by two FBI agents. One lock of hair fell onto his forehead, his heavy-lidded eyes made him look like he'd just woken up.

I started to say something, but Arthur broke in. "Don't say another word. I don't want you to open your mouth. They're close. And you're next."

We drove out of town, up along the Hudson on Route 9 for about an hour. At Croton-on-Hudson, we peeled off and up a winding road to a hilltop. The town had become an enclave for artists and left-leaning socialists back in the 1920s, to the extent that it was referred to as Red Hill. Arthur followed a narrow dirt driveway a few hundred feet, until it opened out onto a compound of small houses. None of them interesting, with shutters or porches or gardens. Just boxes, really, with doors and windows.

He parked around the back of one of the houses and we entered through a back door. "We don't want to be seen, even here." He pointed to a small room off to the side. "Wait inside and don't come out until I tell you to."

I sat on a small bed with a worn orange coverlet, the only furniture in the room. Outside, the sun danced on the trees—it was a gorgeous summer day—but what little breeze there was didn't make it through the screened-in window. A ladybug skated across the sill.

That's when I started thinking about the truth. About telling the truth. As if it might set me free. So far, I've kept my promise not to put pen to paper about this. This mess. I've kept this secret for years. On orders. But I can't keep the secret any longer.

Arthur is my controller. Among other things.

I'm a spy.

I've kept it out of my diary, but I can't anymore. The act of writing calms me, takes away the dread and panic for a little while. It's the only way I can make sense of it all. I've found a hiding place for these pages, under a loose board on the mantel of my fireplace in the Chelsea Hotel. Not even the hotel maids will discover it there.

For the first time, I'm really scared. Of the Party, of Arthur.

Of what I've done.

Growing up, I saw my German grandmother horribly abused by Americans. I watched as capitalism destroyed my father and turned him mean. It's true, I found a haven in the acting company, but what I didn't mention is the founders were supporters of the Communist Party. They introduced me to the American League against War and Fascism, a Communist-front organization. The members listened to me when I spoke, they cared about what I thought. Even though I was a girl, they gave me responsibilities. My gender wasn't a hindrance for the first time ever, and I found respect there. When I wasn't at school or working on plays, I served as financial secretary and studied Marxism-Leninism. Arthur encouraged me, pushed me. This gave me purpose, and I blossomed.

They figured I'd be useful in New York City, where membership in the Communist Party was surging during the mid-thirties, especially among theater folk and others still reeling from the Depression. I continued to be shocked by the racism and poverty in America. The economic free fall had cut a raw wound in society's skin, and exposed the maggots and filth deep inside. I truly believed that Communism would eradicate these evils.

At the Chelsea Hotel, I felt finally at home. It was an artistic community, full of creative people who disagreed and fought and then met for drinks, and Lavinia took me under her wing and made me feel like I belonged. At the Chelsea, it didn't matter how much money you had in your bank account, what schools you attended, or where you were born. Neighbors treated each other as equals, and talent and wit carried the day. The way the world should be.

Soon after arriving in New York, I got the ultimate praise. I was taken underground.

The Communist Party USA had a secret department, a clandestine arm that coordinated with Soviet intelligence agents. We stayed low, out of sight, and were given missions via our controllers. A couple of times, I was asked to go on a date with a journalist or rabble-rouser who seemed sympathetic to our cause, to see if they could be convinced to spy against America. Hazel's brother, a card-carrying member of the Party, was a ripe target. We went on a few dates, but I got the distinct impression he didn't hold enough of a grudge to flip. And after he brought me to that demonstration—the last place I wanted to be seen—I broke up with him fast. I couldn't risk being exposed.

I believed in this cause. I believed that the world would be a better place if we were all equals. Not American equality, which really meant the ones with the most money had the most pull, but truly equal.

Through it all, Arthur was my glue, what kept me together. I'd fallen in love with him right off, and did whatever I could to please him. As a team, we were magnificent. Arthur rose higher in the ranks; I stayed by his side through it all. Reliable, dependable.

A couple of years into the war, I was instructed to audition for the USO touring company and relay what I could to Arthur, but soon after arriving in Europe, I got the message that it was too risky, and to shut down all contact. I liked having that reprieve, I have to admit. Of just being an actress, not an operative. If I'd still been working for the Party, I might not have let myself get so close to Hazel, but I was vulnerable, and the war unsettled my pre-conceptions about America, as you couldn't help but root for the soldiers. But when Paul was killed, because the Americans screwed up and put him in danger, my resolve returned.

I headed to California, hoping to marry Arthur and continue our work, only to discover he'd been married off to another agent, on orders of the Party. They did that all the time, as married couples tended to attract less attention, but I'd thought it would be me. The Party knew best, Arthur said. And we were still a couple, in every way but that.

Determined to impress, I threw myself into my assignment to infiltrate the film industry. And boy, did I. The faster my star rose, the more excited Arthur and the others became. With success would come access to powerful men across the country—Mr. Butterfield being a perfect example—where I could listen in on conversations and report back what I heard, all while play-ing the role of silly actress.

The night we found out that Marilyn Monroe had gotten the part I was up for, and was so close to landing, was the same night Arthur cut off my hair, as punishment for my failure. In Hollywood, you don't get a do-over. Once an up-and-comer has been passed over for a lead role, there's a pretty good chance of being sidelined forever. Arthur's brutality got his point across, and when I read about Hazel's play in *Variety*, I figured I could redeem myself by landing a starring role on Broadway, by being a big fish in a smaller pond, at least temporarily. They agreed it was a logical step, one that might get me back on track.

I tried to keep Arthur happy, but he didn't like this new alliance, of me and Hazel. I was nothing without him, he'd made that clear enough. And I knew that if I were found out, he'd do nothing to protect me. I'd be taken off to jail right behind Mr. Rosenberg.

❖

I heard low voices, Arthur's, and then another man's. With one of the spies in our network arrested, the plan had been thrown into disarray. As the afternoon sun over Croton-on-Hudson crawled westward, panic began to set in. What if they kept me here? Or sent me away? I had to be back in the city by tonight's performance. With only four more shows left before opening night, each one was an opportunity to fine-tune the role. No way would an understudy be able to cover for me, as they usually only got their own rehearsals once the show was up and running. I couldn't jeopardize the show. I couldn't do that to Hazel, after everything she'd done for me.

More voices. Jumping off the bed, I put my ear to the door, when it suddenly opened. Arthur glowered at me and motioned for me to follow him.

In the kitchen, a woman was making bologna sandwiches with white bread and offered me one. I was starving at that point, having forgotten to eat breakfast before rehearsal, and accepted the plate and a seat at the wobbly Formica table. A severe-looking man, with black hair so thick it looked like a wig, sat across from me, chewing on his own sandwich. He nodded at me solemnly. Arthur leaned against the kitchen counter, arms crossed.

I knew better than to ask their names, this mysterious couple. They appeared to be siblings. The woman's profile mirrored the man's, and she had a similar low hairline, although her hair was pulled back in a tight bun.

I glanced over at Arthur, trying to get a read on his mood. He was hunched over, and scratched at a patch of skin under his short-sleeved button-down shirt, the one I'd bought for him back in Los Angeles, attracted to its needle-thin lines of turquoise. He seemed cowed, childlike.

This new subservience chilled me. Arthur had trained at the School of Special Assignment in Russia. For a year, he'd taken six courses a day in the basics of being a handler. He'd passed many of these skills on to me, like how to break a tail or work a meet, but he also knew how to kill silently and quickly. He was all-powerful, or so I'd thought, but clearly these two comrades were much higher up in the organization.

He saw me looking at him and stopped scratching.

"What does the organization suggest we do?" Arthur addressed the man and woman equally.

The man put down his sandwich and wiped his mouth with a paper napkin. "We need to get you both away from here, it's too hot."

"Gold and Greenglass have been passing secrets since '45," said Arthur. I recognized both names, agents who'd been caught in the FBI's sting. "Julius since 1942. They should have been phased out. We brought this on ourselves."

"The information they retrieved has been invaluable," said the man. "Until now, the benefits have outweighed the risks."

"Do you think Julius will talk?" asked Arthur.

The woman didn't give a direct answer. "He's been working for us for a while, which means he's accumulated valuable knowledge." She snapped her head in my direction. "How is it going with the play?"

"Fill them in on what you've told me," directed Arthur.

I tried to hide the worry in my voice. "The play's going well, and people are coming to the previews, in spite of the fact that Hazel had to testify."

Arthur spoke up. "The play's excellent, and Maxine stands out. It's exactly what we hoped for. Everyone's already talking about it, and it hasn't even opened."

"When is opening night?" the woman asked.

"Friday."

"All right. After the reviews are out, come up with a reason to quit. We'll relocate you both to California."

My heart sank. "But I'm under contract for the next four months."

"It's too dangerous for you to stick around New York. Not with what's going on with Rosenberg."

The thought of leaving the play made me sick. I didn't realize until now how hard it would be to relocate, again, and leave behind the friends I'd made. To leave Hazel behind. "The press will be terrible if I suddenly up and quit. No one wants to hire an actress who cuts out on her contract."

The woman stared at me. "I'm sure it happens all the time."

"Maxine's up for another film role, right, Maxine?" Arthur nodded at me. "Tell them about it."

It was true. A Hollywood director had seen an early preview of the play and set up a meeting soon after, gushing that I'd be perfect for the female lead in his next movie. I tried not to get too excited about it. After all, I'd been burned last time this happened. "It's a possible part in the new James Mason film," I offered.

"The female lead," said Arthur. "The perfect excuse to get her out of New York."

"If it works out," the woman reminded them. "We've been down that road before. Unsuccessfully. What if she blows it again?"

Arthur didn't answer right off, letting the moment hang. "I've been thinking about it, and there might be another way, if she doesn't get the role. One that would create a diversion from Julius as well as close the show down entirely."

This was news to me.

The woman narrowed her eyes. "What's that?"

"Charlie Butterfield." Arthur practically growled the name.

"Who's Charlie Butterfield?" asked the man.

"He works with American Business Consultants, and has been assigned to monitor Hazel Ripley to make sure she stays patriotic. His father is Laurence Butterfield, the one stirring up all the fuss in New York. Charlie's by Hazel's side constantly." Arthur gave me a pointed look. "We saw them together at Coney Island. I got the impression he's in love with her."

I wished Arthur weren't so astute. I'd picked up the same dynamic between them, but hoped Arthur hadn't noticed. Recently, during rehearsals, Hazel and Charlie had behaved like a couple of turtledoves, practically cooing to each other when they thought no one was looking.

"What do you think is going on?" asked the woman. "Is she stringing him along in order to get his father off her back? Or is it more than that?"

Arthur looked to me to answer the question.

"I'm not sure," I said.

"Either way, the situation could be a valuable tool for us," said the woman.

The conversation was not going the way I'd expected. Even though it wasn't what I wanted, ultimately I didn't care if they dragged me away from the play, as long as they didn't ruin Hazel's life as well. God knew what they were thinking, but it wouldn't be good, for Hazel or Charlie.

"Maxine, is something wrong?" The man eyed me suspiciously.

I swallowed. "I'm sorry, it's just that I'm opening a play in three days. I know you want the reviews to be raves, and it's a big role. Let's just focus on that for now, all right?"

The man picked up his plate and tossed it into the sink, the sound of it shattering echoed in the tight room. No one moved. "Your first priority is the Party. You seem to be forgetting that fact, Miss Mead."

"No, I'm not at all." My denial sounded thin, even to me. "I'm simply trying to do what you've asked of me."

Arthur pointed a finger in my face. "I'm not sure where you stand anymore. You and Hazel are joined at the hip these days. I don't like it."

"Really, Arthur," said the woman, "first Caroline, now Maxine? Your track record with your agents is certainly problematic."

I sat frozen in place, digesting this piece of information. I'd figured Arthur's wife's illness had developed out of the stress of being an agent. Not everyone was cut out for the job, and her psychological weakness certainly fed my own ego. But had she in fact turned on the Party, questioned her role? Was she mad, or had she been silenced?

The woman went to the sink, picked up the broken plate pieces, and threw them in a garbage can. When she was done, she brushed her hands together. I got the impression that she was the toughest of the three, her face pinched and mean.

"You've done so much for us already, Miss Mead." She said the words without a hint of gratitude. "We are all indebted to your support and good work over the many years. So many years. Perhaps once this is all over, you deserve a reward, not a punishment."

Arthur's eyebrows raised.

She continued. "A journey to the Soviet Union, where you will be lauded and heralded and can continue your good work for us. We should have done so with Julius, but we left it too late. We ought to learn from our mistakes."

They all observed me for my reaction to this glorious invitation. Go to Russia, a country I'd never been to and whose language I didn't speak. This was a warning wrapped up in a big pink ribbon. The bologna sandwich in my stomach threatened to come back up. I coughed, covering my mouth as I did so, trying to rearrange my expression into something unreadable. I was an actress, after all. This was what I did for a living. But with someone else's words. I didn't usually have to be playwright, director, and actress on the spot.

I had to respond appropriately, make them believe me.

So I drew on a tried-and-true theater technique, sense memory. I thought back to a time when I was happy as a child, when I felt safe. My grandmother and I used to pick mushrooms on the shores of a lake near our house. We'd come home and sauté them in butter, and the crunch and savory flavor of the dish made me swoon with delight. I could practically taste the mushroom on my tongue and, like magic, a peaceful calm swept over me. I raised my head up high and let my shoulders fall. "I would be thrilled to accept such an honor."

The woman seemed flustered. "You would?"

"Of course." The words came out strong and sure. Confident. "The Party has been my family for many years now, and I'm here to do whatever you need, in whatever capacity you require."

"Good. That's what I like to hear."

I silently gave thanks for my profession.

"Still, I like this idea of a distracting scandal. If we haven't heard back about the movie by Friday, let's use it to our advantage."

"That's exactly what I was thinking." Arthur straightened, eager to prove his own loyalty. "We set up Charlie Butterfield and Hazel Ripley in a compromising position—no doubt Maxine can pull that off—and expose the fact that Butterfield's son is sleeping with an accused communist who's written a play that the Feds hate. The press will go mad at their hypocrisy, particularly if the show's a big hit."

And no doubt the show would close. Hazel would lose everything: her name, her livelihood.

The woman smiled, pleased. Arthur had redeemed himself. "Report back through the usual channels."

I stayed silent during the long ride back to the city.

What had I done?

CHAPTER NINETEEN

Hazel

July 1950

F ive hours to go until opening night. Hazel stared at the gown
hanging from her closet door, the one Maxine had insisted she
buy during a Bergdorf's shopping spree a couple of weeks ago. It
wasn't her usual style, which was a subdued color and cut. This
was flashy, more like something Maxine would wear, and she'd
tried it on only because Maxine had insisted. Strapless, white
satin with a tulle overlay that faded from black to pink and scal-
loped edging, it shouted, *Look at me!*

"I simply won't allow you to show up as Hayseed Hazel for your
Broadway debut," Maxine had declared. "This dress is perfect for
who you are now: Hazel Ripley, director and playwright."

Hazel had bought it, happy that it came with a matching tulle
shawl. Add long white gloves and she wouldn't feel quite so con-
spicuous. Hopefully.

There was nothing more she could do. At this point in the
game, her job as writer and director was over. It was up to the

cast and crew to pull off the show, and then keep on doing it for however long Mr. Canby allowed it to run.

Hazel's mother was coming to the show tonight, and she couldn't wait for her to see the marquee with her name in huge red letters: *"Wartime Sonata* by Hazel Ripley." Evidence of her success that was irrefutable, finally.

At five thirty, she knocked on Maxine's door and they caught a cab uptown. Maxine was unusually quiet, but it made perfect sense that she was nervous. Hazel squeezed her hand. "Here goes nothing."

"Thank you for this chance. You've done so much for me." Maxine looked down at their clasped hands. She also wore white, in a pale floral pattern. Like two brides off to be married in a dual wedding. In many ways, it was true. The theater was like a church to both of them, a safe haven from the real world.

"Ever since Naples, we've been a team, and a good one at that," said Hazel. "This play wouldn't be nearly as great with Brandy in your role. Thank goodness you came to New York to save the day."

"Yes, thank goodness," she echoed.

Hazel couldn't stand it any longer. She had to share her news. They'd come so far, from performing on a flatbed truck to mounting a show on a historic Broadway stage, that it seemed a shame to keep her secret on their big night. "There's something I have to confess to you, the one bright spot in all this negative attention on the show."

"What's that?"

"Charlie and I, we're in love. I'm sorry I didn't tell you sooner, but with the play and rehearsals, we were trying to keep it quiet. I know we seem like a mismatched pair, politically, but he's really open-minded."

"Really?" She tilted her head.

"You seem skeptical."

Maxine spoke as if she were choosing her words carefully. "He's the son of the big bad Butterfield. Maybe it's smart to stay away from him, at least for the time being."

"What do you mean?"

"I just think it would be prudent, for now, to stay away from Charlie. You don't want to muddle things."

"Charlie's the one thing in my life that's not muddled." Hazel studied her friend. "This is the first time I've truly been in love. I thought you'd be happy for me."

"Of course I'm happy." Maxine hugged her, hard. "Of course."

Maxine's obvious reluctance was about more than their superficial mismatch, Hazel was certain. She remembered Floyd's caricatures in Naples: Hazel as the plain Jane and Maxine as the femme fatale. There was no question that Hazel's countenance and carriage had changed with her newfound power, augmented by Charlie's love. She'd finally blossomed. Could Maxine's status as the most beautiful woman in the room be that easily threatened?

They separated once they arrived at the theater, Maxine to her dressing room and Hazel into the house, where Mr. Canby was looking over the seating arrangements with the press agent.

Opening nights were like high-stakes dinner parties: Where certain reviewers required the best seats, others could be placed a little farther back, all while accommodating backers and industry royalty and hoping that no one left the theater offended before the curtain even lifted. Gossip columnist Walter Winchell needed to be placed far from Dorothy Kilgallen, due to a long-standing feud about who knows what, while Brooks Atkinson, the reviewer for the *Times*, required an aisle seat not too close to the stage but not too far back, either. At curtain call, the reviewers would scurry up the aisles before the rest of the audience began filing out, in a race to make the late-edition deadline.

All looked good, and Mr. Canby and the press agent headed to the lobby to finalize the last-minute changes with the box office staff. Charlie passed them, shaking Mr. Canby's hand, and did the same once he reached Hazel.

It was torture, to not be able to kiss properly.

"You look marvelous," he said. "That dress is beautiful, as are you."

Charlie looked dashing in his tuxedo, Hazel hated to pull herself away. "I should go see the cast and give them a preshow pep talk."

"Are you nervous?"

"Right now I'd rather be anywhere else. Seriously, I have half a mind to run down to the basement and curl up in a ball in the corner."

"Then you'd ruin your pretty dress, and you don't want that, do you?" He took her arm. "Come with me."

He pulled her up the stairs to the balcony, to the very back of the theater. In the shadows, he kissed her, long and slow, before drawing her in front of him and wrapping his arms around her waist. They looked over the rows of seats lined up like velvet soldiers down to the set, where the actors warmed up with stretches and vocal exercises, joking around and teasing one another, all in high spirits.

The tensions of opening night had succeeded in finally pulling the company together, in spite of the ongoing blacklist and the various factions that had developed among the cast. For the next three hours, the critics served as a common enemy, uniting all sides.

After the show, they'd all go to Sardi's, as was expected after an opening, and drink to the show's success, everyone wide-eyed and buzzed from the excitement as well as the anxiety of waiting for the first reviews. Mr. Canby would meet a messenger on the sidewalk outside the restaurant, get handed a stack of newspapers, and scan through each in search of the theater section. If he entered holding the issues aloft, champagne corks would begin popping. If he tossed them in the trash and came in empty-handed, the party would turn into a wake.

Hazel had to enjoy the moment, this moment. Because anything could happen. She'd done her very best, and that would sustain her.

"I should go." Reluctantly, she kissed Charlie, before leaving him to gather everyone on the stage to thank them for all their hard work, for believing in her and in the play, and also to express her gratitude to Mr. Canby for giving them the opportunity to present it to the world. Everyone clapped and kissed, but then the stage manager called half hour and the moment passed, as the nerves kicked in and the actors scrambled back to their dressing rooms to finish getting ready.

In the house, she greeted her mother, who looked splendid in a pink gown Hazel hadn't seen her wear since before her brother's death.

"You look lovely." She kissed Ruth's rouged cheek, pleased to have given her a night out, the first one in a very long time. One of the neighbors was looking after her father that evening. She wished he could have come, to share in her success.

Hazel made sure Ruth was settled in and then popped over to where Lavinia sat with several residents from the Chelsea, who offered Hazel kisses and congratulations. Finally, she took her place next to Mr. Canby at the top of the center aisle, greeting the incoming agents, lawyers, and industry people. How far she'd come, from the shadows of understudying where no one really knew she existed, to this.

She checked her watch. Ten minutes after eight o'clock. Not bad for an opening night. The curtain finally lifted and she relished the collective gasp as the audience took in the set, an intricate replica of a war-torn, formerly majestic hotel, complete with a crystal chandelier, a scarred grand piano, and a pile of rubble stage left. That gasp was a good sign. It meant they would suspend their belief and enter the world of the play easily, happily.

The first act moved along fast, buoyed by the actors' nervous energy, but not so fast that the lines got lost. Excellent.

At intermission, Hazel and Mr. Canby shared hesitant smiles. So far, so good.

The final act began well. But about halfway through, Maxine seemed off. Hazel couldn't put her finger on it, and probably the audience, seeing the play for the first time, didn't notice, but the other actors sensed it and became slightly more careful when they should be diving in, building the emotion and the tension. There was tension, sure, but it wasn't the right kind.

Beside her, Mr. Canby straightened up, alarmed. Hazel clenched her fists, willing the cast to keep up the momentum, not lose it.

The audience began to cough. Never a good sign. It meant they were getting fidgety, bored. At the crucial moment near the second-to-last scene, Maxine paused. She'd never paused at that place in the script before. She turned out, facing the audience. Her face was frozen, eyes wide. Her lips parted, but no words came out.

She'd been thrown into that desperate oblivion, one every actor fears.

She'd gone up on her lines.

Hazel knew that horrible feeling from her acting classes. She imagined it was similar to a fighter pilot ejecting from a plane. One minute, you were the pilot, fully in charge, and the next you were drifting in the open skies, vulnerable, at the mercy of the winds.

When Hazel had gone up doing a monologue from *Macbeth* in acting class, she'd been thrust out of the world of the play, where she portrayed a Scottish noblewoman bent on murder, and was suddenly just Hazel, a plain girl standing all alone on a stage, everyone staring and judging her. Blood had pounded in her temples as adrenaline flooded her body. It had felt unbearable.

The audience began to murmur and shift in their seats. Hazel said the line quietly out loud, vainly hoping that somehow Maxine would pick up the cue and get back on track. Tears came to Maxine's eyes, magnified by the lights, but she didn't wipe them away.

Maxine stood there, in terror, lost, as the seconds stretched on and on.

<hr />

After what seemed like hours, one of the other actors fed Maxine her line and the show finally lurched forward. Hazel swore she heard a collective sigh of relief from the audience members, but recovery proved futile. The cast was unnerved and Maxine overacted the final scene, as if to make up for her misstep.

The magic was gone. Maxine's last line rang out over the theater, drifted up to the mezzanine and the top balcony, and dissipated. Where in earlier performances, Hazel had heard gasps—sobs, even—in the interval between the last line and the first burst of applause, tonight a splatter of limp clapping broke out. It grew louder as the cast assembled onstage for the curtain call, but not by much. Audience members were already scuttling out, turning their backs on the work of these actors who'd slaved so hard the past few months and tried valiantly to bring Hazel's words to life.

If only the critics could have come the night before, or on any other night but this one. If only.

Without saying a word, Mr. Canby sprinted up the aisle before the curtain call was finished. Hazel sat for a moment, stunned, before slipping out the side door of the house and heading up to Maxine's dressing room.

The door was ajar. Hazel pushed it open and stood there, unsure of what to do next. Maxine sat in front of her mirror, wiping off the stage makeup, her shorn hair sticking up as if she'd run her fingers through it in frustration.

"Sorry, Hazel. I blew it." The bitterness in her voice brought tears to Hazel's eyes.

"You went up on your lines. Happens to everyone, at some point."

"Not on opening night, at the most crucial moment in the play. You should have never cast me, I was terrible."

"What happened?" Hazel knelt down at her friend's side, one hand on her leg and the other on the back of the chair.

The touch broke Maxine's fierce defensiveness. Tears fell down her face, streaking her cake foundation. "I forgot one line. Then everything went blank, and then it was like I was paralyzed, frozen in place. Which made me panic even more. I'm so sorry."

"It was over before you knew it."

"Do you think so?"

"Of course," lied Hazel.

Maxine grabbed a tissue and wiped her cheeks. "Hey, the play is strong, so maybe the critics will see beneath my flub what a great script it is."

"Exactly. Don't be too hard on yourself. Think of all those

times in Naples we made stuff up because we'd learned the play the day before and were completely lost."

Maxine wiped her eyes. "We did, didn't we? At one point, you did a monologue from George Bernard Shaw to fill the time. The guys loved it."

"Hey, whatever works. See you at Sardi's?"

"Thanks, doll. Let me get cleaned up and we'll drink to Naples."

Hazel congratulated the cast members she ran into on the stairway, a forced cheer in her voice. Charlie was waiting in the corridor. She craved Charlie's touch, wanted to fall into his embrace and be comforted instead of having to offer comfort, but that wasn't possible in public. He smiled at her and offered a "good show," but they both knew it had been a disaster.

"Have you seen Mr. Canby yet?" she asked him.

"No."

"Probably ran back to his office to calculate how much money he'll lose if we get panned."

"Stop with that. It'll be fine, you'll see."

She couldn't bear it. "Give me a moment, I should see my mother off in a cab."

She found her in the lobby. Most of the crowd had thinned out, thank goodness.

"My darling. You poor dear." The words were followed by an awkward hug, but the effect was as if Hazel had been slapped across the face.

Her mother was practically giddy. Hazel realized, in a sickening rush, that tonight's debacle was everything her mother had dreamed of. Hazel had failed, miserably and publicly, which meant Ruth could come to the rescue and reinsert herself in her daughter's life.

Hazel desperately wished her father could have attended and

blunted the bitter impact of her mother's joy. As quickly as possible, she shuttled her mother into a taxi, found Charlie, and together they walked to Sardi's. Charlie didn't say much but offered his arm, which she gratefully took, happy to feel the connection to him, the strength of his muscles underneath the sleeve of his tuxedo jacket. Inside, the cast stood around the bar laughing as if everything were normal. Hazel worked her way into the middle of their group, clinked glasses and wound from one to the next, giving each a nugget of thanks. Same with the crew, from the wardrobe mistress to the stage manager.

Maxine finally arrived, Arthur skulking behind her. She looked radiant in her red wig, the bitterness she'd revealed to Hazel in the dressing room replaced with a wide smile and too-loud laughter. Hazel's heart went out to her friend. Showing up at the bar tonight and acting happy was sure to be one of the toughest performances she'd ever delivered.

A movement outside the window caught Hazel's eye. Mr. Canby. He took a pile of newspapers from a messenger and awkwardly tucked them under one arm as he rooted around in his pocket for some change. The messenger sprinted off as Mr. Canby thumbed to the arts section in the first paper. He scanned it, then tossed it in the trash. Same with the next one. And the next.

Hazel slipped out. Charlie was busy chatting with the soundboard operator and didn't notice her leave.

"Let me read one."

Mr. Canby whirled around, his face revealing nothing. "These critics know nothing, my dear. Trust me, I've been down this road many times before."

"Are they that bad?"

He didn't answer. "If you read any of this, the words will be embedded in your head for years to come. You'll sit down to write another play and this is what you'll think of. I don't want to subject you to that kind of torture. You're a gifted playwright. Go back home tonight and start on your next play."

"Hand one over."

He did, finally. She had to see it, had to know what people would be saying about her, thinking about her.

The review belittled her attempt, as a "woman playwright," to handle a subject as serious as war, although the critic did say several moments in the early scenes held promise. Maxine was taken to task for trying to be a stage actress, when clearly she should stick to movies. Silent ones, preferably.

The door opened and Maxine came out, her wrap slung over one shoulder and a hand on her hip. Ready for a fight. "Let's have it, then."

Hazel knew better than to soften the blow for Maxine the way Mr. Canby had done for her. All those qualifiers made it worse. Maxine read through it and handed it back. Hazel couldn't read her expression. If anything, she seemed almost relieved, the furrows in her forehead smoothed out as she rearranged her fur stole so it sat evenly on both shoulders. She seemed calm, serene.

"Sorry I blew it for you," Maxine said. "I guess it's all over now."

Not the response she'd expected. Hazel stared at Maxine, confused. She wished Charlie were here, so she could get his reaction to Maxine's lack of one. Something was off, and it wasn't just the play.

In Naples, Maxine had been the strong one, the unflappable one. It was hard to believe that the opening of a play on Broadway had thrown her. Even in rehearsal, when she forgot a line, she'd blithely play through it until she found her way. Until opening night.

But the pressure had been enormous, on both of them.

"They didn't like either of us, so you didn't blow it alone," offered Hazel. "They'd probably have hated the play no matter how splendidly you performed the role."

"We can't control the critics." Mr. Canby balled up the last newspaper and tossed it into a nearby trash can. "I'm glad I took the risk on you both, and I don't regret a thing."

"Do you think word of mouth might make up for the reviews?" Hazel knew she came off as desperate, but had to ask.

"Not in July. Sorry, kid."

Maxine rejoined the party, but Hazel wanted to get home. Charlie insisted on coming up, and as she sat on the sofa, her head resting on his shoulder, staring out into the night sky, she was glad he had.

"Well, that's that, then." She sighed. "My show was a bust."

"So was Arthur Miller's Broadway debut. *The Man Who Had All the Luck* closed after four performances. You're in good company."

She had to laugh. "How do you know that?"

"Because I went to the last performance."

"I like the way you think."

"Look, I know right now the bad reviews sting, but I have no doubt that you will write another play and get it up on Broadway, just like Miller. In the meantime, I'll take care of you." He cleared his throat. "I have some news."

"What's that?"

"I got my conditional letter of acceptance. They said my test scores were through the roof, which means with time, I might get a shot at the Soviet Espionage squad. It's about as far from American Business Consultants as you can get. No more bungling amateurs, this is the real deal."

She blinked. "You mean you're joining the FBI?"

"Yes. It's what I've been waiting for."

His enthusiasm stunned her. "You should turn it down."

"What? I can't do that."

"Can't, or won't? Stop trying to impress your father, running around after spies that don't exist."

He drew back, defensive. "We've been over this, Hazel, they do exist. That's been proven. Just look at Julius Rosenberg. Sure, the HUAC is barking up the wrong tree, going after actors and writers, but our country's secrets are being stolen. If more get into the hands of the Soviets, we'll be in big trouble. We're already in deep trouble, to be perfectly honest. Don't you want someone like me on the inside, someone who sees the big picture? By going after the actual spies, I can put a stop to this insane focus on entertainers."

A primal anger surged through her. She had to protect herself. Everyone was a suspect, anyone might betray her. Including Charlie. Maxine had been right. "You're not on my side. If you were, you'd walk away from your job and your father. Now. This very moment."

"Look, we're both under a great deal of pressure. You're pushing me away because you're scared, but you don't have to do that. Let things unfold as they will. I promise you, it will all work out."

"What makes you think we could be together once you're in the FBI? Federal agents aren't allowed to be with blacklisted actors."

"Maybe not at first, sure, but I promise you this witch hunt will pass over."

"In what? One year? Five? Ten? I can't believe I almost bought into your story. If you really love me, you'll tell me right now that you'll turn it down."

He pulled away. "I can't. I'm sorry."

"Then you should go."

He tried, once more, to convince her, but the words meant nothing.

She sat, arms and legs crossed, fuming, until the door clicked softly shut.

Then she burst into tears. She walked over to the living room window and wept, letting the sounds and smells of New York wash over her through the open window, a reminder that she was just one of many who'd tried and failed, who'd been decimated by the city.

CHAPTER TWENTY

$\mathcal{M}axine$

July 22, 1950

After getting the bad news from Mr. Canby and Hazel, I re-joined what was left of the cast party. Arthur hovered behind me, trailing me wherever I went, and I purposely ignored him and flirted with others, laughing too loudly and letting my hand linger too long on the stage manager's arm. I took whatever champagne was offered and downed it fast, knowing that it was the only way to blunt what was ahead.

"Let's go."

Arthur at least let me bid goodbye to the group before yanking me out into the street and gripping my arm hard as we waited for a cab to pull over. When one finally did, he opened the door and shoved me inside, to the point that a man walking by called out, "Hey, that's no way to treat a lady." Arthur ignored him, went around to the other side, and directed the cabbie uptown.

I'd hoped he'd wait until we got wherever we were headed to start in on me, but his anger boiled over, fueled by our close proximity.

"You threw it. On purpose."

"No, Arthur. I went up on my lines. It happens to actors all the time. I was too rattled by that meeting up in Westchester, all the menacing talk. I'm an artist, and can't be handled like that."

He slammed his hand into the side of my face, palm out, so that my head hit the window hard and bounced off. Everything went dark for a couple of seconds, and I wondered if my neck would still hold up the boulder that had been my brain. The thick loopiness of shock was quickly replaced by searing pain that brought me out of my champagne buzz fast.

The taxicab driver glanced at me from the rearview mirror, then looked away, eyes on the road. No one was going to save me now.

We headed into Central Park, along the winding road that ran parallel to Fifth Avenue. I knew better than to ask where we were going. The blow had calmed Arthur, temporarily at least, and I didn't want to risk another smack. I gingerly rubbed my head and tried to come up with a plan. Nothing.

The first act of the play had gone beautifully, just as we'd rehearsed. Which made what I had to do even harder. Earlier, when everyone was milling around, warming up on stage, I spotted Arthur—who'd stopped by to deliver a dozen anemic roses—staring at Hazel like a wolf. He asked me if I'd heard about the movie role, and I'd had to admit there was still no news. "Any day now, I'm sure," I said, but he just shook his head. Right then, I'd realized that the only way to save Hazel from Arthur's scheme was to tank the play. Short term, it would be painful. The thought made me ill. But less so than initiating the scandal they'd cooked up to divert the press's attention from the arrest of Julius Rosenberg. If Hazel and Charlie's relationship came to light, if Hazel was discovered sleeping with the enemy, she'd be attacked by both sides, the theater community as well as the militant right. She'd never write, never work, again.

At least this way I'd get the heap of blame. I would be the flighty Hollywood star who blew it, big-time. While the reviews would be scathing toward me, Hazel would eventually go on to write another play. I could then hightail it back to California to mourn the fact that I'd thrown away the best role of my life.

When the moment came, I'd stopped short, looked out into the audience, and let my eyes go wide, in the most sublime imitation of an actor forgetting her lines ever performed. Meanwhile, the words went around and around in my head. *If not for Matthew, I'd be dead, part of the rubble. Never remembered, even by those who hate me.*

I said them silently in my head three, four times. The audience stirred, murmured, the pressure building. It was as excruciating for me as it was for them. I fought against every good instinct I had to keep going, to say anything at all, to cross the stage and sit in a chair, anything, anything but stand there like a fool.

Another actor eventually came to my rescue and said my line for me. From there, everything and everyone slid downhill, fast. We staggered along aimlessly until the curtain finally fell.

If Hazel had been a painter instead of a playwright, it was as if I'd slashed her best artwork with a surgeon's scalpel.

Before tonight, I'd desperately wanted to show everyone what a star I am, prove how perfect I was for this role. It wasn't easy to let go of my own ego. But I had to. I had to in order to save a friend, all while destroying what she believed in most.

I had my reasons. That's what I kept telling myself. I'd succeeded in tanking the play and, in doing so, saved Hazel and Charlie from the Party's clutches. They were of no value anymore. A twisted triumph.

❖

"Pull over here."

Arthur threw some bills at the driver as I stepped out. We were just north of the boat pond in the very heart of the park. During daylight hours, the area would be rife with tourists and city dwellers out enjoying the shade of the giant sycamore trees. This late, the place was empty. Silent. No one would hear me out here.

He dragged me along a dirt path. The hilly area was called the Ramble, where pathways curved in, around, and across each other, winding over a hill covered with shrubs and trees and back down the other way past a gurgling waterfall. During the day, it was like a maze, where you couldn't tell which way was east or west due to the dense greenery. In the dead of night, the place was frightening. I tried to keep my sense of direction. We passed no one.

We ended up standing on a rocky outcropping overlooking a small inlet. He shoved me down and my knees banged hard on the stone. To think that this boulder had existed in this same spot for thousands and thousands of years, long before humans, long before the Soviet Union or the United States even existed. Small glints of light shone up from the surface of the rock, and for some reason their beauty almost brought me to tears.

"Why did you do that?" asked Arthur.

"I didn't do anything." My words came out as a whimper.

"You're useless to us now. You'll never be a star after that. They'll kill you, and me. Everything is closing in and you chose this moment to protect your friend? Don't think I don't know it. And they will, too. They're not dumb, Magnild."

Magnild. The name I was given as a child. What my grandmother used to call me.

He kicked me hard in the upper thigh. I rolled over and gripped it with both hands. "Stop. I don't deserve this. Please, Arthur."

He stood over me, panting, both hands on his hips. "You do deserve it. Traitor."

"We love each other." The words made me sick but I said them anyway, anything to buy some time. "You can't let them tear us apart like this. We're more than the Party. Let's break away, together."

"You're saying you want out? Is that what kind of a comrade you are? What about everyone who supported you on your way up to the top? Do you think you would have attained your success without us backing you? You belong to us, to me. Don't forget it."

I didn't care. I'd saved Hazel, that was all that mattered. "It's no good anymore. The Party's not the same, we're all under fire."

Arthur knelt down on one knee, like he was about to propose. "You've lost your way, Magnild. You have been pretending all this time, haven't you?"

"No. But we don't know what it's really like in Russia. I don't want to go there. I want my freedom."

In response, he grabbed me by the neck and choked me. I tried to punch him but he was too big, too strong. I grabbed at the hands around my neck and tried in vain to pull them off. Finally, I let go and stared up at the stars beyond his red face, at the way the trees gently brushed the dark sky with their leaves, until the sound of the wind was replaced by the pounding of blood in my ears, and I passed out.

❖

Arthur left me on that rock in the middle of the night. I came to, briefly, and then fell asleep, too sore to move. I let the humid air, which smelled of rotting wood and wet dirt, drift over me like a ghost. Moving in and out of dreams and the sleep of the exhausted, I woke just as orange streaks began to burnish the sky.

I tested my bones for damage. Nothing I couldn't handle. Nothing broken. After making my way down to the side of the lake, I splashed water on my face like a vagrant. Two ducks watched me from a distance, curious but wary.

I caught a cab at Fifth Avenue and told the driver to take me back to the Chelsea Hotel. Luckily, I still had my purse and my wallet. The driver eyed me in the rearview window. I probably looked like a whore who'd been tumbled hard. Which pretty much summed me up. I'd whored myself out to Arthur, to the Party. They'd groomed me from when I was a teenager and didn't know how to say no, or how to assess what was being asked of me. As I grew older, and realized the world wasn't as black-and-white as they depicted it, I tried hard to justify my role in their master plan to spread communism to the States, but it became more and more difficult. All capitalists weren't awful, nor were all communists morally superior. Working on Broadway with Hazel had opened my eyes to another choice, a world where I could simply act, stripped of any ulterior motives, and deepen my focus on my craft. Because that's where my sympathies lay now, with the artists, the ones who struggled to make sense of the world. That's what I wanted to be.

What to do now? I could turn myself in. Tell the Feds everything I knew. Which wasn't much. As an underground operative, I was only told bits and pieces of the puzzle, never the entire thing. I didn't even know the names of the couple I'd met up in Croton. It would make news, sure. The Feds would parade me about just like they did Julius. In handcuffs, on the front page.

I thought of my grandmother. In her letters, she'd told me how my fame had brought with it not only the check I sent along each month, which she said made her cry whenever she received it, but also the approbation of the people who'd once reviled her. She'd found acceptance, having a well-known actress as a granddaughter, but they would turn on her like a pack of dogs if I outed myself. She'd be persecuted, isolated, and shunned once again.

I concealed the fingerprints around my neck with makeup and made it to the theater for the matinee. Before the curtain went up, we were informed that tomorrow's matinee would be the final performance, to no one's surprise. Onstage, it was obvious the bad reviews had infected the audience's response, which was remarkably different from previews. Where there had once been guffaws, now there was silence. Hardly a sniff during the big scene where Matthew and I reunite. They'd been told what to think and weren't going to let anything going on onstage change their puny minds. While we started with great gusto, the lack of energy from the people staring back at us couldn't help but dampen the performance. Where two days ago, bolts of emotional electricity sizzled, this afternoon's show felt more like a funeral for a distant aunt who hadn't left you any money. A muffled misery that's soon forgotten.

Back at the hotel after the evening's performance, I crawled into bed and fell into a deep sleep. The phone woke me up Sunday morning.

"It's me."

Arthur. His baritone brought all the aches and fears racing back.

"Yes?" I wasn't sure why he'd called here, knowing that the phones were tapped. It had to be important.

He spoke carefully, measuring out each word. "I hope you're feeling better."

"I am."

"That's good to know. We're going forward, as planned, creating a diversion for our friend. Let us know a good time and place for a rendezvous."

Meaning a time when I'd know that Charlie and Hazel would be together, in a compromising position. They were going forward with the plan anyway.

"No." I scrambled for the right words. "There's no point. No point in doing that."

"That's not your decision. If you don't agree, I've been told to give our regards to your grandmother back in Seattle. We'll be sure to reach out to say hello from you."

I let out a weak moan. Arthur knew my deepest vulnerability, and would have no problems giving orders to hurt my grandmother if I didn't do what they wanted.

Hazel and I shared a cab back to the Chelsea Hotel after the final show, after the maudlin goodbyes and promises to stay in touch. She insisted we meet up on the roof for a final toast, and I agreed, eager for anything to dull the pain.

"How are you doing?" Hazel asked, once we'd settled into our usual places.

"I should ask that of you."

"I'm fine." She laughed when I looked askance. "I guess I'm fine. I mean, I'm still breathing."

"Is there anything I can do?"

"Funny how when things are really, really bad, you look around and appreciate the tiny things—like the taste of this wine, you by my side—because the big picture is so scary that the small things are what keep you grounded." She smiled softly. "Who knows? Maybe, eventually, I'll write another play, one that's even better, even if that seems impossible in the moment. It's strange, but whenever I'm stuck, I come up here and stare out at the city and, before I know it, I'm back on track. Something about this place is magical, in that way."

"It's your muse."

"You're my muse. No, don't shake your head. It was your boldness on the USO tour that inspired me from the very beginning:

the way you handled the other girls, the soldiers, the officers. How you're not afraid to jump into the thick of things without over-thinking matters or being nervous about screwing up. I haven't forgotten you're the reason why I landed the director's job in the first place. That would've never happened without you sitting at the table, pushing Mr. Canby, pushing me, and it was my dream job. So thank you."

It was like a punch in my gut, to hear those words. "Not any-more, no way. I can't be bringing you down like I did. You're on your own from here, chum."

"Please don't be hard on yourself."

I hated that she was worried about me, and looked away, study-ing the reflection of the setting sun on the skyline, as the gray facades of the neighboring buildings turned a shimmering pink.

Hazel stared hard at me. "What's that on your face?"

Without thinking, I had tucked my hair behind my ear, expos-ing the bruise. I quickly covered my cheek with my hand. "Noth-ing, just some reaction to that awful stage makeup."

"Let me see." She reached out and gently cupped my chin, her touch so tender I wanted to weep. "Is that from Arthur? Did he hit you?"

There was no point in lying. "We got into a tiff, nothing major. I fell while we were arguing."

Hazel wasn't having any of it. "No. You're lying. What happened?"

I tried again. "He saw me flirting at the opening-night party. It was my fault, I'd had too much to drink."

"And so he hit you?"

"He didn't mean to, I swear." I had to deflect her attention away from him, for her own sake.

Hazel shifted forward in her chair. "We're going to the police.

I'll back up your story, and we'll get him arrested and carted off to jail. He deserves no less."

God, no. That was a terrible idea, for dozens of reasons, none of which I could share with Hazel. "You can't. I won't."

She pulled back, incredulous, eyes wide. "Why not? Are you that scared of him?" She watched me as I tried not to squirm. "What's going on? Is there something you're not telling me?"

I struggled to figure out how to answer.

"I love him."

I don't think I've hated myself as much as I did when I said those three words.

Hazel shook her head, confused. "If he hits you, why would you love him?"

I waited a moment, trying to figure out how to derail her demand to go to the police. "Just leave it alone, that's all. I'm fine. If you've never been in a long-term relationship, you wouldn't know what it's really like."

She inhaled sharply. The concern on her face was replaced with a stunned bewilderment. "I see. I'm not sure who you are anymore, Maxine."

I wondered that myself. "Look, give me some time, okay? I promise everything will be fine. I just can't be pushed right now, after the bad reviews and now this. I need a little time to get my bearings, reassess everything. You can understand that, can't you?"

She nodded, but I could practically see her mind spinning, trying to figure out what I'd left unsaid. Where the missing pieces of the puzzle lay.

"Look, I'm sorry. I spoke out of turn. You and Charlie, I know you're close. I just worry about it, that's all."

Hazel's face grew pinched. "After opening night, he told me that he'd been accepted into the FBI and we had a terrible row. I told him to break off from his father, from all the spy hunting, right there and then. He refused, and that was that. We're done."

I took a sip of my drink, unable to meet her eye or offer a word of comfort. Relief poured over me. They were done. She'd gone and saved herself without knowing it. I'd meet with Arthur tomorrow first thing and tell him that Charlie and Hazel were no longer a couple and to go jump in a lake.

Hazel was safe, that was my main concern. Whatever awfulness she'd gone through, I wouldn't be adding to her woes any further. Not as long as she and Charlie stayed apart.

I took a deep breath, spoke in a soothing tone. "I'm so sorry. That must be difficult. But I think you did the right thing."

"I thought I'd be enough for him to let his family's legacy go. For the sake of us."

"He's a guy with a chip on his shoulder and something to prove to the world. To his father. You wait, you'll meet someone smart and lovely and see Charlie for what he really is."

"What's that?"

"A boy. He's not a man. You deserve a man. We both do."

She considered that for a moment. I worried I was being too . pushy.

"I think you're right. Thank you, Max." She reached out and put her hand over mine. "I don't know what I would have done without you, through all this."

Guilt tugged at me, hard. I ought to confess everything, get it all out. But I could already imagine how her features would rearrange themselves, grow hard and cold, and then my best friend would be lost to me forever.

The roof door opened and Lavinia appeared, holding an empty wine bottle in one hand and a glass in the other. Her hair, normally up in a bun at the nape of her neck, hung in loose strands down her back, and the colorful caftan she wore had slipped to one side, revealing a bare, bony shoulder.

"Girls, my girls." She settled into one of the chairs and poured the last few drops of wine from the bottle into her glass. "Don't worry, I've sent one of the porters out to the liquor store. The perks of hotel living."

"Lavinia, are you drunk?" asked Hazel.

"I'm smashed to pieces, my dear. Don't mind me." She sat back in her chair, looking up at the sky. "What a view. I'll never get tired of this view."

Hazel and I exchanged looks.

"Oh, before I forget, Maxine, the switchboard operator said to make sure you got this." She pulled a folded piece of pink paper out of her pocket and handed it to me.

As I read it, my mouth dropped open. My agent had called. I'd been offered the role, my first as a leading lady. His message said that he'd already booked me a flight to Los Angeles for Wednesday. I wondered how this was possible, with my listing in *Red Channels*. Maybe my single "offense" hadn't been enough to raise the alarm.

"What's the news?" asked Hazel.

Lavinia spoke up before I could answer. "I'm nosy, I read it on the way up. She's been offered the lead in a movie with James Mason."

I didn't deserve this. Hazel was having what was probably, after her brother's death, one of the worst weeks of her life. Yet here I was on the rise, being handed a career opportunity most actresses would die for.

"How thrilling," exclaimed Hazel, though her excitement didn't reach her eyes. "Tell us all about it."

I tried to play it down. "I don't know much yet, to be honest. Haven't even read the script."

"It's a once-in-a-lifetime chance, one that may set you up as a huge Hollywood star," Lavinia declared. "You deserve it."

"Not after blowing opening night."

"Stop with that," said Hazel. "You got the part because of the play, right? I remember you mentioned something about the meeting last week."

I admitted that the director had seen one of our early previews, when the play had been at its peak and the audience reaction unsullied by negative notices, and had gushed breathlessly to me afterward. The fact that he'd still offered the part to me despite the bad reviews showed an unusual amount of courage, by Hollywood standards. If only I'd found out two days earlier.

"Then you deserve it. You deserve this success." She nodded emphatically, almost as if she was convincing herself. I knew Hazel well enough to know that underneath her kind words, she was putting on a brave face and had to feel frustrated or even resentful. She hid it well.

I didn't deserve this grand opportunity. I'd betrayed my best friend. Even worse, I'd tanked the play, which, after all that, hadn't even been necessary.

"At least one of us will make it into the big time. In spite of all this blacklisting craziness." Lavinia was watching me closely.

"What about your television role, Lavinia?" asked Hazel. "You could be a household name soon enough. Think of all those people who'll be watching you week after week."

"They've rescinded the offer."

"What? Why?" Even in the fading dusk, I could see that Hazel had gone pale.

"I've been blacklisted."

"When did this happen?"

"This week. At least they got my entry right. I was a card-carrying member of the Communist Party until 1939. A proud member, I'll have you know. Got out when the Soviets made a pact with the Nazis, an alliance I could not abide."

The same year I first questioned the cause myself. Arthur had pointed out to me that the Soviet Union had no choice in the matter, and if they didn't sign, Hitler would attack anyway. He said we had to keep our mother country alive at all costs and the alliance was merely for show. I believed him.

Lavinia gave me a crooked smile. "So you see, you're the last one standing, as the rest of us drop like flies. It's all on your shoulders."

All on my shoulders.

Maybe that was my way out.

Maybe there was another choice, besides turn myself in or continue toeing the party line. An option I'd never even imagined before, perhaps because it was so simple, so obvious. The perfect plan, if I could pull it off.

The more I considered the idea, the clearer the answer became. I could rise above my own fear of Arthur, my panic and helplessness, and turn that into brilliant rage. The rage of a diva.

The roof door opened and a large man appeared in silhouette.

Lavinia slid forward in her chair. "Aha, refreshments have arrived!"

The man headed our way, but he wasn't one of the porters, nor was he holding a wine bottle. He held a white envelope.

"Oh my God. It's a subpoena," said Hazel.

Lavinia got to her feet, wobbling slightly. "Well, that was fast. Bring it on."

The man came to a stop and stared at each of us, before settling his gaze on me. "Maxine Mead?"

I nodded.

"You've been asked to appear before the FBI tomorrow, in a private session, here in New York. I've been told to let you know it's only a formality."

Because of the film role. I took the envelope and watched as he walked away. Lavinia collapsed back into her chair.

"At least it's a private session," said Hazel. "That's a good sign. They don't want to make an example of you."

My worry slowly started to dissipate. "It'll be smooth sailing, I'm sure."

❖

"Miss Mead, what a pleasure to meet you in person. I'm Roy Cohn."

I shook Mr. Cohn's hand, amazed at how the soft voice didn't match the man's pugilistic appearance. His eyes bulged out like Elmer Fudd's from the cartoon, and a garish scar ran down the length of his nose. I tried not to stare.

He fell over himself to accommodate me, holding out the chair, asking if I'd like some water or coffee. He introduced the other two men, who were with the FBI, but I didn't catch their names, he spoke so fast. We were all squeezed into a tiny, bare office, a stenographer wedged in the corner, poor thing.

"This is simply a formality to clear you to work, as requested by a movie producer, Miss Mead. We are terribly sorry to inconvenience you. This is a pointless enterprise, but we must do what we're told to do."

I nodded, wary. While Hazel had said I should wait and bring a lawyer with me, I didn't want to put the meeting off. Arthur had been instructed to lie low, up in Croton, on orders from Moscow, and I was relieved at the reprieve. It gave me more time to position myself the way I'd planned. The news of the new movie hadn't hit the press yet, thank goodness. I wasn't ready to let Arthur know, not yet.

Enough of Arthur and the Party. I had to stay focused. Act the part of the silly actress with nothing to hide.

"Mr. Cohn, of course. How can I help you?" I let my eyes go wide. I'd dressed the part, in a bright green suit nipped at the waist and baby doll pumps, and accentuated my eyelashes as I would on the stage, to make them pop. The better to bat them at my prey.

"We just have to clear up a couple of questions." Mr. Cohn looked through his notes, reshuffled them, and took a nervous sip of water. He seemed jumpier than I was.

We ran through the basic questions, Mr. Cohn smiling blandly as the stenographer clicked away behind me.

He tapped a pen on his notes. "Tell me about this demonstration that *Red Channels* says you went to. Back in, oh, 1938. Seems so long ago, right?"

"Sure does. I can barely remember what happened yesterday." We shared a chuckle.

"Of course. But tell me, do you remember that day?"

"I suppose so. A boy asked me out on a date, and I said yes. That's where he took me."

"To a communist rally?"

"Well, it wasn't a communist rally. It was a rally for the evacuation of European Jews. To convince the United States government to allow them to immigrate, and save them from Hitler."

He sat back. "You remember a lot about it, then."

I'd overplayed it, trying to be helpful. "I remember because it was the one rally I ever went to."

"Well, of course." He looked back down at his notes. "Who was the boy who took you to this rally?"

"I don't remember his name."

"Really, Miss Mead?"

Mr. Cohn took a long time writing something down. As I waited, the room turned incredibly hot, as if the vents had begun blowing in desert air. I wanted more than anything to reach into my purse and pull out a handkerchief to dab at the shine on my face, but I didn't dare.

Finally, he put down his pen and spoke. "I must remind you, Miss Mead, that you are testifying here, just as if you were before the Committee in Washington, DC."

I threw him a girlish smile, hoping he was joking with me. "Really? That wasn't made clear to me."

"We take our role very seriously, Miss Mead." His nervous mannerisms had all but disappeared. He even seemed to grow taller in his chair.

"May I ask your position, exactly?" I asked. "Are you a member of the Committee?"

"No."

I tried to hide my relief. "I see."

"I'm Senator McCarthy's chief counsel."

"Joseph McCarthy?" The worst witch hunter of them all.

"Senator McCarthy. Yes. So no more nonsense."

I was trapped. Inside, I chided myself for not heeding Hazel's advice and bringing a lawyer. This was bad. "I wasn't aware that I was being nonsensical."

"I understand you're a good friend of Hazel Ripley. Is this correct?"

"We've worked together, yes."

"Did she or her brother, Benjamin Ripley, ever try to lure you into joining the Communist Party?"

The twisted irony of the statement made me laugh out loud. I apologized immediately, but it was too late.

"Do you think this is a joke?" A drop of spittle flew out of his mouth and landed on the table between us. "Our country is being assailed by forces that want to destroy everything we have here. And you're laughing? Who do you know who has links to communists?"

I remembered Hazel's tactic. "I'm happy to answer any questions about myself, but not about others. I don't think that's right."

His mouth twitched with excitement and I kicked myself for underestimating him. "You know as well as I do that, in the eyes of the public, not being completely honest with us is as good as an admission of guilt. You have a big movie coming up, right? I'd hate to see that part taken out from under you. I hear you're perfect for it."

"That's not fair."

He looked back down at his papers. "I'm sorry you feel that way." He continued rattling off names, including several who I knew had been in the Party.

"I don't know, really, I don't!" Tears came to my eyes, and I hated myself for it.

He softened, though. "I'm sorry, Miss Mead. I don't mean to put you into a bind. Look, this Benjamin kid isn't around to be angry at you for naming him. You're not doing anything wrong if you tell us that he was involved. It was a long time ago, as you said yourself."

I stayed silent.

He erupted, making me flinch in my chair. "If you don't respond, you will never work again. I personally will make sure you can't even find work as a salesgirl in a drugstore."

I had to work. It was integral to my escape from the Party, to saving myself and my grandmother, and helping Hazel in one fell swoop. A plan that would fall to pieces if I couldn't take this job.

A surreal calm came over Mr. Cohn. I could barely keep up with his changing demeanor. Either this man should be in the theater, or he was a sociopath. "Ben Ripley's no longer with us. Tell me the truth, that he was a communist sympathizer."

In that moment, I only had to answer one question and I'd be free. A question concerning someone I barely knew, and who was no longer on this earth to be affected by my betrayal. It was as if Mr. Cohn was pulling the response out of me, against my will.

I nodded.

But that wasn't good enough. "Tell me yes, Miss Mead."

It came out a hoarse whisper. "Yes."

"Good girl." He made a notation on the piece of paper in front of him and offered an encouraging smile.

"Hazel Ripley?"

I tried to stay still, not move a muscle, as if I were a fawn in the tall grasses, hiding from a predator.

"Look," said Mr. Cohn. "We have these names already, you're not telling us anything we don't know."

"Then why bother to ask me?"

He didn't respond, just gave me a reproachful frown. I knew the answer already, anyway. Because then they could go and frighten someone else, and transmit terror like a virulent contagion.

He went back through the list of names. Roy Cohn wasn't going to let me out of there until I gave up the information I had, but if I hadn't been a Soviet agent, I would have stood my ground. I would have shown the backbone that Hazel had and let him bully me until he had to jail me for contempt, knowing there were those who could vouch for me, make it right. But I was being attacked on all sides. Arthur, the Party, the HUAC.

And so, I broke.

I did what I could to save myself, to set myself free.

I named names.

CHAPTER TWENTY-ONE

Hazel

July 1950

H azel stared out at the city from her window. She'd sat there, motionless, for probably an hour now, watching the patterns the pigeons made as they burst into flight, then settled back down on the rooftops for minutes at a time before bursting off once more. She couldn't really figure out what triggered the flights. Maybe one pigeon got a funny feeling, thinking that a hawk was scoping them out from far above, and jerked its head up, which caused another one to flap its wings, which caused another to leap into the air, until finally the entire flock fled in panic.

A hard knock on the door brought her to her feet, the sound like a shotgun in the quiet afternoon calm.

"Who is it?" She knew better than to open it right off.

"It's me."

Charlie.

She opened the door and ushered him inside. Confusion and

panic crowded his features, and her worry overrode some of the anger from their last meeting.

Charlie looked her up and down. "I got your note that you wanted to see me. I rushed right over. Is everything all right?"

"What note?"

He pulled a folded piece of stationery from his jacket pocket. "Maxine said you were in trouble, to come right over."

Hazel studied it. She hadn't seen much of Maxine the past few days, and missed her. They'd run into each other in the elevator yesterday as Maxine was leaving for a quick trip to Los Angeles, for some preliminary costume fittings for her movie. She'd told Hazel that the meeting with the FBI had gone just as they'd expected, a formality. Thank goodness one of them was in the clear. Once filming began, she'd be moving to L.A. permanently; the very thought made Hazel heartsick.

The stationery had a cursive, flowery *M* printed at the top—Hazel recognized the stock from Maxine's opening-night cards to the cast and crew—and underneath was a quickly scribbled note. "I guess she's back from L.A. already. Strange, though. Why would she send this to you?"

"I have no idea. So you're not in trouble?"

"Other than that I've lost my career while holding on to my principles, no. I'm bored, really, but otherwise okay."

Charlie's shoulders dropped several inches and he blew out a breath. "Thank God. I was worried."

"I'm flattered. Look, I'm sorry about our fight, I was edgy and looking to blame someone. You were in the wrong place at the wrong time."

"I hated the way we left things. There's so much to explain. So much to talk about. Do you have time?"

She laughed. "All the time in the world." She sat on the sofa, and he did the same, leaving space between them.

"I'm not joining the FBI."

She stayed quiet for a moment, studying him. "Why is that?"

"My father admitted he was behind your subpoena. He didn't like the way you spoke to him in Coney Island, and decided to teach you a lesson. If this is what our government's become . . ." He trailed off. "The way the politicians are going after every actor or director who ever said the word *red* is a waste of time and taxpayers' money. I want no part of the country going off the rails like this." He counted on his fingers. "Denial of due process, no impartial judge and jury, no cross-examination. It's a travesty. You were right all along. I had blinders on, and didn't see until it was too late how far the witch hunt had careened out of control."

"I've been saying this for months."

"Look, I was brought up to respect authority. My father, with all his government contacts, made me believe the nation was being kept safe by the FBI, by our politicians, that they had our best interests at heart."

"What about you working from the inside to change things?"

"Maybe, eventually. But right now it's too toxic. Anything I uncovered or did would be turned around to make their argument. Politicians like McCarthy and Wood have already made up their minds, I won't be able to change them. Somehow, I had it in my head that this would blow over fast, that public opinion would shift when they saw how blatantly people were being persecuted. I was wrong, and I see that now."

"Have you told your father?"

Charlie nodded. "He said that I'm a traitor to my country. Especially when I told him what I'd like to do instead."

"What's that?"

"Work in the theater."

She gasped. "Really? You actually said that to your father?"

"His head pretty much exploded."

"I can imagine. What kind of job are you looking for?"

"I don't know yet. I'll reach out to Mr. Canby, see if he needs an assistant producer. Or I'll assist you."

"No one will be producing any of my plays, not after that flop."

"Remember Arthur Miller."

She smiled. "True. And he's doing okay. Although I wouldn't be surprised if he gets summoned down to Washington one of these days. I'm glad you told me, Charlie. I'm glad we're on the same side."

"We are. Please understand that I want more than anything to be with you."

"I do understand."

He leaned in and kissed her. "I suppose that now we're both out of a job, we'll have to find something else to do to fill our time." He ran a finger down her bare arm and she shivered.

"I can't imagine what that might be."

They barely made it to the bedroom, kicking off shoes, unbuttoning shirts, shedding every scrap of clothing between them. Their feverish start melted into a more sultry lovemaking that left Hazel gasping for breath. The afternoon faded into evening, the sky eventually turning all shades of purple as they dozed on and off.

A knock at the door brought Hazel out of her groggy sleep. Maxine, probably, here to explain her note. As she tied on a robe, Hazel laughed out loud at the thought of Maxine setting Charlie and her up to reunite in the most dramatic way possible. So typical of that girl. She was probably stopping by to find out how it all worked out.

"I'll be right there," she called out.

Charlie rubbed his eyes and rolled out of bed. "What time is it?" he asked, as he pulled on his pants. His chest was shiny with sweat.

The sight of him, along with the thick July air, made it hard for Hazel to think, to breathe. She was overcome with wanting more of him. She'd scoot Maxine out as soon as she could. "I have no idea. Around eight, I guess."

She opened the door in her silky robe just as Charlie ventured into the living room, half his shirt unbuttoned, not yet tucked in. Instead of seeing Maxine, Hazel was blinded by the flash of several cameras. She blinked, uncomprehending.

"Miss Ripley, who's your mystery pal?"

A reporter, pad in hand, leaned in. More flashes. Hazel stuck up her hand, trying to ward them off, before slamming the door, hard, putting her back against it. Charlie, all color drained from his face, began to shake.

The flashes had set off another fit. She rushed to him, crying out his name over and over again, as they slid to the floor in a crush.

❖

Hazel and Lavinia scuttled through the tunnel that connected the hotel to the brownstone, following the stretcher where Charlie lay, falling in and out of consciousness. Up in Hazel's room, as Charlie's body flailed with no sign of subsiding, she'd managed to grab the phone and reach Lavinia, who'd immediately taken charge: calling for an ambulance, ordering the porters to toss out the press, and relaying the address of the brownstone on Twenty-Second Street so as not to attract attention.

The two women followed the ambulance in a taxi to the hospital, where they waited for an hour before being told that they wouldn't be permitted to see him, but that he had stabilized and his family had been notified. Hazel stayed cooped up in the hotel all weekend, waiting for Charlie's call and leaving notes for Maxine, but not hearing a peep in return.

The photos in the newspapers on Friday had been damning. Hazel's loosely tied robe revealed an unseemly amount of cleavage—but not enough to keep it from being published—while Charlie stood behind her, buttoning up his shirt with an astonished expression on his face, tufts of hair sticking up, proof of their recent roll in the hay. COMMIE CHASER CAUGHT WITH COMMIE SYMPATHIZER, blared the headline. The article described Charlie as an employee of American Business Consultants, and the son of Laurence Butterfield.

The damage had been done. Over the weekend, Hazel tried to reach out to several of the actors from the play, who might understand her explanation, and had been rebuffed at every turn. Her mother had shaken her head with disdain, and refused to discuss the matter. Only Hazel's neighbors at the Chelsea carried on as they always did. Thank goodness she lived here, where being ostracized at one time or another by the outside world was simply part of living an artistic life, something to be expected, if you were doing your job well.

Most everyone else had turned their backs on her because, in their minds, she was a traitor for being associated with American Business Consultants. Her theater family had no use for her, and her testimony in Washington had displeased all the right-wingers. She'd managed to be vilified by both ends of the political spectrum, no easy feat.

She had her part in it, of course. She should never have dallied with Charlie. A terrible idea from the start, but one she did not regret. He'd reach out to her as soon as the noise died down. Once he was back on his feet.

Finally, on Monday, Maxine reappeared and agreed to meet her at El Quijote.

Hazel slipped down to the lobby and through the side door that connected the restaurant to the hotel, grateful to avoid going outside. Mr. Bard had warned her the press was still gathered on the sidewalk, hoping for another ambush.

Maxine was already seated at a table in one of the back rooms. The place was empty save for the waiters, who couldn't care less about the political leanings of their customers as long as they tipped well. Maxine looked tired, with dark circles under her eyes, and gave Hazel an awkward hug. "It's awful, what they've done to you. I'm terribly sorry that I was away, and I have to go back tomorrow. I hate that I'm abandoning you in your moment of need. I really do."

"Are you going with Arthur?" Hazel had to ask.

"No. Definitely not. How's Charlie?"

"Who knows, now that he's back in his father's clutches? I thought he might have called by now. It's been four days." She took a deep breath, trying not to cry. "Maybe, since my life has come to a screeching halt, I'll come out and stay with you in California. I could use a change of scenery."

"Sure. But you'll muddle through, I know you will."

Not exactly a warm invitation. The waiter approached with coffee.

Hazel waited to continue until he'd poured two cups and was out of earshot. "What made you send Charlie to me last week? I have to ask."

"What do you mean?" Maxine poured sugar into her cup and stirred it.

"You looked so relieved when I told you we'd broken up, I was surprised, that's all. It seemed like you were trying to set us back up together, which was sweet. I wanted to thank you for doing that. It worked, until the press caught wind of it."

"I'm sorry, but I don't understand. How did I send him back to you?"

"With your note. He came rushing over as soon as he got it."

"My note?"

It was as though they were speaking two different languages. "Yes. It was on your stationery, with that big flowery *M* at the top, and said that he had to come to me right away or something like that."

"Do you still have the note?"

Hazel considered it. "The maids came on Saturday, so probably not."

"I didn't write that note."

Was she joking? "Okay, then who did? I don't know any other Maxines."

"I'm not sure." Maxine had gone white, which made the gray circles under her eyes even more pronounced. "Listen, I have to go back to California, like I said, because it's better if I'm not around. You'll be better off without me. At least for now. But know that I'm your very best friend, and always will be."

"You sure? It seems like you're pulling away, like everyone else." Hazel couldn't help it, tears of self-pity burned her eyes.

"I swear, no. Oh, please don't cry. Please, Hazel. I adore you and I'd do anything for you." Maxine leaned close, smelling of lemons and lotion.

Hazel took a deep breath and pulled back, exhaling for what felt like the first time in forever. "Is this about Arthur? Is he bothering you again?"

"No. Just, no." Maxine was closing down again.

"Okay. Well, on the bright side, I'm excited about your new movie, Max. I guess that means you aced your interview with the FBI. Well done."

"I suppose. Any word from Floyd?" It was as if Maxine wanted to change the subject, fast.

"Not a thing. It's like he's fallen off the face of the earth." Enough with the bad news. She didn't want to think about that right now. "Tell me more about your new job. What's your part?"

"It's a silly role that I could do in my sleep. Nothing like the amazing parts you've written. You've spoiled me." Her words rushed out with an artificial burst of energy. "I leave this afternoon, but I had to say goodbye to you, and thank you for everything. You've been so generous, and this way I can be generous back. With this salary, I mean. It was all worth it, because now I can help you out and make sure you're taken care of until all this craziness blows over. Which I'm sure it will."

As Maxine rambled on, one phrase stood out.

"Wait a minute. What do you mean, 'It was all worth it'?"

Maxine delicately wiped her mouth with her napkin. "You know, all this craziness."

"What exactly did they ask you at the hearing?"

"Oh, gosh. The usual, 'Was I a communist?' That sort of thing."

"Did they ask you about anyone else?"

"No. Not really." Maxine shifted uncomfortably in her chair.

For a moment, neither spoke. The truth rippled through Hazel, like a snake slithering up her spine and wrapping itself around the curves and dips of her brain.

In Maxine's meeting downtown last week, the one that wasn't really official, just a formality, she'd turned. Hazel was certain of it. The only way Maxine could have been offered such a juicy role was if she'd cooperated. Which explained why she'd been so elusive the past week.

Hazel stared at her in the dim light of the restaurant. This was a person she did not know. Another person entirely.

Maxine, from that first day in Naples, had inspired Hazel's work. The play had soared because of her dear friend, and failed because of her. Hazel couldn't imagine a life without Maxine in it, without her fire and flippancy coming to life on the page.

Yet Maxine had betrayed her.

When she finally spoke, her voice cracked. "Who did you name?"

"What?" Maxine looked down at the table. "It was just a formality, like I said."

"You and I both know that's not true. Tell me. Who?"

Hazel stared as her friend's glamorous facade contorted into ugliness as she began to cry. The waiter looked over from where he was wiping down the bar and yawned, unconcerned.

Hazel slammed her closed fist down on the table.

"Tell me everything now. Everything."

CHAPTER TWENTY-TWO

Maxine

July 31, 1950

The conversation with Hazel had slid into dangerous territory. All of the secrets I'd kept for the past sixteen years whirled through my mind as we sat
in the gloom of El Quijote. I had to say something, to explain, but I couldn't
tell her everything and I only had myself to blame. I'd placed myself in this
situation, by wanting to be free to be an artist while still yielding to the pres-
sures from the Party. You can't have both, but I'd realized it too late. Realized
that, when it all comes crashing down, it's the people you love most who get
caught in the landslide.

I took a deep breath, knowing I only had a few minutes to make
this right, to make it make sense to Hazel without revealing
too much.

"They tricked me, Hazel. I was set up. I went into that meeting,
stupidly, with my guard down."

"I told you to bring my lawyer with you."

"I know, I know." I nodded but couldn't meet her eyes. "You were right. Roy Cohn talked around me and over me and I was intimidated."

In fact, Mr. Cohn had not been happy with my initial lukewarm responses to his list of names. I'd tried being as vague as possible, danced around giving any definite answer, and finally he'd leaned in so close I smelled his stale breath. "Your real name is Magnild Keller, I understand."

"It is." I'd tried to stay still, not recoil.

"An ugly name. I understand why you'd want to change it."

I remained silent. Waiting.

"And your *oma*, isn't that what they call a grandmother in German? An *oma*? She's living in Seattle, I've been told. She's not well."

"No, she's not." The money I'd been sending had enabled her to hire a helper around the house. In my last letter, I'd invited her to come live with me in California, where I could keep a closer eye on her. But now Roy Cohn had his talons in her.

"It would be terrible if she was suddenly deported back to Germany. I'd hate to see that."

The fact that both Mr. Cohn and Arthur, who sat on opposite sides of the political arena, would use the same tactic almost made me laugh. Instead, I broke out into a sweat.

Coming in, I'd thought that I had the power as a pretty young starlet. But he'd done his research, while I'd wandered in blind; I was a butterfly about to be pinned to a corkboard. "You can't do that," I said. "She doesn't know anyone back there, there's no one left."

"That would be tragic."

I began to shake. "You're threatening to hurt an old woman in order to get me to talk?"

"Look, Miss Mead, please don't get upset." He put down his pen. "Here's the truth: Any names we already have are people who have been confirmed, it's not like you're adding anything new to the mix. All you have to do at this point is concur. That's all we're asking. Is that really too much?"

Overwhelmed with fear, all of my training—both as an actress and as a spy—fell to the wayside. I could only imagine my grandmother stepping off an airplane in Germany, bewildered, clutching her purse to her chest as she looked around for a familiar face, and finding none.

So I'd cracked.

Hazel was staring at me oddly, and I realized I'd been lost in thought.

"Did you name me?" she asked.

"You aren't a communist and I told them that."

Hazel gave me a look of disgust. "You and I both know that's not the point. They asked me about Ben; did they bring up his name with you?"

I paused a moment. "He's gone, so really what does it matter either way?" The words sounded worse out loud than they had in my head. Sarcastic, derisive.

Hazel's face went from alarmed to appalled. "You're a monster. Even if he's the one who drew you into this, you would ruin the name of a good man, a soldier, just to get yourself out of trouble? To keep your fancy life in the limelight?"

Ben Ripley hadn't drawn me into this. In fact, I was the one trying to turn him. If I spoke those words out loud, I would be free from all the lies. But I couldn't.

Hazel sat back, arms crossed. "You're playing their game. That's the whole reason for this ridiculous exercise, to make you bow down to their level. How could you?"

I stayed quiet.

"Who else did you name? Tell me now. Tell me everyone."

"They had the names already, I wasn't telling them anything new." I tossed them off, one after another, as if by saying them fast, it would minimize the damage. "Philip Loeb, Clifford Odets, Burl Ives, Zero Mostel. They were already listed in *Red Channels*. Or had been named by someone else. I didn't add anyone new."

"You told Cohn they were communists?"

"I only mentioned people who were open about their affiliation in the past. I mean, it's public record. He wouldn't have let me off the hook any other way. And this way I could use my earnings to help you."

"All your excuses," sneered Hazel. "'He's dead.' 'She'd already admitted it.' You're a traitor and a snitch. I'll never forgive you."

The enormity of what I'd done hit me, hard. "They threatened to go after my family, my grandmother."

Hazel stared at me, fury in her eyes.

"Cohn said he'd deport my grandmother if I didn't cooperate. I had no choice. She only has me, I had to protect her. If Mr. Cohn sent my grandmother back to Germany, she'd never recover. She's too frail. It would kill her."

The waiter came by with refills but Hazel waved him away. "By renaming those who have already been named, you confirmed the politicians' view that there are subversives lurking around every corner who might be a danger to this country. You reminded everyone in the artistic community that they could be fired, have their career upended, have their lives ruined, if they don't do what you just did. You've prolonged the agony for all of us. These aren't just names, they're real people who'll be turned into pariahs because you added fuel to the fire."

"But the communists *are* everywhere, even if you don't see it."

"What do you mean?" Hazel gaped at me.

I'd said too much. "Mr. Cohn told me that by naming people, it showed that I'd broken with my past."

"You have no past. You went to one rally."

If she only knew. Confirming the names he already had was my way of declaring that I was done with the Communist Party, done with Arthur, and regretted all my terrible misdeeds.

"You know what Nazis did to people they suspected of not being on their side?" Hazel didn't wait for me to respond. "They asked people who were under suspicion, 'Who recruited you?' and 'Who did you recruit?' They did that in order to break down the social ties between them, to prevent any kind of organized resistance. It's no different here in the United States, where we're being asked to betray our friends. They're ripping our community apart, ripping it to shreds."

I had nothing to say to that. She was right, of course.

"You sicken me. Get out of my sight. Now."

I stood, shaking, feeling as if my bones were so ancient they might crumble into dust at any moment.

Up in my room, I packed up the last of my suitcases and trunks. I wouldn't be coming back to the Chelsea Hotel. I whispered goodbye to my room, to the place I'd come to love more than anywhere else on the earth, then called for the bellboys to bring my luggage downstairs before taking the elevator down to the lobby. Mr. Bard's office door was open, and I knocked softly. He looked up from his ledger.

"Miss Mead. How are you this morning?"

"I'm leaving, Mr. Bard."

He clicked his tongue. "I hear that we'll be seeing you soon on the silver screen. California, I'm guessing, is your destination. When shall we expect you back?"

"It's for good."

He looked as if I had broken his heart, and even laid a hand over his chest. God, I would miss this place. "Where shall we forward your mail?"

"I'll let you know once I'm settled. Thank you for everything." I stepped into the office, shut the door behind me, and moved closer. "If you don't mind, I'd like to take care of Miss Ripley's rent going forward. Well, not right away, but she may have trouble ahead."

He inhaled dramatically. "I've been reading the papers. She's in for a rough ride. But you know I always take care of my tenants in any way I possibly can."

"You do. We all appreciate that." The eclectic mix of art along the lobby walls and up the stairwell attested to that, works he'd accepted when a tenant wasn't flush. But it wasn't as if Hazel could write a play for him in lieu of rent. "When her troubles come, I'll cover her expenses. But you have to promise never to tell her. It'll just be between you and me."

He gave a toothy grin, enthralled by our intimacy. "Of course. You have my word."

With that, I left New York behind. Left Hazel behind.

I had no choice. At least, that's what I told myself.

❖

When I pulled into the MGM film studio in my cream convertible cabriolet, a gift from the movie's producers, everyone turned and stared. Not only at the car, but at the girl inside it, my bright red hair streaming in the wind, a perfect complement to my emerald silk dress. Exactly the reaction I'd hoped for. Several photographers and fans clustered around the car as I eased it into my spot, and I posed, preened, and signed until the very last one of them was satisfied.

I'd also hit up the studio heads for a low-slung, Spanish-style bungalow in Brentwood with a pretty pool out back. A magazine had taken photos of me in a bathing suit, lounging away, last week. I hoped Hazel would never see them.

So far, my plan had worked.

Up on the roof with Lavinia and Hazel, stunned by the news of the movie role, I'd decided to burn bigger and brighter than ever. The one way I could stop Arthur and his cronies from coming after me was by becoming a big movie star. No, not big. A huge movie star, one whose every move was covered by a panting public. By placing myself in the spotlight, I'd make myself untouchable. I hired a publicist to set up interviews, offered to talk about the making of the movie with any reporter who'd have me. I got myself written up in every rag out there. That was step one.

We only had another week of shooting in California before the entire cast and crew flew off to Costa Brava in Spain to do the bulk of the scenes. The farther away from the United States, the better.

I reached into my car to grab my purse, and when I looked up, there was Arthur leaning over the other side, smiling at me with a quiet fury.

Step two. If I didn't lose my nerve.

He looked like a native Californian, dressed in a Panama hat, crisp cotton pants, and a plaid shirt. Almost like he was trying too hard, in fact. He'd lost weight and when he took off his sunglasses, I noticed the skin under his eyes sagged like an older man's. "I missed you, Max. We were surprised when you stopped answering our phone calls, didn't leave us a forwarding address. That's not like you. Luckily, you're not that hard to track down."

I reminded myself to stay calm, not show fear. "I'm shooting the movie."

"It's great to see you." He walked around the car and placed a hand on my arm, gave it a squeeze. He smelled of coconuts, the final touch in his tropical ensemble. The thick scent made me nauseous, and a trickle of sweat ran down my back.

I stayed silent.

"Don't be afraid, Max. You know you're always safe with me. I'm not going anywhere. Is there a place we can talk?"

I didn't want to bring him into my dressing room, best to stay in public. I gasped for air, my lungs betraying my anxiety at the sight of him.

"You all right?"

"I'm fine," I whispered. "I need some coffee. Do you want to join me in the commissary?"

He considered it a moment. "Sure, babe."

I checked my watch. "I have to be in hair and makeup in twenty minutes."

"Whatever you say. I have all the time in the world."

I shook as I carried the coffees to a table at the back where Arthur sat, waiting. He'd probably been tailing me, watching me, for some time now. I looked around. The commissary wasn't very full, it was too early for lunch and too late for breakfast. Still, enough people stopped me and asked questions about the movie as I made my way through. I had a small army of supporters nearby in case he tried to pull anything sneaky.

I sat down, reminding myself to breathe. The thought of even having one sip of coffee made me sick to my stomach, and I pushed it away.

"You're not thirsty anymore?" Arthur poured a teaspoon of sugar into my cup. "I know you like it sweet."

I decided to go on the offensive. "Did you steal my stationery and set up Charlie and Hazel?"

He tried, and failed, to keep a straight face. "What makes you think I'd do such a thing?" His eyes crinkled with amusement.

"It's not a joke. You wrote that note to Charlie, didn't you, and said it was from me?"

"It worked like a charm. The tabloids ran with it for days, and our boy Julius was moved to the inside pages, at least temporarily."

"I thought we'd decided against it." The words came out girlish and weak, plaintive.

He stuck a spoon in my coffee and stirred it, over and over. I watched, not wanting to meet his eyes, hypnotized by the clinking of metal against ceramic. "Yeah, well, you ran away from us, Max. They didn't like that one bit. Did you really think you'd be safe in California?"

"I wasn't safe in New York, what with Roy Cohn interviewing me and all."

"We don't like the idea of losing track of you, though."

I threw up my hands. "I'm an actress who came to Los Angeles for a part. It's not like I was trying to shake you." I knew he didn't believe me. "You got want you wanted, right?"

"True. Hazel and Charlie's scandal took the heat off. I was eventually able to get out, as were a couple of others. So the question remains, 'What's next?'" His knee touched mine under the small table and I stopped myself from recoiling.

"I'm shooting a movie, that's what's next."

It was as if he didn't even hear me. "We have to rebuild. Start over. It'll be like when we first met. That time was special to me. Do you remember?"

I did. Back when he was charming and kind. He'd sweeten me up and then catch me off guard with an offhand insult, a sarcastic remark. At the time, I dismissed it, thinking he'd had a bad day, that he was under too much pressure. I did whatever I could to soften him up and avoid another caustic sneer.

How I wish I could go back to that moment and do something different, knowing that I could manage on my own and didn't need to twist myself into the smallest person possible to please him. I would've sneered right back and told him to go screw himself. I would've used the biggest, most booming voice I had—and I could boom when I needed to, just ask the folks in the back row of the Biltmore—and sent him running for the door.

It wasn't too late, was it?

"Arthur. I'm out."

"No, you're not.

I recognized the steely edge to his voice from when he was dealing with a reluctant operative. No one went against Arthur's wishes. All I needed to do was forget to lock a window one night and I'd be a cold corpse by the next morning.

Arthur finished his coffee and took mine for himself. "You're not alone. You must remember that. You have me, you have your grandmother . . ."

The threat was implicit. Waves of panic poured off my body. I looked around, but no one else seemed to sense the danger. Only me.

He reached over to smooth a curl behind my ear. I flinched as if I'd been hit.

I never wanted to be touched by him again.

"Look, Arthur. I'm no longer interested in working for you, or for the Party. You should move on, find someone else without my complicated history. Really, why take a risk?"

He licked his lips. "Don't forget the reason you're here is because of us. Because we paved your way." He waited a beat. "No. You can never leave the Party. Or me."

I sat back and crossed my arms. "You don't get to call the shots anymore."

"Watch it, Maxine. You're going to be very sorry if you continue to talk like this."

It was now or never.

Before I'd left the Chelsea for good, I'd made one more stop, at Lavinia's. A young woman stood in the middle of her living room—Lavinia had started taking on private acting students as a way to supplement her income since being blacklisted—and I apologized for the interruption. "Lavinia, I have to give you something."

"I'm in the middle of a lesson, come back in an hour." Lavinia turned back to her student. "Once again, and remember the character is trying *not* to cry. The tension comes from her fighting against the tears."

"No, Lavinia," I insisted. "I'm leaving, for good."

She walked over to the door and stood close, concern in her eyes. "What's going on, Maxine?"

"I want you to take this." I handed over a sealed, brown-paper package consisting of all the pages I'd stored in my mantel: my diary, as well as detailed records of what I'd done and who I'd met with, of Arthur's involvement in the Party, and my own. "Keep it hidden. Please don't read it. If anything happens to me, give it to the FBI."

"Maxine, are you in trouble?"

"I won't be, if everything works out."

"This means you're leaving us all behind. Me, Hazel?" Lavinia sensed the truth, I was sure. She'd known me since I was so young, knew where I came from, who had influenced me. So many times I'd considered confiding in her but then pulled back, worried that I would be putting her in danger. Yet here I was doing so now. A miserable shame washed over me.

"You can trust me with this, Max." Lavinia's voice was a hoarse whisper. "Go wherever you need to go and keep yourself safe. I think I know what this is about, and I don't blame you, if so. You were just a girl, I should have stepped in."

I'd hugged her goodbye and left.

As the California sun poured through the commissary windows, turning the room gold, I squared my shoulders, lifted my chin, and looked Arthur in the eye. "I kept a diary. A detailed diary, about my involvement with the Party. Yours, too. If anything happens to me, instructions have been given to hand it over to the Feds."

He studied me to see if I was telling the truth. "You think you're so smart."

"No. I think you're desperate. You said yourself that the Party had been compromised."

"We will rebuild. It may take some time, but we will."

"I'm stronger than you are now. People will notice if I go missing, or turn up dead. My fans will want to know the truth and so will the police. If anything happens to my grandmother or anyone I know, I will make a commotion like you've never heard before. I will roar and you'll go down."

"What, you'll publish your silly diary and expose all our secrets? You'll get sent to the electric chair with the rest of us."

"I'm willing to lose everything. Are you?"

I caught a flash of fear in his eyes. He flicked his fingers at me, an odd, persnickety gesture that didn't suit him. "You're a flea."

That's when I knew that I'd got to him, that I finally had the upper hand. Arthur had been trained to be economical, stealthy. With that superfluous flick, he revealed what we both knew: Arthur was no longer the controller, he was the controlled.

"Miss Mead, is everything all right?"

A beefy young security guard, whom I'd chatted up the first day on the lot, stood just behind Arthur, the buttons straining on his uniform.

Arthur turned and looked up. The cords of his neck stood out, white and thick. I wondered what it would be like to wrap my hands around his neck and strangle him as he'd done to me. To tighten my grip and feel his throat under my fingers.

I spoke clearly and loudly, from my chest. "This man needs to be escorted off the lot and banned from ever coming here again."

Arthur held his palms out. "I'm leaving. I'm leaving."

I wondered if he had any last words for me, but the guard grabbed him by the collar before he could say a thing.

In my dressing room, I sat still, calm and composed, as the makeup artist painted my face. I thought of Hazel and how I'd betrayed her in ways both big and small. A terrible choice had to be made, and I'd taken the coward's way out. I'd make it up to her, though, make sure she was well taken care of. I'd reach out to her again when things settled back down.

When the world righted itself.

CHAPTER TWENTY-THREE

Hazel

December 1950

Hazel practically fell out of the taxi onto the pavement outside the Chelsea Hotel, she was so tired. A bellman took her luggage from the trunk and helped her over the curb. She tipped him as much as she could spare, knowing that the bellmen at the Chelsea rarely had the opportunity to perform the more profitable hotel duties of escorting guests and their belongings up to a room—one of the drawbacks of employment at what was really an artists' commune.

The Christmas tree in the lobby had been commandeered by Winnifred and Wanda, Hazel guessed, glistening with baubles and tinsel that overwhelmed the poor pine. An enormous golden angel at the very top listed precariously to one side, ready to be toppled at any moment by a wayward gust of wind from the open door.

At least she was home, if only for a two-week break for the holidays. Hazel was back to understudying—the only job she'd been offered since the debacle, and only because the producer had been eager to see her grovel for the part—this time in a tour of an Ibsen play across the sadder towns of America in an effort to bring the classics to the masses. The masses didn't care much for Ibsen, and the stage manager had whispered to Hazel that the second leg of the tour was up in the air as the big bus hurtled through New Jersey.

It was a paycheck, one that she could really use right now.

The thought of money stopped her from going right up to her room. She backtracked and knocked on Mr. Bard's office door.

"There you are! Welcome home!"

His effusive greeting and hug almost made her weep. She attributed her silly emotions to the fatigue of travel, and dug into her purse for an envelope.

"Mr. Bard, I have rent money for you for the next couple of months. Thank you for being so patient with me."

He shook his head. "No, my dear girl. You are a gift to our city, to our community, and I will accept half of it only." His generosity moved her even further, and he chuckled and handed her a handkerchief. "No need to cry."

"It's been a long couple of months, and it's so nice to be back. Thank you. I'll be out again on tour in a couple of weeks, so there will be more money coming in." Hopefully.

He plucked the envelope from her hand, gathered up half of the bills, and returned the rest to her. "Buy yourself something pretty for Christmas, all right?"

She turned to go but he called after her. "Wait a moment, I have some mail for you. Special delivery, one of them."

Ugh. In the five months since she and Charlie had been caught in flagrante delicto, she'd hoped the hate mail had died down. That terrible summer seemed so long ago, and she hadn't heard from Charlie since. One day she'd even stopped by the offices of American Business Consultants in the hopes of finding out where he'd disappeared to, but they'd rebuffed her, which came as no surprise. His absence, and that of Maxine, left a dark hole in her life, though she hated herself for thinking so.

She grabbed the stack of mail and thanked Mr. Bard once more.

Her preference would have been to fall into a tub of hot water and soak, letting the muscles tensed from days on the road work out their kinks. But two weeks wasn't much time, and she had to make the most of it. She changed into clean clothes and refreshed her face with some cool water before heading uptown. Her mother hugged her and brought her inside the apartment, where the smell of a pot roast made Hazel's stomach growl. For all Ruth's faults, she was an excellent cook.

Ruth embraced Hazel and took her coat. "Come in, see your father, and we'll eat right off."

Hazel handed over the bag of groceries she'd picked up at the store on Broadway. While she was earning money, she wanted to share the largesse. Or perhaps it was a proud gesture, to prove that she was still a successful artist and that nothing had changed. Even though everything had changed.

"You are a dear." Ruth kissed her on the cheek and laughed—a light, tinkling sound better suited to an ingenue. Hazel and Ben had been certain she'd cultivated the giggle as a schoolgirl and refused to part with it, despite her advancing years.

Both her parents had aged greatly since Hazel's fall from grace. Their theatrical friends had mostly abandoned them after the news of Hazel's affair with Charlie broke, and they were left outcasts. Her father had faded into himself more and more, no longer making any grunts of approval or even raising his eyebrows, while her mother had become a constant source of noise, either humming or talking back to the radio, as if to make up for the silence.

How far they'd come. When Hazel was a struggling understudy, Ruth had been angry at what she perceived to be her lack of ambition and refusal to take direction. When Hazel made it into the big time, Ruth resented her independence. Yet these days, her mother was nothing but supportive and kind, and no longer controlling. She'd stood by Hazel, unlike most of the others, and only wanted her daughter to be happy. Hazel's trajectory had allowed her mother to finally work through her sticky grudges and come out the other side a softer woman.

"You don't have to go back to that hotel, Hazel." Ruth placed a large slice of beef on Hazel's plate before turning to her husband and cutting his food with a practiced efficiency. "You could move back into your old room."

"I'm fine there. Thank you, though."

"Why pay all that rent money when you're on the road most of the time, anyway?"

"Mr. Bard's been very understanding."

"He'll get tired of it before long, trust me. I really don't understand it."

Hazel knew there was no point in explaining. True, economically it made sense to move back home. But there was no place like the hotel, her oasis of crazy calm. She loved hearing Mr. Kleinsinger's piano compositions as they drifted down and around the serpentine stairway from his room on the tenth floor, like a melodious ghost. Sure, his pet boa constrictor occasionally turned up in the hallway, but no one really seemed to mind. Artsy and crazy were one and the same here, no questions asked.

It was the only place she could write, as well. The only place she wanted to write. Not that she'd had much luck lately. The two scripts she'd tried to submit under a different name had been rejected. No doubt the radio producers had asked around and figured out her true identity. All the blacklisted writers were trying the same scam.

Back at the hotel later that evening, determined to not waste a minute, Hazel sat at her desk by the window and rolled a sheet of paper into her typewriter. Really, she should go to bed and start fresh in the morning, but waking up to a blank piece of paper tomorrow would be the end of her. Better to get something down now, even if it was just a page, something she could shape and edit, than to have nothing at all.

What, though? A new play? A novel?

She could write about her terrible experiences of the past year, but it was too close. No one cared, anyway. Her voice had been stifled and that particular fire within her extinguished.

For a split second, she thought of stepping down the hallway and talking it through with Maxine, before remembering that Maxine was gone and had betrayed her. On the tour bus back to New York, Hazel had opened a magazine that one of the actresses had left lying on the seat to a full-page spread of Maxine and her leading man somewhere in Europe, posing for photos, Maxine's mouth wide and smiling. But Hazel knew that smile. That smile meant she had something to prove. That smile was her defense when she felt small.

Hazel ripped the sheet of paper out of the typewriter, rolled it into a tight ball, and pitched it across the room, before instantly regretting wasting a perfectly good piece of paper. The stack of mail sat on the very edge of the desk. A diversion.

Only one was an anonymous letter of fury, which she dumped right into the trash. A couple were from playwrights she knew in passing, offering their support. That was an unexpected surprise.

Maybe eventually the tide would turn and she'd no longer be a pariah.

The one that had been sent special delivery had no return address. She sliced it open, wary, as if a goblin might jump out, but when she saw the scrawl at the bottom, she gasped.

Charlie.

He apologized for not reaching out sooner, but wrote that it was safer for him to remain at a distance. He'd sent the letter to Mr. Bard inside a larger envelope, with instructions for him to pass it directly to Hazel.

The note was terse, lacking any warmth. He said he'd be in town over Christmas and asked if they could meet December 26 at noon, at the New York Public Library on Fifth Avenue. He'd be waiting by the information desk in the Reading Room.

She imagined walking into the Reading Room, sun pouring in through the arched windows, and finding Charlie standing there. Maybe he'd smile and reach out his arms to her. God, how she missed him.

She shook off the image. Charlie had abandoned her right when she needed him most. He was probably upstate, doing his father's bidding, or had joined the FBI after all and wanted to continue on with his spy hunt.

She put his letter to the side and opened the last one in the stack.

It was from Floyd, dated two days ago. He said he was in a terrible state and needed to see her, that he was staying at the Taft hotel in midtown.

The hotel operator put her through, but there was no answer in Floyd's room. Hazel left a message, saying she was on her way, and rushed out into the night.

❖

The Taft hotel rose out of the sidewalks of Seventh Avenue like a prison, brown and imposing. Hazel went straight up to the room number Floyd had given her and knocked on the door.

No answer.

Finally, after what seemed like ages, she heard footsteps on the other side of the door.

"Hazel, my darling!"

Floyd welcomed her inside as if he were throwing a garden party, all smiles and cheek kisses. He looked paler than she remembered, but maybe it was just from the dimness. Only one lamp over by the window was lit, the bulb too weak to reach the corners of the small room. Floyd gestured for Hazel to take a seat in the lone chair as he poured her a drink from the bar.

"Is the open window all right? I can close it if you like."

The cool breeze offset the smoky, stagnant air inside. She didn't remember ever seeing Floyd with a cigarette before, but the overflowing ashtray on the nightstand pointed to a serious habit. "No, it's perfectly fine. Refreshing." She took a sip of her drink, pure vodka. "I'm sorry I didn't get here sooner."

"No matter. You're here now."

How he'd changed from that sweet boy in Naples, sketching caricatures of the men, handing the paper over with a shy smile that spread to a blush as the soldier burst into pleased laughter. Hazel wondered how he'd draw himself, now. His ears still stuck out like a schoolboy's but his forehead was lined, his eyes puffy and red. He'd filled out since the war, his shoulders and arms thickening with muscles, but now seemed to be reversing course, his limbs and even his fingers longer and thinner than she remembered.

"What's happened? We've been so worried about you."

He perched on the bed with his drink. "I didn't name names, just so we're clear about that."

Rumors had flown since Floyd had disappeared, that he'd turned on his friends, that he wasn't who he appeared to be. Hazel had swatted down every one and defended him, and would continue to do so until she knew the truth. It was such a relief to see him, after all this time.

"I know you and Charlie were close." He took a big sip of his drink, spilling a little and wiping it with his sleeve, like a kid. "I don't blame you one bit for what came out in the papers, he is a delightful man. Not like his father."

A flash of heat went through her. "We're not together anymore."

"I'm sorry to hear that." They sat silently for a minute, before Floyd let out a sharp laugh. "Did you know they apparently have box scores for us now? They're released every month and passed around to all the ad agencies."

"What do you mean?"

"It's a guide to who's in and who's out. For example, it'll say, 'José Ferrer: Avoid his latest movie.' I was told that mine said, 'Floyd Jenkins: Done for good.'"

So many decent people, like Floyd, were being bulldozed. "I know it seems awful now, but you must hang in there. You're so talented and a delight to work with. You'll have a bang-up career again, I'm sure."

"They're still bringing me in for interviews," said Floyd.

She brightened. This was a good sign, that the producers were still seeing him. Maybe all was not lost. "That's great, who?"

"No. Not anyone in show business. The FBI."

The fight drained out of her.

"I keep telling them it was a silly comment in front of friends.

'Oh, right, all of us are commies.' It was sarcasm, I tell them. But they don't care." It was obvious Floyd replayed the conversation in his mind, over and over, reliving the moment when he'd unknowingly sealed his fate. "All because of an orange dress. Sorry, *tangerine.*"

Like Maxine, Brandy was working nonstop these days.

Hazel was still unsure of why he'd called her here. "Maybe I can help with your situation. Do you have a lawyer?" She opened her purse, searched for a business card, and laid it on the side table. "Mr. Stone was quite helpful to me. Here's his number."

He offered up a half smile. "Right, thank you for that. I'll ring him."

Floyd had no money to afford a lawyer like Stone, Hazel realized. She offered to loan him some, but he wouldn't accept it.

Another uncomfortable silence.

Floyd's gift as an artist was his sensitivity. But that same gift made the real world much harder for him than it was for Hazel. The terrible sanctions against him had wrecked him.

"Don't lose hope," she said. "You can do other things, you're a brilliant artist. Let's see what else we can find you. A job in an art gallery, perhaps. Or wait, what about teaching?"

"No one will hire me after next week. They've made that much clear."

"Next week? Who've made it clear? What do you mean?"

"I'm not who you think I am. The deadline has finally arrived, and since I refused to cooperate, they're going to tell the world who I am."

By now she was utterly confused. "Who are you?"

"They called me back, week after week, hoping I'd cave in. I suppose they've finally realized who they're up against. That I won't turn on my friends." He let out an anguished sob. "You see, they know that I love men. They have photos, proof." He waved one hand in the air. "And with that, the curtain falls."

A chill ran through Hazel. That would be the end of Floyd's career, no matter what he chose to do. While Hazel couldn't care less who Floyd loved, as long as he was happy, no one in the industry would hire someone who'd been exposed as a homosexual. He'd be shunned, even worse than Hazel was. That the FBI would stoop to this level infuriated Hazel.

"That's not acceptable," she said. "We will not be railroaded. I've got your back, Floyd, and don't you forget it." Floyd wavered a tiny bit from side to side. Hazel glanced at the vodka bottle, which was two-thirds empty. Tonight was probably not the best time to figure out his plan B. "Look, you get a good night's sleep and I'll come by tomorrow and take you out for breakfast. In the light of day, it won't seem so bad. We'll find you a decent job, I promise."

His eyelids drooped and stayed closed. She rose and gently extricated the glass from his hand, placing it on the bar next to hers. "For now, lie down and get some rest."

"Thanks, Hazel." He was awake again, his blue eyes shining. "Thank you for coming to the rescue."

"I'm sorry I've been away for so long. I know how lonely it can be when you feel like you've been abandoned."

"We've all been abandoned. I hear Maxine's star is ascending rapidly, just as ours is falling." He began to cry. "They say she talked. She told them whatever they wanted to hear. How could she have done that?"

She didn't want to discuss Maxine. "We have each other." Hazel leaned over Floyd and gave him an awkward hug. "Enough being maudlin. One day I'll write a zany comedy about this year and you'll do the costumes and everyone will love us once again."

"We'll do that, Hazel."

When she left, she closed the room door behind her, quietly, in case Floyd had already fallen asleep.

Not for the first time, she wished she had Maxine—the old Maxine—by her side. She would have cajoled Floyd out of his funk, got him back on his feet. With her film earnings, she also would've been able to help out financially. But neither Hazel nor Floyd would ever touch a penny, knowing that her riches came right out of their own pockets. She got to work precisely because she'd thrown them and others like them to the wolves.

The elevator opened but Hazel hesitated. The elderly couple inside glared at her.

"Sorry, I forgot something," she called out as the doors slid shut.

She hurried back down the hall. It didn't feel right, leaving Floyd so fast; he shouldn't be alone.

She pushed open the door, quietly, and saw the curtains flapping in the breeze. She walked in intending to close the window so he wouldn't wake up in the morning with a cold, but stopped short.

The bed was empty, the door to the bathroom shut. She stood next to the door, listening for sounds of water running, of movement. Nothing.

"Floyd?" She knocked gently. "I came back. I wanted to make sure you're really all right."

Nothing.

She opened the door a crack, embarrassed to be doing so. Then farther. The bathroom was empty.

She glanced around the small room as her throat closed with panic. The closet door was ajar, he couldn't be hiding in there. The bedclothes were rumpled. As she leaned over to check under the bed, because that's the only other place he could possibly be, someone outside screamed.

Hazel straightened. The window was fully open. She hadn't noticed it when she first came in the room, that it wasn't just cracked like before. It was wide open. Wide enough for someone to put one leg over, then the other.

She rushed to it, horrified and certain she was wrong. Floyd had decided to go down to the bar. He'd taken the stairs and that's why she couldn't find him. That's why he wasn't here.

More screams.

She made herself look down, where his crumpled form lay ten stories below. He'd landed on his side, and lay there like he'd just fallen asleep, hands tucked under his cheek, the only sign of violence the red blood pooling around him.

ACT THREE

T *he ghosts of the Chelsea Hotel draw closer, eager to greet their latest member the moment the soul leaves the flesh. Over the years, the dust of the hotel's many occupants has spread thinly over the walls, the floors, the mantels, and the hallways, though only a small number remain in spirit. The handrail on the stairs holds the residue of actors and poets, singers and dancers, passed from guest to guest. Great successes and bitter failures, or bitter successes and great failures? No matter.*

The dust lingers in the air, and when the woman breathes it in, her lungs fill with the heady hope of the innocent. Breathe again and it's the desolation of the lost. Close now, but she keeps breathing.

CHAPTER TWENTY-FOUR

Hazel

March 1967

The cloying scent of marijuana wafted across the lobby of the Chelsea Hotel as Hazel returned from her morning walk, the obvious culprits yet another group of long-haired musicians, judging from the mix of duffel bags and instrument cases scattered about. They looked like they'd been waiting for their rooms for a while, and had dug in for the long haul. One man was fast asleep on a low banquette, another slung a jean-clad leg over the arm of a chunky Victorian chair and strummed a guitar.

In the past several years, the hotel had attracted a different sort of artist than had come before: Beat poets and beaten ladies of the night, rumpled folk singers and vacant-looking pop artists. They scurried down the halls and stumbled down the stairway, making the place feel overwhelmed, congested, and unseemly. Even the walls of the lobby were chaotic, filled with a riot of paintings whose tight arrangement—less than an inch between frames in some cases—rendered any serious appraisal of the works impossible.

Hazel stepped over a guitar case and breezed forward, not wanting to appear like some fussy old lady—after all, she was only forty-seven—who remembered with great nostalgia the days when the Chelsea Hotel was, if not elegant, at least respectable. The place had acquired a dirty mystique in the past seventeen years.

The communists on the first floor had been usurped by languid, underdressed prostitutes and their pimps, but none of this seemed to bother the permanent residents, who had gotten used to the parade of new bohemians who made the hotel their home for days or years at a time, the hippies, the groupies, the international artists and novelists who came and went.

She'd just completed her daily, brisk walk up to Central Park and back down along Seventh Avenue, although she always crossed to the west side at Fifty-First Street, not wanting to pass the spot where Floyd's broken body had landed.

Floyd's funeral had fallen on the same day that Charlie had asked Hazel to meet him at the library. Hazel had decided it was a sign that she be done with all that, done with the fierce pain of fighting against a machine that was so much bigger than she was. Floyd's death had closed her down, she had nothing left. On her way to the service that morning, she'd dropped off a letter with the information clerk at the library and asked her to give it to Charlie when he appeared. She told her to look for a dark-haired man with a dimpled chin who would show up around noon. She'd written him that she'd moved on, found someone new, and it was best they not see each other again. It was the only way she knew that she could force him out of her life completely.

"Hazel, Stanley wants to see you," said the Chelsea's day clerk.

When David Bard passed away three years earlier, his son

Stanley took over his duties with the incompetent enthusiasm of a golden retriever. Not that David had been the most efficient hotel manager, but where the maids tended to blandly disregard David's directives, they openly mocked Stanley, who often laughed along with them, as if he were in on the joke.

Hazel stepped back over the guitar case and turned into Stanley's office, where the Spanish leather padding on the walls reeked of cigarette smoke and the clutter had reached epic proportions. Stanley rose as she entered, a lanky man wearing a stretched-out sweater badly in need of a trip to the dry cleaner's.

"Hazel, how are you?" He gestured for her to sit.

She looked at her watch. "My shift starts in five minutes."

"That's fine. If you're a little late, it won't matter."

She'd been working the switchboard of the hotel for what felt like forever. It was a ghastly old piece of wiring beside the front desk, a throwback to another era that badly needed updating. The antiquated system often crossed lines, so Hazel would end up connecting a stoned actress on the second floor with the maudlin dress designer on the sixth, the two of them making no sense at all while refusing to hang up. There were days when Hazel was excoriated for not putting a call through fast enough, or was stuck chatting with Mr. Thomson because she was too polite to interrupt his musings. But David, and then Stanley, had let her work a couple of shifts each week in return for a free room, and for that she was thankful.

The rest of her living expenses Hazel covered with a weekly beat reviewing theater for a downtown newspaper. Lavinia, once again coming to the rescue, had connected Hazel with the editor, who allowed her to write under the pen name W. S. Pear and gushed over her reviews, which he said bristled with sharp observations. While reviewers for *The New York Times* and the *Post* still carried a lot of weight, the "in" crowd knew to look for Pear's column for the real skinny. The work kept Hazel connected to the theater world, which she still adored in spite of how it had mistreated her in the past.

"We need to make a couple of minor changes," said Stanley. He rifled through the pile of yellowed papers on his desk before giving up on whatever he was looking for. "There's a rock group here, called something crazy like the Chipper Skulls. These bands, I can't keep track of them anymore. Why are they so confusing?"

She shrugged, unsure of what this had to do with her. Better not to interrupt, as he'd make his way back to his point sooner or later.

"They want to rehearse but say the rooms they're staying in are too small. I said to them, 'We're not a music studio,' but they won't listen, and told me they'll just practice right there in the lobby. Can you imagine?" His voice rose an octave, a sure sign that he was irritated. "However, I think I've finally straightened it all out. You see, they need a large room to rehearse, and I thought we could do a little switcheroo."

"How do you mean?"

"Well, your room is one of the original ones. It wasn't chopped up, and so for a little while, let's put you in 732."

"You want me to change rooms?"

"Just for a little while."

She knew what that meant. He could get more money for her current room. A paying customer. Unfortunately, she had no lease to protect her, as his father had tended to not bother with leases after the first year, either unable or unwilling to deal with the paperwork. In any case, it wasn't as if she paid rent, so she really had nothing to stand on.

She'd lived in the same room for so long, the idea of moving scared her more than she'd care to admit. Her parents had died within six months of each other a decade ago. This was her home. "But 732 is tiny, a cubbyhole. I won't be able to fit everything in there."

"Right. We can put some things down in storage, in the basement."

No way. Stanley often offered new tenants a crack at whatever was in the storage room when they first came on board, in order to get in their good graces. She imagined some wasted poet fingering her favorite lamp with the beaded shade, or the subdued watercolors she'd picked up at the flea market.

"When do you need my room by?" Panic made her voice shaky.

Stanley ducked his head. "Is it too much? I'm so sorry. It's too much. My father would be so unhappy with me."

David Bard would also be unhappy at the way the more valuable paintings tended to disappear from the lobby walls every so often, most likely to enhance his son's private collection. Stanley might be goofy, but he wasn't dumb.

In any event, Stanley wasn't going to change his mind, and she had nothing to negotiate with. "It's fine."

"Great, how soon do you think you can pull the trigger? We'll have the staff help out, you won't have to lift a thing."

"I guess I can be out by the end of next week."

He looked up into space, as if calculating some complicated algorithm. "How about Monday?"

"That's three days away."

"It's an easy move, you won't even notice the difference."

Room 732 could barely fit a twin bed. The one time she'd been inside, invited by a choreographer whose name she couldn't remember, Hazel had noticed that the curtains were stapled to the window frame. Stapled.

But she couldn't leave the hotel. After all these years, it kept her connected to the heart of the city. Mr. Thomson still held his memorable cocktail parties, where a few times she'd spotted Arthur Miller and his third wife, a photographer, who lived in room 614. No one mentioned Hazel's play, probably out of politeness, and that was fine with her. She'd refilled drinks and acted as an ersatz maid, passing around the canapés and delighting in the lively conversation between artists, filmmakers, writers, and composers. She didn't mind being on the outside looking in, as long as they let her look, and as long as she still got to write. Luckily, Lavinia was still going strong, confined to a wheelchair but making appearances at the Lavinia Smarts Acting Studio when the mood struck, and between the lively gang at the Chelsea and her nightly forays to the theater, Hazel's life was full, if not particularly joyous. And that was fine.

"Very well. I'll start packing."

"I'm sorry, Hazel. I promise it won't be forever. Just until the band's finished up. They might even play a concert on the roof this summer. If they do, I'll make sure you get a ticket."

She couldn't imagine anything worse. "Thank you, Stanley."

After her shift, she popped into Lavinia's apartment, where her friend was dozing by the window, her gray hair almost translucent in the sunlight. She stirred as Hazel entered. "Hello?"

"It's me, Hazel. Sorry to wake you, I'll come back later."

"No, no. Come, sit."

Lavinia had grown thinner with every passing year, her bracelets flopping around her tiny wrists, often falling off onto her lap. Her eyes, though, were as sharp as ever, her opinions strong and strident. God help the acting student who showed up unprepared for class, as Lavinia's thundering tirades were legendary in the theater community.

After the news of Floyd's terrible death, as well as the injustices he'd suffered, spread throughout the theater district, the Broadway community banded together to mount a bulwark against the blacklist, with theater owners successfully employing actors who otherwise couldn't get hired. The ever-changing list of producers behind each production, as well as the fact that no one knew if a show would run for three performances or three years, made organized boycotts too difficult, and so after that terrible year, the theater world began to flourish once again, unimpeded by the political machinations of Washington. Hazel, of course, was shunned from this support due to the scandal with Charlie, though even her pariah status had faded with time.

At least Joseph McCarthy was no longer around to cause trouble. He'd tried to go after the US Army in '53 for communist subversion, but his bullying tactics finally fell flat and his popularity plummeted. When he died in 1957, Hazel was not sorry.

"I have something for you," said Lavinia. She reached for an envelope on a side table, but her shaky hand couldn't grasp it.

Hazel picked it up and took the chair opposite. "What is it?"

"Open it up."

Inside were two tickets to the Tony Awards, to be held at the Shubert Theatre in two days' time. The note inside explained they were a gift from Jeffrey Hubert, a former student of Lavinia's who'd recently mounted a revival of *Wartime Sonata* to some acclaim at a claustrophobic downtown theater. While Hazel had granted the rights for the production, she'd avoided most of the rehearsals and sat through only one performance, her words too dear and painful to hear spoken out loud. The production had a small budget and a bare-bones set, and Hazel had kept her expectations low.

"How nice," she said. "That Jeffrey is a lovely boy. Too bad I'm not going."

"Yes, you are. I insist." Lavinia pounded her closed fist on one knee. "You deserve to get some kudos already, kiddo. Look at that article in *The New York Times*, you're on the rise."

In a way, Lavinia was right. To Hazel's surprise, the play had sold out and been extended, twice. Soon after the glowing reviews appeared, Hazel and the director had been interviewed for a feature in *The New York Times*, where Hazel spoke with bitter honesty about her experiences during the McCarthy era. When the reporter inquired about her current relationship with the famous movie star Maxine Mead, Hazel had hedged, mumbling something about how actors were always falling out of touch, that it was the nature of the business.

She examined the two tickets. "It's out of the question. There's no way I could sit in the audience and watch playwrights and actors accept awards, knowing that I'd been snubbed, cast out. Knowing that if I'd begun my career in the late 1950s, after McCarthy was censured and the blacklist drifted into oblivion, I would have had a clear shot at a career as a playwright."

"Oh, stop with the self-righteous pity. You were caught in bed with the enemy, let's not forget." Hazel began to protest, but Lavinia cut her off. "I know, I know, true love and all that. In any event, what happened happened, the good and the bad. I would go myself if I wasn't stuck in this wheelchair. Before you know it, you'll be like me, an invalid, and wish you'd said yes more than you'd said no."

"You're far from an invalid."

Lavinia's voice dropped to a lower register, one that she used only when she was dead serious. "Please, Hazel. Jeffrey insists and he'll be quite upset with me if you don't."

Up in her room, Hazel put the envelope with the tickets on the mantel of her fireplace. She couldn't decide anything right now, first she had to deal with this ridiculous move. She started by blindly sorting through her clothes, tossing them into a suitcase. The dress she'd worn to the opening of *Wartime Sonata* on Broadway, the old winter coat she should've replaced a few years ago, the inside of the pockets reduced to shreds, but still couldn't afford to throw out. She stopped and poured a glass of wine to steady her nerves. Hazel spent too much time alone these days, which meant that she could get lost in her head if she weren't careful, the memories churning past like thunderclouds.

A knock on the door interrupted her bleak thoughts.

"Who is it?"

These days, it wasn't smart to open your door without checking first—drug dealers roamed the hallways, and every so often someone went out in a body bag, from either an overdose or a murder—but the peephole to Hazel's door had been painted over years ago.

A muffled voice responded.

"Who? I can't hear you."

The familiar voice, louder, echoed in her ears.

"Hazel, open up. It's me. It's Charlie. Charlie Butterfield."

❦︙❧

Hazel opened the door. Charlie stepped back as she did so, as if a gust of wind had blown him off-balance.

She put a hand to her hair, suddenly aware of how different she must look to him. In the past decade, she'd let it grow long, like the hippie girls who paraded through the halls in cutoff shorts and see-through tunics. Well, perhaps not quite as hippie as all that. But her formerly blond locks were now streaked with gray and her face, she knew, showed evidence of the hardship of her middle years.

Like many men with boyish features, Charlie didn't seem to have aged much in the almost two decades they'd been apart. Just a few speckles of peppery gray along the temples and some lines at the corners of his eyes, but that was it.

"Charlie."

He looked past her to the scattering of clothes and suitcases on the floor. "You going somewhere?"

She stepped back, surveying the mess. "You could say that."

"I was hoping we could talk. Can we talk? I don't want to intrude, but I have something important to tell you."

She studied him, uncertain. After all this time, what did they really have to say to each other? She didn't want to bother explaining her decisions. Nor did she want to hear his.

Charlie must have sensed her reluctance. "Look, I don't have to come inside. Is that diner down the street still around? Can we go there and I'll buy you a coffee or something?"

She could use a coffee. Her stomach growled. She was starving as well. Back when they were lovers, they'd order grilled cheese at the diner after their romps in bed. Back when.

"Fine. Give me a minute." She left him standing out in the hallway as she gathered her purse and coat, smoothing her hair in the mirror by the front door. This unexpected reunion hadn't sent her spiraling into confusion the way she might have expected it to. Then again, she'd dated men in the intervening years, even fallen in love a couple of times, although nothing lasted more than a year, usually because she got bored or annoyed. Life had moved on.

The elevator descended slowly, stopping on the fourth floor to pick up a shaggy, deep-voiced kid—Stanley had mentioned he was some Canadian poet/rock star—and a rough-looking woman he called Janis who wore a blue fur coat that looked like it'd been run over by a truck. They barely noticed Hazel and Charlie, murmuring gravelly whispers to each other as the car descended.

Embarrassed, Hazel stared straight ahead.

Out in the street, Charlie let out a breath. "Wow. The hotel's really changed since I was there last."

Her defenses kicked in. Only the residents had the right to disparage the place. "Not really. It's still full of artistic types, it's just that the mediums have changed. Films are different, songs are different. So the people who live in the Chelsea reflect that. Classical composers have been replaced by rockers, compositional painters by pop artists. Who knows what it'll be like in another twenty years?"

"You sound like you don't mind it."

"The entire city is different. You can't expect your little piece of the pie to stay the same."

They made it to the diner and she slid into a booth, happy to have the table between them. They both ordered coffee and grilled cheese.

Charlie placed his napkin in his lap, not looking up. "My father was eventually sued, did you hear about that?"

She had. In 1962, a radio show host named John Henry Faulk had won $3.5 million in a libel suit against Laurence Butterfield and Vincent Hartnett, for damage done to his name and career during the blacklist. In a strange twist, Charlie's father had died the night before the judgment was announced.

"I had heard. I'm sorry you lost your father." And she was. Having lost her own, she knew how disorienting it was to lose a parent. Even one as pigheaded as Laurence Butterfield.

"I'm glad Faulk got his day in court and won. After everything my father did."

"Right." They ate in silence for a while. She waited him out, mainly because she had nothing to say.

He finally cleared his throat. "That note you left for me at the library, you mentioned you'd met someone else. Who was he?"

She couldn't lie anymore. What was the point? "There was no other man. I didn't want to see you. Floyd Jenkins had just jumped to his death. I was there when it happened. I couldn't take it any-more." Her sentences came out short and sharp, like Morse code. "I wanted to stop fighting, stop everything. Live my life like a normal person, whatever that is. So I left that note, knowing it was the only thing that might stop you from reaching out."

He sat back, looking like he'd been hit. "It wasn't true?"

"No."

"Oh." The look on his face reminded Hazel of a sped-up clock, whirling away. "You lied."

"I did. Why didn't you come back sooner, Charlie? Where were you for five months, not calling or writing, leaving me to fend for myself?"

He took a moment before answering, as if gathering courage. "My father had me hospitalized upstate, supposedly for my epi-lepsy, but basically he wanted to keep me out of the way. I'd made too much trouble."

"You were involuntarily committed?"

"Yes. They drugged me, I had no idea where I was, or what day it was. As soon as I got out, I tried to contact you through Mr. Bard—I figured the FBI was still tapping the phones. Then, at the library, I got your note."

For years, she'd assumed he'd deliberately stayed away, re-pulsed by her toxicity, like so many others. Her heart broke for him, for both of them. "I thought you were keeping your distance because you didn't want to be associated with me."

"I should have been clearer in my letter, but I was worried they'd find out somehow and come after me again. After I got your answer, I just took off. I traveled abroad for a time, before coming back and getting a job with the government. Not as a federal agent—the hospitalization dashed any hope of that—but I worked my way up, and it's a decent job, a good one, to be honest."

"What exactly do you do?"

"I work for an agency that tries to decipher Russian codes."

After all this time. "So you're still obsessed with Russian spies?"

"I am." He pushed aside his plate. "To be honest, that's why I reached out."

He hadn't come to declare his love, then. Of course not. She chided herself for even considering the possibility.

"We recently uncovered some Soviet cables. It turns out a Soviet agent called Silver was the linchpin of all the activity that was going on back in 1950: Julius Rosenberg, David Greenglass, Harry Gold."

Other than Rosenberg, who'd been executed along with his wife in '53, the names meant little to her.

Charlie continued. "I saw your interview in *The New York Times* and I realized you might be able to shed light on some questions I have."

"I doubt that. I don't know anything about those people."

He tapped a finger on the table. "In that article, you mentioned that Maxine convinced you to cast her in the play when you were both in some tunnel under the Chelsea Hotel."

The journalist had pushed Hazel for stories about her and Maxine during the original production, catching Hazel off guard. She wouldn't have brought it up otherwise, but he'd seemed to love the drama of it.

She nodded.

"I wouldn't have thought twice about it," Charlie explained, "except that it brought back strange memories, of after we'd been ambushed. I remember being pushed through a long, dark passage. There were bare light bulbs and a dank smell. Was that the tunnel?"

"Yes. That's how we got you to the ambulance, to avoid the press."

"Where is it, exactly?"

"It runs between a town house on Twenty-Second Street and the hotel on Twenty-Third. Before that, we'd used it to avoid the photographers lurking out front for Maxine."

Charlie, unable to contain his excitement, knocked over his water glass. He waited until after the waiter cleared up the mess with a dish towel to continue. "One of the cables discussed a near miss one night, back in 1950, when the Feds were on the trail of Silver, but then he disappeared. On Twenty-Second Street. I looked up the FBI's reports, and they say Silver went into a town house and vanished into thin air. They staked it out for days, but never saw him leave."

"You think he went into the tunnel and out through the hotel?"

"That's what your article made me wonder. How did you get access to the town house?"

"David Bard gave Maxine a key."

"Did he give any other residents a key?"

"For God's sake, Charlie, I have no idea." She noticed him flinch, and regretted her harsh tone. "You think that maybe this Silver was connected to the hotel in some way?"

"I wondered about it."

"In that case, he could be any of the commies who lived on the first floor in those days. The place was full of them."

"He wouldn't have been that obvious." Charlie looked around, as if he was worried someone was watching them.

She almost laughed. As if anyone cared at this point. The world was full of tragedy, on the brink of disaster, if you read the news-paper headlines. Charlie's hunt for a communist spy was almost quaint. Poor guy was stuck in the past. His colleagues probably ridiculed him. Hazel considered herself lucky she'd been able to move forward with her life, even if it had been stunted, instead of living in the past the way he was.

He lowered his voice. "One of the ways the spies confirmed each other's identity, when they first made contact, was with a Jell-O box top that was ripped in half."

A vague memory of Charlie talking about Jell-O box tops drifted back to her. She played along. "Right, they each had a sec-tion. Proof they were on the same team."

"You remember!" He sat back, pleased. "As I was reading that article, something else occurred to me. Do you remember the man Maxine dated, Arthur something?"

"Arthur. Right. I don't recall his last name."

"Arthur was in food packaging."

She couldn't help it, a bubble of laughter escaped. "As were sev-eral hundred thousand other people at that time. Arthur was an ass and a manipulative son of a bitch, but he was just a boring corporate guy in the end. Nothing special about him."

"Which would make him the perfect spy."

She pushed her plate away. "You've got to be kidding." Now she was no longer hungry, and exhaustion overcame her. All she wanted was to go back to her room and sleep. How disappointing Charlie had turned out to be. It would have been better if he'd never come back, so she could retain her memories of their glori-ous affair without this melancholy overlay. "Why would you care about a spy from years ago? He's probably dead by now, or gone back to Russia."

"Because we've connected Silver's identity with that of an agent who's still going strong, according to recent cables. Different code name, but all our data points to it being the same guy. We know he's in his mid-fifties now, which would make him around thirty-seven or -eight back then. If we can identify him, we'd bring down an entire network." He paused, eyes steady on hers. "I was wondering if you might remember the night in question, when they lost Silver's trail, in case you maybe saw the person but didn't know it."

"I can't remember what happened last year, never mind in 1950."

"It was July third."

Ben's birthday. Every so often, Hazel wondered what it would have been like if her brother had lived. She would have had someone by her side during the crisis, the kind of guy who'd have charmed Laurence Butterfield within five minutes and in the next breath convinced him to invest in the production. Then again, if her brother had been alive, she doubted she would have achieved the heights that she did, writing and directing a show on Broadway. That drive had sprung from her need to live up to the family legacy but had been replaced by ambition of her own, ambition that she never even knew existed. The taste of success had been delicious, but left her grasping for more, just as Ben's death had taken a chunk out of her heart.

Charlie wasn't letting up. "Your play opened a few weeks later."

A sharp memory came back to her, clicking into place like one of those View-Master stereoscopes. She was dressing to go out. Maxine was upset. "July third was Maxine's birthday. She was weepy because Arthur hadn't reached out to her."

"I see." Charlie waited. "Nothing else?"

"We went to an opening of a show, some awful musical revue. I took her to cheer her up."

"Any sign of Arthur?"

"Later, after the show. We all went to a bistro and had coq au vin." Hazel gave herself a mental pat on the back for her acuity. "Really, you actually think Maxine was dating a spy?"

As she said the words, a strange feeling ran through Hazel, like a shiver, or a warning. She remembered all the intrigue surrounding Maxine's relationship with Arthur, the hold he had on her. The bruise. He'd been around that age—mid-thirties—give or take a few years.

No, Charlie was just getting her all worked up again. The idea was ridiculous. "Why don't you ask Maxine about him? She's the one who'd know if he seemed spy-like." Still, after all these years, she couldn't talk about Maxine without a bolt of fury shooting through her.

"Have you seen or heard from her recently?" asked Charlie.

"No. Not at all. Not once."

"Right. I'd heard she gave names to Roy Cohn."

"She certainly did."

The waiter came by and dropped off the check. Charlie pulled out his wallet and left a few bills. "She's in town, she's been asked to present an award at the Tonys on Sunday."

Hazel's mouth went dry. She wondered if Lavinia knew and hadn't told her. "Is that so? She hasn't been on the stage since *Wartime Sonata*."

"She's a movie star now. Everyone wants a piece of her. Trust me, I've been trying to reach her through her agent and her manager to ask her some questions, but can't get a response for the life of me."

Hazel stifled the urge to punch Charlie in the face. *A movie star.* The idea of Maxine being welcomed back by the theater folk she'd betrayed, of all of them applauding while she glided onstage in some fancy gown, smiling and blowing kisses, of Charlie calling her a "movie star," brought back everything Hazel had held so dear and lost. She'd suffered mightily, and no one cared.

How dare Maxine even show her face? The grudge Hazel had carefully nursed since the blacklist turned malignant and dangerous.

Charlie tucked his wallet into his pocket, oblivious.

Hazel kept her voice even. "I have two tickets to the Tonys. I hadn't planned on going, but maybe you could speak to her there."

Maxine wouldn't get away with it, not this time.

CHAPTER TWENTY-FIVE

Hazel

March 1967

"What's with all the cameras?"

Hazel inched a little closer to Charlie as they wended their way down an aisle in the Shubert Theatre, past dapper gentlemen in tuxedos and women dripping with jewels.

"They're televising the awards for the first time." Charlie found their seats and led the way into the row.

"So all of America will be watching?"

"I suppose so."

"Just great. As if Maxine needs more exposure."

Hazel had been in a foul mood since Charlie had picked her up at the Chelsea. Going to the Tony Awards was a stupid idea on her part. First of all, she didn't have the right clothes. She'd put on a black satin gown that looked frumpy and out-of-date among the stylish actresses surrounding them. Hazel's hair was twisted back into a simple bun at the base of her neck, while all the other ladies had their hair teased up into fancy creations that, to Hazel, looked like wigs. What was the point? Just wear a wig.

Second of all, she'd figured their seats would be way up in the top tier, where she could observe the scene from afar. To her shock, they were seated three rows from the stage, right on the aisle.

She craned her neck around and looked up. Both balconies were packed, all the boxes full. So this was what it was like if you made it big. How nice for them all.

"Miss Ripley, I'm so glad you made it." Jeffrey, the director of *Wartime Sonata*, swooped over, shaking her hand and introducing himself to Charlie, followed by several other producers doing the same. The bare-bones production of *Wartime Sonata* in a downtown factory building was all the rage, apparently. Too little, too late, though. Hazel was polite but curt. No doubt some of these folks had been around back in the day and pushed aside the scripts she'd submitted, scared of facing blacklist backlash. Say that three times fast. She chuckled to herself, her nerves rising to the surface.

"You all right?" Charlie asked.

"This is bringing back some strange memories."

"I had the same thought. At one time, we sat in a theater much like this one and ran the show."

"We?"

They both laughed. Those days, when they parsed her play against the looming deadline of opening night, were still a bright memory. Hazel hated to admit that she enjoyed sharing an armrest with him again.

"Do you have any new plays up your sleeve, Hazel?"

"Nothing came easy after *Wartime Sonata*. What about you, you consulting on theater productions in DC?"

He turned red. "I work with a small community theater, to be honest. Behind the scenes, not onstage," he added quickly. "We do four shows a year, and some of them, I must admit, are quite good."

"I think that's wonderful. Good for you."

"Seems neither of us can shake it, Mr. Pear."

Hazel regarded him anew. Charlie was still full of surprises. "How did you know about that?"

"I'd recognize your particular turn of phrase any day. Your reviews always make me smile."

The idea that he knew Hazel well enough to recognize her writing gave her a small thrill, but before she could question him further, the curtain rose and the hosts for the evening, Mary Martin and Robert Preston, came out and welcomed the crowd.

Hazel barely heard a word. Right now Maxine was probably getting her makeup touched up in a dressing room, flirting with the stage manager to kill her nerves before presenting whatever award it was she'd be presenting. Ridiculous.

After the first musical number—Joel Grey singing from *Cabaret*—they paused for a commercial break. Hazel rolled her eyes. "Next thing you know, all the Broadway shows will be televised, and writers will have to add in commercial breaks between scenes."

"I doubt it will come to that."

"How do you propose we approach Maxine? What's your plan?"

"No plan. We'll find her at the party afterward, at the Plaza, and I'll pull her aside." He cocked his head. "You're going to behave, aren't you? Don't mess this up."

"If you were worried about that, you should've come alone."

"You're the one who invited me."

"So basically you're using me."

"No." His voice was firm. "I wanted to see you. That article, the way it described how you'd been treated, it got me boiling with anger."

"I don't want people's pity. I would have preferred to be able to work back when I was inspired and young."

"You're far from old. And things seem to be going better for you now, with the revival of the play."

"I suppose so. Keep in mind the actors in this so-called revival had to compete with the rats for space in the dressing room."

The ceremonies continued, with *Cabaret* and *The Homecoming* garnering most of the big awards.

"And now, we'd like to introduce the shining star Maxine Mead to hand out the award for best actress in a play." Robert Preston motioned to the wings as Maxine swished out in a dress of silver lamé.

Maxine walked with confidence, her shoulders back. Her hair was longer, wavier, than Hazel remembered. In the past almost two decades, Maxine had carved out a respectable career. Her film with James Mason had been a hit, and since then, her face had graced all the magazine covers—*Life, Time, Harper's Bazaar.*

Hazel wished she was sitting farther back. What if Maxine spotted her? While everyone else clapped, Hazel crossed her arms in front of her chest. Charlie gave her a sideways glance, checking in.

Up onstage, the reflected light from Maxine's dress gave her a shimmering aura. Fake lashes had been plastered on her eyelids, while her lips glistened with a pinker hue than she used to wear. Maxine had kept up with the changing fashions. Yet while age hadn't been exactly kind to Hazel, Maxine hadn't been spared either. Her formerly sculpted cheeks were transitioning into jowls, and thin, horizontal wrinkles crisscrossed her neck. Her voice, though, with its familiar raspy tone, brought out of their interment all the memories Hazel had buried. That voice, booming in El Quijote, whispering a snarky comment backstage, speaking

German in the radio room in Naples. The voice of a woman she had once adored.

Maxine listed the nominees for leading actress in a play, and called out the winner, Beryl Reid, for her performance in a show called *The Killing of Sister George*. Hazel had seen it and enjoyed it thoroughly. Nice to know that a play with an all-women cast could hit it big these days.

At the end of Reid's speech, there was a moment of confusion as Maxine began to lead her offstage but was stopped by Robert Preston. Reid disappeared behind the curtain, while Preston guided Maxine back into the spotlight. A look of bewilderment flashed over Maxine's face, but she kept a steady smile in spite of whatever glitch had occurred.

"And now, ladies and gentlemen, we are going to give a special award." Robert Preston pulled a piece of paper out of his pocket.

Dear God. Were they going to give Maxine a Tony for gracing their stage with her presence? If so, Hazel would storm off, never mind protocol. She tensed, at the ready. Maxine looked out into the audience with a raised eyebrow, as confused as the rest of them.

He read out loud. "After so many years, today is a day of reckoning. The theater community was, for the most part, unaffected by the terrible events of the blacklist, when the McCarthy era threatened the very creativity and freedom that America stands for."

The blacklist? If they gave Maxine some kind of award and mentioned the blacklist in the same breath, Hazel wouldn't storm off, she'd run screaming onto the stage, snatch the award away, and bludgeon Maxine with it.

"What the . . . ?" murmured Charlie.

Preston continued. "Yet while the film, television, and radio industries are best known for coming under direct fire, several of our

theater community's members were also affected. Tonight, we acknowledge them. We acknowledge brilliant artists, like Lavinia
Smarts, Lillian Hellman, Uta Hagen, Zero Mostel, and Floyd Jenkins. We acknowledge that they suffered, that they were denied un-
alienable rights. We acknowledge that a terrible miscarriage of
justice took place, and that too few spoke up, spoke out, at the time.
Alas, some who've been harmed cannot be with us tonight. But we
are lucky to have one virtuoso present who stood up to the madness."

Maxine looked as if she were going to crack wide open, her
smile turned to fear. Hazel's heart pounded, and she gripped Charlie's hand, as if that might stop what was coming.

Preston chuckled merrily. "I actually have two special an-
nouncements to make. First of all—breaking news, folks—I was
informed earlier this evening that the acclaimed revival of *Wartime Sonata* will return to the Great White Way next season."

Hazel had known the producers were trying to raise the money
for a Broadway transfer, but had written it off to the misguided
enthusiasm of neophytes. Very rarely would a play make such a
leap, hardly ever. Yet they'd pulled it off. The audience erupted in
applause. Her mind reeled, trying to process the unexpected good
news. This was why Lavinia had insisted Hazel take the tickets.

Preston gestured to Maxine. "Even better, we're lucky enough
to have the star of the original cast here to present a special award.
Once again, Maxine Mead."

He handed the paper he'd been reading from to Maxine, who
took it with shaking hands.

She scanned it and then looked out into the audience with a half
smile. "Actors hate it when the playwright changes the script
right before a performance. Or during."

The audience laughed as the mood in the room shifted, curious
to know what was next.

Maxine took a deep breath. "For valor and strength in terrible circumstances, the American Theatre Wing would like to award a special Tony Award to the playwright, and my friend . . ." Her voice cracked on the last word.

This was spiraling out of control, not at all what Hazel wanted. It was all a terrible mistake, a terrible mess.

Maxine looked out into the audience like a prisoner of war.

"Miss Hazel Ripley."

◆┊◆

Hazel turned to Charlie, confused.

What is going on? she mouthed.

Around them, people clapped and cheered.

"You've got to go up and say something," Charlie finally said.

She shook her head. "I don't know what to say."

She couldn't hear his reply, the noise of the crowd was too much. He helped her rise to her feet. Once out of her seat, she located the stairs with what felt like tunnel vision, focusing only on what was directly in front of her. If she looked up, she feared she might trip or freeze. She didn't want to go up on that stage, up to Maxine. Everything about this was wrong.

Trumpets blared a generic melody as she climbed the steps while holding her skirt in one hand, her mind racing. How could they have put her on the spot like this? They thought this was some kind of honor? That shaggy-haired director, she was certain, was behind all this. A way to get his show an injection of publicity. And a way for all of these people, the ones clapping until their hands hurt, to feel better about themselves for staying quiet when they should have stood up for justice when it mattered, or others who'd turned in their colleagues and stolen careers out from under them.

She wondered if Lavinia had been in on this. Over the years, Lavinia had inquired about the rift between Hazel and Maxine, gently encouraging Hazel to reach out and forgive her friend. But Hazel had shut down any further discussion, and eventually Lavinia had stopped bringing it up.

The stage. She'd made it. Maxine stood to the side of the thin microphone, clapping her hands. Another woman handed a small plaque to Maxine, who in turn handed it to Hazel, their fingers not touching.

The solidity and weight of the plaque helped ground Hazel. The applause didn't die down; in fact, it grew even louder as the audience rose from their seats. A standing ovation. *Well, isn't that something?*

For years now, in spite of the success she'd achieved as a reviewer, and in spite of the life she'd made for herself at the Chelsea, Hazel still walked around with a ball of fury deep within her, like a cancer. Fury that she'd never again had the chance to achieve much of anything on the stage, after so much early promise.

Unexpectedly, tears sprang to Hazel's eyes. Looking out at these strangers, who stood cheering her on, acknowledging her existence for the first time in seventeen years, Hazel realized that her fury was in fact grief. Terrible, inconsolable grief, at what could have been. At the loss of her best friend, and her theater family, in one fell swoop.

She swore she wouldn't break, she wouldn't let them see her pain. She'd lived with it this long. But looking out over the crowd who'd gathered tonight to celebrate the splendid world of live theater, in all its eccentric, superstitious glory, her heart broke. She stifled a sob with her hand, the suffering of so many years now evident to all.

Which only made them applaud harder.

Hazel looked down at Charlie, who stood with the rest of them, his face beaming. Maxine waited awkwardly by Hazel's side. They should kiss or embrace or something, that's what the crowd wanted. Two best friends, reunited after all these years.

Hazel turned to look at Maxine, who had that same silly smile on her face, but her eyes revealed fear. Fear of what Hazel was going to do next: Would she play the game? Or attack her on live television?

Hazel's fingers itched. She'd heard that expression a thousand times before but never really understood it until now. They itched to physically hurt this woman who'd betrayed her so terribly. Who'd left her behind. Who was a traitor.

As the cheering finally died down, Hazel looked out to Charlie again. He was sitting back down, her empty seat beside him. Something about that unsettled Hazel, but before she had a chance to figure out why, she heard Maxine weeping beside her, her mouth a grimace. The ugly show of emotion dried up Hazel's own tears in a flash. Leave it to Maxine to draw focus on herself when this was supposed to be Hazel's moment. Chewing the scenery, as always. Hazel refused to be upstaged, not this time.

She stepped up to the microphone and took a deep breath.

"Thank you for this remarkable, and surprising, honor." Her voice rebounded up the balconies, up to the rafters, through the cameras and into the homes of millions of Americans.

For years now, she'd wanted a way to right all the wrongs, an opportunity to be heard. This was it. Maybe Charlie was right. It was a new era, perhaps her anguish hadn't been for nothing.

"Back in 1950, when *Wartime Sonata* first graced a Broadway stage, we were young and full of hope. We'd won another world war, defeated the enemy, and were the leaders of democracy, of the free world."

She didn't want to lecture. How to make her point, make them understand?

"It's true that secrets were being ferried out of the country back then, secrets that were shared with the Soviet Union when they should not have been. Brave federal agents hunted for those spies, and they should be commended." She looked down at Charlie. Again, that empty seat beside him nagged at her. Reminding her of another time, another empty seat. On the third of July.

"But then a terrible infection took hold in America. One of paranoia and witch hunts. Others in politics decided to use the fearmongering as a way to decimate the entertainment industry. They said that communists were poisoning the minds of their children, were out to destroy democracy. And many of you bought the lies." She looked right into the television camera. "You didn't question them. You didn't fight back. You let this happen.

"The entertainment industry was hounded by bullies as the rest of America, including its top newspapers and news organizations, went along for the ride. The press, who should have exposed the contagion for what it was, let it fester for far too long, cowed by the credentials of the bullies in charge. Because of this, we lost a generation of talent. Screenwriters became typists to earn a buck. Brilliant actors sold shoes to make a living. My friend Floyd Jenkins, who had so much hope and promise, was forced out of the career he loved because of an offhand remark, then killed himself."

Her throat threatened to close up, but she swallowed, took a breath, and kept on. "This is how a society is corrupted, from the inside out. We must make a promise to not ever let this happen again. We must promise to be vigilant against our own worst tendencies. Only by doing so will our country sustain its ideals of freedom."

She stopped. There was nothing left to say.

The men and women in the audience sat for a moment in silence, before a wall of sound, of cheers and stamping feet and clapping, surged forward.

Hazel looked up into the darkness to the very last row of the top balcony, grateful that her message had been heard.

She heard Charlie give a whistle, the same one he used to catch a cab, and caught his eye and smiled.

Again, the empty seat. On the night that Charlie had asked about, the third of July, Maxine's birthday, they'd gone to a show. Maxine had been harassed by a fan and seemed out of sorts during the first act, fidgeting in her seat. Then she'd disappeared.

The seat next to Hazel's had been empty the entire second act. Hazel had emerged from the theater to find Maxine waiting outside. And Arthur right across the street, watching them. Just enough time . . .

No. It couldn't be.

In shock, Hazel drew back, as if a burst of feedback had screeched out of the microphone that only she could hear. She felt Maxine's hand on her arm, steadying her.

Maxine leaned close, speaking directly into her ear. "I didn't know, I'm sorry about all this."

Hazel couldn't speak. Sorry for what? For this muddled awards ceremony? Or for worse?

She felt Maxine's hand on her waist, guiding her off the stage.

"That was a beautiful speech, Hazel," Maxine said. "You've certainly got a way with words."

Her delivery was wry, playful. She wanted to once again be in Hazel's good graces now that Hazel was back in fashion.

But Hazel was having none of it.

"I know your secret, Maxine Mead." Her tongue tasted of metal as she spoke. "I know the truth."

CHAPTER TWENTY-SIX

Hazel

March 1967

O nce backstage, Maxine was swept up in a sea of handlers, leaving Hazel in the wings. Soon enough, though, the stagehands surrounded her, thanking her for her rousing words and shaking her hand. If anything, that was the most gratifying moment so far at this insane awards show, that she'd made the crew proud.

More than ever, Hazel wanted Charlie to have a chance to confront Maxine. Especially now that Hazel had figured out the truth. But any kind of confrontation was sure to be noticed and covered by the press. This had to be played out very carefully.

"Hazel."

Charlie appeared, and she'd never been more relieved to see his face. She waited until they were safely in a taxi, on their way to the post-awards party at the Plaza Hotel, to fill him in.

"Maxine was part of it."

"Part of what?"

"Arthur's spy ring. Silver's spy ring. Whatever you want to call him. Arthur is Silver, I'm certain. And Maxine was a spy, too."

Charlie frowned. "Maxine Mead, a spy?"

"That evening, July the third, when we went to the theater, Maxine wasn't with me the entire time. I only realized it when I was onstage giving my speech and saw the empty seat next to you. I remembered that Maxine never returned after the intermission, leaving me alone for the entire second act. I saw her later, outside. I spotted Arthur across the street, watching us, and insisted we all go to dinner so I could finally meet Maxine's mysterious beau."

"Slow down. I'm not understanding the connection."

Hazel started again, thinking it through as she spoke. "When we were first entering the theater, a fan waylaid her, a rude one. After that, she seemed flustered, like something was bothering her. She got up as soon as the curtain fell for intermission, told me she was going to the bathroom, but never came back. Later, she said she'd missed the bell and didn't want to make a fuss scrambling back to her seat in the dark. But I think the fan was connected to Arthur in some way, and had told her to get back to the hotel and let Arthur in through the tunnel. I remember the second act of that play was interminable, which means Maxine had more than enough time to grab a cab and help Silver-slash-Arthur escape by disappearing into the town house, through the tunnel, and out the hotel's front door. Then they jumped in a cab back to the theater district."

She sat back, pleased.

"What if she just missed the bell?"

When he said it like that, the story did seem improbable. Still.

"I don't think it's just a coincidence. Arthur treated Maxine terribly, he hit her, abused her. But she never left, which didn't seem like Maxine at all. The Maxine Mead we knew would have dumped a loser like that in an instant. Whenever I questioned her, she'd say that she loved him, but there was something empty in the words, like she didn't really believe them. I always thought there was something odd going on, but I could never put my finger on it. Now it makes sense. Arthur and she were more than lovers, they were both spies. Which was why she couldn't escape his clutches. Or maybe she really didn't want to." She let out a sharp laugh. "To think I just made a speech chastising those who were paranoid about spies, when one may have been standing right beside me."

"What did you say to her, as you were going offstage?" Charlie asked.

"I told her that I knew the truth." She should have never let on, but she couldn't help herself. "Do you think I've ruined your opportunity? What if she runs for the hills?"

He considered it. "She's too famous. She has to show up at the party, and probably thinks it's safer in a crowd. We have to figure out a way to get her alone."

"It's better if I do it. It's the only chance that she'll open up."

"You're not trained, no way."

"She's emotional, vulnerable, and we have a long history. I've got this, I promise. Inside the ballroom, there's a long balcony that overlooks the room. I'll lead her up there for a private talk, and you take the opposite stairs and sneak over. Don't let her see you, though, or we'll lose our chance."

A band played as they entered the grand ballroom of the Plaza Hotel, a space that would have looked at home in Versailles, with its gold leaf plaster and mighty columns. They were escorted to a table where Lauren Bacall and Carol Burnett sat engrossed in conversation.

"Well, this will be easy." Hazel pointed to the placards, where she and Maxine were seated next to each other. For a brief moment she doubted herself. Maybe she was just jazzed up with adrenaline from the unexpected turn of events, indulging in conspiracy theories. But the guilty look on Maxine's face after she'd spoken the words out loud was undeniable. She'd known what was going on, one way or another.

"Excuse me, coming through." An older man Hazel recognized as Maxine's agent pulled out a chair. Maxine, behind him, didn't take it. Instead, she froze when faced with Hazel and Charlie. Her mouth opened and closed a couple of times but no sound came out.

"Max, it's been too long." Charlie leaned over and gave her a kiss on the cheek.

Maxine responded with an enigmatic smile. "Look at that, the gang's back together. Lovely to see you, Charlie."

Just then, a couple of photographers pushed Charlie aside. "We need a photo of the two of you, Miss Ripley and Miss Mead."

Hazel put her arm around Maxine's waist and drew her close. "Say 'cheese.'"

After a couple of flashes, Maxine tried to pull away but Hazel spoke through gritted teeth. "Come with me. We have to talk." To her surprise, Maxine softened in her arms.

"Fine."

They cut through the surging crowd and up a wide set of stairs. Hazel unhooked the velvet rope that limited access to the balcony and let Maxine through, before clicking it back in place behind them.

Once they reached the top, Maxine moved into the shadows, out of the view of the crowd below. "I'm so sorry about this evening, Hazel. I had no idea they were going to pull that stunt. I would have never agreed if I'd known. But your speech was marvelous. I hope you know that."

"Don't flatter me."

"I'm not. It's the truth." Her hand fluttered to her hair, a nervous tic Hazel knew well.

Better to get straight to the point. "Maxine, I know about your activities with Arthur." Out of the corner of her eye, she saw Charlie approaching. He stayed glued to the wall, out of Maxine's line of vision but well within earshot.

"My activities?"

Her pretend innocence infuriated Hazel, she couldn't hold back. "You were a spy, just like Arthur was. You were spying on all of us. How could you?"

"I wasn't spying on you. What on earth are you talking about?" Her face was open, childlike. Confused.

What if Hazel was completely wrong about all this, and had simply gotten caught up in the drama of the evening? She charged on, anyway. "I know it all, Maxine. I know that Arthur was known as Silver, that he was at the top of a network of spies that included Julius Rosenberg. You were his protégée."

A leap of faith, that last statement, but Maxine wouldn't know it was just a guess.

"No, that's not true. None of that is true." The words came out robotic, the worst line reading ever.

Hazel softened her voice, let her hands fall to her sides. "That was all a long time ago, Max. A lot has changed since then, we all know that. I'm just trying to make sense of it all. We all did what we could to get through, in a terrible time. I want to hear your side of it."

Maxine responded with a tiny sigh. The air around them shifted, and Maxine's face went slack. Not with fear, but with relief. Hazel suspected she was desperate to confide her side of the story.

"You can tell me, Maxine," said Hazel. "It's water under the bridge. After all this time, I deserve the truth. That's why you stayed with Arthur, right? Even though he was a beast. I realize now that you didn't have a choice."

Her gaze flickered. "I wanted to tell you for so long, but I couldn't. It would put you in danger, but hell, let's be honest, I didn't have the courage." Maxine paused. "I met Arthur, like I told you, long ago, when I was still in Seattle. I didn't realize it until later that he was grooming me, training me from the very beginning. I was young, a teenager, and he was powerful and smart. I thought I was in love. With him, with the Communist Party. The two were one, in my mind."

"Did he bring you to New York?"

"Yes. I was sent there, to work as an agent. Soon after, I was told I'd been made a member of the underground. It was an honor, it meant they regarded me as important. It also meant I cut off all contact with regular communists, didn't go to meetings, distanced myself from the Party. Not even the communists knew I was a communist."

A terrible realization dawned. "What really happened with you and my brother? Was he trying to recruit you or was it the other way around?"

Maxine's face crumpled. "He was on our list of potential recruits. I was told to get a sense of where his political sympathies lay, but when he took me to that protest, I was completely blindsided. That was exactly the type of scene I was supposed to avoid, being deep underground. I let him go after that. I told them that he was too patriotic, that he wouldn't be turned."

Hazel wasn't sure whether to believe her or not. In fact, she was having a difficult time aligning the woman before her—someone who had been trained to lie and scheme—with the changeable drama queen she'd met in Naples and practically lived with in New York. Which one was the real Maxine?

Hazel backtracked, returning Maxine to more comfortable territory. "Did they make you join the USO tour?"

"They thought it'd be a good way to monitor what was going on in Europe, but the controls were too strict, I couldn't get word back to Arthur, so for a time I was told to cut off all communication. That was the first taste of what it's like to be a normal person. When we met, when we were trying to help Paul. That was all true. You know that, right?"

Hazel stayed silent.

"After the war, I went back to California to help them infiltrate the film industry, but after I lost the part to Marilyn Monroe, they sent me to New York, to try to revitalize my career on the stage."

"In my play."

"Yes, in your play." Maxine's voice trembled. "It was a calculated move on their behalf, but I wanted to play Lina more than anything. It was a beautiful part, the best I've ever had. Then Julius Rosenberg was arrested, and everything fell to pieces. Arthur came up with the idea to use you and Charlie as a diversion, once the show had opened to raves. But I couldn't let them do that to you and Charlie, so I, I . . ." She trailed off.

The image of Maxine standing on that stage, floundering like an amateur, came to mind. "Oh my God," said Hazel. "You threw the show. On purpose."

"I was protecting you."

"How?"

"I hated to do it, Hazel, I swear. I figured by screwing up, I'd get you out of the spotlight, keep you out of Arthur's reach."

Her excuses enraged Hazel. "I had one chance. Only one. And you ruined it."

Maxine shuddered. "I wasn't in my right mind."

"What about the evening of your birthday?" Hazel demanded. "That was the night you helped Arthur escape, right?"

She nodded, slowly, surprised. "An operative followed me to the theater, said I had to return to the hotel and let in Arthur through the town house, that the Feds were closing in on him."

"That man who wanted your autograph?"

"Yes. So I left at intermission, took a cab there, let Arthur in, and then he insisted on coming back to the theater with me. I was trapped."

Playing the victim again. Hazel couldn't stand it. "So after all that, you not only flopped the show, you still set me and Charlie up that day in the hotel. You told the photographers where to find us, and ruined Charlie's career as well."

"No! I had nothing to do with it. My guess is Arthur stole my stationery and wrote that note. You have to believe me."

Hazel tried to conjure up the memory of the note, what the handwriting had looked like, but it had been so long ago. "I don't know what to believe anymore. You can't deny that you named names."

"I had to. You don't understand."

"No one *had* to. Sure, you might have not had the career you do now. You might have been destitute like me, but you didn't *have* to." Hazel started to laugh in spite of herself. Maxine looked at her like she was mad. Maybe she was.

"What's so funny?" asked Maxine.

"I'm picturing you being questioned by Roy Cohn, and how he had an actual spy right there, right in the room with him, and didn't even know it. The incompetency of it all."

Maxine didn't crack a smile. "I went in there thinking it was just about paperwork, and then I'd be on my way. But they started questioning me and, yes, I had a lot to hide. As Cohn dug in deeper, I panicked. I never meant to name anyone, never, but they knew my weak spot. They threatened to deport my grandmother if I didn't cooperate and tell them what they wanted."

Acid dripped from Hazel's voice. "You poor dear."

"I'm sorry for everything, I really am. I was trying to protect you, protect my family."

Hazel would have none of it. "You've been living large on other people's pain for years now."

"I tried to help. I took the job in Hollywood so that I could support you, make it up to you. I figured by burning bright I could escape Arthur's grip and free myself from being a Soviet agent, and it worked. Once I was out, I could take care of you."

"Take care of me? What are you talking about?"

"I had an arrangement with Mr. Bard, and later his son, that I would pay your rent every month. I wanted you to share in the spoils. I knew I didn't deserve it."

Hazel burst out laughing. "You're an idiot. Stanley Bard must have been pocketing your blood money for years now. I've never seen a penny. I paid what rent I could, and worked the switchboard when I couldn't."

"You never received it? But that was the whole point." Maxine's words faded away into the general noise of the party going on below them. She put one hand on the wall to steady herself.

Charlie stepped forward. "We'll need you to tell the FBI everything you know."

Maxine's knees seemed to buckle at the sound of his voice, but she caught herself and recovered. "Charlie?" For a split second, the vamp from Naples reappeared, all smiles and charm. "What are you doing, eavesdropping on a lady's private conversation?"

"Charlie works in the government now."

Maxine snapped to attention. "Huh. I see. I've been set up." She turned to Charlie, her voice ragged. "It's all meaningless. I was a nobody, really."

"Then you make a statement to that effect," said Charlie. "The cables that were passed between spies and the Soviet Union are still being decoded and analyzed. It's important that you share what you know."

Hazel cut in. "Is your grandmother still your excuse?"

"No. She died years ago. There's no one left to protect." She looked at Charlie, then over at Hazel. "Hazel, I would have never hurt you. Anything I did was so that you wouldn't get caught up in it, that you wouldn't get hurt. But it was bigger than I could have imagined."

"You seem to have made out pretty well in the bargain. For all intents and purposes, you're a huge success."

"No. I'm completely alone. I haven't let anyone else into my life since then. I was too nervous that they'd come after me all over again, come after the people I love. There's no one left. You're the success, Hazel."

"Is that so? Please, enlighten me."

"You stood tall when everyone else was caving in. Don't you see? That's why you were honored tonight. All the trappings of fame mean nothing, not when you've sold your soul."

"How easy to say, when you're the one living the dream."

Maxine straightened and looked over at Charlie. It was over, and she knew it. "Let me get my affairs in order this evening, and I'll come to you first thing in the morning. You'll get your due, I promise."

Charlie nodded. Hazel stared at him in disbelief. "You're going to just let her walk out of here? Are you crazy?"

"She has nowhere to hide, Hazel. Her plan worked for the

Russians, and it works for us, too. She's too big of a star. One night won't make a difference, right, Maxine?"

Hazel didn't wait for Maxine to respond. "Once again, you're leaving destruction in your wake. I make the speech of my life, and then tomorrow you go out there, front and center, and admit to being a spy, take up the spotlight. You really know how to cap me at my knees every time, don't you?"

Maxine began to cry. "No. That's not what this is. Remember Naples, when we did so much good for the soldiers, made them forget where they were, for a little while? Same at the Chelsea Hotel, running lines and working on the play, I had that glorious feeling of freedom and creativity and not having any chains to hold us down. You will have your time in the spotlight. You are brilliant, and your play is brilliant. Everyone will see that now."

Maxine's facade, the one built on movie star glamour and a breathless beauty, had completely slipped away. She looked faded and lost.

"I'll accept my responsibility, I promise," said Maxine softly. "I'll do whatever I can."

CHAPTER TWENTY-SEVEN

Maxine

March 27, 1967

The worst, with Arthur, was when we were driving somewhere together and he asked me to pull out the huge atlas and figure out the directions. It didn't matter if we were cruising around the Hollywood Hills or looking for some unmarked door in Queens to make a drop-off, the very request would get my heart pumping like I was running alongside the car, not sitting in the passenger seat. I would look up the name of the street in the back as quickly as I could, then locate the appropriate square on the map, but I was never fast enough.

Looking back, I can see that he got great pleasure in flustering me, in getting angrier and angrier until he was screaming at me to tell him which way to turn, swearing until I wept. He'd apologize afterward and I'd stupidly presume that the balance of power had shifted over to me, which generated a rush that was probably equal to his own. The same rush I felt when I passed off secret documents, or raced to the Chelsea Hotel to rescue Arthur. Arthur was my life. I had attached to him like one of those round-mouthed fishes on a shark, and I wasn't going anywhere.

This is no excuse for what I went on to do, for having ruined the lives of the people I loved. But being kept off-balance like that was a terrible, terrible fate. Never mind walking on eggshells, I tiptoed on shards of glass whenever he was around. I was so eager to please, and never quite measured up. I placed my passion in our mission, in our cause, to prove to him that I was worthy of his love.

I thought I had reason to hate the same things Arthur did: capitalism, American greed. Only later did I realize I was viewing my life through Arthur's particularly warped perspective, as if we were standing in front of a fun-house mirror that elongated certain truths and shortened others.

Magnild. An ugly name, he'd told me. He only used it when he was angry at me, hitting the consonants hard with contempt.

I wonder who she might have become, this Magnild, if she hadn't been twisted into Maxine Mead.

Instead, I became a follower, content to do what other people told me to do. As an actress, that worked in my favor. If a director told me to cry, I cried. Laugh? Done. I could bring any emotion up from my very bones and let it cascade through my mouth, my eyes, so that you knew exactly what I was thinking. Or what you thought I was thinking.

It's kept me employed for a long time, eons in this industry. I graduated from dishy ingenue to wisecracking dame, and that's perfectly fine with me. More substance to play with, even if the lines are fewer. Shooting movies suits me, as the cast bonds like long-lost family members for the course of a couple of months and says goodbye at the wrap party with giddy promises to be in touch, but never does. I have the illusion of being part of something, without the closeness.

I've missed Hazel terribly these past many years. Missed being able to pop down the hall and have a laugh, to meet at El Quijote for a drink after a long day of rehearsal and let all the insanity fade away. That's what good friends do—all that stuff that builds in your head into something terribly important that might bring you down at any moment—it dissipates when you see each other, turns into feathers that float away.

Seeing Hazel onstage, standing just a few feet away from me, had almost been more than I could handle. There she was, my dearest friend, yet she might as well have been a total stranger. Sure, she looked terrible, in dire need of a makeover, but I adored the fact that she didn't care. That was my Hazel, all right. She was fierce in her gray streaks and her blazing eyes, and I wanted to hold her in my arms and tell her how much I loved her, how much I'd missed her.

To my surprise, after that terrible confrontation with Charlie and Hazel, they let me go. It would have been better if they'd hauled me away, right then and there. Instead, I went back down to the party and drank whatever came my way, until my agent guided me upstairs to my room and told me to get some rest, closing the door behind him. I didn't do what he said. I ripped off my gown and put on some dungarees and a sweater. The clock said two in the morning, but I wasn't tired. This was my last evening of freedom before my carefully constructed world came crashing down, and I wouldn't waste a second of it.

I pulled on a hat with a wide brim and caught a cab downtown. We cut through Times Square, where the lights were still as bright as ever.

Part of the reason I'd been a good actress—and how funny that I am already speaking in the past tense—was that I had a terrible fear of disappearing, of being a nobody. That's what I thought the Party was all about. That's why I fought so hard for a country that I'd never even been to. Because communism stood for everyone taking care of each other, for being valuable and worthy, being equals.

In the intervening years, we were all proven wrong. Wrong that I was valuable, and wrong that communism would protect us from economic ruin or fanatical leaders. Stalin killed millions who disagreed with him, they simply disappeared. For a long time I denied the reports, unwilling to believe such a thing. But even the most authoritarian government can't evade the truth, it rises like steam from the fissures of a volcano. Still, the world is run by men who want power, who will say anything to attain it, and do anything to retain it.

Outwardly, I was Hollywood royalty. Inside, I was a nobody, just like Arthur had said.

❖

I had the taxi pull up on the far side of Twenty-Third Street. The Chelsea Hotel, where I'd been embraced and felt safe, where nonconformists were the norm. When I came back to New York for a quick visit a few years ago, I put on glasses and a scarf and watched from the bar across the street until I saw Hazel appear. She walked to the newspaper stand, exchanged a word with the owner, then down the street to buy flowers, before disappearing back through the lobby doors. I knew exactly what vase she'd put them in, the white ceramic one with the narrow neck. I missed her so much.

This evening, I could see a few lights on, even at this late hour. Not surprising, in a building full of artists and musicians. I crossed the street and entered the lobby, which had hardly changed. There were more paintings on the walls, and some kind of awful papier-mâché sculpture hung from the ceiling, but these were hardly a distraction from the room's decaying Victorian splendor.

A man behind the counter looked up from a dirty magazine.

Suddenly, I was so tired. I motioned to one of the couches. "Do you mind if I sit here a moment? I'm waiting for someone," I lied.

He shrugged. "Do whatever you like."

If David Bard had still been alive, he would most likely have been up at this hour, overseeing a midnight installation of new carpet in the hallways so as to avoid paying union wages or some other ridiculous enterprise. He would have sat with me and talked on and on about the hotel, filled me in on the latest gossip. That would've been nice.

What was I doing here? I wasn't sure. I suppose I wanted to feel part of Hazel's world one last time.

The lobby door opened and a couple of young rockers stomped by in matching black boots. The girl, who had acne-scarred skin and a head of blond corkscrew curls, turned and scrutinized me. "Hey, I know you."

I shook my head and pulled my hat lower. By now the booze was beginning to wear off. I'd have a terrible headache soon. "I don't think so."

"Sure, you're that lady. My mom loves your movies."

I nodded but didn't answer. Luckily, her boyfriend hadn't broken his stride, and she hurried off to catch up. A minute or so later, a high scream echoed down the stairwell, tapering off to a muffled yelp. I moved to the edge of the couch, ready to spring into action, but the desk clerk didn't even look up.

"Is everything all right?" I asked.

He stared at me as if I were the one who'd screamed. "Some junkies having a fight. Nothing I can do about it."

I worried about Hazel living in a place like this. It no longer had the innocuous, creative vibe of the fifties. Today, a different kind of creature lurked about, desperate and dangerous.

I wished I had the courage to get up and knock on Hazel's door, insist she invite me in. Tell her that I loved her.

The clock said five in the morning. I had four hours before I was due to be at the address Charlie had given me, downtown in Foley Square. In spite of the changes, it felt good to sit in the Chelsea, to feel part of the hotel once again. I thought of all the people who'd found their creative muse here, created poetry and plays, music and art. I had missed out on the best of it by heading to Holly-wood, missed Mark Rothko, Dylan Thomas, Arthur Miller, Jack Kerouac. What if I'd stayed, and not headed west to the antiseptic wasteland of Los Angeles? I could have been part of the legend of the Chelsea Hotel. Like Hazel would be, once her play was revived on Broadway and her career resurrected. No chance of that now, for me.

I rose and approached the counter. "Can I get a room?"

He looked at the wall of keys and plucked one from it. "How long you staying?"

"Just for one night."

"It'll be twenty-eight dollars and seventeen cents."

"That seems like a very arbitrary figure."

"Just saying what's in the book here."

"That's fine." I pulled the bills out of my wallet and counted out the change.

"You got any luggage? I can call a porter to take it up for you."

I shook my head. "I'm traveling light these days." I put my hand in my coat pocket, checking that my second-most important pos-session was still there. It was. The most important one was in my satchel: my diary, which I'd kept writing even after turning over the earlier pages to Lavinia. How ironic that Hazel didn't write anymore, yet I'd never been able to stop.

"The room's on the second floor. You can take the elevator or the stairs."

"I know the way."

Room 225 was in the west wing of the building, the door lo-cated off a side hallway. The hotel had been carved up since I'd been in it, larger suites divided into two—more profit and less space. The chamber lacked all of the glorious details of my old room, with just a twin bed and side table squeezed between two dingy walls. Something sharp had sliced through the lampshade, leaving a six-inch vertical scar. The stained-glass transom above the door was the only reminder of the hotel's original elegance.

I reached into my coat pocket and pulled out the bottle of pills, placing them carefully on the side table next to a smudged water glass. I carried the glass down the hallway to the shared bathroom and filled it up to the top.

Then back to my room. All was silent. The night sky outside the window had turned from turgid black to a dark gray. The sun wouldn't be up for another couple of hours. I could feel the ghosts of the hotel gathering around me, keeping vigil.

I closed the curtain, a dusty damask that had seen better days, and sat back down on the bed. I undid the bottle, took a couple of pills in my hand, swallowed them down, took a couple of pills, swallowed. Over and over until there were none left. As I lay down on the bed, waiting for whatever was going to come next, a memory of my grandmother giving me a pill when I was sick came back to me. She'd crush the white tablet into a chalky powder and mix it with raspberry jam on a spoon. The pill was bitter, as I'd known it would be, but the sweetness of the berries and the pretty way they glistened on the spoon overrode my distaste.

I wished I had a jar of raspberry jam next to me now. And a spoon to taste it with. If only I had that.

If only.

CHAPTER TWENTY-EIGHT

Hazel

March 1967

Hazel put on her most comfortable shoes and skipped the elevator—it was stuck on the second floor again—and instead plodded down the stairs, around and around, her hand gliding along the bannister, to the ground floor. After Charlie had dropped her off in front of the Chelsea last night, she'd yanked off her gown, not even bothering to hang it up. She'd never wear the dress again. It was as though it had been stained by Maxine's denials and excuses, invisible damage that only Hazel could see. Sleep had finally come as the sun rose, and she'd awakened abruptly at ten to the garish ring of the alarm, checking the hands of the clock in panic, like a schoolgirl who'd missed an exam.

By now Charlie would be with Maxine at the Bureau's field office in Foley Square.

Walking west until she could go no farther, Hazel turned south, the Hudson River sluicing along on her right and the crumbling elevated highway to her left. Not the most peaceful stroll, but she liked the idea that she was getting some fresh air, even if she was sandwiched between car exhaust and polluted waters.

Before she'd headed out, the phone had rung. It was Stanley, saying that he'd watched the Tonys and loved her speech. She'd thanked him before explaining that she wouldn't be moving from her room, and that he'd have to find somewhere else to put his rock band.

She was done with getting pushed around, by anyone.

He'd quickly agreed, and asked how Maxine was, said that they'd looked swell together onstage. She'd thanked him and hung up.

Maxine. The panicked look in her eyes last night had haunted Hazel in her sleep. They'd cornered her. What a fall from the brash, brassy woman Hazel had met in Naples, who owned the joint and made no bones about it. The one who fearlessly drove a Jeep into a frenzied crowd in order to save a couple of frightened boys. Whom Hazel had once considered her best friend in the world.

She'd said she thought she was protecting Hazel. The way Maxine spun it, she'd tried to deflect dangerous attention away from Hazel. If only she'd opened up and told Hazel what was going on, about the depths of the abuse by Arthur.

Hazel had witnessed his crass bullying firsthand, and hadn't done enough. Hadn't said enough. She should have insisted that Maxine leave him, taken her somewhere safe and out of his clutches. Maybe that would have changed things. But she could never have guessed the wicked winds that were swirling around them both. And Arthur was a master at turning on the charisma, at hiding his true self, just as he'd done over dinner that warm summer evening. All shy smiles and self-flagellation.

Another call came through soon after she hung up with Stanley, this time from her agent, a husky-voiced woman who hadn't reached out to her in years.

"Do you have a play ready to go? We're getting lots of inquiries." She didn't wait for an answer. "The Coast will want to know if you have any screenplays. Do you have any screenplays?"

Hazel had agreed to come in to her office for a meeting that afternoon. Over the past many years, a number of ideas had floated by, before dissipating in a puff of disapproval of her own making. Nothing had clicked. But even with all the newfound approbation, she knew better than to rush the process. She would never be bullied again, either by a movie producer or by a corrupt politician, that much she knew.

Her life hadn't been the happiest, but it *had* been full, and Hazel was finally ready to appreciate that. Maxine and Hazel's early definition of success, which had left Maxine corrupt, lost, and alone, would no longer be hers. This latest interest in Hazel's work could be as fleeting as the last, but she would do this on her terms, relying on the grit and courage she'd always had, the rest of them be damned.

This time around, she'd please herself first. If that didn't make the grade with the critics or audience, so be it.

She just needed an idea. A good one.

She also had Charlie back, possibly. Seeing him again had brought on a rush of emotions, one that she'd never felt for any of her other lovers. He'd kissed her lightly on the mouth as he dropped her off.

"You're remarkable," he'd said.

"I know," she responded, which made him laugh. "You are, too, for sticking with this spy hunt for years and years."

"I knew it was my way back to you."

But she was getting ahead of herself, thinking about all that. Hazel stopped and stared out at the cliffs of New Jersey. She wondered when she'd hear next from Charlie. Maybe when they took a break for lunch. Turning back home, she picked up the pace.

When she was writing the first draft of *Wartime Sonata*, a walk by the water always helped her overcome whatever obstacle was bothering her, whether a weak plot point or a particular turn of phrase that needed to be fine-tuned. She'd enjoyed those early, quiet days in the hotel, when she felt she was part of something larger. A ship, Wanda or Winnifred had called it. A ship of fools, maybe, but at least they were trying to achieve something great, even if everyone was rowing in a different direction.

That was when she'd soared. Poor Maxine—and how strange that Hazel was already forgiving her, a tiny, tiny bit, imagining the terror she'd gone through at the hands of that brute Arthur—never had that chance. She'd never found her own center, always struggling to please everyone around her. Hazel's lingering jealousy and resentment of Maxine's success were slowly chipping away, like flakes of marble from a statue. In spite of it all, Hazel's moral center had held, and she'd stayed true to her beliefs and values when so many others hadn't. Just as Maxine had remarked last night.

Approaching Eighth Avenue, Hazel considered what forgiveness might look like. Could she forgive a friend who had ruined her, all in the guise of protecting her?

It hadn't been a guise. Maxine's whimpered pleas last night, with the party raging below them, came from a dark, dreadful place. She'd done some terrible things—no doubt Charlie could set Hazel straight on that front once they were done interrogating her—but she'd gotten tangled in the machinery of an organization that was much stronger than she was.

Outside the hotel, an ambulance had pulled up to the curb, and

Hazel's heart flipped. Over the past several years, she'd gotten used to seeing the elderly residents being trundled into the back of an ambulance and never reappearing. Give it a few decades and she would be the one being transported off to an old folks' home, having fallen and broken a hip, losing her dignity and independence in one fell swoop. But right now, her first concern was Lavinia.

The front door opened and a stretcher appeared, the body on it covered with a blanket. Behind the stretcher walked a young man in a leather jacket, next to a woman with frizzy curls.

Hazel stopped them. "Do you know who it is?"

The woman snapped her gum. "It was one of the transients, not a permanent. Someone who was only here for the night."

Relief settled through Hazel. Another drug addict, probably. Last year, a drug dealer had been shot dead on the fourth floor. Stanley denied it ever happened. If anyone asked, he said the man they'd seen slumped in the stairway in a pool of blood had just been taking a nap, before quickly changing the subject.

"Someone famous," offered the woman.

The man looked annoyed. "Come on, we've got to go."

"Did they say who?" Hazel asked.

"Hmmm." The woman considered the question, much to the irritation of the man. "She was an actress from the 1950s." She looked at her boyfriend. "What was her name?"

He shrugged and stared off down the street.

Her face lit up with a dopey joy. "I remember, it was Trixie something."

A shiver ran through Hazel.

Now the man was engaged. "No, stupid. Her name was Maxine."

"Whatever." The woman turned back to Hazel. "I saw her sitting here in the lobby last night, just hanging out. At, like, four in the morning. So sad."

Hazel's breath came in short gasps, she struggled for air. It couldn't be possible. Maxine was downtown, with Charlie. The ambulance had already pulled away. Hazel rushed inside the hotel, almost slipping on the floor as she made the sharp turn into Stanley's office.

The radiator hissed with steam in the too-warm room. Stanley was behind his desk, rifling through a drawer. He looked up when she came in and from the expression on his face, she knew it was true.

"What happened?"

"I didn't even know she'd checked back in until this morning. The police said they found an empty pill bottle by her bed. This is terrible. The hotel will get a macabre reputation. I'm trying to make this into a decent, respectable residence, and now this. How could Maxine have done this to me?"

Hazel knew the answer. As she spoke, her voice broke.

"She wanted to come home."

Hazel waited up on the roof for Charlie, shaking. He'd called soon after she'd arrived back at her room and she'd told him the reason Maxine had never shown up to her appointment. After hanging up, she had to get out of this room, where every corner held some memory of Maxine, dancing around with a martini glass in hand or pacing back and forth as she ran her lines, stamping a foot whenever Hazel corrected her or had to give her a cue. "Really, this script is terrible," she'd joke. "God knows where they found this playwright."

The memories crashed down on her. The two of them, in the ruins of Naples. Backstage at the Biltmore. In the safety of the Chelsea, where Maxine had found her final refuge.

The night before, while Hazel had been upstairs, staring up at the water-stained ceiling and trying to sleep, Maxine had been sitting down in the lobby. Had she approached the desk clerk to ask him to ring up, but then decided not to? If only Hazel had known.

Charlie burst through the roof door. Hazel ran to him, sobbing. "We killed her."

"No. She made some terrible decisions, one after another. Including taking her own life."

"I wanted to forgive her, eventually. She was the first person to believe in me. She gave me the confidence to write and direct. I'd forgotten that, in all of the resentment and betrayal."

Who knew what Maxine could have become if she hadn't met Arthur at such a young age? But Hazel would never know the answer to that. And in spite of it all, Maxine had shined onstage, been brilliant on film. Her talent was undeniable.

"What a terrible waste." Hazel wiped her eyes. "A terrible waste."

CHAPTER TWENTY-NINE

Hazel

April 1967

A memorial for Maxine was held at St. Malachy's on West Forty-Ninth Street, a neo-Gothic sanctuary long considered the spiritual haven of New York actors, where Douglas Fairbanks married Joan Crawford, and where Rudolph Valentino's funeral mass drew thousands. Maxine's memorial didn't draw quite as many spectators, but Hazel was sure she would have been pleased with the turnout.

Hazel sat next to Lavinia's wheelchair near the back of the church. Curiously, the grand show of emotion by the people who barely knew Maxine canceled out any grief of her own for those two hours. After, she wheeled Lavinia back up to her room at the Chelsea, both of them eager to get out of the public eye. Only once they were back in the safety of the hotel did Hazel curl up on one of Lavinia's armchairs and weep, a messy mix of sobs and crumpled tissues. So much had been lost.

"Oh, Maxine would have loved all this drama," said Lavinia, patiently pouring out two cups of tea.

Hazel laughed in spite of herself. "Yes, she would've been very pleased." She took a sip of tea and regarded her friend. "I have to ask you a question, Lavinia. Did you know she was a Soviet agent?"

Lavinia pursed her lips and didn't answer right away. "I had moments when I thought she was, and others when I didn't. She was a changeable creature, and she came from a tumultuous time." She pulled a handkerchief out of her sleeve and wiped away a tear of her own. "It was grand watching you both on the television, on the Tonys, what a speech you made. I've never been prouder. But I didn't think it would end quite like this. I feel terrible."

"None of this is your fault. Please don't blame yourself."

Charlie had told Hazel that with no official confession on record, the FBI had no real proof, so Maxine's treasonous activities wouldn't be made public. However, they had apprehended Arthur this morning in a raid, and taken him into custody. The spy hunt was over.

"I have something for you, Hazel." Lavinia waved a hand at two packages that sat on her dining room table. "One I received directly from Maxine the day she fled the Chelsea for California, back in 1950. The other, a porter brought to me this morning. Apparently, Maxine left it on the nightstand last night, with my name on it."

"Then you should have them."

"In her note, she insisted they were both meant for you."

Reluctantly, Hazel took the packages up to her room. For the rest of the day, she ignored them. It wasn't until the sun began to set that she poured herself a Scotch, untied the string on the package that was noticeably older—the brown paper crinkled and thin—and began to read.

It was the first half of Maxine's diary, beginning in Naples in 1945, a detailed account of her creative endeavors, both theatrical and treasonous. The other package continued on after her final move to California. It took Hazel a few days to get through all the pages, as she often had to stop and step away, catch her breath. Maxine's accounts of her triumphs and failures were vivid, her fear leaped off every page. Of being caught, of being discovered. Of losing Hazel's friendship.

It was almost as if Maxine were still alive.

Hazel always believed, deep down, that they'd find each other again someday. They'd be somewhere around Lavinia's age, wobbly and croaky, but their prior tribulations would have smoothed over with time, like a rocky shore that's been reduced to clattering pebbles. Maxine would move back down the hall at the Chelsea Hotel, begging forgiveness at every turn, and Hazel would pretend to hold out, but not really. They'd come back together.

Instead, Maxine had left Hazel alone to try to unravel the truth from the lies. She'd snatched away the possibility of reconciliation, and Hazel wanted to hate her for it. But really, she hated herself, for being cruel and not knowing how broken Maxine was. How desperate.

Hazel sat at her desk, staring dumbly at the sheaf of papers. To think, while Hazel had struggled with writer's block, her friend had been scribbling away all these years, day after day.

Hazel laughed out loud, the sound a solemn echo.

Maxine had always pushed her to the precipice, whether onto a stage in Naples, or to mount and direct her own play. At the same time, Maxine was pushing herself, straddling two worlds and rising to the top in one while successfully escaping the other. Hazel couldn't blame Maxine for getting caught up in a cause. After all, she'd done it herself, at Ben's urging. But Maxine had fallen into a nasty web of characters, while Hazel had not. In spite of it all, Maxine had done what she could to take care of Hazel, including that ham-fisted attempt to protect her on opening night. There were more shades of gray to Maxine's existence than Hazel had been able to see previously. With this diary, Hazel finally understood the larger struggle beneath the betrayal.

If Maxine were here right now, standing next to her, what would she say?

She'd tell Hazel to stop whining and write another play already. *Get on with it,* she'd snap, *and meet me on the roof at sunset.*

Hazel placed her palm on the top page. What a story lived within these words. A rip-roaring plot in three acts: Naples, the McCarthy reign of terror, the tragic aftermath and what could have been.

The last ray of sunlight shone on her typewriter, and she idly tapped the space bar.

What if?

She slid a blank piece of paper into the roller, her hand feeling as if it was being guided by someone else's. A play in three acts. One that would speak of Maxine's legacy, both good and bad.

The story of a friendship.

Hazel began typing.

EPILOGUE

The sound of typing draws the ghosts close, watching, nodding. The woman, their newest member, stands apart, weeping. She cries in grief because her absence is so much worse than what she'd escaped. She cries in happiness to see her friend, head bent forward, furiously typing away once again. Her friend would have forgiven her—the ghost understands that now—but it's too late; they will not embark on this new journey together.

She cries for all the souls of the Chelsea Hotel, who climbed the stairs, opened the door, and found their way home.

As she has now.

AUTHOR'S NOTE

For over a decade, beginning in 1947, the House Un-American Activities Committee (HUAC) set out to rid the entertainment industry of suspected communists. The names of individuals accused of being members of the Communist Party were compiled on index cards, a stack that ultimately stretched ten feet high. During those terrible years, careers were derailed, finances drained, and lives destroyed. Although this is a work of fiction, I hewed closely to the stories of several blacklisted artists. For example, much of Hazel's experience with the HUAC parallels writer/director Lillian Hellman's, as described in her memoir *Scoundrel Time*.

The publications *Red Channels* and *Counterattack*, as well as the organization American Business Consultants, existed, as did Vince Hartnett and, of course, Roy Cohn. The character of Laurence Butterfield is based on Syracuse grocer Laurence A. Johnson, who threatened to lead boycotts of programs that hired blacklisted artists, demands to which the advertising firms of

Madison Avenue readily yielded. The despicable "clearance indus-try" described in the novel, where artists could pay the people who blacklisted them to get exonerated, is also factual.

Books that proved vital to my research include *Inside the Dream Palace* by Sherill Tippins; *Naming Names* by Victor S. Navasky; *Unfriendly Witnesses* by Milly S. Barranger; *Red Spy Queen* by Kathryn S. Olmsted; *Red Channels: The Bible of Blacklisting* by Ja-son Hill; *In the Enemy's House* by Howard Blum; *It Happened on Broadway* by Myrna Katz Frommer and Harvey Frommer; *The Chelsea Affect* by Arthur Miller; *I Said Yes to Everything: A Memoir* by Lee Grant; *Just Kids* by Patti Smith; and *Over Here, Over There* by Maxene Andrews and Bill Gilbert.

Despite early threats from the American Legion and the HUAC, New York's Broadway community proudly welcomed blacklisted artists to continue working in the theater. Many found refuge on the stage as opportunities in film, radio, and television dried up. Still, the impact of the blacklist—the many movies and television programs never made, the careers and lives ruined—is immea-surable, and remains a heartbreaking loss.

ACKNOWLEDGMENTS

Several survivors of the McCarthy era blacklist were kind enough to talk with me about their experiences, and I'm indebted to the late Virginia Robinson, Michael Howard, and Lee Grant for taking the time to recall a turbulent period in their lives. Thanks also to Florie Seery and Jim Joseph from the Manhattan Theatre Club for giving me an insider's tour of the Samuel J. Friedman Theatre (formerly the Biltmore) and offering a peek into its history. I'm indebted to Sherill Tippins, Gerald Busby, Judith Childs, Patricia Lancaster, Andrew Alpern, Martin Davis, Kathleen Carter, Hannah K. Davey, Madeline Rispoli, Brian and Dilys Davis, Molly Steinblatt, Adam Hobbins, Nikki Terry, and the New York Public Library for the Performing Arts.

Huge thanks, as always, to the team at Dutton, including Stephanie Kelly—your creative input is a crucial part of every novel, I'm truly indebted to you—as well as John Parsley, Christine Ball, Amanda Walker, Carrie Swetonic, Alice Dalrymple,

Becky Odell, Elina Vaysbeyn, and Christopher Lin. Stefanie Lieberman, I'm so grateful for your wise guidance and generous support. Finally, a shout-out to all the former members of the Willow Cabin Theatre Company for memories and friendships to last a lifetime.

ABOUT THE AUTHOR

Fiona Davis is the nationally bestselling author of *The Dollhouse*, *The Address*, and *The Masterpiece*. She lives in New York City and is a graduate of the College of William & Mary in Virginia and the Columbia Journalism School.